SECRETS
IN THE
DARK

DARCY COATES

Poisoned Pen
PRESS

Published by Poisoned Pen Press, an imprint of Sourcebooks
P.O. Box 4410, Naperville, Illinois 60567-4410
(630) 961-3900
sourcebooks.com

Library of Congress Cataloging-in-Publication Data

Names: Coates, Darcy, author.
Title: Secrets in the dark / Darcy Coates.
Description: Naperville, Illinois : Poisoned Pen Press, [2020]
Identifiers: LCCN 2019050867 | (trade paperback)
Subjects: GSAFD: Horror fiction.
Classification: LCC PR9619.4.C628 S43 2020 | DDC 823/.92--dc23
LC record available at https://lccn.loc.gov/2019050867

Printed and bound in the United States of America.
VP 10 9 8 7 6 5 4 3 2 1

CHAPTER 1

"CLARE? IF YOU'RE THERE, please answer. It's me. Beth."

Clare stood at Winterbourne Hall's kitchen sink as she stared, shocked, at the crackling radio. Gusts of freezing wind howled through gaps in the old mansion's stone walls. Even wrapped in the cotton dress she'd inherited from one of the manor's former maids and a fur jacket borrowed from Dorran, the kitchen would have been too cold for her without the fire. The blaze both warmed and illuminated the room, bathing Clare and Dorran in its orange glow.

Dorran stood close enough to touch. He still wore bruises and scratches from the monsters that inhabited Winterbourne, but his dark eyes shone in the candlelight as he looked toward the radio.

"Beth…" Clare's heart missed a beat, then returned with a vengeance, thumping furiously until her pulse was all she could hear. The last time she'd spoken to Beth, she'd been driving to her sister's house in an attempt to escape the spreading stillness. That had only been seventeen days before. It felt like half a lifetime. She had kept the radio running constantly since she'd retrieved it from her car, but her hope of hearing from Beth had been whittled down to almost nothing.

Dorran moved first. He strode around the wide wooden table filling the kitchen's center and snatched the two-way radio off the shelf, then returned and placed it on the table in front of Clare. He didn't try to speak but bent forward to listen, watching expectantly.

The radio crackled. Clare struggled to breathe. In a flurry of urgent panic, she dropped the dish towel and darted forward, then pressed the button to transmit her voice.

"Beth? Beth, I'm here. It's me. I'm here."

She released the button and bent close to the speakers. Her hands were shaking. Her throat was tight, and every nerve in her body felt on fire with a desperate need to hear her sister's voice again.

Beth, who was the closest thing Clare had to a mother. Beth, who at the vulnerable age of twenty had taken Clare to dental checkups, to netball practice, to school recitals. Beth, who had never stopped worrying about her when she'd moved into her own home.

The transmission was faint and distorted by a weak signal, but the voice was unmistakable. Beth took a gasping, hiccupping breath. "Clare? Is that you? Is it really you?"

She's still alive. She's okay. "Yes! I'm here!"

Beth was crying, and Clare couldn't stop herself from following. She wiped her sleeves over her face as tears ran. At the same time, a grin stretched her cheeks until they ached.

Dorran moved silently. He nudged a chair in behind Clare so she could sit, then a moment later placed a glass of water and a clean cloth beside her. She gratefully used the cloth to wipe some of the wetness off her face. Dorran took a seat on the opposite side of the table. He was tall, towering over Clare, but he moved smoothly and carefully, even his breathing nearly silent. He folded his arms on the table, his dark eyes attentive, his black hair falling around his strong jaw, as he listened to the conversation.

"Sweetheart, are you okay? Are you hurt?"

Beth never called her *sweetheart* unless she was frightened. Clare guessed, after more than two weeks of no contact, Beth was about as frightened as she'd ever been. "Yeah, I'm fine."

That was a half-truth at best. She still had red lines running across her arm and abdomen from where the hollow ones had attacked her. She grew tired too quickly. Her muscles ached. A bite on her wrist and thigh still needed dressing every day.

But she was alive. And, if the hollows were as prevalent as they seemed, that was better than what could be said for a lot of the world.

"What about you?" She pulled the radio closer, struggling to make out Beth's voice under the distortion. "Are you in your bunker? Are you okay?"

"Yes, don't worry about me. I'm in my bunker and getting

thoroughly sick of staring at these four walls." Beth laughed. "I paid for every add-on I could for this place…air filtration, water filtration, generator, aquaponics system. The only professional I didn't think to hire was an interior decorator."

Hearing Beth's laughter made Clare feel lighter. She couldn't stop her own grin. "I guess people don't really think about throw rugs and wall hangings when they imagine the end of the world, do they?"

Beth chuckled, but the noise didn't sound quite natural. Clare's own smile faded. For a moment, the only noise in the kitchen was the soft static and a distant drip.

"It's all gone to hell, sweetheart." Beth's voice had lost its color. "Everything. It's all gone."

"Yeah." Clare swallowed. "But you're okay. And that's what matters."

"Are you at Marnie's? Is she there? Can I talk to her?"

The questions were like being dunked in a freezing bath. Clare closed her eyes. She took a slow breath and tried to keep her voice steady. "I never reached Marnie."

"Oh."

Clare's aunt, Marnie, was the third piece of their tiny family. She lived on a farm two hours' drive from Clare's own home. On that last morning, Clare had been trying to pick Marnie up on her way to Beth's. She'd never made it out of Banksy Forest.

"Well." Beth sounded like she was choking. "At least you're okay. At least…at least…"

"I'm so sorry." Clare stared down at the chipped wooden

counter and shivered. The kitchen no longer felt as warm as it had a moment before.

There had been very little chance to think about the world outside the forest during the previous few days. But whenever she had, her mind had turned to her family and what might have happened to them. She'd felt sick every time she imagined it.

She felt sick again, knowing that Marnie must have been waiting for her. Beth would have called her to say Clare was on the way. She'd probably been standing by her front door, a suitcase on one side and a cat carrier on the other. Clare could picture her easily. Brown hair that had started to develop streaks of gray. A body that had been made strong by a lifetime of working in the garden but was always a little on the plump side. She would have been wearing floral clothes and a knit cardigan, like she always did. She was a short woman but had a huge smile and an even bigger heart.

Did the hollow ones get her? Was it fast, or painful and slow?

A warm hand moved over hers. She met Dorran's dark eyes as he squeezed her fingers.

"But you're okay." Beth's voice crackled through the radio again. She seemed to have rallied. "After your phone went out, I tried reaching you through the radio almost constantly. For days. You didn't answer, and I thought...I thought..."

"I'm so sorry. I left the radio in the car. It took me a while to get it back."

"That's fine. You're alive. I can forgive everything else as long as you just stay alive. Where are you? If you didn't get to

Marnie's, does that mean you're in your cottage? It's not going to be safe—"

"No, no, I found a new house. It's in Banksy Forest."

She could hear the frown in Beth's voice. "There aren't any houses inside the forest."

"That's what I thought too. But it was well hidden. The owner, Dorran, is letting me stay with him."

Again, Beth hesitated. "Is he a good sort of person?"

"Yes, don't worry. He's nice. And we have plenty of food—and a garden. Winterbourne was designed to be self-sufficient and it's hard to break into. I was lucky. Really lucky."

"Be careful, Clare. Don't trust him just because he's friendly."

Clare looked down at her hand, which was still enveloped in Dorran's. She followed it along his arm, covered by the green knit sweater, and up to his face. Thick black hair, grown a little too long, framed a strong, reserved face. His dark eyes, shadowed under a heavy brow, smiled at her. She thought there was no one she trusted more.

"He's good, I promise. You don't need to worry about me. How are you doing there?"

"Holding up at least." There was a speck of hesitation in Beth's voice.

Clare frowned. "Are you sure? Do you have enough food and water?"

"Yes, that's all fine. But the generator's out. I've been trying to fix it, but it's been a challenge without the lights."

A chill ran through Clare. She pictured Beth, sitting in a dark box, having to feel her way through the space every time she needed food or the bathroom or water. There would be nothing to see. Nothing to do. Just her, alone, listening to the seconds tick by.

"I'm doing *fine*, sweetheart." Her voice took on the familiar hint of warning she used whenever Clare was doing something she didn't approve of. "I have a flashlight. I'm using it judiciously— apparently an excess of batteries still isn't enough—but I'm hardly suffering down here."

Clare wasn't sure if she could believe that. But she tried to keep her voice bright for Beth's sake. "We can talk on the radio as much as you want. I can carry you around with me and keep you company."

Beth laughed. "Oh, that would be fun. But I think it's better if we keep our chats short."

That was unexpected. "Why?"

"Ah…"

"Tell me, Beth."

"Too much noise attracts them."

Dorran's fingers laced through Clare's, trying to reassure her. She barely felt it. Her hands were turning numb. "The hollow?"

"Yeah." Beth's voice cracked. "I was the only person on my street who had a bunker."

Clare understood. Without shelter, all of Beth's neighbors would have been affected by the stillness.

Under the static's crackles and her own too-fast breathing, Clare thought she heard another sound. The noise had dogged her for weeks, following her even into her sleep, and every fiber of her being revolted against it. Fingernails, digging. Clawing. Scratching. They were at Beth's bunker door.

They'd heard them. They were hungry.

CHAPTER 2

"WE'LL GET YOU OUT," Clare said. The words left her before she could think them through, before she could even glance at Dorran for his agreement.

Beth snapped, "No! Clare, listen—"

"I can be there this afternoon." Clare stood. She stared about the kitchen, frenzied, trying to piece together a plan. She didn't have a car. Her own little red vehicle was a crumpled wreck. But if she could get out of the forest, she was sure she could find some other form of transport. There would be street upon street of abandoned cars, their owners long gone.

As long as the temperature hasn't frozen their engines too badly. As long as I can find the keys. As long as the snow isn't too thick on the road—

"Clare." Beth's voice boomed through the hissing speakers, and Clare instantly froze. "Sit *down*."

Beth only yelled when Clare was in trouble. It had been years since she'd last heard that tone, but it still held power over her. She meekly sank back into her seat, licked her lips, then tried again. "I can bring you back here, to Winterbourne. It's safe. At least...saf*er*."

"No, you absolutely will not." Beth's voice softened until she only sounded snippy, not angry. "You said you had food there, didn't you?"

Sort of. "Yes."

"And shelter. You're warm enough?"

"Yes. Firewood."

"And that person you're with. You're sure he's okay? He's not strange or creepy or..."

Clare glanced at Dorran. He had both hands clasped under his chin as he studiously watched the table, apparently not sure what to do with himself under her scrutiny. "He's good."

"Then you'll stay there. It's probably the safest you can be right now."

"But if we can get you here too—"

Beth sighed. "Clare, baby, it's not going to happen. You must be hours away. There are hollows all up and down my street. If I try to leave, I'll die. If you try to reach me, you'll die. And how can you expect me to handle that?"

Clare closed her eyes. She took a moment to gather her thoughts. "You've been in there for two weeks. How much longer can you handle it? People aren't designed to survive isolation that long—"

"I'm not *completely* isolated." A thudding noise came through the speakers, and Clare pictured Beth tapping her radio. "I have this. I've been listening to the world. Humanity isn't dead yet. People are trying to rally."

"Do they know what happened?"

"No. There are endless theories. But none that make much sense." Beth exhaled again.

Whenever she stopped speaking, Clare could hear the faint scratching noise. It seemed to be growing louder.

"After our phone call was disconnected, the news station I was watching lasted another four hours. They stopped updating the maps of the quiet zones and instead started listing places they still had contact with. Isn't that horrible? It was faster to list the surviving cities than the lost ones. After each name, they posted the time they had last spoken to someone there. Gradually, the times for some cities grew further and further away…and eventually they were taken off the list. Toward the end, they were talking about entire countries being gone."

Her voice was pained. Clare bent close to the radio as the distortion worsened.

"One of the newscasters said he needed to get a glass of water and almost ran off the stage. The other followed about a minute later. Finally, it was just an intern—this miserable, dead-eyed kid—reading off a list of names from a piece of paper. I think his supervisor had told him to do it, and he didn't know any better. Everyone else had left. Trying to flee somewhere. Trying to reach their families. It was just this kid on national TV, doing his best not to cry as he faced a camera in an empty studio. Then the building's lights went out. I could hear the kid screaming. I don't know why. Just scared? Or had the hollow gotten into the building? I don't know. But that was the last news broadcast. I still have the TV in my bunker, and when the generator worked, I turned it on a few times a day and tried to find some kind of life through it. Nothing."

Clare stared at her hands. Bandages wove around one, protecting her wrist. "You said there were still people out there though."

"Yes. I catch them on the radio sometimes, talking to each other. Not the people I would have expected. No government. No military. From what I can figure out, those kinds of people are pretty much gone. Whatever happened started in large cities first. They were overrun before they even realized there was a problem…before they could even start evacuating." She took a shuddering breath. "Some of the prepper types survived. People who lived out in the wilderness. People who had their own bunkers. But they're dropping one by one, and I'm hearing fewer broadcasts each day. The preppers take too many risks. They try to push their luck, to venture outside, to fight back."

"The preppers can't be the only people out there. Are there any other survivors?"

"Mostly? People who are hiding. Do you understand what I'm saying, sweetheart? The heroes are dying. If you want to survive, don't take risks. You have a good thing where you are now. Stay there. Weather it out. We might be able to meet up afterward."

"Afterward?"

"It's got to end at some point, somehow. That's what people are saying. Either we find a way to kill them effectively, or they starve."

Or humanity dies out. Clare tried not to follow that third option. "Are they capable of starving?"

"No one knows. They're hard to kill. You can hurt them—cut them open, bash parts of their heads in, whatever—but they'll just keep walking for days afterward. One man talked about a hollow he caught in his barn. He chopped it in half at its waist, he said, and it just kept dragging itself along the ground. After three days its spine had started to grow...well, he described it as little claws. It was sprouting crablike legs out of its back and was using those to scuttle around faster. He killed it properly before it grew anything else."

Clare remembered the hollows she'd seen. They were monstrous, contorted beyond what a person should ever have to endure. Skin grew. Bones grew. They broke out of their confines, and somehow, the creatures neither felt pain nor collapsed from infection.

Beth chuckled. "They make us humans look awfully fragile by comparison."

"They sure do."

"Here's everything I know about them. They're like animals. They're hungry, but they still have some kind of survival instinct. They don't like light or fire, and they'll hide if they think you're a threat, so if you ever get trapped, make a lot of noise and use light to chase them away. But they won't stay away for long, so safety—somewhere they can't get to—is always your first priority."

They won't stay away for long. Clare knew that firsthand from her time in the forest. The hunger was always pushing them. Eventually, it won over caution. They would never give up until they ate.

"They don't fight each other," Beth continued. "But they don't work together either, thank heaven. They'll eat another hollow if it's already dead, but they always prefer warm-blooded things. Humans or animals."

"They can't infect you, can they?" Clare tried not to stare at the bandages on her wrist.

"People say they can't. It's not like a virus. It's… I have no idea. Some people say leaking radiation. That hundreds of nuclear bombs went off without anyone realizing, and that's what's deforming us."

"But radiation would kill you long before anything like *this* happened."

"That's what I mean about the theories. Most of them are half-plausible, but none really makes complete sense. Aliens. Government experiments gone wrong. Some people say this is the rapture, except good people seem to be dying alongside the bad. But whatever it is, they agree that you have to be *exposed* to something to be affected. No one is immune; nobody's come walking out of a city that was affected. If you come in contact with it, you become a hollow."

Clare's heart skipped a beat. "Whatever caused this…is it still out there? Could it change *us* as well?"

The radio was silent for a moment. Clare stared at it, fixated, and felt Dorran lean in closer as well.

"I don't know." Beth sounded tired. "I haven't heard any stories of people surviving the event only to turn monstrous afterward. But people *are* disappearing. Their radios just go silent. Are the hollow finally getting them? Infection, dehydration? Or are they changing too? I don't know, sweetheart. I don't know how to keep you safe."

Clare thought back to the two weeks she'd spent in Winterbourne. As far as she could ascertain, the stillness event had happened shortly before she entered Banksy Forest on her last day of freedom. She'd survived unscathed. But Winterbourne's owner, Madeline Morthorne, along with her entourage of staff and maids, had all succumbed to the stillness no more than an hour outside the same forest.

The woman had been deranged, but she'd kept at least part of her mind from before the change. When Clare had asked her what the experience had been like, she'd said the air had turned sour. *"Oh, it burned when it was swallowed."*

"Keep your air filtration unit running no matter what. Whatever this is, I think it's in the air. Your bunker's filter might be the only reason you're safe."

"I'm all right here. I'm more worried about you."

"We think..." Clare glanced at Dorran. His expression was grim. "Maybe this thing was targeted. You said it started in cities before spreading to rural areas. It's like it was focused on where people live. This house is in the middle of the forest, hours from any other kind of habitation. We think that might be why it's safe here."

"I hope so." Beth's voice sounded ragged. When she paused, Clare could hear the scratching sound again. This time, it was accompanied by a metallic banging. It sounded like some kind of lid being lifted and dropped repeatedly. "I need to go now. I'll talk to you again soon, okay? Tomorrow, at the same time?"

"Those hollows outside your bunker…"

"They'll give up after a couple of hours. They always do."

"They don't have any way to get in, do they?"

"Not right now. Goodbye, Clare. I love you."

Clare opened her mouth to say *I love you* back, but the radio clicked off before she could. She sat back, blinking at tears, still staring at the little black box clasped between her hands.

CHAPTER 3

CLARE HELD THE RADIO for several minutes after it went dead. Her emotions rose like a tide, growing overwhelming. There was joy. Beth was alive and, for the moment, safe. There was hope. But dread and fear were growing too, and they were swallowing the small patches of happiness until all Clare could feel was horror.

Dorran pulled his chair around to sit beside her, but he didn't try to talk. He seemed to understand that Clare needed time to process what she'd heard. She pictured Beth, sitting in the lightless, lonely room, trying her hardest to stay silent for the hours it would take for the hollows to stop scrabbling at her door. *I can't just leave her there.*

But Beth had been vehement. Hollows were everywhere. They were ravenous and hard to kill. Clare and Dorran had been spared the worst of them thanks to their location, but even then, they'd nearly lost their lives just by going to the forest.

And even if she could get through the hollows, the fear of becoming just like them made Clare's stomach turn. Beth didn't know if whatever had changed them was still out there. From what Clare had gleaned from the few radio broadcasts she'd caught, people were traveling across the country. They were surviving—at least for a couple of days. She didn't know if that meant the air was safe or whether the effects were simply delayed.

And if the air isn't *safe, can it blow over Winterbourne? Are we going to be exposed to it, no matter how cautious we are?*

She felt herself start to hyperventilate and pushed away from the table. She crossed to the sink and splashed water over her face. It was cold enough to make her skin sting. It helped though. She gave it a moment, then returned to the table where Dorran waited.

"What do you think?" she asked, desperate for someone else's thoughts to distract her from her own.

Dorran faced her, one elbow resting on the table and his hand running over his mouth. He watched the radio, like Clare, almost as though it might come alive again.

"I think your sister has good advice. Knowing what the outside is like, Winterbourne is probably the safest house we could find. And we have the garden. As long as we can find fuel to keep the lights on, it will be sustainable. We could conceivably live decades by harvesting new seeds from the plants we grow."

Clare imagined spending the rest of her life in Winterbourne. She wondered if she could ever feel comfortable in it. The mansion was towering, imposing. Every item cluttering its endless rooms had been chosen for its prestige. And now, at the end of the world, it was all worthless. The gilded-framed paintings. The ornate furniture and brushed rugs. They were living surrounded by unimaginable wealth, but with no one to care about it.

Dorran lowered his hand and let his fingers trace across the wooden table. "Your sister also advised us to be cautious. And, as sturdy as Winterbourne is, it is still far from completely safe. Hollows were able to get inside once. They can do so again easily."

Clare nodded. "The passageways."

"I have no idea how many there are or where they lead. Until they are sealed, we must be on guard." He took a slow breath and closed his eyes. "But I would also like to try to find a way to bring Beth here."

Clare's heart jumped. She clenched her hands, but it wasn't enough to stop them from shaking.

"It won't be today. It might not be for a while. But we will know soon whether the hollow can starve. If they cannot, we must try to find a way to get Beth out of where she is. It is not a life fit for any human."

"Thank you." Clare dropped forward, resting her head against Dorran's chest, and he wrapped his arms around her in return.

She'd been so afraid that he would take Beth's side and refuse to leave Winterbourne. Dorran liked to be cautious. She knew he was pushing himself to even make the offer. "Thank you so much."

"Shh. Don't thank me now. There is a long way to go yet." He kissed the top of her head. "But we will make it possible."

They sat together, wrapped up in each other. Clare struggled to get her emotions back under control. Dorran's knit sweater was warm under her cheek, and it moved subtly as he breathed. He felt as steady as ever, but she could feel conflict under the surface. He was worried.

A loud thud echoed from the floor above them. They both turned to stare at the ceiling. A trail of dust, jostled free, trickled through the dimly lit air. Dorran tensed. "Stay close to me."

Clare kept at his side like a shadow as he lit a candle and collected two fire pokers from where they kept them beside the stove. He passed one of the pokers to Clare, then they left the relative security of the kitchen and crept into the foyer.

The noise had sounded like it came from the second floor. Above it was the third floor—where she and Dorran had their room—and the attic. At that moment, Clare hated how rambling the house felt. The dizzying number of rooms were crisscrossed with roving hallways, and she still didn't know where all of them led.

Dorran moved with purpose. He gave the foyer a brief scan, then led the way to the stairs, keeping their backs to the walls. As they climbed, he tilted his head toward her and whispered, "If it is one creature, I want to either drive it out or kill it. Stay behind me and watch my back. But if there is more than one, we retreat. We get to the bedroom if we can. Better to be safe and live to fight another day."

Clare nodded. The stairs creaked under their feet, the noise muffled by thick carpet. On a normal day, morning's light would have glowed through the windows, but the manor had been swallowed by a perpetual haze that dampened the sunlight and dimmed the sky. Clare had the sense that more snow would be arriving soon. The weather had been increasingly unpredictable since the world had gone silent. They could have clear weather, immense hail, and a snowstorm all in the same day. She didn't know how the hollows were managing to survive the brutal conditions in the forest, except that they didn't seem to feel the cold like she did.

They stopped on the landing. Clare waited for her eyes to adjust to the gloom. The hallway stretched in both directions. With no maids flitting through the space each day, dust had started to accumulate on the gilded frames and furniture. Wood paneling filled the spaces between the pillars embedded in the walls. The hallway's runner, a dark maroon, complemented the narrow tables and displays arranged in the area. It somehow managed to feel cluttered and refined at the same time.

Dorran waited, listening to the silence, then led Clare right. She tried to visualize the house's layout. She thought if they continued on a little farther, they would be standing directly above the kitchens.

Blurred shadows lingered over the furniture. Clare fought to make out shapes as the thin light from the window and the gold glow from Dorran's candle played tricks on her eyes. Dorran moved steadily, each step measured, his center of gravity low and his weapon held expectantly. Closed doors bracketed them on both sides, leading into dark rooms with thick drapes and heavy shadows.

Dorran came to a halt. His hand shot out to hold Clare back, and she took hold of it, anchoring him to her side.

Ahead, shapes cluttered the hallway. Chairs. Pedestals. Narrow side tables. Shelves. In among their straight lines and symmetrical designs, something organic stood out. Something jagged. Clare stared, and realized the shape was staring back.

The creature was invisible except for its silhouette and one rounded eye, which glinted in the light. Clare tried to trace its outline, but it was maddening. What should have been its arm split into two. The place where its hand should have been had too many knuckles. Too many *fingers*. Twelve of them, Clare thought, splayed at its side. Matted, thin hair cascaded over its shoulders and draped down, passing the shredded ends of its maid's dress, to brush against the floor. Clare's eyes flicked from the hair to the elongated feet with a multitude of toes.

Dorran slowly nudged her back until she was sheltered behind him. The poker glinted as he adjusted his grip on it.

The creature's head tilted back. The lower jaw stretched farther than Clare would have thought possible, exposing rotting teeth in black gums. A hissing, chattering noise ripped out of its throat, then the monster slid into the wall and vanished with a sharp *bang*.

"Ah..." Dorran moved forward with smooth, quick steps. Clare, knowing she was supposed to watch their backs but incapable of looking away from where the woman had stood, followed. The candle's glow flowed over uninterrupted paneling. Dorran handed his light to her, then felt across the wood. He paused at one place near a pillar, gave it a hard shove, and stepped back as the concealed door rocked open.

Clare had to give credit where it was due. Madeline Morthorne had hidden the compartments well; the door's edge lined up with the paneling in a way that made it nearly invisible. They had been disguised well enough to make Clare doubt her own sanity. And enough that Dorran, a prisoner in the building for his whole life, hadn't known they existed.

"So, here is another one," Dorran said. He took the candle back and reached it through the opening. Clare felt a squeeze of panic as she watched his arm disappear inside, the fearful part of her mind jabbering that it might never come out again. But Dorran only stayed inside the passageway long enough to make sure it was empty, then he stepped back and let the door creep closed again.

"At least now we have our answer. There are hollows left inside the building." His eyes were hard as he turned from the concealed door to the window at the end of the hall, where the sky was steadily darkening. "We must make the doors a priority. Sealing them is the only way to ensure we will be safe."

Clare nodded slowly. She thought she could hear distant noises moving through the house. They were hard to pinpoint; they could have been wood flexing under the biting wind, hurried footsteps, or even just her imagination.

In the two days since facing Madeline in the basement, they hadn't seen or heard any sign of the hollows. She and Dorran still moved cautiously, bringing weapons whenever they ventured out of their room and locking doors behind themselves, but this was the first time the monsters had actually shown themselves.

Dorran rubbed his hand across the back of his neck. He sounded tense. "I suspect the only way to seal them effectively will be from the inside."

Clare watched the way his narrowed eyes flitted across the exposed wood. The idea of creeping through the lightless, musky passages left her clammy. But she understood why it was necessary. Dorran didn't know where the doors led out. Without seeing the inside of the passageways, their only alternative would be knocking against every square inch of the building—and that would take months. "It'll be dangerous."

"Yes. I'll take precautions. You should—"

She knew what was coming and narrowed her eyes. "I'm not sitting in the bedroom."

They glared at each other, both trying to win the war of wills. Dorran took a breath, and his voice softened. "Let us make a compromise. I will go in. You stand at the doors and mark their locations on a map."

Clare gave his chest a light prod with the tip of her poker. "How about this for a compromise? We both go into the secret passageways and neither of us dies."

"That is not a compromise." He was trying, and failing, to hide his laughter. "That is you winning yet another argument."

"No, that is me not going insane because my Dorran selfishly keeps all of the danger to himself." She reached up and pressed her hand to his cheek. He was warm and solid, and closed his eyes as he leaned into the touch. "We agreed. We're in this together."

He tilted far enough to kiss her palm, then sighed. "Very well. Together."

CHAPTER 4

HOW MANY OF THEM are there?

The question had refused to leave Clare since she'd discovered Madeline and her maids had taken up residence in the secret parts of the house. Clare had thought she'd killed the woman. But when Dorran had gone to bury his mother's body, he'd found it missing.

No one could survive a metal rod through the head, Clare kept telling herself. *She was dead. The other hollows took her body away. That's all.*

But doubt still lingered. The monsters could withstand incredible damage. Their own bones shredded their flesh, and they continued moving as though nothing was wrong.

They could die. But they didn't go down easily. And still in the back of Clare's mind was the small terrifying thought that the matriarch continued to stalk the halls after she and Dorran went to bed. Maybe she watched them. Maybe she had plans for them, some way to punish them for what they'd done to her.

Even if Madeline was gone, the memory of her certainly wasn't. The figure they'd seen in the hall proved at least one of the maids lingered. Possibly more. Clare's mind chewed over that question again and again. *How many? How many?*

Clare knelt by the fire in their bedroom and rekindled the embers. Out of every room in the house, it was the most secure. They had checked the walls to make sure there were no secret compartments. They had bolts on the doors. They kept their food there in case they weren't able to reach the kitchens. The adjacent bathroom supplied water.

Dorran stood at a little side table behind Clare. He'd laid out three sheets of paper and drew the house's layout, one floor on each sheet. It was a labor-intensive process. He was completely silent as he worked, and Clare gave him space.

The flames caught on one of the larger logs. The muffled hissing and popping were the only noises inside their room. The radio, which Clare had kept at her side constantly, sat on the mantel. She knew it would be smarter to turn it off and conserve the batteries since Beth wouldn't be reopening communications until the following morning, but she couldn't bring herself to shut the machine off. The euphoria from speaking with her sister was still fresh, and if Beth tried to make contact again, she didn't want to miss it. Even if it meant burning through their limited supply of batteries.

Her car had spare batteries, along with cases of food, water, and gasoline. They were all things she and Dorran needed. But the car was an hour's walk from Winterbourne, in Banksy Forest, which was home to an unknown number of hollows, and the last time they'd ventured there, the creatures had almost killed them.

"Clare."

Dorran had the sheets spread out across the floor in front of him and beckoned for her. She knelt at his side and admired the sharp, intricate lines he'd drawn.

"Here we are," he said, indicating their room on the third floor. "The kitchen is here. The foyer is here. These are the stairs."

He'd drawn the hallways cleanly, Clare saw, but instead of butting the rooms up against each other, he'd left space between them. She understood. The hidden passageways could be anywhere; he intended to add them into the map when he found them.

Dorran took out a red pen and drew three short, thick lines. "Here are the passageway entrances I know about. There is also a doorway into the attic that will have to be dealt with."

"There's going to be another one here," Clare said, pointing to the hallway a little farther on from their room. "That's where I first saw one of the creatures."

Dorran marked the paper. "All right. What will be the best way to handle it? Start at the top and work our way down, or go from the ground up?"

"Ground up, I think." Clare chewed on the corner of her lip. "They came in through the holes in the roof. If it's possible to chase them out, and I think it might be—that one we saw in the hallway earlier was nervous enough to run rather than confront us—then going up will herd them outside without making us more vulnerable by opening the main door."

"I agree. It will also make it safer to reach the gardens, which still need water daily." Dorran clipped the top back onto the pen. His jaw worked as he examined the maps. "I don't know if it's possible to eradicate the creatures from the house entirely. As long as there are holes in the roof—and that will not be a small project—then they can get back in. But as long as we can seal all of the doorways, we can keep them contained. They will have the hidden passageways, we will have the rest of the house."

The idea of sharing her home with the monsters, no matter how contained they were, left her stomach squirming. But Dorran was right; there was no way to get rid of them completely.

She realized he was watching her and forced a smile. "Do you have nails?"

"Yes. In the basement. As well as boards. The house was constantly in need of repair during my mother's reign; we will not be short of supplies."

"Let's get this done, then."

He smiled at her, and the fondness in his expression was almost enough to melt the queasy sensation.

They collected the equipment they would need from the bedroom: thick jackets to ward off the cold, gloves and scarves for protection against bites. Dorran strapped a sheathed knife under his coat, then fussed over Clare, making sure she had small blades tucked into pockets within easy reach. Then they both retrieved a main weapon: the poker for Clare and a hatchet for Dorran.

Clare carried the maps and a lamp as she followed Dorran. She sucked in a breath as they left the warmth of their bedroom and pulled her scarf up to cover her mouth and nose.

Getting from their room to the basement was a short hike. Clare watched the sun through the windows they passed. Small flakes of snow were snatched at and hurled around by the wind. Gradually, natural light was filtered out as they descended deeper into Winterbourne.

The staff areas were shabby and old compared to the rest of the house. Dust, which hadn't been tolerated in any of the family's many rooms, had gathered across a lot of the tools. Dorran picked out a can full of nails from the shelves behind their indoor garden and passed them to Clare. "Would you carry these?"

"Sure." She took the hammer as well, then Dorran bent to reach a stack of wood piled underneath the shelves.

"I can help." Clare reached toward Dorran as he hauled out eight of the planks.

"I have this." His voice was a fraction tighter than usual, but he didn't hesitate as he hefted the planks to carry them across his shoulder.

Clare pressed her lips together. Dorran never complained, but she worried for him. Neither of them was in peak shape. They had run out of meat, and the canned soup—their only source of food left—wasn't meeting their caloric needs. Both of them were trying to recover from injuries while simultaneously dealing with the cold, the stress, and the exertion that Winterbourne demanded.

Sometimes she had the sense that they were being held together by will alone. She didn't know what would happen when their resilience finally failed.

Dorran, breathing heavily, stopped in the cathedral-like room that connected the basement, wine cellar, garden, and hallway back to the main parts of the house. He adjusted the boards on his shoulder and glanced at Clare. "Wine cellar?"

"Yep." She knew why he was asking. Out of all the rooms in the house, she hated the cellar the most. The cold stone space seemed to leak hostility, and her skin prickled whenever she neared it. But it needed to be dealt with first; it held an entryway to a hidden chamber the hollows had been living in.

Dorran hesitated, his dark eyes questioning. She made herself smile. He gave a brief smile in return, then stepped toward the cellar stairs.

Clare shivered as she passed through the massive stone archway. The change in atmosphere was palpable. The hairs rose along her arms, and no matter how thick the jacket was, it never seemed enough to keep out the damp, frozen air.

She held the lamp ahead of herself and kept close enough to Dorran to light his feet. As the steps led down, the gray stone created endless echoes that bounced across the walls. The candle's light felt muted. It shone off Dorran's back, shimmering in his dark hair and across the wooden planks, but never reaching far enough to see ahead of him.

The steps leveled out into a stone floor. Shelves rose around Clare, the bottles glinting in a way that reminded her of eyes in the dark. She kept her breathing shallow, her ears straining to pick up any unnatural noises as Dorran wove between the shelves. In the distance, she caught the sound of dripping. Behind her, something that might have been a sigh or might have been an echo. Dorran was moving too fast. Clare started to lose him between the shelves. She broke into a jog and staggered as her shoe clipped an uneven stone. She caught her balance against one of the shelves. Its bottles clinked as they rocked in their holders.

Dorran had stopped. Even though he faced her, he looked half like a stranger. His deep-set eyes were full of shadows. The candlelight painted unnatural angles over his face as its flame guttered. They stared at each other, unmoving, and Clare's heart felt like it was about to burst.

"Clare? Are you all right?"

His voice was distorted by the wine cellar's echoes. Clare didn't trust herself to speak, but she gave two quick nods. Dorran adjusted his hold on the boards and held a hand out, and Clare moved to his side. He wrapped his arm around her shoulders. They walked side by side, and for a moment, all Clare could hear was their breaths.

They reached the back wall. Clare recognized the place she'd seen a hollow one scrabbling at the ground. She nodded toward it. "The door must be somewhere here."

Dorran bent and let the wood fall against the end of the closest shelf. "Keep the light steady."

She held it high while Dorran explored the wall. His gloved fingers dug into the gaps between the stones, feeling for any sort of opening.

A soft noise intruded. A shudder ran through Clare and the candle flickered. The scratching noises were back. Fingernails on stone, digging, digging, digging.

"Dorran." She kept her voice to a whisper. "Do you hear that? The scratching noises?"

He stopped his search. They both held their breaths. The scratching ran around them, distorted, persistent. Clare strained to hear where it was coming from. The cellar was disorienting, and the noise was so faint it was almost possible to lose it under the sound of her pulse.

Dorran watched her, his expression unreadable. "Do you still hear it?"

"Yes. Don't you?"

He frowned, staring into the blackness, and after a moment, shook his head. "I do not."

Clare swallowed around the lump in her throat. "I'm not imagining it."

"No. You're not." He stripped his gloves off as he stood. A finger brushed loose hair back behind her ear. His eyes were sad but intense. "I promised you I would not doubt you again. And I don't. You are better at hearing them than me. Please, stand guard. Tell me if they come closer."

She nodded. Dorran's fingers lingered a moment, grazing her jaw, then fell away. He turned back to the wall and ran his hands across the surface.

He believes me. She couldn't hear the scratching noise any longer. Part of her already wanted to believe she'd imagined it. The cellar was making her paranoid, and it would be easy to extrapolate a simple echo into something malevolent.

But the other part of her held steady. She'd doubted her senses once before, and it had nearly killed Dorran. She wouldn't make that mistake again.

Dorran pressed his shoulder against part of the wall. It shifted back. Hinges, old and rusty, groaned as they turned, and the door drifted inward.

"There." His smile glinted in the thin light. "We found it. Are you ready?"

She didn't feel ready. Dorran waited in the opening, his dark eyes trying to read hers. She knew he would let her return upstairs, into the safety and warmth of their room, if she asked. He would probably even be grateful for it. But that would mean he would have to enter the passageway alone. Clare's fingers ached from how hard she gripped the lamp, but she lifted her chin and stepped through the doorway.

CHAPTER 5

THE WOODEN HALLWAY WAS wide enough that Clare and Dorran could stand side by side. The pathways would have been built by the house's original owner, Dorran's ancestor, a woman who had constructed Winterbourne in one of the family's forests to hide away from the world following her husband's death. Clare guessed she had designed it to be her refuge—a way to move about the house without staff or relatives knowing.

Dorran stopped inside the door and glanced down the passage-way's length. It stretched away in both directions, the smooth walls vanishing within feet. The lantern wasn't as bright as Clare would have liked; already she couldn't see much of the wine cellar, just the glint of two bottles that looked horribly like eyes.

"We will have to nail this one closed from the inside," Dorran said. He ran his hands across the wood door. On the other side was stone, designed to blend into the cellar's walls. Clare nodded.

They had no way to drill into the stone without special tools. She tried not to let her panic rise as they stepped inside the passageway and pulled the door closed behind them.

With their exit sealed, the hallway's sickly, musky scent was intensified. It smelled like rancid meat and rats. The hollows were responsible: a mixture of wet, decaying clothes, greasy hair, and injuries left open and allowed to fester. Clare tried not to imagine how many of them had paced the hallways for their smell to permeate it.

Dorran lifted one of the pieces of wood, braced it across the door, and held out a hand. Clare passed him a nail and the hammer. For a moment, her ears were filled with the hard thuds of metal impacting wood. Dorran drove the nails in at opposing angles, ensuring they could not be pulled out easily. Once the first board was secured, he picked up a second but paused before positioning it.

"I have been thinking. About your car and about Beth."

"Yeah?" She offered him the nails.

"If we are to reach your sister, we will have to learn more about the hollows, about how to handle them, how to fight them, how to escape them."

"Right."

He drove the first nail in, then lined up the second. "And the supplies in your car would be a boon. As it is, we will run out of food in four days."

Clare squeezed her eyes closed. She hadn't expected it to be so soon. "Is that all we have?"

"Yes. Initially, I had planned to ration it. But you were not well. Your body needed fuel to heal."

And Clare had refused to let Dorran ration his own food. When she'd found out that was what he was doing, she refused to eat unless he ate at the same time. She didn't regret that, not even when faced with their dwindling supplies.

"The garden is growing well," Dorran continued. "A few of the plants, especially the leafy ones, could be harvested within five or six days. But it will not be enough to survive on, and we are still a few weeks away from sustainable food. I considered sprouting some of the seeds. But the amount we would need to eat to even last a week would wipe out our store, and that, of course, would put an end to our garden."

"You're thinking about going to the car."

"Yes. If we can find a way to reach it and to bring the food home, we will not have to go hungry."

"And it's like a practice run for getting to Beth."

"Exactly."

The passageway didn't feel as cold or dark as it had a moment ago. Clare bit her lip, a cautious sense of hope starting to form. If they could reach the car, then surely they could make it to outside the forest. And if they could get outside...

Dorran kept his head down as he finished nailing the second piece of wood. He hadn't voiced the idea just to make idle conversation, she realized. He'd felt her stress and brought up the plan to give her something less grim to think about. Not for the first time, Clare felt a pang of gratitude that they were together.

She pulled the hand-drawn maps out of her pocket as Dorran put his hammer down. They unfolded the pages against the stone wall, and Clare held her lantern close. Dorran marked off the entrance they'd sealed, then drew two red lines through the empty space to indicate which direction the passages went.

"Left or right?" Dorran asked.

"Right." Clare could see stairs leading upward. More than anything, she wanted to put some distance between them and the wine cellar.

Unlike the main parts of the house, the wooden passageways weren't flat. They constantly led upward and downward with sets of two, three, or four shallow steps at a time. It disoriented Clare. For a house as proud and rigid as Winterbourne, the uneven stairs felt like a dirty secret hidden away where no one could see.

She hated having her back exposed. Every time she tilted her head, she glimpsed leaping shadows in her peripheral vision. She thought she heard the scratching again, except this time it faded in and out of hearing, never close or loud enough for her to be certain it was there, but teasing her senses and terrifying her subconscious.

The familiar question kept playing through her mind. *How many are there? How many?*

She imagined them creeping up behind her. Scuttling. Moving so quietly that their noises were buried under her footsteps and gasping breaths. She could almost feel them behind her, close enough to snatch at the hem of her dress, close enough for their bony fingers to tangle in her hair and yank her back into the yawning darkness. When the tension grew too immense for her to bear, she turned. The pathway was empty.

She hated the tunnels. She hated the house. But Winterbourne was the only thing keeping her and Dorran alive. She squared her shoulders and lifted the lamp higher to light their path.

Behind her, the soft scrabble of grasping fingernails seemed to seep out of the house, coming from every corner, every crevice, unstoppable and repugnant, like a stain bleeding through the walls.

CHAPTER 6

THEY SAT IN THEIR nest of blankets in front of the fire, shoulder to shoulder, as they watched the flames. A pot of soup sat in the coals, warming. Clare felt as though she could finally breathe again.

Even after two trips into the furnace room for more wood and eight sealed doors, they hadn't finished working through the ground floor. Her nerves were raw. She imagined she could still hear the scratching sounds in the back of her mind.

Dorran reached forward to stir the pot as wisps of steam began to rise. As he settled back at Clare's side, he kissed the top of her head. "Today was a challenge. You did well."

"You did most of it," she countered. Still, she relaxed against him, enjoying how solid and safe he felt.

He murmured happily, his fingers running over her arms, his eyes closed. For that moment, everything felt right again. Clare could forget about the monsters crawling through their house. She could forget about the world outside the forest. She could even forget the scratching noises. She had Dorran. And, in that moment, she realized she'd found the answer to a question she'd asked herself earlier. *Could I spend the rest of my life in Winterbourne?* She smiled. *Yes. I could. As long as Dorran is with me, I could live anywhere.*

The moment ended though. The soup bubbled, and Dorran reached forward to take it from the heat before it spilled over. He divided it into two bowls and placed one in Clare's hands.

"Let's eat," he said, his fingertips trailing over her shoulder as though he were as reluctant to let her go as she was. "And you must be ready for some rest. It's been a long day."

Through the window, Clare could see the red and gold of a sunset spreading through the falling snow. The weather outside could be ferocious, and it could be terrifying, but it was the first time she'd seen the property look so beautiful.

They ate in silence. Dorran was never very chatty, but he seemed quieter than normal. She snuck glances at him. He was tired, but there was something more in his expression. She tucked her feet up under herself and put her bowl aside. "Dorran?"

He startled, and some life returned to his eyes. "Sorry. I have been ignoring you, haven't I?"

"I don't mind that. But…something's worrying you."

He opened his mouth, then closed it again. Clare waited. After a moment, he said, "There is a lot to do. That's all."

"You're worried about going to the car, aren't you?"

He chuckled. "You read me too easily."

"I'll go with you. I'll be there to help."

His smile cracked. She'd touched on a sore spot. Clare found his hand and wrapped hers around it, twining the fingers together. He felt cold.

"You can tell me," she whispered.

His voice was raw. "I cannot even fight you on accompanying me. This is not something I can accomplish alone. I would need your help. But that would mean asking you to step into a situation that…that may kill you."

"That's fine. I want to come. And by now you should know I'm not letting you go alone."

A chuckle broke through the tension masking his face. "Yes. You are strong. Stronger than I expected. But this, Clare…" The flames made shadows leap across the planes of his face. He was quiet for a beat, then continued in a calmer voice. "This will be dangerous—more danger than I ever wanted you to be in. And I do not know if I can keep you safe out there."

"We can prepare. We'll have weapons, maybe even some kind of armor."

"Yes. But I keep thinking of what your sister said this morning: The heroes are dying. The ones who take risks are never heard from again. And her advice seemed so wise: do not take chances. Choose the safest path. Hide."

Clare didn't know what to say. She and Dorran sat so close she could feel his chest rise with every breath and see dampness shining in his eyes. He blinked, trapped in some kind of mental battle, then spoke again.

"And yet, I feel like we must try. Yes, we could sit here, hidden, always taking the cautious option, always guarding ourselves, but what life is that?" He was holding her hand almost hard enough to hurt. "That is not the kind of life I want to give you: hungry, unable to see your sister, always flinching at the noises in the walls. That is not the life you deserve."

"Dorran."

His eyes were growing increasingly frantic. "But I am afraid. Oh, Clare, I am afraid. I have never cared about anything so much. I must keep you safe. I want to see you happy, if I can. Why must these goals be so thoroughly opposed?"

"Dorran." She shuffled around so she could sit in his lap, carefully detangled their hands, and wrapped her arms around him. She could feel his heart through his shirt. It thundered. She held him tightly and whispered, "It won't be your fault if something bad happens out there."

"But—"

"I want to go. I'm ready to go. And, yeah, I'm frightened too, and I'm hoping you'll stay near me if things get bad. But…if it goes wrong…that isn't your fault. It's a choice we made together."

He didn't answer, but his arms enveloped her, as though he never wanted to let her go.

Clare buried her face in his chest. She knew very little about his childhood, but what she had learned was painful. His mother had controlled him through guilt, and he'd never learned how to let it go. It was like an invisible weight on his shoulders. She wished she could do more to ease it from him, but she worried that it might be too deeply ingrained, that he would always accept more responsibility than he deserved.

Instead, she stretched to put her head closer to his and kissed his neck. He shivered. His fingers tangled in her hair. She tilted her head back, and his lips brushed hers, then pressed closer for a kiss. He was sweet, moving carefully and tenderly. She held on to him, warming him, and felt the tension fade from his body.

They stayed like that until the fire began to burn down into coals. As the room's shadows deepened, Dorran's hoarse voice disturbed the stillness. "How soon would you like to make the journey to the car?"

Clare bit her lip. The longer they put it off, the more she would dread it. Already, it loomed like an impassable mountain. "Soon. Tomorrow?"

He nodded. "Yes. It is probably wise to go early, before our stores grow too low. That way we will still have some time to adjust our plans if anything goes wrong."

It's not going to go wrong, she told herself as she closed her eyes. *Dorran will look after you, and you'll look after Dorran.*

She fell asleep at the fire's side to the sensation of Dorran stroking her hair. The scratching sounds continued to follow Clare into her dreams. She wrestled with them, sometimes trying to run from them and sometimes trying to find their source, but no matter what she did, she couldn't escape them.

Clare woke early. The pale light coming through the windows told her the morning would be clear. It didn't have much significance for the rest of the day, but she wanted to take it as a good sign.

She rolled over. Dorran was already up. He stood at one of the tall, narrow windows, hands clasped behind him as he surveyed the land outside. Clare rose, bringing one of the blankets with her to wrap around her shoulders. Dorran held out an arm to welcome her at his side, and together they looked out over the pure-white field.

"I have a plan," he said. He looked tired; dark circles ringed his eyes.

She wondered how long he'd been awake. The melancholy seemed to have lifted, though, and Clare smiled. "Yeah?"

"It is an hour's walk to the car. All of yesterday afternoon, I was trying to think of how we could be faster. Improvised skis? Lighter loads? Under the best conditions and if we jog the whole way, we could be there in half an hour and back in the same amount of time. But that is still an hour spent outside. An hour when we are vulnerable."

The air was clear that day, and the forest stood out more sharply than normal. The pine trees wore their familiar caps of white, but the trunks were still dark. Clare searched the spaces between them for movement. She knew hollows lived in the forest, but it came back to the same question that continued to plague her: *How many?*

She tilted her head back to look up at Dorran. "What did you decide on?"

"I changed my way of thinking." He flashed her a smile. "Instead of trying to be fast, we will be slow."

"Okay." She wasn't following, but she trusted he knew what he was talking about.

"Instead of packing light, we will bring a sled. There is chicken wire in the storage shed behind the garden. With a good, strong cloth, I believe we can create something like a tent, something tough enough to protect us if the hail returns."

She'd been so focused on avoiding the hollows, she hadn't considered the temperamental weather. But the first time they'd attempted to reach the car, they had been caught in a hailstorm that had risen unnaturally quickly. The storms didn't seem to strike often, but when they did, they were brutal.

"We will have weapons," Dorran said. "But more importantly, we will have armor. This time, instead of trying to kill them before they bite us, we will make ourselves unbiteable. Do you understand?"

"Yeah. Defensive, rather than offensive." Clare nodded. "It's smart."

"Good. Eat first; you will need energy. Then we will see about our equipment. I would like to leave no later than midday. If we are being slow, we must be prepared for all eventualities, including being waylaid. I would not want to be outside after dark."

CHAPTER 7

CLARE AND DORRAN CROUCHED in the stone room connecting the garden, the basement, and the wine cellar. The room was cold, but it was closest to the equipment they needed. Dorran had laid out a sheet to work on. One of the immense, heavy woven red drapes had been wrenched off its holder in the dining room and lay in a pool beside them. Dorran unspooled chicken wire from its roll and, by buckling it and tying it, created a dome shape.

"We will be like a turtle," he'd joked.

When it was completed, it would be just large enough for them to huddle underneath. Once the frame was ready, Dorran layered the drapes over it, then a second layer of the wire, followed by more drapes. The fabric was thick; it added to the construction's weight, but Clare hoped it would be enough to keep the weather out at least.

Clare had her back to the cellar. She couldn't tell if that was better or worse than facing it. Her mind was constantly hunting for the scratching sounds, the shuffling, and the quiet breaths that would be the only warning she had of someone creeping up behind her.

Dorran rocked back on his heels, wiping his forehead with the back of his hand. "It will be heavy. But I would rather carry this weight than have it fail on us when we need it most."

Clare finished tying off one section. She couldn't help but admire their handiwork. The vivid red cloth would stand out against the white snow, but it was a solid construction. Dorran lifted one end, and Clare tried picking up the other side. Between the two of them, they could heave it up, but Clare knew they wouldn't get far carrying it on their backs. They dropped it back onto the floor.

"It won't be such a burden when we have the sled," Dorran said. He packed up the toolkit they'd been using, then scooped up the unused chicken wire and carried it back to the shelves in the storage area. As he put the equipment away, Clare brushed her hand across some of the tools: gardening gloves, so old and worn they were starting to fall apart, trowels, bottles of fertilizer. They were all well used.

A sense of regret washed over her. Dorran's family had issues, but he'd talked fondly about some of the staff. Someone had dedicated their life to tending to the garden. They had worn the gloves daily. And they would never be back.

She turned away. A pitchfork caught her notice. She picked it up and shook dust from its handle. "Dorran, what about this?"

"Yes." He felt across the prongs, testing their sharpness. "This will be useful. I will try to find a second long weapon too. And a knife of some kind, perhaps. I wish this family had been interested in swords—"

He broke off and his eyes flitted toward the ceiling. Clare looked up, too, a spike of panic catching in her throat as she thought Dorran had heard something. But then he smiled.

"My uncle used to be involved in fencing. They will not be any use for weapons, but the masks will make a good defense for our faces. Come. Let's see if I can remember where he stored his equipment."

They dropped the pitchfork beside the protective dome and crossed to the stairs. Clare was faintly aware of how quickly the time was passing. She had a sense that, if they didn't get there that day, they might never make it. The sky had stayed clear all morning. It was almost as though the outside world was waiting for them, staying on its best behavior as it coaxed them outside. If they missed their chance, the following day might be storming. And then the next. And then, all of a sudden, they would be out of food.

Dorran moved carefully. They still hadn't found most of the concealed passageways, and as long as they stayed open, the house wasn't truly theirs. Anytime they passed through a new room, he paused at the door and listened.

The constant guardedness was beginning to wear Clare down. Every noise, every creak, made her flinch. By comparison, Dorran was like a rock. He was cautious but never flighty.

When Clare's nerves started tightening beyond endurance, she looked at his face, watched how steady and confident he was, and made herself relax.

Dorran tried one of the second-floor rooms first but, after a minute of sifting through a closet, backed out. "Not here. Which means it's either in his bedroom, or—"

Clare grabbed his arm to silence him. In between the house's natural noises, the buffeting wind, and their own movements, she thought she'd caught a hint of another noise. A *human* noise.

Dorran held still while they listened. Under the house's hollowness, Clare was sure she could hear a voice. Words. Coming from above them, on the third floor.

Madeline? No…she was so careful about not letting us hear her before. She can't be back. And the others don't talk.

Dorran silently unsheathed his knife and beckoned for Clare to stay close to him. Together, they stepped into the hallway and faced the stairs.

The voice had fallen silent, but Clare could still feel its echoes, seemingly hovering around her ears like invisible moths. Dorran was at the stairs before Clare could hiss a warning to him. His dark eyes scanned the upper landing as he ascended, and Clare, her own heart beating against her ribs, followed closely.

What if it's a trap? They could be trying to lure us toward them.

They stopped at the top of the stairs. Neither of them breathed. The silence held for a moment, the voice came again, floating out of their bedroom.

"I hope you're okay. I'll try again tomorrow."

Clare took a sharp breath, half in relief, half in shock. The voice was Beth's. They'd agreed to speak again that day. She'd been looking forward to it—but she hadn't realized the morning was *that* late. She slipped past Dorran and ran along the hallway, jarring the cuts on her leg but barely noticing. She caught herself on the bedroom door and fumbled to unlock it, then darted inside. The radio sat next to their fireside bed. She grabbed it and turned her signal on. "I'm here! Sorry!"

Static answered her. Clare dropped back onto her heels, burning disappointment stinging her throat and her eyes. She should have watched the time more closely. Or at least thought to bring the radio with her.

Dorran hesitated in the doorway, his eyes tense. "I am sorry."

"Not your fault." The words were automatic. She swiped her palm across her eyes to clear them and took a ragged breath. "She'll try again tomorrow. And I'll make sure I don't miss it."

He approached, and his hand gently rested over her shoulder. "Would you like some time?"

"No." It was later than Clare had thought, which meant they didn't have time to spare. She pushed onto her feet and took a slow, steadying breath. "Let's keep going. Where did you say we were looking next?"

They followed the hallway around a corner, where Dorran unlocked and opened the door to a bedroom. A strange sensation spread through Clare as she stepped over the threshold. Most of the house had been maintained so impeccably that it was hard to imagine someone living there, but this room was filled with signs of life. At the same time, it had an odd feeling about it—one Clare couldn't put into words.

A bed, not much different from their own, had been neatly made. A jacket hung across the back of a chair, with a scarf carelessly draped over a side table beside a hairbrush and watch.

Clare, feeling like she was intruding on something private, didn't let herself touch anything. She stayed to the center of the room, with her arms wrapped around her chest. "What was his name?"

"Eros." Dorran stepped around the bed to approach one of two large wardrobes.

Clare knew the name. Dorran had told her about Eros when recounting the night half of his family had died at Madeline's whim. Cyanide in their wine, culling the family of any sign of dissent. Eros had taken Dorran's side in the disagreement. He had lost his life for it.

Shivers traveled through her—she understood why the room disturbed her so much. The scarf and jacket had been carelessly arranged, making it look like Eros had risen from bed just that morning, but he had not lived there for many years.

Madeline had not left the room locked up and forgotten either. The furniture had been kept free from dust. The sheets must have been changed regularly. Each morning, the jacket would be lifted to allow the chair to be dusted, then carefully placed back the way it had been.

"Found it." Relief bled into Dorran's voice as he pulled boxes out of the base of the wardrobe. He hadn't been impervious to the room's atmosphere either. He tucked two objects under his arm, shoved the box back into the wardrobe, then crossed to the door with steps that were slightly too fast to be casual.

"Great." Clare followed him, trying not to show how relieved she was. "What else do we need?"

"I think we're ready, actually." He held out a hand and pulled her in for a hug, then kissed her forehead. "Are you all right?"

"Absolutely." She took a moment to rest against his chest, as though she could absorb some of his confidence. Then she stepped back and put a genuine smile on her face. "I'm ready."

Dorran collected their equipment in the foyer. The sled looked old and shabby, and Clare instinctively knew it had been used by the staff, rather than the Morthorne family. On it, Dorran stacked the pitchfork and a hatchet, along with two thermoses filled with hot tea and a spare jacket. The red-covered dome rested over them, just barely fitting on the sled. Dorran tied it down with twine, then began gathering jackets and insulated pants from where they kept them on a side table by the door, and handed them to Clare one by one.

She remembered how cold the outside had been last time she'd ventured into it. The clothes had been enough to stop her from freezing but still hadn't quite managed to keep her warm, so she didn't complain as Dorran bundled her in layer after layer.

"These should also help protect us from the hollows," Dorran said. "The clothes shouldn't tear easily, and with this much padding, we will only need to watch our hands, necks, and faces. In theory."

Clare was already wearing knit gloves, but Dorran passed her a leather pair as well. They were a men's size and too big for her, but she knew why she was wearing them: knit would be easy to bite through. Leather not so much. The gloves extended over her wrist, and when she rolled down her jacket sleeves, Dorran tied a piece of twine around them to hold them in place. As he worked, his fingers grazed over the bandage on her wrist, and his eyebrows pulled a little lower. Clare wondered how closely his thoughts mimicked hers.

Will it be enough?

Even with the layers, even with the gloves, even with every heavy, bulky protection they could find, she didn't know if they could stay safe. But she was ready to try. Because if they could get to the car, it meant they were that much closer to reaching Beth.

"Hm." Dorran paced around her, tugging on bits of her clothing, checking everything was secure. The pants had been tied over the boots. A belt had been looped through holes in one of the jackets to ensure it couldn't be pulled up to expose her stomach. Still, he kept pacing, scanning her, brushing stray hair away from her cheek.

"I feel like the world's puffiest astronaut." Clare gave an exaggerated waddle, trying to break some of the somberness.

Dorran cracked a smile, but he didn't laugh. "Come back. You're not ready yet." He scooped her hair away from her neck and tied it into a bun, fit a knit hat over it, and tied a scarf around the lower parts of her face, so only her eyes were free. Then he returned to the table and picked up the fencing face guard.

The mesh shield fit snugly over Clare's head. Thick padding pressed against her cheeks, forehead, and chin, to protect her from the metal. The oval mesh ballooned out from it, extending just far enough that she had about an inch between her nose and the superfine metal. Her joke about astronauts suddenly felt much more appropriate. The mask was as good as a helmet. As it fit over her head, the world turned a shade darker.

Dorran adjusted it, checking that it was comfortable and making sure it wouldn't come loose. Flaps of padded fabric draped over her neck, and he tucked them into the collar of her jackets, then stepped back. She couldn't be completely sure through the mesh, but she thought he looked paler. Still, he nodded as though he was happy. "I think that is the best we can do."

She hoped she looked cool. She knew she probably didn't. She gave Dorran two thumbs up, then rested against the wall while he donned his own gear. He was faster about dressing himself. By the time he was ready, Clare was starting to feel overheated. She was almost looking forward to the first blast of icy air as they opened the doors.

Dorran took up his own mask and fit it on. She hadn't expected the mesh to hide his face so perfectly. It left her with an odd sensation, as though she were facing a stranger. The dark, expressive eyes she loved were gone. The straight, strong nose. The lips that could look so serious and so happy. All of it vanished under a blank, smooth sheet.

"Follow the same rules as last time," Dorran said. Even his voice seemed muffled. "Stay close to me. If you feel unwell, tell me immediately. If you hear or see something, let me know. If we have a choice between fighting and sheltering, always choose shelter. Are you ready?"

She prayed she was. "Yes."

He wrenched the doors open, and welcomed winter into their home.

CHAPTER 8

THE FIRST BLAST OF cold air was as welcome and refreshing as Clare had hoped it would be. But then the second gust came, and she scrunched her face up against the chill.

Snow was packed nearly to the top of the door. Dorran took up a shovel and attacked it, alternately pulling it into the foyer and shoving it out. The snow would drench the tiles when it melted, but they didn't have much of a choice.

Dorran carved a channel through the middle of the buildup, effectively creating a ramp leading up to the ridge. Clare understood his plan and got behind the sled. He joined her, and together, they shoved their luggage over the peak. The wire-and-drape shell rattled as the wind tried to get under it, then the sled tipped over the ramp's balance point and disappeared down the slope.

Dorran extended his hand. Clare took it, and he helped her

climb over the snow. She slid down the other side, tumbling and unwieldy in her outfit. Flecks of snow became trapped in the mask. As she righted herself, she tried to beat them free and restore her vision. She heard, more than saw, Dorran skid down beside her.

The good weather had held. The sun felt a little stronger than it had the previous few days. Clare let herself hold on to the thin, risky hope that they might have turned a corner and milder, warmer weather was on its way. Then she looked behind them and saw a patch of gray over the house's broken roof.

A storm? Coming toward us or going?

She blew a breath through the scarf in an attempt to melt the last ice flakes clinging to her mask, then turned to face the field. As far as she could tell, it was empty. The hollows seemed to prefer dark, quiet spaces when they could get them. The forest. The house. They only ventured into the sun when they had no way to avoid it.

The sled had come to a rest not far away, and they hiked to it. A rope had been tied around its front, creating a loop, and Dorran took one side while Clare picked up the other. Then they turned toward the forest.

"Normally I would want to go between the trees, where it's more sheltered." Dorran's voice was almost lost under the wind's howl. "But the sled will have trouble on the roots. I think it will be easier to go along the path my family used when leaving the property, then backtrack along the main road. It will add perhaps ten minutes to our trip."

Clare nodded. They had left later than she'd wanted, but even so, energy was in shorter supply than time. The sled was heavy. Their clothes weighted them down. And the snow, which had developed an icy sheen over its surface, was slippery and treacherous. Even with snowshoes Clare struggled to find a good footing.

She alternated her attention between the ground in front of her, the forest's edge, and the sky behind them. Dorran was watching the gray patch too. It was hard to be certain, but Clare thought it was moving toward them. At least it was slow. With luck, they would be inside the forest and at least partially protected before it hit.

Her breathing was ragged. The face mask felt as though it was smothering her, and the frozen air burned her throat and lungs every time she inhaled. Her body was starting to settle into that uneasy middle ground where it was both too hot and too cold at the same time.

Ahead, a gap between the trees loomed. The way the boughs hung over the road made it feel like walking into a tunnel. Banksy Forest was ancient; initially planted as a pine forestry but never harvested, its once-neat lines were breaking apart as old giants collapsed and younger generations grew to take their place. The oldest trees seemed to rise up forever, as though they were trying to blot out the sky.

The road was straight, and even though snow lay dense, it wasn't quite as thick as where there was wind to whip it up and build it into drifts. The world seemed to grow quieter as they entered the forest. Clare could hear both of them breathing between the steady crunching of their snowshoes. And, underneath that, the scrabbling.

Clare stared upward, into the forest's boughs. She thought she saw motion, but as soon as her eyes locked on it, the branches were still.

The hollows liked to climb. Beth said they hunted animals; Clare guessed the boughs held birds and squirrels for them to catch. She flicked her gaze over the branches, searching the interlacing silhouettes for any sign of life.

The scratching noise was following them. And yet, the creatures weren't trying to attack.

How sentient are they? She flinched as a branch snapped behind them. She turned but still couldn't see anything. *Do they remember what happened to the others that attacked us? Are they frightened of us? Or...are they cleverer than we know? Are they waiting, planning, looking for an opportunity?*

"Not far now." Without the wind snatching away their words, she could hear Dorran more clearly. She tried to smile for him before remembering he couldn't see her any better than she could see him.

Their path opened up unexpectedly. One moment, they were encased in what felt like a never-ending hedge of trees. The next, Clare stumbled as the vegetation thinned into a familiar channel.

She'd driven the road through Banksy Forest at least once a week for as long as she'd lived in the area. She thought she could recognize the part they were in thanks to a bend to their right. If she was right, they were still in the heart of the forest.

Dorran indicated to their left. It took a moment to get their sled lined up on the new path, then they set off again. Clare's muscles were waning, but she walked a little faster. Being on the main road meant they were close to her car—and the hollows still hadn't shown themselves.

The road led them around a gentle bend, then, up ahead, Clare glimpsed her car. The little red hatchback had been driven up on the side of the road. Its hood was crumpled from where it had smashed into one of the ancient trees. The front driver's door hung open, but it was at an angle that meant relatively little snow had ended up inside.

She and Dorran exchanged a look, and she was pretty sure that, under the mask, he was smiling just as broadly as she was.

A branch cracked behind them. Clare turned, and her heart dropped. In the distance, almost perfectly blended into the forest, stood a figure at least two heads taller than she was. It leaned out from between the trees, one elongated arm dangling. The limb had been broken. Bone fragments jutted out, and they seemed to have grown, the sharp spikes fanning out like early plumage. Clare stared at it. It stared back.

"Dorran," she whispered.

"I see it. Get to the car."

She pulled on the rope again, pushing tired muscles to move faster. The car was close. The hollow wasn't following. *Please, let it stay there.*

Dorran gave the sled a final shove as it slid around the car's back, unfastened the dome shelter, then pulled the ax out from underneath. He turned to face the hollow. "Can you get the supplies by yourself?"

"Yes." She wrenched on the rear door's handle. Snow and ice had formed a seal around it, but a sharp kick cracked it free. The door fell open, revealing the two travel cases she'd packed for the trip to Beth's.

They held necessities—long-life food, batteries, clothes, a small first aid kit, a couple of books, which would have been essential to survive weeks in a cramped room with little other entertainment. Clare hauled them out, gasping as she moved the heavy cases to sit on the sled. She stacked them, then used the twine to tie the shelter down on top of them.

"Got it," she called to Dorran.

He stood by the car's front, one hand resting on the lifted hood as he alternated his attention from the wrecked engine to the hollow between the trees. "Is anything else in the car useful?"

She looked in the trunk. It held jugs of water, long frozen; she left them there. Winterbourne had its own water supply. "Not unless you can get the gas out of the tank."

"It is spilled." Dorran stepped away from the car's front, still keeping his eyes on the figure posed between the trees. "We will need to retrace our steps to reach the road. Are you ready?"

"Yes."

CHAPTER 9

DORRAN FACED THE CREATURE blocking their path. "If it attacks, be prepared to run. We can retrieve the sled another day if need be."

Clare picked up her end of the rope and heaved the sled back onto the path. It rocked before stabilizing, and Dorran took up his half of the rope. With the extra weight, Clare had to dig her feet into the snow to get it to move. She was grateful she had Dorran with her. He'd been right when he'd said it wasn't something he could do alone.

She tried not to stare at the hollow, even though a morbid curiosity kept pulling her attention toward it. The creature watched them, not blinking, its jaw hanging open. As she got closer, she had a better view of its features. She thought it might have been male before it became warped. It no longer wore any clothes. The skin over its face was drooping as though it had been melted, and the nose was little more than a bump. Its chin seemed to have receded into its neck, until its entire head and throat looked like one form.

They were nearly level with it. The hollow leaned farther out from its cover. Its throat began to vibrate as a low chattering noise came from it. The sound left Clare feeling cold. The face was human, but the mind definitely wasn't.

Clare kept her head down. Dorran pulled the sled with one hand, but in the other, he held the ax. The blade was raised—not high, but at the ready.

To their right, a narrow, dark gap appeared between the trees: the path leading to Winterbourne. They were giving the hollow the widest berth possible. Even so, the creature was reacting to their presence. It sank low, drawing tension into its legs. The chattering grew louder. Its small, watery eyes followed them, seeming too close to the badly spaced teeth in its slack mouth.

Then they were at the path and turning away from the hollow. Clare lifted her head again as she tried to keep moving despite the shaking in her limbs. She could see Dorran out of her peripheral vision. He kept the ax at the ready, his head tilted to watch the monster behind them.

We did it. We walked right past one.

An idea rose. Maybe the hollows weren't attacking because they couldn't recognize her and Dorran as human. With the masks in place, neither of them had a face.

It almost felt too good to hope for, but if she was right, the possibilities were incredible. It meant they could venture past the house's walls without being afraid. It meant they could get to Beth—

A branch snapped behind them. She looked over her shoulder. The elation faded.

The hollow had followed them. It kept its distance, nearly twenty feet back, but when they took a step, so did it.

She wished she could see Dorran's expression. He flexed his grip on the ax, his shoulders visibly tight even under the layers. They both increased their pace.

The hollow matched them. *No. Worse than matched,* Clare realized. *It's gaining.* It seemed to be picking up speed, its long legs loping forward, its torso bent, the melted, deformed face still fixated on them.

And it was no longer alone. Clare could hear them at their sides—the rustle of dead pine needles being crushed, creaks as branches were strained. She tilted her head and glimpsed scuttling movement among the boughs.

No. Please, not now, not when we're so close.

She didn't dare speak to Dorran. Making any kind of noise felt like too much of a risk. They kept their heads down as they dragged the supplies back along the path. Dorran's mask turned from side to side as he watched their surroundings. He adjusted his hold on the ax again.

The path ahead was growing lighter. They were at the edge of the forest. But the noises around them were surging. The animalistic chattering came again, first from the hollow following in their wake, then echoed from the ones in the trees. Clare strained to breathe through the stress choking her. She tried to guess how many there might be. Too many. Every time she thought she had them located, more noises emerged from the underbrush, from the branches above, from every side, and even from ahead. A small shape darted across the path. Clare prayed it wouldn't attack. She could fight the larger hollows if it came to that. She didn't know if she would be able to kill a child.

Then they stepped through the edge of the forest, and the clear white field, glaring in the late afternoon sun, stretched ahead of them. Winterbourne loomed in the distance.

Not far now. Twenty minutes, if that.

She chanced a look over her shoulder. Dozens of eyes glittered from between the trees. They'd stopped at the edge of the forest, holding to their shadows.

Above, the storm clouds stretched across the entire sky. The wind felt colder as it gusted through the mask. Clare couldn't stop shaking. She fought to keep her footing steady, to keep herself upright and moving.

Snow crunched behind them, and Clare flinched. She didn't stop to look. Neither did Dorran. They both faced the manor, shoes digging into the show, adrenaline battling exhaustion.

Then Dorran cried out and fell. Clare turned in time to see him swipe the ax at a hollow that had raced in their wake with deceptive quietness. The creature, a stocky, buckled one, pulled at his leg. Its spine rippled like an accordion. Its flesh was almost as white as the snow. When it opened its mouth, a tongue with a deep split down its center arced out, flicking through the frozen air, before coiling back inside like a snake's.

Clare dropped the sled's rope. Dorran's ax connected with the hollow's shoulder and dark-red blood sprayed across the white field. The monster coiled back, snapping and hissing, then dove forward again, aiming for Dorran's throat.

Instead, it hit the end of the pitchfork. Clare yelled as she forced the implement forward, the tines plunging through the hollow's chest. She could feel the bones cracking and cartilage breaking. The hollow barely seemed to notice. It reached forward, lumpy arms and knobbled fingers scrabbling along the wood, trying to grasp Clare.

Dorran was back on his feet. He had a better shot this time. Clare held the pitchfork as still as she could while he swung. The ax sunk into the hollow's skull, cleaving it in half between its eyes. More blood bubbled out of the hole, but there was less than Clare would have expected. It seemed thick, almost as though it had been dehydrated, as it dribbled over the creature's torso. The bulging eyes turned in opposite directions. The jaw fell slack, and the cleft tongue slid over the bottom lip. Dorran pulled his ax free as Clare shook the creature off the tines.

They stood for a moment, staring down at their work, panting and shaking. Then Clare looked up. Three hollows had stepped out of the forest's edge. They watched her. To Clare, their expressions almost seemed curious.

A slow, muffled rumbling noise made prickles run along her skin. The storm was coming. It progressed slowly, creeping across the landscape, heavy drops of sleet hitting the trees, the snow, the house.

Dorran found her arm and tugged on it. "Move," he whispered. "As quickly as you can."

She grabbed the rope, stumbled, and caught her balance. The hollows stood in front of the forest. They were still, but she thought they must have come closer when she wasn't looking. Another two had appeared between the trees.

Dorran took up the other end of the rope. His ax was stained black, specks of blood scattered over his arm and his chest. It smelled foul. Rotten. She bit her tongue to stop from gagging. They moved forward. The sled was too heavy to run, but they took fast steps, panting in lungfuls of burning air.

Chewing noises came from behind them. The hollows descended on their fallen comrade. They huddled over its body, fingers digging into the skin to expose the softer insides, teeth tearing off strips of fat and muscle. They ate like animals. Horrible wet smacking noises floated through the frosty air.

She turned back to the house. Rain blurred it. Running through the water as it trickled under their clothes would be hell, but it was better than lingering outside. They only had half of the field left to cross before they reached the blocks of white that marked the front yard.

Under her pounding footsteps, she thought she caught another noise—rasping breaths. Low, eager chattering. She felt the sled jerk, and turned. A hollow clung to the top of their domed shelter, bony joints poking out at unnatural angles. It had teeth everywhere. At first, Clare's mind revolted against the image, unable to understand what it was seeing. Bulging yellow teeth poked through its shoulders. Something like a deformed jaw gaped below its collar bone. The skin around its mouth was shredded, and additional teeth poked through the holes. Hundreds of them. Clare yelled.

That second of shock cost her. The hollows moved at a blinding pace, scuttling on all fours, some grasping at the sled, others swarming around it and reaching toward Clare. She moved on instinct, lifting the pitchfork and driving it into the nearest creature. The impact forced her back, and in a heartbeat, the others were on her.

CHAPTER 10

A BODY SLAMMED INTO her chest, winding her. Hard pressure dug into her forearm. Teeth, she thought, fighting and failing to get through the jackets.

A new face loomed over her, just inches away, peering through the mesh mask. Saliva dripped from its open maw. The mouth stretched from one ear to the other like a gash. Its right eye bored into her. The left was missing, only a rotting, dark-red socket in its place.

Dorran yelled. The pressure on her arm disappeared in time with the *thwack* of an ax. She heard scuffling as he was overrun by the creatures.

Clare pulled on the pitchfork, trying to use it to knock the monster off of her, but one of them was still impaled on its tip, weighing it down, its body contorted as it stretched to reach her.

The hollow perched on her chest reached long, bony hands up to her mask. Its fingers traced over the mesh, trying to pry its way through. It was so close that she could see the whorls of its fingerprints. See the dirt trapped under its nails. Smell the rot from where a green infection spread around a cuticle.

The nails dug at the mesh. When it couldn't get through, it lifted its hand and brought it down as a fist. Clare grunted. The impact crushed the mesh against her skin. Now, she could feel the fingers. Through the barrier, through the freezing wire, she could feel the clammy, spongy skin poking at her cheek.

Then the hollow whirled away. Dorran crouched over her. Blood painted a streak across his mask, dripping from the wire. He kept low, one hand braced over Clare, the other holding the ax at the ready. A hollow came forward. The ax cleaved through its neck, and Clare gasped as the head bounced over her stomach, then tumbled away.

Dorran was yelling, but Clare couldn't make out the words. Noise swallowed everything—a rumbling, deep, like a mountain's scream. She tilted her head back and saw the sleet was racing toward them.

We can run through the rain. But we can't fight in it. It will sap our strength. Freeze us before we can get free. And it's still so far to the house. We can't outrun the hollows.

"The shelter," she yelled to Dorran. She didn't think he heard her. He moved sharply, furiously, stabbing at the creatures as they darted forward, still holding himself over Clare. She rolled to her side. The sled was less than five feet away. Hollows stood between them, but she thought, if they moved quickly, they might be able to make it. "Dorran! Follow!"

She grabbed his arm and yanked him as she moved. He obeyed. Together, they raced toward the sled, tripping over their snowshoes, staggering through the churned-up snow. Two of the hollows in their path scattered as they neared. The third crouched and sprang. Dorran swiped at it. The ax missed its mark, skimming across the hollow's ribs, but it was enough to knock the monster aside. They were at the sled. Clare grabbed the dome, leaned back, and wrenched it up and over them. The twine holding it down snapped, and the sled jolted as the dome came free. She and Dorran pulled together, on their knees and pressed against each other, as the structure dropped over them.

The hollows hit the shelter's surface. The scrabbling was back, worse than it had ever been before. Above her. Around her. Inside her own head. The smell of hollow blood filled the space. Clare choked. Her arms had no more strength left in them, but she clung to Dorran. He held her in return.

"Shh, shh." The murmurs should have been comforting, but distorted through the mask and trapped in the tiny shelter, they just made Clare shake harder.

Then a new sound joined the scrabbling: sleet, hitting the ground outside. Hitting the fabric. Hitting the hollows. Strangely, it helped. It drowned out everything else—the chattering, the scrabbling. The rain's rhythmic, unrelenting pounding soothed something deep inside of her.

Clare lifted her head. Her mask was badly dented, pressing against her cheek, and it felt like it was rubbing her nerves raw. She fumbled to take it off. Dorran helped. He unfastened the straps from the back of her head, and finally, she felt as though she could breathe properly again.

The space was claustrophobic. Kneeling, pressed as close together as they could get, their heads and shoulders still brushed the chicken-wire frame. The curtains were too heavy to let anything more than a distant trace of light through. Still, it was a respite. They were out of the rain and away from the scratching fingers.

Dorran unfastened his own mask and dropped it at his side. His skin was pale and glistened with sweat. Clare reached up, her fingers brushing over his cheek and trailing down to his chin. She'd never thought she would be so happy to see his face again.

"Are you all right?" He was still panting.

She was breathless, too, and nodded. A drop of icy water landed on her cheek, and she flinched away from it.

Dorran's eyes tightened as he looked up. "This will not be waterproof. I designed it to protect from hail more than rain."

"We were so close." Clare huddled over even farther to avoid the drops that were appearing on the wire frame. Dorran adjusted his position so they could sit side by side. His arm ended up wrapped around her waist. She leaned into his shoulder. Flecks of blood stuck to her cheek, but she was too tired to care.

"We are still alive," Dorran said. "That is something to be grateful for."

She let her eyes close as she rested against him. Outside, thunder crackled. The fingers, persistent, groped at the thick cloth. She could feel the creatures climbing over the dome. When lightning flashed above them, she could see the dark bodies silhouetted above them. Then the frame shivered. Fingers were prying under the edge of the dome. They wiggled through the snow, feeling, seeking. Dorran pulled his hatchet free from his belt. The sound of crunching bones was accompanied by low, angry hisses.

"Hold it down," Dorran said. He took hold of the chicken wire above his head and pulled it toward him. The dome bowed slightly as Clare added her weight to his.

The fingers continued to try to squirm under the shelter's edge. Whenever they got too close, Dorran stabbed at them. Clare closed her eyes and tilted her head back. The sight of severed fingers and red-stained snow seeping around them turned her stomach. She breathed through her mouth, the smell of blood making her dizzy as she clung to the wire and held the dome down.

Beth had hollows outside her bunker. When they hear her, they come looking for her. But she said they go away after a while if she stays quiet. A couple of hours, she said.

Clare opened her eyes a fraction. In the hazy, failing light, Dorran's features were barely visible. He raised one gloved hand and hovered a finger over his lips. He'd had the same idea. Clare nodded.

They held as still as they could, their breathing slow and quiet enough to fade under the unending sleet. Water dripped over her gloves and soaked into Clare's sleeves. She shivered. Dorran tapped her wrist, telling her to let go, but she shook her head.

The hollows continued to creep over their shelter. She felt their pressure sometimes, as they stepped over her fingers. When they moved, they shook drops of water free. Sometimes they hissed. Sometimes they chattered. She heard fingers prying around the edges of the dome again, but with the extra weight, they couldn't get under.

Her head drooped. She was too tired to cry. Too tired to think. Instead of listening to the monsters outside, she tried to listen to her silent companion. His soft breaths. The nearly inaudible rustle of his coat's collar as he tilted his head. She could hear when he swallowed. That was enough to focus on.

Minutes blended together like a fractured nightmare. The scratching noises were trying to send her mad. They burrowed through her head, digging in under her nerves, winding her up.

Dorran released his grip on the wire beside her. He tapped her chin lightly to get her attention. She opened her eyes.

Inside the dome was so dark that she could no longer see Dorran's face. And, she realized, the noises outside had faded. Not just the hollows, but the sleet, as well.

She released her hold on the mesh. Her arm muscles screamed as she lowered them, but she bit her tongue to stay silent. There was no guarantee that the hollows were gone. Any noise, no matter how small, might revive the attack.

Dorran moved as well as he could in the cramped space. He scraped away some of the snow at the dome's edge and bent over, face to the icy ground, and looked through the gap. Then he put his head near Clare's to whisper into her ear. "Can you run?"

"I think so."

"Get ready. Leave the sled if you have to. We can get it later."

She felt him lift his arms again, this time to brace against the dome's ceiling. He pushed. A cracking noise echoed around them. Dorran froze, waited, and when the silence persisted, he pushed again. An inch at a time, the dome lifted. The structure was built to be heavy, but not so heavy that it should have resisted him so much. Clare lifted her arms and pushed too. More cracking noises surrounded them. *Ice*, she thought. The sleet had frozen over their shelter.

The edge of the red fabric lifted from the snow and wan light rushed in. The day had entered twilight. If they stayed any longer, it would be night. They continued pushing, straining against the weight, to lift the structure. It broke free with a snap and tipped away.

Clare pressed a hand to her throat. Hollows were scattered around them. The sleet had coated the monsters. It encased their warped bodies, freezing them into horrible, deformed ice sculptures. She recognized the one closest to her feet, the one with too many teeth. Four of its fingers had been cut off, leaving raw, red stumps. Clare stared at it, revolted but unable to look away. It was perfectly preserved under a solid inch of glassy ice. Its wide eyes stared into the distance. Then they rotated, swiveling to fix on Clare.

She stumbled back and felt for Dorran's arm. "They're not dead," she whispered.

"Let's go."

Dorran left the dome where it was, encased in ice and fused to three of the hollows. They found the sled's rope and strained to free their precious luggage from its own ice prison. The sled jolted free with a crunch, and they both staggered, then regained their feet. Clare kept her eyes fixed forward, even when she thought she heard the crunch of fracturing ice echo through the field.

The sleet had left their path slippery, and each step was an ordeal. But the house grew closer with every passing breath, and just as the sun vanished over the horizon, they stepped under the arching front porch.

"You first," Dorran said, and picked Clare up. He lifted her while she scrabbled up the snowbank at the front door, then tumbled inside the house.

The drop jarred sore muscles, but she moved to the side to make way for Dorran. A moment later, the sled came over the rise. The two travel cases broke free as they slid across the floor, closely followed by Dorran. He slammed the doors closed behind them.

The house was too dark to see well. She heard Dorran feeling for matches along the side table. The sound his gloves made felt too close to the grasping, scratching noises the hollows made, and Clare shuddered. Then a match flared, and pale golden light spread around them.

"Well. We are home." Dorran looked exhausted. Spots of blood coated his clothes. Dark circles filled the spaces around his eyes, enhanced by his pale skin. But he still smiled. He reached out a hand, and Clare took it. Together, they shuffled toward their final obstacle: the flight of stairs leading to their room.

CHAPTER 11

CLARE SAT IN THE wingback chair in front of the fire. She rested her cheek on the fabric, staring into the flames, her mind wandering in and out of conscious thought.

Where's Dorran?

She blinked. She remembered walking up the stairs. She remembered him feeding wood into the fire and helping her peel the damp layers of clothes off. Then a cloth soaked in warm water, running over her arms and her face, cleaning her. After that was a daze, but she thought he'd said something as she fell into sleep. *"I will be back soon."*

Clare frowned. He shouldn't be wandering the house alone, especially that night. He would be exhausted; he wouldn't be able to defend himself properly if something attacked.

She rose, and the muscles in her legs screamed. She'd made it two steps toward the door before it creaked open, and Clare sank back into her chair with a sigh of relief.

Dorran carried bowls of food and a bottle tucked under one arm. She thought he might have washed. He wore the green knit top she was fond of, and his wet hair was brushed back from his face.

"Here," he murmured, placing a bowl in her lap. "You must be starved."

It was warm and smelled good. What was more, it wasn't soup. Clare stared in wonder at a generous portion of cheesy pasta.

"I didn't realize you were cooking dinner," Clare said. "Aren't you tired?"

He settled into the chair beside her, cradling his own bowl. "I thought we should enjoy the rewards of our mission. I hope you don't mind; I opened your cases."

"No, I'm glad." She picked up the spoon and scooped some of the pasta into her mouth. "Oh, this is good. Sorry, Dorran, I know you put so much effort into the soups—"

He chuckled as he licked his spoon. "But we were both thoroughly sick of them."

Clare was ravenous, and the food, so tasty and rich compared to the watery vegetable blends they had been living off, made her want to shovel it into her mouth until she couldn't fit any more. But she paced herself, trying to savor it and not make herself sick. "So much has happened since I left home, I can't remember what I packed. Or how *much* I packed. Will it be enough?"

"Yes. We should be comfortably set until the garden is ready for harvest. Pastas, rice, canned sauces, canned fruit. You did well."

It was a ridiculous thing to be proud of, but she felt herself turning pink at his praise. "At least the trip was worth it."

"We made it back in one piece. I do count that as a success."

Clare laughed. But at the same time, the images returned: the creatures, frozen under their layers of ice, still alive, still watching. The blood. The way they had swarmed over Clare and Dorran as though willing to bury them alive.

It had been so near impossible to get to the road, and that was only an hour away. She couldn't imagine how they could go farther. Simply walking to the forest's end would take at least four hours, and they would probably need to go much farther than that to find any kind of transport. Beth might as well be on another continent.

"I got something to celebrate with." Dorran put his bowl aside and picked up the bottle of wine. "I hope you won't mind drinking out of mugs."

Clare realized her face had fallen and tried to put some cheer back into it. "That's my favorite way to drink wine."

He used the end of his spoon to force the cork into the bottle, then half filled two of the mugs. Clare gratefully took hers. The wine would at least help chase off some of the melancholy. Dorran was right; they'd gotten back alive and mostly unharmed, and that was as much of a success as they could ask for. The wine burned as it went down, and the sweetness lingered. "This is nice."

"It's merlot," Dorran said. "We have owned this bottle for decades, but when it was bought, it was worth nearly six thousand."

Clare choked on it and pressed the back of her hand over her mouth. "For wine?"

"For prestige more than the drink, I think." Dorran laughed. "My family was passionate about their collection. The staff drank cheap wines, and I liked them just as much. But I wanted you to have something nice tonight."

"Well, it's by far the most expensive thing I've put in my body." She smiled down at the mug. Then a thought occurred. "Did you have to go into the cellar for it?"

"Only briefly."

"Hah. It really doesn't bother you, does it? I'd rather drink water for the rest of my life than go back down there again." She pressed her lips together. "But thank you."

Dorran's smile was warm. For a moment, Clare was enraptured, enjoying the way he looked at her. Then he took a slow breath, his thumb tracing around the edge of his cup. "I think I know how to reach your sister."

Her heart missed a beat. She stared, food and wine forgotten.

Dorran reached into his pocket and took out a small, black shape. "While we were getting the supplies, I had a brief look at your car. And I found this in the ignition."

He passed her the key. Her throat tightened as she wrapped her hand around the small fob. She realized, with a shock, it was the first time she'd held a personal possession since arriving at Winterbourne. Everything had been borrowed: the clothes, the shoes, the food. She supposed that would change now. She had her luggage downstairs— two cases that now encapsulated the entirety of her life.

But the keys meant more than that. She lifted her gaze to meet Dorran's. "Do you think we can get it to start?"

"I'm afraid it's almost certainly dead. While I stood guard, I looked into engine. I was hoping I could repair it, but I am not familiar with the system. It is more complex than what I know."

"I guess your family still uses mechanical cars, whereas mine is full of digital parts."

"That seems to be the case. But it is not a lost cause. Behind the house is a shed where our cars are stored outside of use. The cars themselves are all gone, taken when my family left for the Gould estate, but there is an engine I was toying with. If we can transplant the engine into your car, we may be able to get it to run."

"If we could…" Clare rubbed the back of her neck. If they could, then Beth would no longer be unreachable. She bit her lip. "This is just a theory, but I think the masks might have protected us. Not just from the attack, but before as well. I couldn't see your face through the mesh; the hollows wouldn't have been able to either, and I think that was why they waited so long to attack."

"You might be right," Dorran said. "We had covered all of our skin. The hollow that watched us move the supplies out of the car—did you see how it looked at us? It was *curious.*"

"Exactly." Clare was growing more confident in her theory. "All of the other hollows, the ones in the house and the forest, they either looked hungry or afraid. Never curious."

"So the masks may have sheltered us…for a stretch. But the creatures are starving. You saw how they descended on the hollow we killed. Even his bones were broken and consumed. After that, they lost all control."

Clare agreed. "Like an animal that becomes so hungry that it ignores every other instinct. Maybe killing that first hollow pushed the rest into a frenzy."

"But even if they do not protect us completely, the masks should at least buy us some time. That will help." Dorran nodded to himself. "The journey will be dangerous, but not unachievable. We would need to find a way to keep the garden stable while we are away. And we would need part of our fuel reserves for the car. But if you are prepared to take a risk, I am as well."

"Yes." Clare's heart felt painfully full. The radio stood on the shelf, turned on but its volume kept low to muffle the static. She wished she could talk to Beth, to tell her what they were thinking, to tell her they were coming.

"I will see about the engine tomorrow and see what it might need to be compatible with your car."

"Thank you."

The gap between their chairs was narrow, but Clare reached across it to be closer to Dorran. He took her hand. They sat in silence, drinking their wine as they watched the fire. When Clare glanced toward her companion, she thought he looked the happiest she had ever seen him. Dorran wasn't he kind of person to grin or pose. But a small, content smile curved his lips, and his heavy-lidded eyes were bright. He ran his thumb over Clare's fingers. His happiness was infectious. When Clare fell asleep that night, she was almost comfortable enough to ignore the scratching in the walls.

CHAPTER 12

CLARE HADN'T THOUGHT IT was possible to be as stiff as she was. Every time she moved her arms, the muscles ached, running from her shoulder blades down to her hands.

Light came through the gauzy curtains to flow across the wallpaper. She'd slept late. Clare sat up in bed, groaning under her breath, and blinked sleep out of her eyes. Dorran's half of the bed was empty. A bowl was on the bedside table, covered with a plate to retain its heat, and a small note, written in ink, poised on top.

I will be back soon. Wait for me. Love, D.

"Seriously? *You* don't let *me* wander around the house alone," Clare grumbled as she threw the blankets aside and slipped sore feet into her boots. "Double standards."

She touched the bowl's side. It was still warm. He couldn't have gone far. A faint worry that he might have left for the shed alone—ventured outside, where she couldn't protect him if anything went wrong—tightened Clare's chest. She tied her hair back as she tried to quiet her mind. Dorran was stubborn, but he wasn't stupid. He wouldn't step into a situation that risky without at least telling her. More likely, he had gone to water the garden or unpack their new supplies.

Still, Clare's mind continued to buzz. She ignored the food and crossed to the door as she pulled on her coat. The house felt strangely quiet. She paused on the hallway landing, squinting in each direction, trying to read the shadows that clung to the walls.

A door slammed, and Clare jolted. She clenched her teeth as she looked toward the stairs. The sound had come from the floor below.

It's just Dorran. Probably.

She stepped back inside the bedroom. The fire poker rested beside the chairs, where she had left it the previous evening. Clare took it up and returned to the hall.

The stairs carried her downward, and she moved carefully to keep her footsteps silent. The second floor was bitterly dark except for one hall: a single lit candle had been positioned on one of the tables clustered along the walls. There was no sign of Dorran. At the end of the hallway, a curtain blocked out the window. Some additional light would make her feel safer. She licked her lips, glancing into the twisting darkness behind her, then began edging toward the window.

"Dorran?" Her voice cracked, and she regretted the word as soon as it left her. It wasn't wise to advertise her position in case something less friendly lurked in the halls.

Dorran rarely left her alone in the manor. She'd taken it for granted until that morning, but, all of a sudden, Clare was aware of how vulnerable she was. She swung the metal bar at her side, her pulse harsh. The walls seemed to be closing in around her, squeezing.

She could return to her room. But that would still leave Dorran out in the house somewhere, in just as much danger as she was. Clare bit the inside of her cheek and moved to the window in three long steps. She grasped a handful of the material dampening the light and pulled it aside.

The ethereal white fields were obscured by ice crusting across the panes. Clare could faintly make out her own reflection. The candle glowed behind her, meager and flickering as a gust of cold air blew across it.

Something else moved in the reflection. A tall creature, stepping through a gap in the hallway walls, its bulging, hairless head tilting as it stared at Clare.

She gasped and swung, bringing the crowbar around as she turned. The metal whistled through the air but missed its mark as the figure ducked. Clare staggered with momentum, then dropped the crowbar and pressed her hand over her pounding heart. "Dorran!"

He pulled the fencing mask off, his eyes wild. They stared at each other for a second, then he broke into laughter. "I am so sorry, my dear. I didn't mean to startle you."

Clare closed the distance between them and pressed her hands to his chest, checking he was really there. "I couldn't see your face... I thought you were a hollow... I could have really hurt you."

He lay his hands on top of hers as he smiled down. "I sometimes forget how fierce you can be. What are you doing outside of your room? Didn't you see my note?"

She narrowed her eyes, relief barely tempering the frustration. "What am *I* doing out here? What about *you*?" Over his shoulder, she noticed an open door in the paneled wood. "Were you seriously going into the passageways *alone*?"

"I know you do not like them. I thought I could get ahead on the work and seal some of the doors near our room." He shrugged. "It is safer now that I have the mask."

"That doesn't matter. We're supposed to do this together. You should have at least woken me so I knew where you were going. Or written it on the note. Or *something*. What if you went missing? I wouldn't even know where to look for you."

No matter what she said, he refused to look chastised. A small smile curled his mouth, and his dark eyes were filled with something Clare couldn't quite pinpoint. She squinted at him, a challenge. "What?"

"You are so beautiful."

She resented the way heat flowed over her face. "Don't think you can sweet-talk your way out of this."

He laughed. His thumb grazed along her jaw, then he ducked in to steal a kiss. Clare was caught off guard but closed her eyes to savor the touch. Warm lips, nuanced and tender, explored hers. He made a faint happy noise in the back of his throat, his nose grazing her cheek as he reluctantly pulled away.

"Don't think you can kiss your way out of this either," she mumbled, but the frustration had drained from her. It was hard to stay angry at Dorran when he was so intently affectionate.

"Of course not. I promise I am thoroughly repentant." Dorran's eyes were bright as he lightly pulled on her hand, leading her back toward the stairs. As he passed the open door, he nudged it closed, sealing off the dark cavern within.

"Did anything bother you?" Clare asked.

"No. No sign of anything." He looked more relaxed than Clare could have felt if she'd been inside the passageways. "I managed to close three doors near our room, so as long as there are none that I missed, we will have bought ourselves a shade more protection. The creatures will have to travel through the main hallways if they wish to reach us."

Clare had to admit, it was a nice feeling. They didn't have complete security, and probably wouldn't for a while, but it was a relief to know she would at least see the hollows coming in that part of the house.

As they moved onto the stairs, Clare asked, "Did you want to keep on with the passageways? I can help this time. Beth will be calling in about an hour. Or we could have an early lunch and maybe spend some time in the garden."

He stretched, flexing his back muscles. "Or we could visit the shed behind the property and look for our motor."

"Really?" She hadn't expected him to be so ready to step outside after the previous day.

"It is directly behind the house. Not far to walk. And not as risky as the forest." He opened the door to their room and let Clare enter ahead of him. "If we are able to bring the motor inside, I can check it to make sure it will work. The weather is likely to stay erratic. We might have a limited window of time to reach your sister, and I want to be prepared."

"All right. I'm game if you are."

He found the untouched breakfast on the bedside table and pressed it into her hands. "Or...consider this. You could stay inside, where it's warm, and keep lookout for me."

She lifted her eyebrows.

Dorran sighed. "I knew it would not work. But you cannot blame me for trying. Very well, eat first, then we will make the trip while the sun is nearing its zenith and the weather is calm."

Clare finished the breakfast in a hurry, while Dorran marked his progress on the maps, folded them, and tucked them away in the drawers. Before they left the bedroom, Clare collected the radio. She wouldn't let herself miss Beth's call for a second day in a row. She checked that the batteries were still good, then tucked it under her arm as they went downstairs.

Her luggage waited in the foyer. Dorran had removed the food and locked it in their room, where it would be protected from any hollows roving the house. He'd left everything else though, and Clare knelt to sort through the cases.

She had to laugh. The final morning in her old home had been so rushed that she'd barely paid attention to what she packed. The stash included shorts and blouses, which would be too light to keep her warm in Winterbourne. The day she left had been a mild autumn morning, she remembered, and her closet had still been full of thin, comfy clothes. But the bag also included shoes, which meant she would finally have some that fit her well, and underwear. She had never felt completely comfortable wearing another woman's.

The batteries would be invaluable, and she set the packs on the side table, where they would be within easy reach. The box also included two books she'd grabbed off the shelf as a last-minute bid for entertainment. One was a thriller she'd already read twice. The other was a dusty, never-used reference book. It wasn't the best selection, but that didn't matter. Winterbourne had vast libraries. The books were all from the nineteenth century or earlier, but she didn't mind classic fiction.

"That's pretty," Dorran said.

Clare looked down at the gauzy, floral print top she held. She felt herself turning pink as she folded it back into the bag. "Not much use here."

"Keep it. We don't know when the weather will warm up again."

The house was so cold that it was hard to imagine spring would ever come, but Clare tucked the lighter clothes away neatly. Even if she couldn't wear them, it felt good to have some of her own possessions. Even just a handful.

It feels as though we're clawing back our lives an inch at a time.

We have shelter. We have food. Soon, once the passages are sealed, we'll have safety. And maybe even transport...

Beth's warning echoed in the back of her mind: *The heroes are dying. If you want to survive, don't take risks.* She frowned and pushed the thought aside. It wasn't as though they wanted to drive across the country; they were just going to retrieve Beth. And for Clare, that counted as a necessity.

CHAPTER 13

THEY WENT THROUGH THEIR routine of strapping on layers of clothes. Dorran promised the walk to the shed would take less than a minute, but he didn't let her skimp on her protection. "The shed doors have remained shut, so I expect it to be empty," he said as he checked that her gloves were tucked in place, "but I still want to err toward caution."

They picked up the snowshoes and fencing masks. Clare used her elbow to knock out the dents in hers. It left the mesh's once-smooth curves wavy, but it was better than nothing.

Instead of opening the front door, Dorran led Clare deeper into the building. They followed a route she hadn't seen before, and soon narrowing passages and bare stone walls told her they had entered the staff's quarters. A minute later, they stepped into a near-empty storage room with a thick metal door. Frost spread out from the door's edges, crusting over parts of the rough stone and freezing the hinges. Dorran nodded to Clare. She tucked the radio into one of the folds of her jacket, then pulled on the mask. He undid the door's bolt and leaned back to use his weight to wrench it open.

The door shuddered as rusted hinges were forced to move. Specks of snow shot through the entrance and swirled over the benches and floor. The snowdrifts hadn't grown so high at the house's back, and Dorran used a shovel to beat them down to something they could climb over.

Through the opening, Clare could make out large, blocky buildings hunched in the field of white. Beyond them, the dark ribbon that marked the forest's edge stretched into the distance. Snow fell, but at least it wasn't a storm.

They latched their snowshoes into place. Dorran offered his hand, and Clare held it to stay steady as she scrambled over the waist-high snowbank. Dorran followed, shutting the door behind them, and they began the march through the snow.

The dark shapes resolved into two large wooden buildings. Both had sharply peaked roofs that had still managed to collect snow. Dorran led her to the largest one, the building on the left. As he'd promised, it was close to the house. Clare kept watch for movement among the trees, but as far as she could tell, they were alone.

Dorran led her to the door, a massive square that was designed to slide to the side, rather than swing. Whoever had built the doors hadn't intended them to be opened in deep snow. Both Dorran and Clare had to put their shoulders to the wood and strain to get it to open even enough to slip inside.

The ceaseless wailing wind faded as Clare entered the barn. The space was vast but dark. Its few narrow windows were crusted with ice. She stopped in the entryway and strained to see through the area. Metal glinted. Something tall stood near the back wall. Then Dorran slammed the door behind them, cutting out almost all of the light.

A shudder ran through Clare. The darkness seemed to press around her. Every movement echoed through the space, and she wasn't sure if all of the noises were from her and Dorran, or whether they might not be alone. An unpleasant musty smell surrounded her. She wished he hadn't closed the door.

Then a match scratched against its striker, and the spark illuminated Dorran's face. He'd removed his mask and his features were placid as he bent to light a lamp sitting on the table by the door. At first, the glow was barely enough to light his arm. But it grew, creating a little circle of illumination and pressing back the smothering blackness.

"Here. You can keep this one." He passed her the lamp, and Clare gripped the metal ring tightly. "We are safe. The seal on the door hasn't been disturbed since my family left, so the creatures will not have gained access to the shed."

As Dorran lit a second lamp, Clare cautiously removed her own mask and unbuckled her snowshoes. Then she lifted her lamp, and the area came into relief.

She could tell it had once been busy. Tool sets were spread across counters and hung on the walls. Spare mechanical parts littered the shelves and were held in old crates. The floor was stained from innumerable oil spills. Partitioning walls stopped her from seeing the whole floor plan. Like everything in Winterbourne, it felt uncomfortably large.

A loft waited overhead, taking up half the space above them. An old staircase braced on the left-hand wall led up to it. Clare craned her neck, straining to glimpse what might be up there but couldn't see more than the ceiling.

"The stable hands used to sleep in the loft," Dorran said. He was already moving deeper into the space, his keen eyes glinting in the light as he scanned the tools. "You might have seen the second building we passed. That was the stables. All of the horses are at Gould with the family—"

His voice caught. Clare bit her lip. His family had been on the way to Gould; they had never reached it. She wondered how far the camper had gotten. Not a huge distance, she guessed. Madeline and her maids had returned to the house within days.

What happened to the rest of the family and the other staff members? Are they dead? Out there, deformed, wandering the countryside? Or, like Madeline, do they remember the house? Do they want to return to it?

Dorran's shoulders were hunched, but his voice remained steady. "I will find the motor. Could you look for something to make it easier to carry? A wheelbarrow or a sled, perhaps?"

"Right." Clare left her mask and radio on the table by the door. Even under the layers, she was shaking, and she didn't think it was all from the cold. Her eyes kept drifting toward the loft. Shadows thrown from her lamp darted across the ceiling. She hated not knowing what was up there.

She stepped around the partitions carefully, not touching anything, but her eyes always moving. The shed had not only been used to store cars, but repair them as well. A host of spare parts littered the place, in some areas piled up into rusty heaps.

A board flexed above her. She looked up, staring at the loft's underside, her heart in her throat. *Just the wind. It's a wooden building. It's going to groan occasionally.*

Dorran muttered something under his breath. Clare craned her neck to see him around a spool of wire. He'd set his lamp down and crouched beside a car's motor. It looked old, grime speckling the once-bright metal. He felt around it, pulling sockets out and running his fingers across connections.

"Is that it?"

"Yes." He kept his head down. "It needs parts though. I will be a minute while I find them."

The windows rattled as a fresh burst of air gusted past them. Clare forced herself to loosen her death grip on the lamp's ring and straighten her back. She stepped away from Dorran, scanning the floor and shelves for anything that might slide easily over icy ground.

A drop cloth caught her eye. It wouldn't be as good as a sled, but if she and Dorran both took an edge, it would be enough to cross the distance between the shed and the house. She pulled it down from a shelf and coughed as dust billowed around her.

Something cracked upstairs. Clare clutched the cloth, not daring to move, as she listened. The sound might have been a strained support beam adjusting. She began edging toward Dorran.

The shed was sealed. There were no signs of forced entry. It should be safe.

Dorran was lost in his own world. He sorted through a tool chest, his lips moving without making a sound as he picked out the implements he needed. Clare left the cloth beside him. She took a step toward the staircase running against the wall.

Long-neglected spiderwebs decorated the structure. They shimmered in the sparse wind. Clare lifted her lamp and squinted up the length of the steps.

Don't do it, her mind whispered. She looked over her shoulder. Dorran was still bent over the motor. It looked like it had been half pulled apart already. She could interrupt him and ask him to check the loft with her but pressed her lips together instead. The memory from that morning, when he'd gone into the passageways alone, was still clear in her mind. He thought he needed to protect her from this new world, but she was capable too. She had to be.

She placed a foot on the lowest step. It groaned, protesting the sudden pressure. The boards were thin and not well supported. Clare looked from her feet and up their length, toward the loft above.

Marks ran through the wood beside the stairs. Long, shallow scores. Clare carefully held out a hand. She pressed her fingertips to the marks and mimed scraping along them. They matched the scores left by long nails.

Don't do it.

She stopped, one foot already on the next step, ready to lift her higher. From her position, a third up the stairs, she could see the lower level's floor plan more clearly. Dorran's light created a little orb of brightness among the jagged metal teeth and dulled blades filling the space. If she climbed just another foot or two, she would be able to see over the lip of the loft.

Her throat caught when she tried to swallow. Shaking fingers raised the lamp farther. She began to climb.

CHAPTER 14

THE LOFT'S BACK WALL came into view. Clare froze, her skin crawling. A hunched shape was silhouetted beside the window. Clare stared and thought she could feel it staring back. The lamp's light flickered. Clare exhaled a held breath. She was looking at a tattered coat hung on the wall.

Another step up. More of the wall was revealed. Old posters were plastered over it. Photos of beautiful beaches, now so old and tarnished that the water looked brown and the sand was tinged green. Pinups from old magazines. The girls beamed at the camera, peeking over their shoulders cheekily or gasping in surprise as a wind blew their skirts up. Every single one of them had had their eyes clawed out. The marks cut into the wood beneath, so much like the scores marring the wall running along the staircase.

A final step up. The wood rocked under Clare's foot, threatening to break. Beth's voice played in her head on repeat: *Don't take risks. Don't take risks. Don't...*

But she could see the attic. The mattresses scattered over the wood, worn down until they were pocked with holes and bits of stuffing bloomed out of the wounds. The old, broken set of drawers that had been co-opted from the house, its dark wood a sharp contrast with the lighter timber surrounding it. Crates filled with possessions.

And the skeleton.

Discolored bones sprawled across the loft's floor. The skull was the closest. It seemed to leer at Clare, even with the lower jaw missing. Spikes of calcium poked out from the cranium, rising up like tiny mountains, protruding from the upper jaw and filling the eye sockets.

A hollow. Not human. At least, not when it died...

Her instincts begged her to step back. She couldn't stop herself from looking further. Femurs and ribs dotted the mattresses, scattered over the place like debris. There were a lot of bones. Not enough for two skeletons. Too many for one. Clumps of hair lay about, as though they had been torn out and flung away. Many of the bones were cracked. They were stained a dark brown, as was the floor, the color spreading in wide streaks. A handprint with seven fingers marred the closest wall.

There was a feast. Not recent. But not quite old either.

Clare pressed a hand over her mouth. Now that she was in the loft, the scent was almost overpowering. It had been nothing but a dusty musk on the lower floor. Now it reeked…of rot and of hollows.

She made to step back down the stairs but froze. Something moved. She fixed on the only window in the loft, a little round circle set into the back wall. It faced away from the brunt of the wind, and even though the glass was mottled with flecks of white, she could see something through it.

Her stomach rolled as she crept between the bones. No part of the floor was clean of gore. All she could do was step over it, doing her best to avoid disturbing the possessions that would never be picked up again. At the window, she had a view of the field leading to the forest. Twisted shapes crawled through the snow. Some of them shambled upright. Others crept on all fours, their spines twisting like a millipede's, unfazed by the cold. One looked up.

Clare gasped and stepped back. She could have sworn the hollow had made eye contact with her. As she stumbled toward the edge of the loft, her shoe bumped into the skull. It skittered, twirling, toward the edge of the wooden platform. Clare grasped for it. She was too slow. It plunged over, the empty eye sockets glancing at her a final time before it disappeared. A second later, the bones shattered on the floor.

No. No. We can't make noise.

"Clare?"

She ran for the stairs, breathless and fighting to keep her feet light, and plunged down the steps nearly recklessly. Dorran was frozen below, staring at the skull, the angles of his face sharp with alarm. He opened his mouth, but Clare motioned frantically.

She stumbled to a halt, and Dorran reached for her. She let him pull her close and rose onto her toes to whisper into his ear. "Hollows outside."

"Ah."

They kept still, holding each other, staring at the walls as they waited. Clare thought she heard snow crunch outside the door. Something was moving closer. Stopping by the door. Seconds passed, and she imagined the creature outside, its bulging eyes staring blankly at the shed.

Then the crunching came again, this time moving away. Clare closed her eyes and let her shoulders slump.

Dorran dipped his head to whisper into her ear, his warm breath gusting across her neck. "The motor is ready. We will wait until outside is clear, then make a run for it. Where did the skull come from?"

"Hollows," Clare said. The fractured bones rested not far from her feet. The cranium had been cracked open like a coconut. It hadn't been clear while it was whole, but now she could see the calcified protrusions reached inside too. They would have been digging into its brain. "I think it died from the mutations. Something—probably *things*—ate it."

He muttered something she couldn't hear, then said, "I had thought the barn would be secure."

"There's nothing alive up there. We should be okay."

The radio crackled. Clare flinched. She'd left it switched on, but with its static muffled by the wind, it had been nearly forgotten on the table by the barn door. As Beth turned her half of the pair on, the volume spiked into a near-painful whine. White noise hissed through the barn. Then, Beth's voice. "Clare? Are you there?"

She ran for the radio, swearing under her breath, and tried to turn the volume down. The dial was stuck. Something heavy hit the barn door beside her, and Clare held the radio close to her chest as she stepped away. Dorran didn't speak, but he picked up a metal pipe from the nearest counter.

"Clare?" Beth's voice was tight and far too loud.

She pressed the button to turn on her audio, and whispered, "I'm here. I can't talk right now."

"What? What's happening?"

"Please! Be quiet!"

Another heavy thud came from the door. The scratching sounds were growing louder. The wood trembled as hands pried at it. *Do they know how to open it? Are they smart enough to figure it out?*

Dorran backed up until he stood beside Clare. His dark eyes darted over the space, watching the walls. She couldn't tell how many of the hollows were outside. But there were a lot. They were closing in on every side. Clare's heart skipped a beat as sudden realization hit her. She tugged on Dorran's sleeve. "They'll have a way in."

The voice crackled through the radio again. "Clare, what's happening? Are you all right?"

"Fine. Can't talk." Clare struggled with the dial, trying to turn Beth's volume off without breaking the radio. It remained stuck. "The door was closed when we arrived, but if there are bones in the loft, there must be another way in."

"Damn it," he muttered. He flexed his hands around the metal pipe.

The front door banged again. A gap appeared along its edge. Long, spindly fingers poked through, feeling, squirming.

"Mask," Dorran hissed, passing one to Clare. She braced the radio between her knees while she fit it on. She was under no delusions that the mask would shield her. The hollows had heard human voices. They were in a frenzy, and their chance to slip out unharassed had passed.

"Clare, I can't hear you." There was something strange about how Beth spoke. Something beyond the usual worry. If she'd had more time, Clare would have been able to focus on it—but the door grated in another inch, and she could see gray skin writhing outside as the creatures jostled for space.

"They might have dug a hole or broken through the walls," Dorran whispered. "Look for the other entrance. We might be able to get out while they're focused on the main door."

They moved away from the shuddering wood and silently stepped between the support beams and dividing walls. Clare cradled the radio against her chest as they passed Dorran's motor. He'd placed it on the sheet, ready to carry it out, along with a stack of tools and supplies. She hated to think that they might have to leave it behind.

A cold breeze stung her cheeks. Clare turned in its direction and beckoned to Dorran. They stepped around the shell of a vehicle, its seats and innards gutted, and Clare caught the glow of pale light splashed across the floor.

In the shed's corner, half-hidden behind a tangle of barbed wire, the wood had rotted. Hollows had clawed at the decaying walls and floors, creating a hole that was just barely large enough for a person to squirm between. Clare crouched to look through. There was no snow blocking the other side. Cold light glared off muddy ground.

"Clare." Beth was crying. "I need to talk to you."

Clare bit her lip until it ached as she fumbled with the radio's settings. She couldn't answer; the noise would give them away. Instead, she flipped a switch, muting Beth.

Dorran held up a finger for her to wait, then dropped to his chest and crawled beneath the barbed wire. He moved quickly but carefully, pipe held at the ready, as he approached the gap. His forearms passed through, then he froze.

"Dorran?" Clare whispered.

He lurched back, pulling away from the splintered gap too quickly. The barbed wire caught across the mask. A long, bowed arm shot through the hole after him, snatching at his face.

Clare moved without thinking. She smashed the radio down onto the hand, hard enough to crush bone. The tough plastic case fractured and the volume boomed. Suddenly, Clare couldn't hear herself underneath the popping, hissing white noise.

"Go!" Dorran yelled, shoving her. He wrenched himself out from the wire, leaving the mask behind. Specks of blood flecked across Clare's arm. She turned and ran deeper into the barn as an elongated, hissing face peered through the opening.

"No, no," Clare whispered. She pressed the volume buttons. It wouldn't quiet down. Beth's breathing echoed around them.

"Clare." Magnified, the regret and sadness in Beth's voice was unbearable.

The hollows responded to the word. Metal scraped as they fought to get through the barbed wire. Up ahead, the sliding door jumped on its runners. Arms stretched through the gap, blindly grasping at the air.

The radio wouldn't turn off. She had no choice. She dropped it, and flinched as it hit the wood floor with a clatter. Dorran grasped her hand, and together, they ran for the stairs leading to the loft. Their footsteps were drowned out by Beth's echoing words.

"I really need to talk to you, sweetheart. Please." She took a tight breath. "It's… Things…things aren't great here."

They were halfway up the stairs. The door boomed as it was nearly wrenched off its frame. Clare kept her eyes ahead, focused on the upper landing, the graveyard for the unknown hollow.

As they gained the loft, Dorran tugged her downward. They dropped onto their knees and crawled through the bones and dried gore to reach the back wall. They didn't stop moving until they were under the window. They pressed their backs to the wall, out of sight of the main floor, their legs pulled close to their chests, and watched the top of the stairs.

The door banged again. Then, the struggling noises transformed into something much worse. Flesh rubbing over flesh. Clare imagined them pouring through the gap, tumbling over each other in their eagerness for food. *How many?* her mind asked, and then answered itself: *Too many.*

"I don't have long, sweetheart." Beth's voice carried clearly through the building, even under the pattering feet and scrabbling fingers. "The...the ventilation system went down this morning. The bunker is airtight. I can't..." Another ragged breath. "The only way to get fresh air would be to open the door. And..."

No. No. Clare shook her head, her heart hammering. The fencing mask was suddenly suffocating her; she wrenched it off.

"I hope you can hear me. I hope you're all right. I don't know how long the air will last me. I'll stay as long as I can. But...I'll see. I'll see. It might be easier to get it over with quickly."

She wanted to scream. The radio was out of reach. She could hear the hollows moving over it, searching for the source of the voice. She leaned forward. Dorran pulled on her arm, dragging her back, holding her still.

"I think this might be goodbye though." Beth said it as though she'd only just realized it herself. For a beat, the only noise came from the monsters—the raw, close sounds of the creatures in the barn, and the distant, tinny noise of hollows prying at Beth's bunker door. Then she took a shuddering breath. "Don't come looking for me. I know you want to, but you can't. Stay where you are. Stay safe. And I want you to know...I...I love you. So much. If I've done anything to hurt you, if there's anything you regret, about how I raised you...or anything I did..."

Clare was drowning. Tears dripped off her chin. She wanted to scream to her sister. The noises were physical pains inside of her, aching worse with every second she held them in.

107

"I'm so sorry. I love you. Goodbye."

The radio clicked. Steady, harsh static took its place. It wasn't loud enough to drown out the furious chatter or the sounds of the hollows spreading across the ground floor.

CHAPTER 15

NO. PLEASE. BETH. NO.

Dorran moved his hand over her mouth. She realized she was moaning. She couldn't stop. He muffled the noise as he rocked her, whispering into her hair, "Shh. Quiet, now. I have you. Shh."

Creatures probed the clutter downstairs. They were spreading out, frantic in their search. It would only be a matter of minutes, if that, until they worked their way up the stairs.

She knew she needed to focus, to be ready, but she couldn't think. Dorran held her, but his face was white. She knew he was making the same calculations as she was. *How long can we hold off the horde when they come up the stairs? How long until our muscles give out, until we're overrun?*

She tilted her head back, staring toward the ceiling, and caught sight of the round window above them. It had a latch to open. It was large enough to fit through…but even if the drop didn't kill them, the creatures would do the job soon after.

The fog of grief and anger swamped her head, clouding her mind. She closed her eyes, trying to think through it. The lowest step of the stairs creaked. Clare opened her eyes. And she saw their chance.

"The window," she hissed. She got to her knees, facing the glass. The sky had grown overcast as a storm brewed, but the field of snow outside was clear of everything except trails of footprints. Every hollow in the near vicinity had been drawn into the shed. She pulled on the handle, straining against the stiff metal, and wrenched the frame open. Freezing wind blew past her.

"Clare?" Dorran's hand rested on her back, but he stayed facing the stairs.

The hollows were climbing. She tried to guess how far up. A third of the way. Maybe half. Soon they would be able to look over the loft's edge and see her and Dorran crouched against the back wall.

Clare crawled to the only piece of nice furniture in the space: the broken set of drawers that had been rejected from Winterbourne. She pried one of the drawers out, crept back to the window, and hurled the wood through.

The drawer created a heavy *thump* as it hit the snow outside. Instantly, the scrambling ceased. The creaking stairs fell silent. Then, from the ground floor, the chattering began again.

Dorran had understood her plan. He was already at the

wooden stand, silently easing another drawer out. He held it at the window for a second as he gauged the distance to the first drawer, then threw it. His aim was good. The half-broken wood crunched horribly as it hit its mate.

The noises below became eager. But this time, they were rushing out of the building. The sliding door rumbled as they forced their way through. Metal jangled as they scrabbled to get under the barbed wire. Clare already had a third drawer ready, and as the first hollows appeared below the window, she threw it.

"Now," Dorran whispered. "Go. Hurry."

They darted around the bones to reach the stairs. Clare paused on the landing just long enough to make sure that the ground floor was empty, then she rushed down, holding close to the wall and rolling her feet to minimize the noise.

The monsters' stench stuck in the back of her throat and made her instincts revolt. But the barn was empty. She reached the floor, Dorran so close behind her that she could hear his breathing, and ran for the open door.

Behind them, the radio continued to crackle. The noise dug into Clare's nerves. She wanted to pick it up—to try to call Beth—but there was no time. The distraction bought them seconds at best.

The hollows had forced a narrow gap in the door. She turned her body sideways and slipped through, then held out a hand to pull Dorran out after her. Cold wind wrapped around her. Ahead, the mansion was lit for a split second by lightning. The metal door was a minute away at a brisk walk, half that at a run.

They hadn't collected their snowshoes—or their masks. There was no time to go back.

The snow came up to Clare's waist. Dorran went first, forging a path, but even with a channel dug out, Clare still struggled to stay upright. She kept her eyes fixed on Dorran's back and her ears tuned to the world behind them. The radio's crackle. The barn door, banging as the wind tugged at it. And behind that, the incessant chattering, clicking noises as the beasts circled back around the barn.

Not far. Not far...

Winterbourne's windows overlooked the field, blank and cold, dispassionate to their plight. The metal door stood out of the stone wall ahead, tantalizingly close.

Something snatched at Clare's heels. Dorran sensed it before she did; she'd barely stumbled when he turned, swinging the pipe. It made a solid metallic noise as it connected with the hollow's skull. Lightning raced across the field closer, harsh enough to blind her.

"Go!" He shoved her past him. The door was less than ten feet away. She fought through the snow, digging through the same path her snowshoes had compressed an hour before. Another *thwack* close behind her. She was at the door. Shoving it open. Tumbling through. She got her feet back under herself and turned to the opening.

Dorran, teeth bared and eyes blazing, swung his weapon a final time, then he leapt back through the gap. Clare was ready. She forced the door shut, hurling her shoulder into the metal to make its aged hinges work. Two heavy *thud*s shook her as hollows impacted with the barrier. She pulled the latch to lock it.

"Are you all right?" Dorran asked. He bent over, panting, hands braced on his knees and his hair damp from melted snow. Tracks of blood ran down his neck and cheek from where the barbed wire had bitten him. Clare nodded, then slid down the wall to crumple on the floor.

Dorran shucked his jacket off and discarded it, then sat down beside her. She stared at her hands in her lap. The hollows were scrabbling at the other side of the door, but she didn't care. The adrenaline was fading, and shock moved in. She felt numb.

Beth.

The last thing she'd said was "Can't talk." Not even a full sentence. She hadn't said goodbye. Hadn't told her sister that she loved her. Hadn't been able to do a single damn thing as Beth cried on the other side of the radio.

Suffocation. Of all the ways she'd feared her sister might die in this new world, she hadn't planned for that. She closed her eyes and tried to remember the bunker. She'd only seen it once, when Beth had proudly shown it off after construction. It was a single room with an en suite bathroom. Not large. She could have crossed it in five steps.

How much air does that hold? How long until the oxygen runs out?

The bunker was a glorified coffin. She pressed her palms into her forehead and clenched her teeth. A repressed sob sent miniature shock waves through her.

All of a sudden, it was so easy to see her mistakes. She'd missed Beth's call the previous day through stupid absentmindedness. And she'd been complacent, believing there was time for her and Dorran to troubleshoot a plan to rescue Beth.

"I need…" Her voice caught. Dorran sat, waiting, at her side. She tried again. "The radio. I need to go back for it."

"Later. Not right now."

A hot anger bubbled up in her insides. She squeezed her gloved hands together as the heat seared through her chest and throat. "I have to tell her… She doesn't know… I didn't tell her about the masks. She needs to know she can cover her face with a mask."

Dorran rested his hand on her shoulder. "We cannot reach the shed right now. Not while the monsters are still out there."

"She needs to know to wear a mask." The anger was compounding on the grief, building until it was uncontrollable. "It could save her."

Dorran's eyes were sad. She hated the way he was looking at her. It was like he didn't understand. They weren't too late; there was still a chance to save Beth if they could just reach the radio. But he sat there, mute, doing nothing.

Clare lurched to her feet. She was dizzy. She caught the door, fumbling for the latch, but Dorran's hands wrapped around hers and pulled them away. "No, Clare."

"She'll *die* without it." Clare hit his chest. He flinched but didn't let her go. So she hit him again. The anger, the revulsion with herself, and the blinding terror boiled over until she thrashed, half-mad. "She'll die. She'll *die*. She'll *die*!"

He wrapped his arms around her, holding her back from the door, and took the beating silently. Clare screamed until her voice was hoarse and struggled until her hands ached. He wouldn't let her go. When she finally slumped, exhausted, he pulled her in closer so she wouldn't fall.

"I am so sorry," he whispered, then picked her up and carried her deeper into the house.

CHAPTER 16

THE FIRE CRACKLED. CLARE had a mug held in her hands, though she couldn't remember how it had gotten there. Her insides felt like they had been scraped raw. Her throat burned every time she swallowed.

She hated the mug. It seemed so normal, so mundane. Like something a person held and sipped after a happy morning in the snow. Not the kind of thing someone got to enjoy when they let their sister die. She lifted it, ready to hurl it into the fire, but Dorran took it out of her hand before she could.

He silently wiped the spilled tea off its side and base, then placed it back on the coffee table. Then he disappeared back into the room's shadows. His expression was unreadable. She hated him.

No. No, you don't. You hate yourself. Stop projecting it onto him.

The scratching noise had followed her inside. It made her wild but, at the same time, filled her with a horrible sense of resignation. Scrabbling, scraping, coming from every direction, coming from inside her head, always there, wearing her down.

This is the reality of the new world. No one gets to escape them. It's just a question of how long you can last.

Tears ran down her cheeks. She was too tired to do anything, even cry properly. The universe had given her a second chance with Beth, and she'd ruined it. Now that the radio was gone—now that *Beth* was gone—she could only think about the things she should have said. Beth had needed to know to wear a mask, now more than ever. She needed to know how to get to Winterbourne. She needed to hear that Clare loved her.

Clare had been given the chance to tell her all of that, but she'd lost it, disregarded it with a curt "Can't talk."

She rubbed her palms over her eyes to dry them. Beth had been right: there was no room for mistakes in the new world. She should have known better.

And now you're pushing away the only other person in your life. You can't rely on second chances with him either.

"I'm sorry." Her voice was hoarse. She turned in her chair and searched the shadows for Dorran, half-afraid that he'd left the room without her noticing. But he was still there. He stepped forward, his expression drawn but not unkind.

"It's all right. Do you want to try again?" He picked up the cup and offered it to her. "It will help."

She took it, holding it tightly to stop her numb hands from dropping it. He'd made her tea with some of the powdered milk

117

from her luggage. She sipped and cringed as it hurt her raw throat. Then she carefully placed it back on the table. "Dorran, I'm sorry. I hit you—"

"Shh, it's all right."

His mother used to beat him. Clare shook her head vigorously. "No. No, it's not."

Moving slowly, he sat beside her in the chair. She reached up and ran her fingers across his cheek. He hadn't cleaned off the blood yet, and it had dried across his face and neck.

He still smiled. "It doesn't matter."

"It does. Did I hurt you badly? Are you in pain?"

"Not at all." He tilted his head, one hand running over her hair. "Why is this upsetting you so much?"

"Because it *should.*" She shuddered. *Because your mother hurt you. Because you don't know how wrong it is. And now I've done the same to you, and you're making excuses for me.* "You shouldn't ever hurt someone you love. Never. And I love *you.*"

His eyes were so full of emotion that she couldn't stand to look at them. He dipped down and kissed her. It was brief but tender. When he drew back, his eyes were heavily lidded. "Take a moment. Drink. When you're ready, we need to talk."

She was afraid of what his answer would be. "What about?"

"Your sister."

Clare still felt numb. But the anger was gone. When she thought about Beth, all she felt was a desperate longing. She would have given anything to turn the clock back just by an hour or two. "I'm ready to talk now."

"Not just yet. You're shaken. Rest a moment; drink the tea. I'll be here when you're ready."

She picked up the cup and forced herself to swallow. It was still hot and burned her throat, but she drained it in one go. She put the cup aside and wiped the back of her hand across her mouth. "Okay. Ready."

Dorran laughed. "Oh, my darling, you are incorrigible. Very well. Come here."

She rested her head against his chest as his hand stroked her hair. He held her a moment before he started speaking. "How far away does she live?"

"Four hours."

"In good weather? With clear roads?"

Clare squeezed her eyes closed. "Yes."

"So perhaps six or seven if we are slowed down." His hand continued to move over her hair in soft, tender strokes. "If we could reach her...would you want to try? Aware of how slim the odds are, aware of how much danger is involved, knowing that it could still be too late?"

She clung to Dorran, a lump blocking her throat. "Are you saying it's possible?"

"Look out the window, my dear. It is raining."

Clare lifted her head. She'd felt dogged by the scratching noise, unable to escape it even for a moment. As she stared at the tall glass panes, fresh tears escaped. It hadn't been hollows after all; she'd been hearing the steady thunder of water hitting the stones and the slate roof. For the first time since her arrival, rain washed the ever-present frost from the glass. She rose, feeling like she was in a dream, and stepped toward the view.

The snow still lay heavily on the ground, but its crisp, rounded edges were turning into slush. The shrubs were poking through the white, and they stood out on the front yard like beacons. In the distance, the dark ribbon that marked the forest was now capped with a deep, heavy green. Streaks of white still painted over the branches, but they were melting by the second.

"Oh," Clare whispered.

Dorran stood beside her. "I noticed on the trip to the shed that the world wasn't as cold as normal. It was enough that I needed to take my jacket off when I got back inside. And now, rain."

"It's beautiful," she whispered. Rivers were beginning to form in the lowest parts of the garden. Thick, glistening drops fell from the roof.

"It's the last thing we needed to line up," he said. "We have the car. We have the motor. We know the hollows…not well, but better. Now, we have clear roads. If we want to risk it."

She turned. Dorran stood tall, his broad shoulders set, his expression passive. But there was an undercurrent to his words that he was trying hard to hide. It took her a second to understand it. Dorran didn't want to leave.

He's doing this because I want it. He's risking everything to make me happy.

She opened her mouth. Closed it again. A war waged inside. Dorran worked tirelessly for her; he tended the garden, prepared food, safeguarded the house, and was an ever-present reassurance if she needed him. It felt almost cruel to ask for more.

If Clare had been the only part of the equation, the answer would have been easy. But her wants and needs weren't the only thing to consider. Beth was out there, trapped in a dark box, slowly suffocating. Or maybe dead. She'd made a comment about *getting it over quickly.* The idea that her sister might already be gone was like a punch to the stomach.

Clare pressed a hand to her forehead, trying to reel her thoughts back in. *Can I risk Dorran's life for a chance to save Beth's?*

"Be calm," Dorran murmured. "Come. Sit. Breathe deeply. We are just discussing it at the moment. You don't have to make a choice right now."

She shook her head. "Why is it *my* choice? You'd be carrying just as much risk."

"Because I have already made my decision. I will follow where you go. If that means staying, I will be happy. If it means leaving, I will also be happy."

"That's not fair. I know you don't want to go. You're only doing this because of me."

He didn't speak for a moment. When he did, he took her hand and traced over her fingers as he talked. "I will not lie to you. I am afraid of what may happen if we go. But I am also afraid of what may happen if we stay. You are close to your sister. I heard it when you spoke to her through the radio. I see it in your eyes when you talk about her. If we stay, if we don't even try, what will that do to you? Already, grief is crushing you...and I am poorly equipped to protect you from it."

"That's not your fault though. And it's not your responsibility to fix."

"It is when your feelings are entangled with my own." His fingers continued to move over her hand, and he watched her fingers intently. "I want to take the best path for you. Until recently, that meant shielding you as much as possible from the hollows. But your sister made contact. The equation is no longer simple. I could preserve your physical health, but what would it do for your emotional health? Would you spend the rest of your life chained by the events of today?"

"Dorran..."

"I cannot see clearly. So I must leave the choice to you. Wherever you go, whatever feels right to you, I will follow."

She tried to smile, but it was shaky. "My choice... You're spoiling me. I'm going to turn into the most selfish person imaginable."

"I don't think you're capable of being selfish."

"Don't underestimate me."

He grinned and bent forward to rest his forehead against hers. Their noses brushed. His eyes were so close that she could see the individual flecks of color in them.

"I love you, Dorran," she whispered.

"And I love you, my darling Clare."

"I want to go to Beth."

"Then we will."

CHAPTER 17

DORRAN FOUND A MAP of the area in one of his relative's studies. He spread it on the ground in front of their fireplace, its corners weighted down by books. He and Clare knelt over it, each holding a red pen as they worked on it.

"That's where Beth's street would be," Clare said, making a mark near the top right-hand side of the map. On the paper, there was nothing but olive-green blocks to signify marshy forest. The map was decades old and out-of-date. It was missing streets and landmarks, but Clare still knew the area well enough to orient herself. The forests had been cut down and the marsh drained nearly two decades before to allow for Beth's suburb to be built. "Don't worry. I'll know where to go once we get in there."

"Do you remember the streets well enough to sketch them?"

"I can try."

As she drew the main road and its dozen offshoots, Clare

fought against the doubtful thoughts that wanted to intrude. Trying to reach Beth was a massive undertaking. Her sister might already be dead. She might have opened the bunker's hatch as soon as she switched off the radio and welcomed in a wave of hollows.

And if she hadn't, the room was a ticking countdown. Clare tried to calculate how much air the box might hold a half dozen times in the previous hour. *Half a day? Two days? More?* She was no closer to an answer.

Clare was trying to coach herself into patience. The only way they were going to get to Beth alive was if they were cautious. But with the snow washing away and the car waiting for them in the forest, it was nearly impossible to resist the temptation to rush into action.

The hollows hadn't left the shed though, and they still needed the motor before they could leave. Every half hour, she and Dorran walked down to a room at the end of the hall and gazed across the field surrounding the two sheds. Patches of their roofs were visible. But so were the gray, spindly creatures, dripping with rain as they stalked around the buildings.

"They'll go back into the forest eventually," Dorran had said. "There's no food for them in the sheds."

But with the radio's static attracting the creatures, Clare had no idea how soon that might be.

She finished sketching Beth's suburb the best she could. She was pretty sure there were at least two more streets she'd forgotten, but it made a rough outline at least. The development held about three hundred houses. She tried not to think about how many hollows that could have produced.

"We're here," Dorran said, drawing an X in the large block of green signifying Banksy Forest.

"And Marnie is here." Clare put the mark down before she could stop herself. Dorran watched her. She smiled sadly. "Not that she'll be... Anyway."

Unlike Beth, Marnie had no bunker. It would be pointless going to her farmhouse. That didn't stop it from hurting though.

Clare cleared her throat. "All right, so this is the route I normally take when I'm visiting Beth. Most of it is a freeway, so it's a smooth drive. The map is missing a road, but it starts about here and goes up to here."

She drew a line along the path they were to take. Marnie's farm was away from the highway, about an hour away, and she tried not to squirm as she effectively cut her aunt out of the journey.

Keep focused. Spend your strength on what's possible, not on the past.

"Is any of it at risk of flood?" Dorran asked. "I'm not sure how far the snow extends, but if it's melting, low streets are likely to be unpassable."

"I've never had trouble with floods before." She capped her pen. "But, uh, I guess the snows have never been this deep before either."

"We will deal with it if it becomes a problem then." He bent over the map, examining it. "There are a few alternate routes in a worst-case scenario. That is good. I want to be as cautious as possible. We will pack food for several days. I believe you said the car had bottled water, correct?"

"That's right."

"We will not have time to seal the rest of the concealed passageways before we leave, like I had initially hoped. No matter. The hollows will have reign over the house while we are gone. We can deal with them when we return."

She bit her lip. "What about the garden?"

"I have given some thought to it. Before we leave, I will fit as much wood as possible into the furnace. It will be hot. Much, much hotter than the garden needs. But the vent will funnel the excess outside. The garden tends to hold its heat. Hopefully, we will have returned before it cools too much. It has an automatic watering system. I never bothered with it since it wastes fuel, but it will be useful now."

"That sounds good."

Dorran took a breath. "We will not be able to leave tonight."

Clare had to bite her tongue to stop herself from arguing with him. The ticking clock was incessant in the back of her head, and the idea of not moving that day seemed nightmarish. "We won't?"

"I am sorry. I know time is pressing. But the day is nearly gone." He nodded to the clock on the mantelpiece above them. It was past five. "The sun sets in an hour. It would be dark before we reach the car, and I need light to fit the motor. And we cannot even access the motor until the creatures leave the shed."

"Okay." It hurt to agree, but he was right. An hour's walk to the car, who knew how long to get the motor working, never mind the time spent preparing the garden and packing. There was no way to get it all done before nightfall…and they were still waiting for the hollows to leave the barn. She forced herself to smile. "First thing tomorrow?"

"That is my plan. Tonight, we will gather supplies and rest as much as possible. We will need the energy for the trip."

They went through the house together, collecting everything they would need and packing it into one of Clare's travel cases. They brought the final two fencing masks from Eros's room; one for Beth and one spare. Cans of food that didn't need to be cooked. Two containers of gasoline, plundered from the generator. Spare clothes. An assortment of weapons: kitchen knives, an ax, and the fire poker Clare had become so used to over the previous weeks.

Once they had the essentials, they debated over which other items might be useful to bring. They packed a bag with toothbrushes and soap. The first aid kit, filled with antiseptic, bandages, and painkillers. Rope. Matches and candles. Batteries. Two thick quilts.

There were a multitude of other items that could have come in handy: the lamp, saws, shovels, and more protective gear. But even though the car could have carried it all, the sled was limited. Every item they brought had to be weighed up compared to its peers. They briefly discussed the possibility of making two trips from the house to the car but agreed that just one was risky enough. Clare was relieved. She didn't like the idea of delaying their morning two hours longer than they needed to.

They laid the equipment out on the foyer's tables. The melting snow bled through under the door, creating a shallow pool of water that spread across the tiles. Clare's boots were leather and protected against the water, but she still splashed with every step. She felt like she'd fallen back in time to when Beth had let her jump in puddles at the park. The memory made her smile. Then reality pushed its way back in, and the happiness faded.

Please hold on, Beth. Wait just one more day.

It was growing late by the time they finished their preparations. Even though outside was warming, the house held on to its chill, and Clare was very ready to retreat to the heated bedroom. They stopped by the kitchen first to cook dinner. They would need energy for the trip and didn't know how many chances they might have to eat on the road.

Back in their room, Clare savored the bowl of warm rice and thick meat stew. She was acutely aware of how quickly the following morning was approaching. If the plan went wrong, it would be her last night in Winterbourne. She was surprised to find she would actually miss the place. Its ornate decorations and dim lights had never seemed very welcoming, but as she looked around the room, she realized she'd somehow grown to appreciate it. Like a snappish aunt who was just barely quirky enough to be remembered fondly.

Dorran had washed the blood off his face, but the cuts still looked red and painful. She put her empty bowl aside as she went to fetch some water from the bathroom. Dorran didn't question her as she heated it over the fire, but he watched her curiously.

She beckoned for him to come and sit with her. "Let me have a look at those cuts."

"They are not bothering me."

"Doesn't matter." She beckoned again. "Come and let me look after you."

He slid out of the chair to sit next to her on the rug, and Clare gently pulled him down so that his head rested on her lap.

"There." She brushed his hair away from his face, and he closed his eyes. The barbed wire hadn't been kind to him. It had nicked his ear and left two more marks across his forehead. She dipped the cloth into the hot water and dabbed the highest scab. His eyebrows twitched, but the rest of his expression stayed serene.

"Okay?" Clare asked.

"Hm. Good."

He's starting to trust me more. She dabbed gently, cleaning the cuts, thrilled to see how he gradually relaxed. Dark lashes grazed his high cheekbones as she ran her fingers through his hair.

"You're beautiful," Clare whispered. She'd thought it secretly a dozen times over the past week but never said it out loud.

Dorran's eyes opened, then he burst into cackling laughter.

"What?" Clare felt heat rise over her cheeks, but at the same time, his laughter was so infectious that she couldn't stop herself from joining in. "What? Don't laugh! I'm serious!"

"You are *not*." His expression was full of mirth, but as it subsided, adoration took its place. He stared up at her, unguarded, happy, loving. "But thank you."

Beautiful Dorran. She kept that one in her mind but returned his smile as she traced her fingertips across the edge of his jaw. Not long ago, every smile and every laugh had been guarded. Very slowly, he was shedding that cautiousness. And it made her so happy it almost hurt.

Her hand drifted to the collar of his shirt. A hint of blue peeked out from under it. Clare's smile faded. She undid the top button to see the bruise across his collarbone, and her stomach dropped as a rush of fresh guilt hit her. "Oh…"

"Clare."

"I'm so sorry. I—"

He took her hand, still smiling. "No. That wasn't from you."

"But—"

"My darling, I say this with the greatest affection and respect possible. You do not hit hard enough to leave bruises."

Clare bit her lip, skeptical, afraid that he was making more excuses for her.

Dorran's eyebrows rose as his heavy-lidded eyes smiled up at her. "I wouldn't lie to you. This was from yesterday, in the snow with the hollows. *They* put some force behind their strikes. Again, I say that with no intent to offend."

"None taken." The tension fell from her shoulders. She let her hand move lower and undid another button. The bruise looked painful, so she kept her fingers featherlight as she traced around it. "Are you scared?"

"About tomorrow?" He rested his hand over hers. His heart was below her fingers. The pulse felt strong, steady, and horribly fragile all at once. "Of course I am. I do not think I would be human if I wasn't." A pause, then, "Are you?"

"Yes." The word, as simple as it was, cracked when she tried to say it. Moisture blurred her eyes.

Dorran tightened his fingers over hers. "Do you still want to go?"

This time, she answered with more conviction. "Yes."

"Then there is nothing to help by worrying. Come. Lie down at my side. I will keep you warm and safe tonight, and for as many more nights as I can."

He lifted himself off her lap so that she could settle down next to him. She lay on her side, one arm wrapped around Dorran, and he kissed her forehead before tucking it into the space below his chin. She closed her eyes and listened to the patter of rain underneath the fire's crackle.

CHAPTER 18

FOUR HOURS TO REACH Beth's if the roads are good. More if they're bad.

Clare's dreams revolved around the map she and Dorran had created. Her mind traced the route again and again. *Four hours. We can survive four hours.*

She saw her hand running over the paper, following their path. A red X marked Beth's house. Her fingers touched it and came away wet. Not ink, but blood, dripping from the bunker, saturating their map.

Clare gasped as she woke. The room was dark. The fire had been allowed to die into embers, but for the first time since she'd arrived at Winterbourne, the room hadn't turned cold.

Dorran's hand rested on her shoulder. He was already dressed, and his eyes were bright as he leaned close. "Time to wake, my darling. We are almost ready."

Beth. She sat up, her pulse leaping, and looked at the window. The black was deep, but in the distance, she thought she saw the first hint of dawn.

Dorran shook a jacket out for her and helped her into it. He kept his voice quiet, almost as though reverent of the early morning's thrall. "Breakfast is ready downstairs. I have set up the garden. Now, all we need is the motor, and I did not see any sign of the creatures around the shed."

"You did all of that alone?"

"Yes. You needed sleep."

She frowned at him but bit her tongue. It wasn't a morning for arguing. If they were going to get to Beth's, they needed to be united.

They hurried down the stairs together, letting the gloom caress them as they worked their way toward the kitchens. For once, the dark didn't bother Clare. She couldn't hear the scratching noises. In fact, the whole house felt strangely calm. As though it were sleeping, waiting patiently for sunrise.

Dorran had laid out plates of porridge and dried fruit on the table, along with steaming cups of tea. The kitchens were cold, and Clare was grateful for the jacket and the drink. They ate in silence.

Four hours to get to Beth's if the roads are good.

Her internal clock counted down. It was ceaseless as it pressed Clare to run, but it refused to show how long she had left. *Hours? A day? Or has the deadline already passed?*

She drained her cup, and Dorran took the plates to wash up.

Clare fought her impatience and picked up a dish towel to dry at his side. It only took them two minutes. Dorran emptied the sink and stood there, palms resting on the edge of the metal basin. Thin-lipped, he stared at the suds disappearing down the drain.

"Dorran?"

He pushed away from the sink. "Let's go."

They were becoming so used to the ritual of donning winter clothes that they completed the task before the sun breached the skyline. Dorran stood at the house's open front doors, staring at the gradually lightening cobalt grazing the tops of the trees. Clare balled her gloved hands into fists as she stared at the sunrise, urging it on.

Four hours to get to Beth's.

As the field gradually lightened, Clare was able to see the gardens clearly for the first time. The snow was gone. A stone courtyard spread ahead of them before four shallow stairs led down to the dirt road that twisted toward the forest. The grass was dead, but the shrubs lining the first part of the driveway were green. Everywhere were the remnants of their winter: water collected in huge puddles in every available dip, sparkling in the brown grass and trickling between the cobblestones.

"Okay," Dorran said. They pulled their masks into place and each took one handle of the sled.

Their equipment was stacked on the structure and tied down with rope. Clare couldn't stop herself from glancing at their supplies as they dragged it down the stairs. The fear that they might have forgotten something—something important, something they would need—weighed on her. But it was too late; the time for preparing was over. They would have to survive with what they had.

The sled's runners scraped over the courtyard stones. Instead of going toward the forest, they turned left, circling around the building. It was surreal to be able to walk outside Winterbourne without wading through snow. The sheds appeared through the mist. Dorran gave a brief nod, and they dropped the rope as they approached the largest building.

Even from outside, Clare could hear the radio's static. It still blared through the building. Dorran slowed as they neared the door, one hand held out to keep Clare behind him and the other holding the ax. The door had been left ajar.

"Watch the field," he whispered.

Clare stepped back to check the grounds surrounding them. She turned in a slow circle, scanning the forest's edge, the stretch of dead grass, and the manor's closest walls. She hunted for movement. She didn't see any.

Wouldn't it be wonderful if the hollows melted with the snow?

The idea made her smile. She'd become so used to associating the deformed creatures with the cold that this new wet, dripping world somehow didn't seem as threatening.

Dorran stood in the shed's open door for a moment, staring inside. Then he pushed on the door. It had been forced off its runners by the hollows and screeched as it tried to move. They both flinched. Clare held her breath, listening for the chatter, listening for the sound of scratching claws. None came. Dorran pushed again, this time keeping the pressure up until the gap was an arm's length wide. Then he beckoned to Clare.

The only light in the place came from the grimy windows. As she stepped inside, Clare's stomach revolted. It reeked of hollows and mildew. The floor, swollen from melted snow, creaked with every movement. The lamps she and Dorran had carried the previous day were left discarded on the side table, burned dry. Toward the back wall, the little black radio lay on the ground, its plastic fractured. It no longer played white noise. Clare tried to turn it on and felt her heart drop as it remained unresponsive.

"Take the batteries out," Dorran whispered. "We will bring it with us."

Clare struggled with the back latch while Dorran moved toward the motor. Four batteries fell into her hand and she tucked them into her pocket. The shed seemed too quiet. She could hear every drip, every squeak of wet wood, every rustle of Dorran's jacket. He bent beside the motor, checking it and making sure all of the components were there. Then he nodded to Clare. She took one end of the sheet and helped lift.

The motor was heavier than she'd expected, and they staggered under the weight. Clare righted herself and led the way back to the door, straining to keep the pile of equipment steady. They shuffled through the shed, past the cracked skull that lay beneath the loft, and, after briefly scanning the fields around them, moved outside.

"On top of the sled," Dorran said. They had packed the rest of their equipment flat, and Clare exhaled as the motor thudded into place. She was shaking and sweaty, and she unzipped her top jacket. The day wasn't exactly warm, but their cautious dressing had left her wearing too many layers for comfort. She took off her outer jacket and tied it around her waist.

Dorran bundled the cloth over the motor to keep everything together, then tied it down with the rope. His movements were sharp and full of energy.

He feels it too. Progress. A way forward. A way out.

They took the ropes and pulled. Their feet sank into the muddy, oversaturated ground, and the sled refused to move as smoothly as it had on the snow. Its runners cut up strips of grass and caught on every stick and rock. They were both panting as they cut across the field, toward where the driveway disappeared into the trees.

To their left, Clare glimpsed the red-cloth dome they had brought on their previous trip to the forest. The fabric had been shredded, the wire dented. The hollows that had been frozen around it were gone. There was no room on their sled to take the dome, so they passed it without stopping.

The pines' shadows stretched across the field like jagged knives. Clare shivered as she approached the forest. In a strange way, it felt more alive than ever before. The branches rocked in the chilled wind, groaning, and Clare couldn't shake the feeling that they were being watched. They got the sled back onto the dirt track. It moved a little more easily through the mud, but Clare still wasn't looking forward to the hike between the trees.

She turned to give Winterbourne one final look. For a second, she thought she saw something in one of the upstairs windows. A curtain moved, gliding back into place, hiding the thin, pinched face. Clare swallowed.

For a while at least, it will be nothing but a home for the hollows.

She pictured them scuttling through the hallways. Intruding on the parts of the house Clare and Dorran called their own. Crouching on the kitchen counter, long fingers probing at the whorls in the wood that Clare herself had traced that morning. Sitting in their chairs, climbing the same stairs she and Dorran had been so familiar with. The garden's door was bolted, at least, but Clare knew they could find a way in if they really wanted to. She tried not to think about it. Instead, she faced the forest.

Dorran didn't look back. That seemed strange to Clare. She'd only been in Winterbourne for a fortnight but already felt reluctant to leave it. Dorran had spent his whole life there. She doubted that he could leave it—possibly for the last time, if their journey went badly—without any feelings of regret.

"Are you all right?" she asked.

"Hm." He nodded but didn't turn his head, not even to look at her.

She was struck by the sense that maybe he didn't look back because, if he did, his steps would falter. Leaving their security was already hard enough for him; he couldn't afford to let sentimentality creep through the growing cracks in his emotional armor.

Clare moved so she walked a little closer to him. She wished there were more she could do. But they were entering the forest, and as the trees engulfed them, it was wiser to keep silent.

In the distance, something chattered. The crackling, bestial noise floated on the cold air. With the mask dimming the world, Clare's other senses tried to compensate. She traced the noise to somewhere on their left. Not close. But close enough.

A grating wail echoed from their right. Like a damaged foghorn, it broke and faded on its last notes. They increased their pace. Clare's muscles were already aching. The sled jostled on uneven ground, its contents threatening to shake free.

Clumps of wet snow, sheltered by the trees, hung around roots and between piles of pine needles. Their boots plunged into deeper mud as the path turned downhill. It stuck around Clare's feet, trying to hold her in place and making wet noises every time she pulled free. Hundreds of tiny streams washed between ancient roots, carrying the slush away.

A dead branch the width of Clare's arm plunged from the canopy, smacking into the ground ahead of them. They barely slowed their pace. Dorran kicked the branch out of the sled's path. As they passed it, Clare couldn't stop herself from looking up. A bow-legged shape clung to the trees above them.

Not far. We're nearly at the car. Then there is only four hours to Beth's. That's all. We can handle four hours.

Every fear and doubt that had plagued Clare through the last days rushed back in, redoubled. *Will Beth still be there? Will the masks be enough to reach her bunker without being attacked? And what if the air is toxic outside the forest? What if we get ten minutes away and start turning into hollows? Will it hurt? Will I know what's happening? What if I stay conscious after the change, like Madeline*

Morthorne? I couldn't live as a monster...or stand seeing Dorran become one beside me.

Dorran was breathing heavily. She didn't think it was just the exercise either. The stress was getting to both of them. She wanted to talk to him, to tell him everything would be all right, to thank him for coming with her. But every second, the creaking noises around them seemed to be growing closer.

How many are there?

The mask was too thick and the clothes too heavy. Sweat trickled down Clare's cheek. It made her itch, and she shook her head but had no way to scratch it. The closest layer of clothes was starting to stick to her back. She didn't think she could go much farther without resting. But if they stopped, she knew the hollows would converge on them, creeping nearer, their wild eyes trying to see through the mesh.

Then, all of a sudden, they were on the main road. Even without the snow disguising it, the entry came up unexpectedly.

They turned left. A figure stood in the middle of the road. Patches of hair sprouted from its body, the strands growing as long as the sparse hair on its head. It trailed from its arms, torso, and legs. Gossamer thin and straggly, it had already become tangled by mud.

Clare looked up at Dorran. She wished she could see his face. He held still for a moment, watching, then tugged on the rope again. They were going to try to pass it.

CHAPTER 19

THE CREATURE HELD PERFECTLY still except for its head. Its long neck turned so the unblinking eyes were always fastened on Clare and Dorran. They kept as close to the road's edge as they could manage. The sled scraped painfully against the asphalt, and the noise wound Clare's nerves tight. Her weapon was on top of the sled, but she didn't dare reach for it. She clamped her teeth together until her jaw ached.

Beyond the hollow, she could see the car. Her poor red hatchback was suspended on the side of the road, passenger door hanging open, front end crushed from where it had rammed into one of the massive pines. The rain hadn't been kind to it. Water glistened on its roof and dripped off of the crumpled hood, and she could already see that the seats would be drenched.

Can he really get it working again?

Dorran's attention was focused on the hollow. They were so

close to the road's edge that one side of the sled was threatening to tip into the ditch. The creature's neck continued to swivel, holding them in its sights, and its lips parted to exhale a low, rumbling hiss.

The sweat coating Clare had turned cold. She kept her head down but, out of the corner of her eye, caught movement ahead. A new hollow stood on the road just twenty meters past her car. This one was missing ribs. A gory hole in its chest gaped every time it breathed through ruined lungs. Bloody froth beaded at the corners of its mouth, but like its companion, it didn't seem to feel the deformity. Its attention was wholly directed at Clare and Dorran.

Focus on the car. We just need to get it to work. Then there're four hours to Beth's. That's all I need to think about.

The chattering in the forest grew louder. Clare knew that, if she looked, she would see their eyes shining in the gloom. Every breath hurt her lungs. Every beat of her heart felt too hard, too pressured.

But they were past the first hollow and closing in on her car. Mud squelched behind her. She looked, and the hollow froze, its mud-caked hair swinging at the sharply aborted movement.

Damn it.

The masks were confusing them but not deterring them. Clare reflexively checked the cloth around her neck. Underneath the fabric and metal, sweat trickled into her eye, and she blinked furiously to try and clear it.

The sled ground to a halt beside the car. The noises around

them seemed magnified. The chattering, which now came from half a dozen directions. The heavy breathing from the hollow ahead, as red-flecked froth dribbled over its lip. The scrape as the hollow behind them took another step closer.

Dorran bent close so that his metal mesh bumped against hers. At that proximity, she could see his dark eyes and long lashes, damp with sweat. He kept his voice soft enough that only Clare could hear it. "Move the supplies into the car, then get into the driver's seat and lock the door. When I wave, try the key in the ignition."

"I can help with the motor."

"No. I need you to start the engine. Do not argue."

The hollow at their backs took another step nearer. Gray flesh emerged from the trees to their left: an arm with three joints, feeling along the ground.

Dorran wrapped his arms around the cloth-covered motor and pulled it off the sled. The thud as it hit the ground made Clare flinch. She opened the back door and began ferrying their supplies inside.

Metal screamed as Dorran forced the car's hood up. He was moving quickly, and although every motion was carefully controlled, there was no way to be silent. Clare felt more eyes fixing on them.

As she bent over the rear seat, shoving the blankets into a spare nook, motion through the opposite window made her look up. A hand slapped onto the glass. A face loomed. Flabby skin drooped over where its lower jaw had once existed. The upper teeth, all it had left, clicked as they bumped into the glass.

Please, Dorran, be fast. Be safe.

She backed out of the car, one eye on the hollow peering through the window, and the rest of her attention spread over the road. The creatures were growing closer. Dorran gasped as the old motor, twisted and broken, clattered onto the road. Then he bent to pick up the replacement.

The sled was empty. Clare left one of the cans of gasoline and the ax beside the front wheel for Dorran. He'd braced the new motor on top of the car's crumpled hood and was using a jack to try and force the space back open so that it would fit. Clare reached toward him, but he motioned her back. She swallowed, opened the driver's door, and slid inside.

Icy water flowed from the saturated seat as Clare dropped into it. The front window had a jagged crack running across it, but at least it seemed stable. Dark stains bloomed across the seats— old blood from the crash. The car wouldn't smell good once it warmed up, but that didn't matter. They only needed it to work for eight hours. Four there. Four back.

Dorran had told her to lock the door, but she didn't. It would keep her safe but leave him vulnerable if he needed help. She found the key in her pocket and fit it into the ignition and waited.

One at a time, with stuttering steps and tilted heads, the hollows were drawing closer. Some had their attention focused on Clare, but the majority were fixed on Dorran, their eyes boring into his back as he bent over the motor. He'd completely removed the crumpled hood and worked on the connections with efficient, sharp movements. Clare tightened her hands over the steering wheel, silently urging him on.

He lifted his head and waved. Hope jumped in Clare's throat. She turned the key. Nothing happened. He waved again, asking her to stop, then put his head back down.

What if he can't fix it? What if it's too broken to ever work? He only knows mechanical cars; mine has digital parts. What if water got into one of them and fried it? There's no way to fix that.

He waved again. Again, Clare turned the key. There was no purr of a motor, no life. Undeterred, Dorran returned to the task.

More of the hollows were coming out of the forest. One ran its fingers across the car's passenger door as it circled toward Dorran. The scrape of nails on metal was physically painful.

She squeezed the wheel until her knuckles ached. The first hollow, the one with stringy hair drooping from its skin, was at Dorran's back. It tilted its head, teeth bared, as it tried to see around the mask.

Can they smell us? Can they feel our body heat? Will that be enough to make them attack?

Its head stretched forward, moving past Dorran's shoulder. Clare couldn't breathe. It was close enough that it should have been able to see through the mesh. Dorran lifted one gloved hand, blocking that side of his face, as his other hand turned a wrench.

Clare was frozen, gripping both the key in the ignition and the door handle. The hollow's bulging eyes rolled slowly as they followed the lines of Dorran's jacket. It pressed against him, the greasy hair dragging over his arm. Clare could imagine how it felt. How it smelled. She didn't know how Dorran could keep his focus on the car.

Then the hollow's hands came up. Wrinkled fingertips prodded along the edge of the mask, dragging in his hair, feeling at the corners of his face.

No, no, no, no. Don't touch him.

Dorran tried to lean away from the contact. The hollow's jaw widened with growing excitement, blue lips stretching back as it chattered at him. The fingers had found the mask's straps. They curled under them and began to pull.

Clare did the only thing she could think of. She smashed her palm into the steering wheel. The horn blared.

They all jumped, including Dorran. He gripped the edge of the motor, his head down. The hollow released a pained screech and stepped back as its eyes twisted to stare about itself.

They hate loud noises. Clare leaned on the horn again, grimacing, and watched as the tightening circle of hollows widened. The ones that had pressed against the car's windows retreated to the shadows at the forest's edge. The one with blood frothing at its mouth took a stumbling step back.

Dorran brought both hands back to the engine. Clare kept on the horn, trying to hold the creatures back for him. Some disappeared entirely between the trees. Others began circling, holding their distance, their distorted faces pinched with frustration.

The nearest ones began creeping forward again. Clare's heart dropped. Their hunger was winning over their repulsion.

Dorran's head appeared above the engine and he waved. She twisted the key. The engine turned over. Sputtered. Died again. Clare tried the key again, holding it, desperate. It wouldn't catch.

No, no, no, come on.

Dorran grabbed a fresh tool off the sheet beside the car. The closest hollow was nearly at his side again. Clare hit the horn. The creature barely flinched.

Metal thudded above her, and she looked up. Feet slapped over the roof, tracing a path above her head, creeping closer to the engine. She felt sick.

Dorran had twisted his body to hide his face from the monster looming over him, but it was no longer staring at his mask. Its eyes had fixed on his wrist, twitching as they followed every movement. Clare's heart turned cold. They had rushed through their routine that morning and he hadn't tied his jacket sleeves in place. One had ridden up, and a sliver of flesh was visible above the glove.

"Dorran!" she screamed.

The hollow lunged. Teeth fastened over the exposed skin. Dorran cried out and pulled back, one hand pressed against the hollow's face, trying to force it off, trying to pry its teeth free. It clung on.

Clare wrenched her door open and the metal hit a hollow that was trying to lunge past. Before she could step out, Dorran yelled, his voice full of pain and urgency, "The motor!"

Help him! one half of her mind screamed. *Trust him!* said the other. She had one leg out of the car as she reached back inside and turned the key.

The engine roared to life. The headlights burst on, bathing Dorran and the hollow in a harsh glow. The creature released its grip on him, screaming, and staggered back. Blood glistened over its jaws.

More were coming, attracted by the commotion and the smell of blood. Dorran snatched up the ax and swung. It impacted a hollow's skull, sticking there as the creature screamed at him. Another latched on to his back, pulling him off-balance.

Door still open, Clare put the car into reverse and hit the accelerator. The car was trapped on the side of the road, facing the tree it had hit, balanced precariously. The wheels skidded in the mud, seeking but unable to find traction, and Clare felt a stab of panic. Then Dorran threw his weight into the bumper, shoving the car back, and the wheels caught. Clare gasped as the car dropped onto the road. Her chin hit the wheel and she tasted blood.

The car jolted as she reversed over a hollow. She slammed on the brakes, switched to drive, and twisted the wheel as she powered forward.

Two creatures disappeared beneath her front wheels. The one on the roof scrabbled as it tried to keep its perch. Clare hit the brakes again, stopping right beside Dorran. He grappled with a hollow, fighting to keep its grasping fingers away from his head.

Clare leaned across the passenger seat to throw the door open. "Get in!"

Dorran fell back, hitting the car's side, and lifted a foot to kick the hollow. His boot impacted with its skull, splitting the bones. Its jaw rolled free as it screeched at him. Clare reached through the open door and wrapped her arms around Dorran, then pulled him back. He fell inside, half in the passenger seat, half in her lap.

She didn't wait for him to right himself or even try to close the door. She just pressed her weight into the accelerator, throwing them both back. The car shuddered as it hit the screaming, scuttling creatures blocking its path. Clare's heart missed a beat as she thought the car might become stuck on them. But her beloved hatchback powered on, tumbling over them as though it had been born for it, and then, before Clare could even draw breath, they were on clear road and the monsters were fading in her rearview mirror.

CHAPTER 20

CLARE CHOKED AS SHE tried to breathe. She squeezed the wheel so tightly she was afraid she might break it as the car rocketed down the Banksy Forest road. She was sliding into the other lane, and as she corrected it, the passenger door slammed closed.

She glanced at her mirrors. The car's taillights washed a sheen of red over the road. The hollows were scuttling after them, heads bobbing, limbs twisting, but they disappeared from view within seconds.

Dorran was tangled in the passenger seat, his arm braced on the cup holders, his long legs against the door. He reached up and wrenched the mask off. His face was sheet white and wet with sweat. "We did it."

He sounded surprised at himself.

"We did." Clare hated how badly her voice shook. She let the car slow until it was only coasting, then pulled her own mask off. They shared an unsteady smile, then Clare pressed her sleeve across her eyes to clear the moisture off of them. "You were amazing."

"And you were clever to think of the horn. Thank you." Slowly, he adjusted himself, sitting up in the seat. Bright blood glistened on his glove and sleeve.

Clare's smile vanished. "Your hand—"

"It's not bad." He wrestled out of his outer jacket and wrapped it around the cuts, then pressed on it to stem the flow. If any color had remained in his face, he lost it then, eyes closed and a muscle in his jaw twitching.

They came to a halt, engine still purring, as Clare turned to dig through the back seat. Her unsteady hands fumbled the items as she sorted through them. "Hang on. We have the first aid kit. I can—"

"I will take care of this." His voice was surprisingly calm. "Please, for a moment, could we keep driving? I want to be out of this forest."

Clare found the first aid kit. She didn't trust herself to speak so placed it at Dorran's side, then turned back to the road. The car's headlights glowed across the trees and the still-wet asphalt. In between the sparkling drops of water were several pairs of eyes. She swallowed and pressed on the accelerator.

Dorran leaned back in the seat, eyes closed and fabric wrapped tightly around his arm. It had to be hurting him, but his face was calm.

Clare kept her speed steady. She wanted to be out of the smothering trees, but she also knew she needed to be careful.

Another crash, or even becoming caught in a pothole or snagged on a fallen branch, could be fatal. Especially as the distance between them and Winterbourne, their only safe haven, grew.

As far as Clare could tell, they were the first people to drive along the road since the world had collapsed. The endless storms and melting snows had left debris. Clare drove over the smaller branches carefully. Several larger branches lay to the side of the road, and she coaxed the car around them. Twice, streams of water flowed over their path. Water sprayed in graceful arcs outside their windows, but the car held together.

The headlights picked up a shape in the road, and Clare slowed again. A thick branch blocked their path.

Dorran opened his eyes as the car eased to a halt. "Stay here."

"No." She pushed him back into his seat. "You're hurt. This one is mine."

"I—"

"No arguments. Sit tight."

She opened her door, motor still running, and slipped outside. Her boots splashed in the water trickling across the road. Her legs were damp from the saturated car seat, and as a wind nipped around her, gooseflesh rose over her skin. Clare strode through the coiling mist, her ears searching for noise. Faint dripping sounds were the only respite from the forest's eerie silence. She grasped the branch's ragged end and pulled.

She'd left her door open, and a sickly yellow light flooded through the car. It washed over Dorran, painting shadows across his face and reflecting off his eyes. He sat forward in his seat, alert, his good hand resting on the door handle. Clare shot him a smile that was more confident than she felt.

Behind her, a twig snapped. Dorran's eyes tightened. Her heart thundered as she dragged the branch to the side, moving it just far enough for the car to slip around, then dashed back to the car. She leapt inside and slammed the door, heart hammering and hands shaking as she released the handbrake and let the car roll forward. "There. No problem."

Dorran slowly relaxed back. His head turned as they passed the branch, and Clare followed his eyes to see a mangled child creeping out of the forest's edge. It used its arms to drag itself forward, a multitude of bones springing from its twisted legs like roots on a fallen tree. Its jaw worked furiously, spilling froth, as it crawled through the debris in their wake.

Just how many of them are there?

She kept her focus on the road as they passed through Banksy Forest. She'd driven the path countless times before, but everything looked different that day. She recognized some of the bends, but it felt as though the world had aged a decade in the past few weeks.

Then, up ahead, a circle of natural light broke through the gloom. The car coasted out of the forest's boundary. As the pines receded behind them, the landscape was taken over by gently rolling hills and sparse trees.

She drove on until the forest was nothing but a band of darkness in the rearview mirror, then asked, "Do you think it's safe to stop for a moment?"

"Yes, it should be." He tilted his head. "Is something—"

She put the car in park, then clambered over the divider to reach Dorran. She kissed his lips, his throat, his forehead, every part of him she could reach. He was salty from the drying sweat, but she didn't care. She thought she could hold him and kiss him for the rest of her life and never do anything else.

Dorran began to laugh in between kissing her back. "Oh, Clare."

"I'm so glad you're still here." She ran her hands through his hair, pushing it away from his face. "Back there…the hollows…"

"Shh." She could feel him smiling against her neck. "You don't need to worry; I will not be leaving you."

She kissed him a final time, lingering over his lips, not wanting to pull away. When she did, she opened the first aid kit between them and sifted through the contents. "Let me have a look at your hand."

"It will be fine. Time is pressing; you should keep driving."

She frowned as she pulled a bottle out of the kit and tried to read the label. "No, this is important. Are these the painkillers?"

He nodded, and Clare tipped two of the tablets out and balanced them on the dashboard. She then kicked open her door and rounded the car to find water and a cup.

The water cartons, sheltered inside the trunk, were still full of ice. Enough had melted that she could pour out a cup for Dorran, which she brought to him. He swallowed the tablets and washed them down. "Thank you. That will be fine for now."

Clare climbed back into her seat and shuffled around to face him. "Not yet. Let me see it."

His good hand rested protectively over the swaddled wrist, and Clare had to lift her eyebrows before he removed it. She picked at the edges of the jacket, and Dorran flinched as she peeled the fabric away from his wrist. Moving carefully, she tugged the bloodied sleeve up his arm to get it clear of the wound. The bite seemed to have landed half on skin, half on the glove. She could see punctures from molars, already filling with blood again.

"Is it okay if I take the glove off?"

He did it himself, moving faster than Clare would have, and clenched his jaw as the leather dragged over damaged skin. Clare brushed stray hair out of her face and bent lower to check the damage. Four teeth had punctured the skin, and they had sunk in deeply. Red bruising showed where the rest of the jaw had failed to cut through the glove.

"Okay." She blinked furiously, trying to keep her emotions in check as she struggled to grasp what needed to be done. "Uh, they need to be cleaned, right? And…and stitches."

"Not for these." He draped the jacket over them. "Stitches are good for pulling skin together when the inside of the cuts are clean. These are not, and stitches will only trap dirt inside. Better to let them scab over and heal that way."

"Right. Okay. So…"

Dorran's healthy hand landed over hers as she riffled through the kit. His eyes were tight, but he smiled at her. "I know this is worrying you, but I am fully able to treat it. What about a compromise? You drive, and I'll patch myself up during the trip."

"Will you be able to?" She bit her lip. "I mean, if the car is jostling you—"

"That will be fine. Besides, we have limited daylight hours. I would feel happier with the road passing beneath us."

"Okay." She gave him a final reluctant glance, then shuffled back to face the road and started the car. The engine ticked over without catching, and a stab of terror hit Clare. She turned the key a second time and it rumbled to life. Gravel crunched under the wheels as they rolled forward. She exhaled, and Dorran echoed the sound beside her.

"I did my best to repair the car," he said. "I hope it will last the trip. But the job was…well, temporary, to put it lightly."

"As long as it gets us to Beth's. She has her own car; we can drive it home." The road outside the forest was straight and clear of debris, and Clare pushed the hatchback to go faster. The driver's door had been damaged by hollows during the initial crash and air whistled through a gap between the window and the roof. The faster Clare drove, the higher the whistle became. A rattling noise joined it. Clare eased off the accelerator.

As he'd promised, Dorran cleaned his cuts. He worked with his usual efficiency, dabbing swabs and antiseptic across the marks. Fresh sweat beaded over his forehead and he took sharp, jagged inhales but was otherwise silent. Clare couldn't stop glancing at him. The jacket he'd used to wrap his wrist was drenched with blood and the cuts seemed deep. She didn't know enough about first aid to guess how serious they were, and it was hard to trust Dorran's self-diagnosis when he incessantly downplayed any injury he got. But she didn't think he would be so calm if the same bite had landed on her.

The empty fields were a relief after the forest. Long grass, brown and ragged after its imprisonment in ice, shivered in the wind. There were trees—thin, straggly ones with kinked trunks and sparse branches—but they were infrequent. The area was sometimes used for cattle grazing, though Clare couldn't see any trace of cows that day. In the far distance, so small that it barely registered as a smear of gray halfway up a hill, was a farmstead. Clare wondered whether its occupants might have found their way into the forest. She could have very well looked the land's owner in the face and not known it.

The road carried on through the countryside for a while. The turnoff to Marnie's property was half an hour ahead, and Clare's stomach tightened at the thought. They would be passing the exit, though, and driving on until the rural road merged onto the freeway that took her to Beth's.

Less than four hours now. You made it this far. Keep your eyes on the road. Less than four hours, and you'll know what happened to her. One way or another.

CHAPTER 21

AIR CREATED A FAINT, breathless whistle as it whipped over the damaged door. They were driving fast, but Clare wanted to go faster. Anytime she increased the speed, the rattle returned, and she didn't trust it enough to live with it. For the time, the car was moderating their speed.

Dorran snapped the first aid kit closed. She peeked at his bitten hand. He'd wrapped bandages around the cut, looping it over his thumb like a half glove. A hint of pink tinged the white wrappings. She hoped it would be enough.

"Where did you put the radio?" Dorran asked.

"Uh…it's back there. I can't remember where exactly. Why?"

Instead of replying, he turned to reach into the back seat. Clare slowed as Dorran braced his elbow on the back of her chair and used his good hand to sift through the supplies. It only took a few seconds for him to return, the black radio and a small leather pouch clutched to his chest.

"Be careful with your wrist," she said.

He smiled as he opened the pouch and took out a small screwdriver. A moment later, the radio's back popped off. He placed the machine on the dashboard and bent over it, screwdriver tip probing as he looked through the nest of cables.

"Do you think you can fix it?"

"Perhaps. I can try."

Clare swallowed. If they could get in contact with Beth, they might be able to breathe a little more easily for the rest of the drive. They would at least know whether she was safe or not. How long she thought the air would last. Whether they needed to hurry, or whether they could afford to be cautious.

Whether she's still alive.

Dorran made a satisfied noise at the back of his throat, and a soft click echoed from the radio. "Do you have the batteries?"

"Yeah." She reached into her pocket and fished them out. Dorran fed them into their slot, then pressed a button to turn the radio on.

Deafening white noise blasted through the car, and Clare flinched, squeezing her eyes closed as though that might save her eardrums. The noise faded to a low crackle as Dorran turned the volume down.

"It was just a bad connection." He reattached the back, then placed the radio onto the dashboard facing Clare. "Would you like to try calling her?"

One eye on the road, Clare checked the settings to ensure it was on Beth's frequency. Then she activated the microphone. "Beth? It's me. Clare. Can you hear me?"

Static answered. Clare flexed her grip on the wheel as the seconds stretched out.

"We're coming to get you, Beth. Less than four hours. Please, if you're there, answer me."

The white noise was like nails on a chalkboard to Clare's nerves. The longer she listened, the worse the anxious ache in her chest grew. It was climbing into her throat, choking her.

"I can't hear you, but if you're there, wait for us. We're not far off now. And…and…wear a mask if you can find one or make one. The hollows can't recognize you if they can't see skin. Okay?"

Hissing, popping, interspersed with nothing. Clare's eyes burned. She pressed the button to end her side of the communication but couldn't bring herself to turn the radio off entirely.

Dorran nudged the volume down until it was barely audible. They sat in silence for a moment, then he said, "Your sister kept her radio off except when she tried to speak with you. She may still be there."

"Yes." She smiled so fiercely that her cheeks ached, but felt dangerously close to hyperventilating. "You're right. Maybe she just can't hear me."

The car's engine rattled again as Clare pushed it too hard, and she forced herself to slow down. She was glad Dorran didn't try to talk. He let her drive in peace as they listened to the faint white noise.

Sickly clouds shifted across a steel-gray sky. A dark smear hovered at the horizon, and as they drew closer, it began to resolve into roofs and trees.

Clare knew the town. She drove through it every time she visited Beth. The closest shop—the one everyone passed on the outskirt of the community—had a bright yellow billboard painted on the wall facing the road, advertising fish and chips. The eatery was at least two decades old, and the sign hadn't been changed in all of that time. A smattering of graffiti tags marked the paint, and the color had worn down in the sun. Clare had always promised herself that one day she would stop there and see what fish and chips tasted like from a shop that seemingly lived in a different generation. She'd never gotten around to it.

The town appeared to be empty. Clare slowed as she neared its outskirts and leaned over the wheel to watch the wide sidewalks and empty windows. Houses were mixed among stores in a haphazard arrangement. Land in that area was cheap, so the buildings all had an excess of space around them, usually filled with weeds or plain dirt. She'd always thought the town was cute, but now, it left her feeling cold and queasy.

Power had gone out a long time before and every window was black. Several doors hung open. A café still had its daily specials sign propped outside, half spilling into the road, but the chalk had run from the snow, and she could barely make out the promise of eggplant lasagna. Clare could only imagine that the lasagna was still inside, sitting on a kitchen counter, slowly rotting as it waited for customers that were never going to come.

It felt strange to see life suspended in that way. People had woken up on that last morning with nothing in their minds except getting through another day. The café's cook would have come in early to prepare the lasagna. He might have doted on it, cooking something he knew would make the regular customers happy. Or maybe he rushed through the prep, cutting the eggplant slices too thick and not caring that the sauce was too watery. It was the last thing he would ever cook. Clare wondered whether he would have prepared it differently if he had known.

Something moved down a side street. Clare kept the car at a steady, cautious speed but watched the shape. A skeletal figure, hunched over a drain at the end of the road, twisted to stare at them with bulbous eyes.

There are hollows here too.

It made sense. If there had been humans, there would be hollows. As they moved deeper through the town, deformed creatures appeared in the open doorways, attracted by the motor's rumble and curious about a potential meal. Several tried to follow them, clambering awkwardly on too-long limbs or scuttling on all fours. Clare watched them in her rearview mirror and increased her speed to outpace them.

They approached a gas station at the edge of town. Clare licked her lips. "Did you put all of the fuel into the tank?"

"Yes. All of it."

The indicator on her dashboard said half-full. That would get them to Beth's. It probably wouldn't be enough to take them home. She wondered if there was any way to get gas out of the station without power to pump it up from the wells.

It was a moot question either way. A pack of hollows was still following them, and shimmering eyes glittered from the shadows around the pumps. There was no room to stop.

Another forty minutes would bring them to the freeway. From there, it was a smooth, straight drive of about two hours to reach her sister's. The freeway was raised, which meant flooding shouldn't have affected it. As long as the roads weren't blocked, Clare thought they would be okay.

She increased her speed as they left town. The shapes continued to scramble after them, and Clare watched them until they became too small to see. *How long will they try to follow us? Until they can't hear or see us? Longer? Is it possible the ones from the forest are still coming down that road, intent on a feast they believe they can still catch?*

She shook her head to clear it. The idea of having their nightmares catch up to them if they ever stopped for too long wasn't appealing. Again, she filed it into the bucket of problems that had no solutions.

Melancholy wouldn't help them. She tried to look for the positives instead. The car was working. Dorran was with her. The freeway was looming on the horizon. She had a lot to be grateful for.

Dorran had been quiet, but his eyes burned with curiosity as they flicked across the landscape. She remembered, with a shock, that he had very rarely seen anything outside the family's estates.

"Is this your first time in this part of the country?"

"Yes." The corners of his mouth lifted. "It is a little ironic. I finally have the freedom to explore the world, but it has all gone to hell."

Clare's throat tightened. He was right; he'd been waiting for this moment for most of his life. Now that he was here, it was hollow. Everything he had been looking forward to, everything he had read about and dreamed about, was gone.

He saw her expression and laughed. "No, don't worry, my darling. I am enjoying myself plenty."

"How can you say that? You're hurt and tired, and I know how stressful this must have been—"

"And we are free from the house and doing something I can be proud of and…" He brushed the back of his finger over her cheek. "I am sitting beside the best woman I have known. I have nothing to complain about."

Pink heat spread across Clare's face, and she looked aside in a poor effort to hide it from Dorran.

He might not ever get to see the cities or go to the movies or ride in a plane, but that doesn't mean everything is gone. "Did you want to listen to some music? I have some CDs, and there's a decent chance the car's player still works."

She reached over Dorran to open the glove box. Inside was a clutter of relics from her old life: her car's registration and insurance details, a pocket pack of tissues, pens, a letter she'd never gotten the chance to mail, a pack of chewing gum, and a small bundle of CDs held together with rubber bands.

Clare hadn't listened to CDs in years, but they had been a staple in her car as a teenager and it had felt wrong to throw them out. Now, she was grateful she'd kept them. They would help drown out the static and give Dorran a taste of the world he had missed.

"What kind of music do you like?" She pulled the CDs free of the bundle one at a time and held them up in front of her so that she could read the names and still keep her eyes on the road.

"I'll trust your taste."

"Don't say that or you'll get one of the boy bands. Here, let's try this." She'd found a mix of rock hits and slid it into the CD player. The compartment hissed and whirred, then the first track started playing. Clare silently cheered for her car. It might have been brought back from the dead by dubious means, but its CD player had survived.

Dorran rested his arm against the door and listened in silence. Clare kept sneaking glances at him, trying to read his expression. As the first song ended and the second one began, he smiled. "I like your music. It has a lot of energy. Just like you."

CHAPTER 22

THE RURAL ROAD SPLIT as it neared the freeway. One passed underneath the pillars and turned south, which would eventually lead to the coast. Clare took the path that funneled them north and entered the ramp leading up to the freeway.

"Oh." She slowed as they turned the corner. A car blocked half of the ramp, facing the concrete blockade, its front and side crumpled. The driver's door hung open.

Clare turned the music's volume down as they approached. Keys dangled from the ignition. Three black drops—*Old blood*, Clare thought—marked the windshield. She tried to imagine what might have happened to the occupant, then immediately shut down that train of thought.

There was enough road left to fit around the car, so Clare did, moving cautiously to avoid clipping the other vehicle. They passed it and Clare focused her eyes on the path ahead that would merge them onto the main road.

We're at the freeway. Just two hours to Beth's.

The on-ramp flattened out and straightened as it grew level with the freeway. The concrete blockades that had blocked the view ended as the roads merged, and Clare finally had a chance to see the freeway clearly.

Cars crowded the space. Some had collided with the concrete walls on either side of the road. Others had crossed over the median strip, breaking the dividing cables and tearing up the plants. They had crashed into each other, creating pileups sometimes eight or ten cars deep. Still others had ended up in the middle of the road, noses slipping out of their lane, their doors hanging open.

How in heaven are we supposed to get through this?

Dorran hunched forward, alert. "I see movement in that car."

Clare followed his gaze and saw a woman in a nearby sedan. A floral blouse still clung to her emaciated body, but parts of the fabric poked out strangely. It took Clare a second to see why. Bony protrusions extended from her flesh. Three split from the back of her skull, sticking out like spines. More grew from her elbows, her hips, and her ribs. She fought against the seat belt, which had locked, binding her in place, but didn't seem to have the awareness to undo it.

She's been fighting in there for nearly three weeks. Clare swallowed around the lump in her throat. She looked at the path ahead and saw movement inside other cars. More trapped creatures, beating their fists against their imprisonment, clambering across the seats, and cracking their teeth on the glass.

Stress pulled her muscles taut. Clare closed her eyes and forced her breathing back to a comfortable level. When she opened her eyes again, she focused on the road. The only hollows she could see were trapped. And, despite the pileups and crashes, she thought she could see a path between the cars.

"Maybe…maybe it's just crowded here because of the on-ramp. Maybe it gets easier a bit farther on."

Dorran gave her a tense nod, encouraging her. Clare eased off the brake and let the car coast forward.

They had to pass the trapped woman's car. The gap was so narrow that Clare was afraid of scraping its side, and she forced herself to keep her eyes ahead as the woman twitched and howled within an arm's reach.

Her CD moved to a new song, a bright, bouncy tune that promised the world was wonderful. She hit the button to turn it off.

Sometimes the cars were so close together that Clare had to slow her hatchback to a crawl and nudge one of the vehicles with her bumper to shift it out of the way. She didn't want either of them to leave the car. The shadows around the piled-up vehicles were too deep to see through, and she didn't know what might be hiding inside.

The trapped hollows never stayed still. The hungry, anguished howling floated around Clare, and a tiny panic sparked that they might figure out the door handles. She was driving too slowly to shake any that attached themselves to the car, and all it would take were ten or fifteen hollows to coat them.

She'd thought that the freeway would be as clear and easy as the road out of the forest. Her estimate of two hours faded into the distance as she was forced, again and again, to slow to a crawl to get around a blockage.

"You're doing well," Dorran said.

Her eyes burned and her head ached, but Dorran's words made it feel a little more bearable. She nodded briefly as she took a sharp turn around a toppled truck.

The clock on the dashboard crawled onward. The car was heating in the sun and odors from the spilled blood and stagnant water began to rise. Clare tried to turn on the air-conditioning, but that was one part of her car that hadn't survived the crash. She reached to open the windows but stopped herself. The freeway wasn't safe enough to risk even that inch of an opening.

Even with their jackets shed, the car was too warm for comfort. They had been on the freeway for nearly an hour. Clare estimated they had covered the same amount of ground she would have normally crossed in ten minutes. Anytime she wasn't watching the path ahead, she stared at the clock. It frightened her.

She clung to the hope that the path would clear, that maybe they were just in a congested part. Every few minutes she found a clear stretch where she could drive, unimpeded, for half a minute before having to slow down again. It was a tantalizing promise of what might have been.

Dorran sat forward. "What's that ahead?"

She pulled her focus away from the nearest tangle she'd been trying to navigate and squinted over the roofs of the cars blocking their path. She could see the road continuing on for forty meters, then, strangely, a dark area. She rose in her seat until her head grazed the ceiling, trying to see clearly, but the view was still too obstructed.

"Hang on." She scraped close to a parked car. What had once been a teenager launched itself against the window, swaying the vehicle. Something that looked like a fragment from a gold necklace was jammed between its teeth. Blood smeared across the front seat and the dashboard told Clare the teenager hadn't been alone in the car.

She corrected her course and squeezed between two parked SUVs. The view ahead became clearer. The asphalt continued forward, then cracked, then began to slope downward, before abruptly disappearing.

"What…" She leaned forward, staring at the gaping hole in the road. The path had been completely torn away. Bent metal and twisted supports jutted out of the other side of the chasm thirty feet away. It was as though a giant had swiped his hand through the road.

What could have done this?

Dorran looked past Clare. She followed his gaze. Fields lay to either side of the freeway. And something large and white shone in one of them.

A plane had come down. Clare could trace its path. It had scraped across the freeway, smashing the gaping hole. Luggage and wing fragments lay scattered over the gouged dirt, which led in a line to the plane's final resting place.

They became hollows. Clare pressed her palm into her forehead.

The pilot. The passengers, probably. Even being sequestered thousands of feet above the ground wasn't enough to save them.

She faced forward again. The chasm gaped, taunting her. Clare rubbed her palms into her burning eyes.

"Breathe." Dorran's fingers brushed over her hair, soothing. "We are not done yet. There are other routes to your sister's."

So much time wasted on a dead end. Clare swiped her cheeks dry, then set her jaw as she put the car into reverse. She hooked one arm over the back of her seat as she steered the car into a gap large enough to let her turn around, then straightened up. They passed the hissing, screaming teenager again, the necklace trapped in his overgrown teeth.

"Where to now?" Clare asked.

Dorran found his jacket in the back seat and pulled the map out of the folds. He smoothed the paper out on the dashboard as he checked the routes.

"There are alternatives. If we travel west for forty minutes, we will be at another freeway that eventually crosses this one farther down its course. But after what we have seen today, I think it might be wise to avoid the major roads."

Clare nodded. "Stay to the rural streets. Ones without much traffic."

"In that case…" His fingertips traced along the map. "The shortest course would be this road here."

Her stomach turned sour. "Okay," she said, trying not to let Dorran hear how much she wished there was an alternative.

They were taking the road that led past Marnie's farm.

CHAPTER 23

THE CAR'S SIDE SCRAPED against a blue sedan. Clare flinched. The gap had been a tight squeeze and she'd been too focused on the other car narrowing their path. She put her hatchback in reverse, backed up, and tried again. Behind her, a chattering wail was followed by a loud thump as a hollow beat against its restraints.

"I'll drive for a stretch." Dorran folded the map up and placed it under the radio, which still crackled and hissed.

"No. I'm fine."

"Clare. You are exhausted. You've been driving for hours and the stress is breaking you."

He wasn't wrong. Clare's nerves were ragged. Her eyes burned and her head ached. Every minute she spent in the locked traffic, listening to the white noise and staring into the broken faces that leered at her through filthy windows, made her want to scream.

But she still shook her head. "Your arm. It would be painful. I can keep driving for a while. Once we're off this freeway—"

His hand landed over hers, and he grazed his thumb across her knuckles, coaxing her to release the grip on the wheel that made her fingers, arms, and shoulders ache. "I can drive with one hand. Move over."

"Really. I'm fine."

"Well, I'm going to drive. You can either move out of the way or let me sit on you."

Clare blinked at him. Dorran smiled back. His jokes were always delivered with such deadpan calmness that they caught Clare by surprise. Slowly, she began to chuckle and put the car in park. "Okay, okay. But be careful with your hand. I can take over again once we're back on a clear road."

They opened their doors. It was the first time Clare had been outside the car in hours, and her leg and arm muscles cried for the freedom. She stretched them as much as she could as she rounded the car, but refused to linger. They hadn't passed any hollows outside of their vehicles, likely because the freeway was too exposed for them to linger, but the fact remained that they were still surrounded. All it would take is for one to finally find a way to break free—or a straggler lurking on the freeway who had avoided their notice—and they could be in a much worse situation.

Dorran slid into the driver's seat and waited until Clare had her door closed before putting the car back into drive. "Do you think you could sleep? We'll be here for a while, and rest might help."

"Maybe."

The car bumped forward, jolting them, and Clare gripped her seat belt. Dorran made a faint noise and tried again. This time, the car moved smoothly.

"It has been a while," he said, sounding apologetic.

"Since you last drove?"

"Yes. One of my uncles taught me how to years ago, but there is not much cause to drive when you cannot leave your property. I tried to keep in practice, but...well."

He steered them around an abandoned motorbike, and Clare began to relax. He seemed to think he needed to apologize, but he actually wasn't bad. He kept his injured hand resting on the armrest, and steered lightly with the other. Clare waited a moment, making sure he was comfortable with the car, then pulled her jacket out of the back seat and bundled it up against the window.

Her skull throbbed with a low-level headache. She leaned against the makeshift cushion and tried to make the muscles relax. Dorran wanted her to nap, but she couldn't. The hollows still surrounded them, clawing at windows and skittering across seats. The best she could do was keep her eyes focused just on the road ahead, not on any of the motion to the sides.

The dashboard clock hit midday. They had passed the four hours Clare had estimated it would take to get to Beth's.

How long will her oxygen last? She watched the radio, silently begging it to give up some kind of noise except for the maddening hisses and pops. *How much air does the bunker hold? Is she already dizzy? I know she kept some bottles of wine down there. Maybe she's drinking them now, trying to steel herself for opening the door and everything that will bring.*

If she'd just pick up the radio. If she would just talk, even once, so I know she's still there...

Dorran drove smoothly. Clare had thought it would be difficult to give up control to him, that the frustration and powerlessness would make her irritable. But it didn't. His bearing was as calm and steady as it always seemed in stressful situations. He didn't drive recklessly, but he was efficient, and soon Clare found it easy to let her attention wander, knowing he would be making the best choices he could.

Dorran brought the car around the outside of another pileup and released his hold on the wheel to tap the CD player's power button. Clare smiled as the bright tunes filled the car again.

He's a good man. The best kind of man. I'm lucky to have him.

With the music drowning out the hollows and the car's gentle rocking, she closed her eyes and let them rest. Time blurred together until she suddenly realized they were moving faster. She peeked through half-opened eyes.

They were back among farmland, racing down the rural road they had covered hours before. Clare sat up and blinked sleep out of her eyes. "We're off the freeway."

"We are. We left it behind a half hour ago."

He'd wound the windows down an inch and the heat had dissipated. Clare stretched and felt muscles in her back ache. "Do you want to swap back?"

"Not at all. I am enjoying this." Dorran was relaxed, one hand holding the wheel steady as the car raced across the asphalt. "You can rest for a while more."

Clare rubbed at the back of her neck. The town they had passed through earlier that day appeared ahead of them, its jagged, low rooftops interrupting the skyline. Dorran didn't slow as they passed through it. Clare caught flashes of motion in the windows and doorways, but they were gone before she could tell what she was looking at.

She pictured the map in her mind. The road to Marnie's would take them through the countryside in a long, rambling loop. Back when the world still made sense, it would have taken miles longer than driving along the freeway. It was strange to think that it was the faster option.

Fast enough to get to Beth's before sundown? Time was ticking away from them. Clare didn't want to think about spending a night out on the road. They had packed for it—they had blankets, food, and water, even toiletries—but only as a precaution. Clare guessed it had been too much to hope that they could make the trip without any hitches. Even so, the idea of being outside at night, in the world that now belonged to hollows, didn't sit well with her.

Then a new thought pressed into her mind, and she glanced at the fuel indicator. The little needle hovered over the lowest marker, just above the ominous *E*.

"We'll need fuel," Clare said, and hated that her voice cracked.

"Mm. Any thoughts of where we could find some?"

She pictured the service station they had passed in the town and how the streets had been teeming with the gray creatures. The hollows lurked in places where they could hide from the sun: abandoned houses, overturned cars, the forest. If Clare could find a service station in a field or down a lonely stretch of highway, they might stand a chance.

She unfurled the map and stared at it. The only service stations she knew about were part of towns or cities.

Dorran didn't know the area and was relying on Clare to guide them. He kept his eyes on the road. She had the impression he was trying not to put her under pressure. In a strange way, that only made it worse.

Think! We can't just keep driving and hope we stumble over a remote station. Where else could we get gas? If we find an empty car off the side of the road, we might be able to siphon fuel out of its tank…but it would be a gamble.

The car would have to be parked somewhere remote enough that there are no hollows around. It would need to run on gasoline, not diesel. And they would need some kind of hose to pull it out of the tank.

Then Clare's mind lit on the solution, and her stomach turned sour with dread. "Marnie's. She lives on a farm. Remote. She keeps cartons of fuel in her shed for the equipment."

On some of Clare's visits, she'd helped Marnie with her chores. She could picture the shed and its clutter of knickknacks. Bright red bottles were stacked on a shelf next to gardening supplies. That was the surest bet she could think of.

"It would be convenient…" Dorran spoke carefully. "It's on our route. But, Clare, you know the risk. She might still be there."

Her remains might still be there. Maybe not a body, specifically, but blood. Torn clothes. Bone fragments that the hollows had failed to consume.

"Yes." The map crumpled under Clare's tightening fingers. "But we don't need to go into the house. The fuel is in the shed. We can grab it and be out of there in less than a minute. It's remote and surrounded by bare farmland, so there probably won't be any hollows there when the forest offers security and more food."

"Then that's where we'll go." Up ahead, a sign poked out of the side of the road, its arrow pointing toward an offshoot. Dorran slowed as they approached it and turned them toward their new destination.

CHAPTER 24

CLARE KNEW THE ROAD well. A big elm tree sat to the left, tilting so badly that it would need cutting down within a few years. That was what Marnie had always said. She'd been saying it for as long as Clare could remember, and each year, the tree grew older and tilted slightly more and still remained undisturbed.

Sentimentality. It needed to be killed, but no one wanted to do it. They all grew up driving past that tree. Sitting under it. Talking about how badly it leaned. It was like a friend.

The car bumped over copious potholes. The road saw a moderate amount of traffic from the rural properties flanking it, but never enough for the government to justify resealing it. Every time a pothole grew too bad to ignore, they would fill it, like putting a plaster over a scab that only got worse through time. Some of the potholes had been filled five or six times, their dark asphalt bowed into a bowl shape as they were gradually worn back down. By that point, there were almost more patch jobs than original road left.

The car's engine rattled with every bounce, but it endured. Clare thought it might actually take them all the way to Beth's and back as long as they could feed it enough fuel.

A dark shape appeared on the side of the road. Clare craned her neck to see it. Dorran's expression darkened, and he took some of the power off the accelerator. "Ah. We're passing it after all."

"Passing it?"

"My family's camper. This is the road we take to reach the Gould estate."

"Oh." Clare had been so wrapped up in her worries about Marnie's property that she hadn't even considered the significance it might have for Dorran. She pressed a hand over her mouth.

"I had wondered how far they might have gotten before… Well, this is the answer."

"Do you want to stop?"

"No. There is nothing for me here."

The car slowed to a crawl as they neared the procession. At the front were six luxury cars. They were older models but maintained well. Even after the snow and rain, their black paint still seemed to glimmer. Behind those were two private buses and horse trailers. *The staff's transport.* The cars all had open doors. Madeline Morthorne had told Clare about the change. She said the air burned. They must have opened the doors to try to escape it. Except, there had been no escape. Not for any of them. A streak of blood ran across one of the bus windows. A child's boot lay on the ground outside the second of the family's cars.

His nieces and nephews. He'd spent years trying to protect them. And now…they're just gone.

"Dorran—"

"I am fine." His voice was a monotone. There was a flash of emotion in his eyes, bright and desperate, then he blinked and it was gone again. "It is in the past now. Regret is not beneficial."

"I won't push." Clare watched him closely. "But…you know you can talk to me. If it would help."

He pressed on the accelerator, and the engine rattled threateningly. But as the abandoned procession faded into the distance, he slowly relaxed. The hardness vanished from around his eyes as he gave her a thin smile. "Thank you."

They followed the slowly curving road. Clare knew what to expect up ahead: the wood post fences and their strings of barbed wire. Then the disused field that bordered Marnie's property. The hill with two straggly birch trees. The rock formations. Then, the smooth driveway leading toward the farmstead.

Marnie had once worked the area with her husband. They grew stone fruit and raised goats and had been two of the most hardworking people Clare had ever known. When Marnie's husband passed away a decade before, some of the neighbors wondered whether Marnie might sell the farm and move into town for a quieter life, since she was in her late forties and on the plumper side. A lot of people wouldn't have been surprised if she'd taken the opportunity to retire.

Clare had asked Beth about it, and Beth had laughed. "If there are two things Marnie hates, it's raisins in her cakes and doing nothing. She'll keep the farm."

And she had. She'd restricted what she'd done on it; their flock of sixty goats was gradually whittled down to her four favorites. The fields no longer carried huge stretches of produce. Instead, she'd built up the area around her house, installing a chicken coop and a garden patch. She must have had money saved up because she never sold any of her land but lived on what her garden grew.

Clare had loved her aunt. When Marnie gossiped, it was only about positive, uplifting news. The barn cats that were supposed to keep the farm free from mice were moved indoors and turned into lazy lap cats one by one. Clare sometimes thought Marnie had the biggest heart out of anyone she knew.

As the farm came into view, Clare squeezed her hands in her lap. It was physically painful to look at the buildings knowing what had most likely happened to their occupant.

"It's the shed up ahead, closest to the house," Clare said. A vegetable garden separated the two buildings. The chicken coop's door hung open, like it always did during the day, to allow the birds to roam through the grass and pick bugs. They would have been eaten. As would the cats and the goats. As the car crept along the gravel driveway toward the shed, Clare scanned the fields for any kind of life and found none.

"Would you like to stay in the car?" Dorran asked.

She didn't think she could speak coherently, so she shook her head instead. He turned the engine off but left the key in the ignition as he opened the door. They stood beside the car for a moment, watching the area and waiting.

The house was uncharacteristically calm and neglected. Clare had never seen it without lights glowing through its curtains and the smell of stews or the sound of music coming from it. She tried to separate her mind from her memories and searched for any shadowed areas that could be hiding hollows.

The barns were dark, but their doors were closed and bolted. There were trees scattered about the yard, but none dense enough to create coverage.

Then she looked at the ground. The field, saturated, had turned to mud. She scanned it but couldn't see any disturbance—from humans or from animals. If hollows were in the area, they hadn't visited the farm recently.

"Okay," she whispered.

Dorran opened the car's back door. He gave Clare the crowbar and took the hatchet for himself. After being inside the car for so long, Clare felt like she might suffocate if she tried to constrict herself any further and shook her head when Dorran offered her a mask. They left the car doors open as they stepped toward the barn.

Thirty seconds. Grab the fuel and get out.

The barn had a large entrance designed to allow tractors in and out. A simple latch door had been set into its corner. Marnie, being more trusting than the world probably deserved, never locked it. Clare undid the bolt and nudged the door inward, then stopped to let her eyes adjust.

183

The space was nearly empty since the larger farm had been closed. Marnie still kept her hobby garden equipment arranged neatly on the tables and shelves closest to the door, though. Shovels and spades, a hoe, gloves, endless varieties of fertilizer, and chicken feed were arranged in neat order.

Dorran stopped beside a basket. He reached toward it, hesitated, then pulled his hand back. Clare approached and saw he was looking at packets of seeds.

"I wasn't sure if it would be…disrespectful." He cleared his throat. "She has some varieties our own garden doesn't. But if you would prefer to leave her property the way it is—"

"No, it's okay. Let's…let's take them. It will be like carrying a little part of her back to Winterbourne."

He gently scooped up the packets. Clare felt a swell of affection for him. His life had been a ghastly example of what family should be, but that didn't stop him from respecting, even caring for, Clare's. He was kind, and a lifetime in a madhouse hadn't been enough to change that.

Clare found the red containers of fuel stacked on wooden shelves, half-hidden behind cartons of feed for the goats. Marnie had eight of them. She usually stocked up in bulk and waited until they were almost empty before driving to the nearest service station and filling them again. Clare lifted the jugs, testing their weight. Five were empty, but three were still full of sloshing liquid. Enough to get them to Beth's and home.

"There should be a funnel somewhere," she said.

Dorran held up a white shape. "Here."

"Great. Let's get filled up and get back on the road."

Dorran reached out to take the jugs, but Clare blocked him. She sent a pointed glance at his bandaged hand.

He raised his eyebrows in return. "At least let me carry *some*."

"One. You may have one." She offered it to him, and he chuckled as he took it. Clare carried the other two as they returned to the shed door.

Scrappy clouds were gathering above them, slowly choking out the sun that had done so much work to melt the snow. Dorran took his carton of fuel to refill the car while Clare closed and bolted the barn door. Marnie wouldn't have liked it being left open. It was a sad gesture—too little, too late—but it was one of the few things Clare could do. A lump in her throat ached as she stored the remaining two cartons in the back of the car. Dorran finished filling the car and left the empty jug beside the barn door.

"Okay." Clare lifted her chin and tried to shake herself free from the memories of being at Marnie's house. They had fuel. They had a seemingly clear road ahead of them. No hollows had disturbed them. There was still a long way to get to Beth's, but it was starting to look a little less daunting.

"Will I drive, or would you like to?" Dorran asked.

"I'll take this stretch. You've been driving for a while; have a rest. We can swap back later."

As Clare rounded the car to reach the driver's door, her eyes drifted toward Marnie's cottage a final time. She would miss its peaked roof. The garden was dead, thanks to the early snow, but she could still visualize how it looked in spring and summer, full of lush, stunning flowers and vegetables. She wished her last time seeing it hadn't been like this, with its rooms silent and its windows dark.

Wait...those are boards.

Clare stopped with her hand resting on the open door. Her mouth felt oddly dry. In the dark windows, in place of the usual gauzy curtains, thick wooden boards had been nailed into place.

CHAPTER 25

"DORRAN..."

He looked from Clare to the house and back. "What's wrong?"

If she boarded the windows, she must have heard about the hollows coming. If she heard about the hollows, that means she survived whatever effect deformed people. And if she survived all of that...she might still be alive.

"I think...I think..."

He rounded the car and put a hand behind Clare's back to steady her. His dark eyes narrowed as he scanned the cottage. "What do you see?"

"She was trying to defend the house."

"Ah—the boards."

It had been three weeks since the last normal day on earth. That was a long time for someone to survive on their own.

But we did. Dorran and I survived. Why not Marnie? She's used to being snowed in on her property. She has food stores and a well behind the house. Is it possible she's still here? Is it possible she made it through the end of the world?

"I have to see." Clare tried to step out of Dorran's hands, but he held her back.

"Wait, Clare. What if she's in there but no longer alive?"

That was a very real fear. But Clare took another step forward. "I have to see. I have to be sure."

"All right." He let go of her and picked up his hatchet again. "Keep close to me."

Clare's heart stuck in her throat as she approached the door. Her mind was fractured. Hope of finding her aunt battled against the knowledge of how slim the likelihood was. If Marnie was still inside, she would have heard their car approaching. She should have come out to see them. And yet, the house stayed dark and quiet.

But Clare couldn't give up. Not while the chance still existed, no matter how slim.

Her boots sunk up to the ankle in mud as she passed through the garden. Marnie's door, bright blue, had always felt inviting, but seemed less welcoming with the windows on either side boarded up.

Please. If she's still here…if she's still alive…

Clare reached for the bronze handle. A cord hung beside it, and Clare knew tugging it would ring bells through the house, a symphony of cheerful little chimes announcing visitors. She didn't touch it. Instead, she twisted the handle, felt the latch click as it unlocked, then watched the door swing open.

The hallway was barely visible in the gloom. Dust gathered across the floor and the myriad of knickknacks perched over cluttered shelves. With the boards over the windows, only narrow slats of light made their way inside to pick through the shadows.

Three items sat near the front door. One was a bucket of nails with a hammer resting inside. Leftovers from boarding up the house. The other two were suitcases, made of faded purple cloth, sitting up on their ends, ready to be carried out the door. Fine dust lay over the handles.

Clare knew the cases. She'd pictured them in her mind a dozen times since waking up at Winterbourne. Marnie would have packed them, ready to be picked up, waiting for Clare to take her to Beth's bunker.

But Clare had never come. And the cases now still sat by the door, unopened and untouched. That was enough to confirm Clare's fears. Marnie was no longer alive.

Hot tears pricked her eyes, but Clare still couldn't stop herself. She took a careful step deeper into the house.

She could picture what must have happened. Beth had called Marnie. She'd told her to be ready. And so Marnie had. She'd stood by the door, just like Clare had imagined, her luggage ready and waiting, staring at the long, empty road.

If there are two things Marnie hates, it's raisins in her cakes and doing nothing.

When the car didn't arrive, Marnie would have rolled up her sleeves and done what she did best: look after herself. She'd hammered the boards into the windows. She'd probably ensured her chickens were outside, just in case she didn't make it through the day to give them food.

The quiet zones—the patches of lost contact that resulted in an area being infested with the hollows—had started in the cities and gradually moved outward. Marnie's remote farmstead would have missed the first waves. *How long did she have? Two, three hours? Half a day? And what happened once it finally caught up with her?*

"Clare."

The word was a whisper in her ear. Dorran's hand fixed over her shoulder and tightened. He began to pull her back.

Clare heard it too. Sounds coming from deeper in the house. Dragging, shuffling.

No. No. No. Please, no, not this.

Something shifted at the end of the hallway. A narrow slat of light passed over it, glancing over a familiar floral blouse. Her aunt's gray hair, normally so fluffy, lay limp against her head. The head that had flattened as though squashed. Bones, rounded and large, made the skin bulge out. Bones around her chin. Bones around her cheeks. And the largest bone, the one on her forehead, that extended forward so far that the swollen skin half covered the eyes beneath.

The eyes were the worst part. The lids drooped. They were bloodshot. It was as though their color had been drained. But they were still Marnie's eyes—broken, damaged, distorted, but still Marnie's.

"No." The sound choked in Clare's throat, along with her air.

She felt dizzy. A ringing noise filled her ears. She couldn't look away.

Marnie shuffled toward them. Her body was swollen, the skin stretched to the bursting point, bright red and shiny. The clothes, half-torn, clung to her and swung about her with every hobbling step.

The mouth opened. A deep, mournful bellow spilled out, shaking the skin around her throat. Her steps were uneven, lurching. A string of saliva fell over the lower lip, spilling onto the stains already coating her blouse. Engorged fingers reached forward, fumbling, grasping at air.

Dorran was speaking to her in short, sharp phrases. She couldn't catch any of them. Her legs felt like they were made of paper and ready to crumble under the weight of what she was seeing. Marnie's slow, shuffling steps were growing faster. She spilled into the entryway, her shoulders knocking trinkets off the closest shelves. Then Dorran's arm moved around Clare's waist and dragged her back through the door, into the outside. Marnie's lips shivered as she released another bellow. It sounded mournful. Pained. Dorran slammed the door.

"No, no, no." Clare dropped her crowbar and clasped her head in both hands as hot tears spilled out.

She'd known Marnie was likely dead. But she'd never properly been able to face the idea that her aunt might have become a hollow. It was worse than death. It was barbaric. Torture. She dropped to her knees, fingers digging into her skull.

"Clare." Dorran's voice was gentle but held an undercurrent of urgency. He crouched beside her, close enough for her to feel his warmth. "We have to go, Clare."

Marnie reached the door. Her fingers, painfully swollen, began to scrabble against it. Clare could hear the phlegmy, gasping breaths underneath.

"We have to go." Dorran tried to pull her up, but she staggered. Her mind felt like it was crumbling. Like a rock that had been squeezed too hard, fragments splintering off, cracks digging deeper. An insane idea entered. Maybe they could go back to that morning. Just go to sleep, and when she woke up, she would be back to a point where there was still hope to look forward to. A world where Marnie was merely dead.

Dorran half carried, half dragged her toward the car. She could feel the stress bleeding out of him as he eased her into the passenger seat. Her door shut with a firm snap, then he took his seat beside her. He didn't try to start the car.

Clare buckled over, palms pressed into her forehead, as she tried not to wail. *That was my aunt.* The thought swirled around in her mind, refusing to give her peace. *That was my dear aunt. My aunt who loved her goats. My aunt who baked me cakes and sang out of tune to her favorite songs on the radio. My aunt who never had a harsh word to say about anyone.*

Dorran stroked her back, but didn't try to interrupt her grief. She could feel him watching the house, though. It was making him uneasy to be so close to a hollow.

That's all she is now—a hollow.

Before, Clare had been able to separate the creatures from who they had once been. It wasn't hard. They barely looked human. They were like some kind of monster out of a video game. Something you could hate. Something you could kill.

But this was Marnie. Not a hollow. Not a monster. Marnie.

And she was in pain.

Clare had seen it in her face, heard it in her bellows. Her skin was bulging, filled with fluid, ready to burst. It was agony for her. And she no longer had a human mind to comprehend what was happening. She didn't understand it. But she was trapped there, and would remain trapped there, suffering. *For how long?*

"We have to kill her." Clare lifted her head. Her voice was hoarse. She thought she might have been screaming, but she couldn't remember the noise, only feel the rawness in her throat. "I…I have to. She's in so much pain."

Dorran looked back toward the door. Beneath the radio's crackles, beneath Clare's ragged gasps, she thought she could still hear the sad digging of fingers at the door.

For a moment, neither of them spoke. Then Dorran said, "I'll do it."

"I can't ask that of you." Clare shook her head, but at the same time, a voice in the back of her mind whispered, *If he doesn't do it, can you?*

She tried to imagine lifting her weapon over her aunt. Looking into Marie's eyes as she brought it down again and again. She retched and threw the door open just in time to be sick over the grass.

Dorran moved around her silently. She slumped back in the

seat, shaking, and a moment later felt a cup being pressed into her hands.

"Drink," Dorran whispered. "I will take care of it. Is there a back entry into the house?"

"Yes." Bile smarted on Clare's tongue, and she tried to wash it down. Her hands shook, spilling water across her lap. She closed her eyes and tried to focus. "In the kitchen. It's a straight line from the front entry to the back door."

"Stay here. Don't try to follow. I will be back within five minutes."

He pressed her hand gently, then stepped toward the house. Tremors ran through Clare, and she couldn't stop them. Dorran paused at the front door to retrieve the weapons they had dropped there, then disappeared around the side of the house.

Marnie. You didn't deserve this. You didn't deserve any of this.

The cup tipped in her hands, and cold water ran across the seat and into the still-damp carpet. Clare barely noticed.

What she'd asked of Dorran was more than should be expected of anyone. But she couldn't leave Marnie there, trapped, in pain and not understanding why. Imprisoned until she starved or died from her injuries.

A muffled *thwack* echoed from the house. Clare dropped the cup and pressed her hands over her face as she moaned. The *thwack* was followed by more. Quick, harsh. Metal hitting flesh. Clare moved her hands to her ears. It wasn't enough to block out the noise.

Marnie. Marnie. I didn't even get a chance to say goodbye.

Five more sharp, short beats. Then silence.

I'm sorry, Marnie. I'm so sorry.

The house stayed still. Its windows were dark. Clare's stomach ached, but there was nothing left to bring up. She kept her eyes fixed on the farmhouse door.

A minute passed. Then another. Dorran didn't reappear.

Clare tried to count the seconds, but it felt as though time was distorting. *How far past midday are we now? Is it close to night? Have we been here five minutes or an hour?*

Perfect silence reigned in Marnie's farm. Now, fear squeezed at Clare's insides. She needed to look for Dorran. She didn't think her legs would carry her. Her ears were ringing again, blending in with the radio's static in a bleak, frightening song.

Then Dorran stepped into view, coming around the house's side. He carried his jacket over his arm. His hair was wet and slicked back.

He washed up, Clare realized with a sickening jolt.

Dorran's expression stayed impassive as he neared the car. He opened the door and slid inside, then threw his jacket into the back seat. It was wet too, Clare saw.

"Everything is all right now." His face might have been expressionless, but his voice was raw. "She is gone."

Clare nodded, and Dorran turned the key in the ignition. The engine rumbled. He eased the car around to face the driveway.

Neither of them spoke or made any move to turn on the music. Dorran kept his eyes on the road. Clare glanced at him once, then leaned herself against the window, breathing deeply as she tried not to be sick again.

Dorran had washed after killing Marnie so that Clare wouldn't see her aunt's blood. But he'd missed a spot. On the back of his shirt's collar, tucked almost out of view, was a little drop of red.

CHAPTER 26

FIELDS PASSED HER WINDOW. They gradually transformed into bare, bleak hills, and the ground was taken over by shrubs and struggling trees as they moved into the valley. In another hour, the ground would start rising again, leading into the mountains that separated Marnie's house from Beth's.

Clare huddled in the car's corner, forehead pressed against the window. Every time she thought about Marnie, her insides ached. It felt like being punched repeatedly. The bruises had no chance to heal before they took another hit.

Dorran didn't try to disturb her, except for once, a few minutes after leaving the farm. He stopped the car to get the blanket out of the back seat and drape it across Clare, and refilled the mug with water. The drink sat in the cup holder, ignored, but Clare held on to the blanket. She felt cold again. The car's dampness continued to soak into her. The air conditioner didn't work, and she thought the outside might be cooling as the clouds thickened.

The clock on the dashboard slowly clicked onward. Past four, approaching five. The later it grew, the less the thought of Marnie hurt. It wasn't that the memories were becoming less painful, but Clare thought she was losing her ability to feel. She was glad for that. Feelings had no place in this new world. She simply had to do what was required to survive.

The road began to snake as it led toward the river. Long before they could see the water, Clare heard it. Rushing, almost screaming. Dorran turned to her, seemingly about to say something, but changed his mind and remained silent. He slowed the car, though, as they navigated through a copse of birch to approach the stone bridge. What *should* have been a bridge, at least. Their passage was gone.

No, Clare corrected herself. *Not gone. It's still there, just underwater.*

She shuffled up in her seat. He back muscles burned, but she barely felt them. She barely felt anything. She stared at the scene, understanding what it meant but not caring.

The path sloped downward. In the space between them and the opposite bank rushed a torrent of water. The snow that had blanketed the region was flooding toward lower ground, and a large part of it had taken the Burbank River as its path of choice.

The water turned white as it surged over things that would normally be clear. Rocks. Signposts. The bridge. Even the *Flood Water* sign had disappeared. The river's edge lapped over the road ahead of their car, as though beckoning them in.

"This is unpassable," Dorran said. "Are there any other ways across the river? Other roads, other bridges?"

She struggled to unfold the map between them. The lines moved in a surreal pattern, and as she stared at them, she could have sworn they were wriggling. She blinked, waiting for them to straighten, but they wouldn't.

Dorran watched her for a second, then leaned closer to read the map himself. "It looks as though there is another bridge upriver. Over here. We might have better luck with it. What do you think?"

"Yes," she said. The word was a croak without any conviction behind it. She rested back against the window.

Dorran folded the map and placed it back on the dashboard. Then he adjusted the blanket around Clare's shoulders before reversing up the road.

The sun danced closer to the horizon. Hazy golds spread across the sky, painting the thickening clouds. It was too early for a sunset, Clare thought. Night wouldn't claim them for another hour and a half. And yet, there it was, gradually tinting the world.

She closed her eyes and visualized the area. They were barely any closer to Beth's and only a few hundred kilometers away from their original path. They were moving perpendicular, not forward. There was no chance of reaching her sister before nightfall.

Tires crunching over loose flecks of asphalt. The car developed an odd, steady rocking rhythm as it bumped over the potholes. The radio remained muffled but ever present. The sounds and sensations seemed to go on forever. Dorran grew restless. He shifted, sometimes rolling his shoulders, sometimes tilting his neck to loosen tight muscles, or letting go of the wheel to stretch his fingers. The red spot on his collar was darkening into brown as it dried.

The sky darkened into dusk. Dorran tried turning the headlights on. One flickered to life, which, after the damage, was a small miracle. The second light must have failed after being used as a bumper to move cars on the freeway.

That scene felt like it had occurred weeks ago. It was hard to believe it was still the same day.

They drove along the edge of a campsite. The stillness had passed through during the off-season and the area was near empty. Eight campers were spaced along the field, their silhouettes standing out of the ground like bleak rocks.

Imagine that. You spend the entire year saving up and planning for a vacation, and when you finally escape the city and all of the stress that comes with your job, the world ends.

Their single light shimmered over the road. The ground was low enough that trickles of water flowed over the asphalt and gathered in its dips, leaving it glittering and damp. As the last daylight slipped away, a sign emerged from the gloom, pointing toward Jenola Bridge. The car slowed as they bumped over the uneven dirt trail. Within a minute, they came to a halt, facing a floor of rushing water extending as far as the headlight could show.

Dorran released a held breath. He pulled the map over and unfolded it, then ran his hand over his face. "Do you know any of these routes? Is there a bridge that will be high enough to cross?"

Clare didn't want to stir from her seat in the car's corner, but she made herself sit up, letting the blanket drop into her lap, and stared at the paper. The lines of red and brown and blocks of green were still incomprehensible.

Thirty hours since we last heard from Beth. A full day of radio silence. And we're no closer to reaching her.

"Let's go home," she said.

Dorran held the map halfway between them. His face was unreadable. For a moment, the only sounds Clare could hear were the buzzing radio and the dull, angry water.

Then he said, "Is that what you want? Is it what you *truly* want?"

"Does it matter? This was pointless. She's dead."

He slowly refolded the map, taking his time to line the creases up. When he was done, he rested it in his lap and stared ahead, through the windshield. His voice was soft. "I think you're suffering from shock and grief. I don't believe you are thinking clearly."

"I am." She pulled the blanket up around her chin again. "We're not going to reach Beth today. Probably not tomorrow either. And even if we did, there would be nothing left to save. Let's go home. We never should have left."

He faced the river. The headlights caught the fine mist floating up from where the water thrashed. His eyes were red rimmed, she noticed for the first time. He looked gaunter than he had that morning, as though the day had drained years off his life.

He never wanted to come. You were the one who pushed him to fight for a cause he didn't believe in. And in the end, we get nothing. Selfish, selfish, selfish.

"I saw campers a few minutes back," Dorran said. "If they are empty, we can sleep in one of them. It will be more comfortable than this car, and I cannot drive much farther today. It is too dark to be safe on the road. Tomorrow, we can look at the map again and find a way over the river."

She scowled. "Didn't you hear me? We're going home. Isn't that what you wanted?"

"No." He put the car in reverse. "And I don't believe it's what you want either. Maybe it is at this moment. But in a week's time, I think you would regret it if you gave up now."

You think you know me. The words, venomous, boiled inside of her, looking for a way out. *You're wrong. You don't know what's best for me. You don't even know what's best for yourself.*

A painful silence surrounded them as they drove back toward higher ground. Clare felt it acutely, like a black cloud had filled their car, poisoning the air and turning her stomach with every inhalation. She wondered if Dorran felt it as well. His face was empty of emotion. Which, she had learned, meant there were emotions under the surface that he was fiercely trying to hide.

His eyes were tired and his lips pressed together. He was unhappy, that was for certain. Unhappy with Clare, maybe. Unhappy that he had to struggle to take the high road, even though he didn't want to.

We never should have left Winterbourne. Things were better back there. We were safe. We were a team. Back there, I loved him.

Her throat tightened.

Don't I love him now?

She wasn't sure. She didn't think so. Her heart felt raw, as though every emotion that had once lived there had been scraped out. There was no love for anything.

He reached the sign for the RV and camper park and turned into it. Poles poked out of the ground, indicating where campers could park and, once upon a time, access water and electricity. Wooded areas surrounded the field. A month ago, Clare would have relished parking in such a picturesque location. Now, she eyed the trees with nothing but wariness. Woods could hide hollows. Woods were unsafe.

"Wait here," Dorran said. The car's internal lights blinked on as he opened his door. She watched in a daze as he walked between the eight campers, stopping at each one to tap on its door with his hatchet. He was listening for noises inside, she guessed, but it was hard to see him in the fresh dark of night. The space felt still, though—almost eerily so. Faint mist ghosted across the dead grass and swirled around Dorran's legs as he paced between the dark structures.

It took several minutes for Dorran to return. When he opened Clare's door, he smiled, despite the stress and tiredness weighing on his features. "We're in luck. They are all empty, so we may have our pick. That one there is the largest."

"It's fine," she said. She didn't care where they slept. Only that she would be allowed to slip into a world where she couldn't feel the aches bruising her insides or remember the look on Marnie's face as she shambled toward them.

CHAPTER 27

THE CAMPER'S DOOR HAD been left unlocked, and it creaked as Dorran pushed on it. His flashlight ran across evidence that the owners had woken up to a mundane morning. The kitchenette had two mugs set beside the sink to dry. A loaf of bread, just barely starting to turn moldy now that the ice had abated, had been left on the shelf. Its bag hung open as though someone was planning to toast another slice. A magazine sat on the pull-out couch. The double bed's sheets were tousled and unmade.

Clare wondered how their morning had been disrupted. A relative might have phoned to tell them about the spreading quiet zones, and they abandoned the camper as they raced to drive home. Or maybe they had heard their vacationing neighbors yelling and stepped outside to see what the commotion was about. Or, possibly, they felt the burning in their lungs as they stood in the very place Clare was standing or lounged on the couch or reached into the bread bag for another slice. What would they have thought—that the air had turned toxic? They could have run outside with just enough sense of mind to slam the door behind them.

Whatever had happened, they were dead. And now she and Dorran were stepping in where they had left off, to sleep in the bed they had shared, to flip through their magazine, to deal with the bread they had left to rot.

Dorran left Clare in the camper as he fetched armfuls of supplies from the back of the car. When he returned a moment later, he carried weapons in case they were disturbed during the night, a jug of water, food, and their blanket. He placed their haul onto the couch and poured out some water.

"Drink," he urged, holding the cup toward Clare. "I'll make dinner. Then we can sleep."

"I'm not hungry."

"You are. You haven't eaten since breakfast."

She shook her head. "I can't. I'll be sick."

An unhappy, barely audible sigh escaped. "Very well. But, please, at least drink some water."

She sat on the edge of the bed and sipped from the cup while Dorran leaned against the kitchenette and ate cold stew from a can. They didn't speak or even look at each other. Clare knew they were fracturing, losing the loyalty they'd held for each other, but she was incapable of stopping it. She put the cup aside and wordlessly crawled into bed, facing the wall.

Her clothes were still damp from the car, but she was too tired to take them off. She coiled up, hands under her chin and eyes burning, as she waited for sleep to give her some reprieve.

A moment later, the mattress dipped as Dorran sat on its edge. He carefully, near silently slipped under the covers.

A word ran through Clare's mind, unbidden. It was a horrible word. A fearful, bitter one. *Murderer.*

She saw the blue door in her mind's eye. Heard the *thwack*s. She tightened her hands into fists as she fought with herself not to cry.

Dorran shuffled closer and, cautious, slid his hand across her waist to hold her.

They had slept like that most nights in Winterbourne. Clare remembered feeling warm and safe, her back nestled against his chest, their legs tangling and his arm a reassuring weight.

Murderer.

Her body stiffened as revulsion ran through her. She stared, wide-eyed, at the off-white wall.

Dorran hesitated, then the hand withdrew. He rolled over to face the opposite direction. The bed was small, but they slept as far apart as they could, not even grazing each other.

Clare felt drained, but sleep still eluded her. Minutes ticked by. She watched the wall and traced the moonlight's progress as it gradually crawled over the panels.

She thought Dorran might be awake as well. He was so still and quiet she sometimes doubted if he was breathing. She opened her mouth to say something, to try to make it right, but couldn't find any words.

She was being unfair. She knew that. She had asked him to kill Marnie—she'd begged and cried for it.

Murderer.

Clare had killed hollows too. She'd stabbed a metal pole through his mother's head. He hadn't held that against her. It was unfair to treat Marnie's death as different. That didn't stop it from feeling wrong.

She was a hollow. A monster.

But Clare had loved her.

Your aunt was gone.

But not completely gone. There was a little of her left in her eyes. Not much, and mostly instinctual by that point. But enough to be confused. Enough to be scared and in pain.

There was no way to save her. Dorran did the right thing by ending her suffering.

The phrase felt wrong. *Ending her suffering.* As though they were talking about putting an animal out of its misery, not a woman who had cared deeply and been filled with love for the world.

She would never be able to forget the noises that had come from the house. The sounds of Dorran beating her skull in. Clare knew he'd had reasons to do it that way. Knives were ineffective. They had no guns. Crushing her skull—thoroughly destroying it—was the only way he could be sure she was dead.

Murderer.

It took hours for weariness to win the battle over Clare's mind. When she finally fell asleep, she didn't even have the respite she

207

had been longing for. Her dreams were full of images of Marnie, her bones poking out of her broken head and her body swollen as she shuffled along the hallway toward Clare.

She woke in a cold sweat. It was still early. Through the small window over the kitchenette, she could see light coming through the condensation on the glass and fog outside. She was cold. The other half of the bed was empty.

Clare sat up gingerly. She pulled her knees up under her chin and wrapped her arms around them. She was alone in the camper. Dorran had left.

She imagined him slipping out of bed in the dead of night, going to the car, and driving out of the RV park. He could be hours away by that point, either returning to Winterbourne or seeking out a new shelter. She deserved it. She'd been a liability for a while.

The idea hovered in her mind, then evaporated. She knew Dorran better than that. He had never looked for an easy way out when things became difficult. He hadn't abandoned her in Winterbourne when they had both thought she was going insane, and he wouldn't abandon her in a camper in the middle of nowhere.

If she went to the window, she would see the car. But still, she didn't move. She was afraid of knowing. She sat shivering, eyes burning, wishing she could go back to sleep but afraid of returning to the dreams.

What are we going to do?

Things had gone bad. It was like sliding down a slope, incapable of stopping, and knowing every extra foot she fell would make the climb back so much more impossible. She didn't know what to do to repair their relationship. Or if it was even possible.

The camper door creaked as it opened, and Clare flinched. Dorran stepped inside. He wore the same impassive expression as he had the day before. Steam rose from a bowl in his hands, and he wordlessly approached the bed and held the food toward Clare.

It took her a moment to muster a response. "I'm not hungry."

Dorran stared at the bowl. Then, with slow, unsteady movements, he placed it on the kitchenette counter. The silence held for a moment, every second of it excruciating. Then Dorran turned to face Clare and took a deep breath. "You hate me. That is fine."

Clare stared at him. Dorran's back was straight and his shoulders set, but one hand rested on the counter, as though he needed it for stability. His face was blank, but his eyes, the only living part in his expression, were filled with desperation. He took another shuddering breath.

"I don't need you to love me. I never asked for it, and I do not expect it now. We don't have to talk. You can avoid me; that is fine. But I *need* you to be well—to eat, to drink, to stay healthy if you can."

The knots in Clare's stomach tightened, impossibly painful. She wrapped her arms around herself. She felt like she would fall apart if she didn't.

"You are the only good thing left in this world. I cannot lose you. I cannot…I cannot do this alone." He pressed his hand to his chest and his fingers dug into the shirt's fabric. For a second, the shell cracked, and emotions flickered across his face: helplessness, despair. "I will not survive in this world alone. You don't have to love me. But if I ever meant anything to you, please, I need you to fight."

Clare shook her head. Tears burned as they slid over her lids, and she didn't know where to look or what to do. Reflexes kicked in, and she stretched her hands toward Dorran.

He responded, stepping forward, his arms wrapping around her. *That* felt right.

"I don't hate you." She mumbled the words into his shoulder. His arms tightened. "Dorran…I don't know what's wrong with me. I'm being horrible. I can't think clearly. I—I—"

"I know."

The word *murderer* resurfaced. It felt hollow. Just like he wouldn't abandon her, he wasn't cruel. He felt lost, like her. He had done his best to make the right choice, even when it was not clear.

And he was scared. Not in a loud, obvious way; he held his fears close to his chest and masked them under steady reliability. But they were there nonetheless. Fear that he wasn't enough. Fear that he would make the wrong choice.

"You did the right thing." Clare's voice cracked, but she knew the words were the truth. She swallowed, trying to clear her throat. "Back at Marnie's house, I mean. I'm sorry I reacted that way—"

"She was your aunt. You are in pain. That is human. It is the most human thing I can think of."

In that moment, Clare no longer felt like she was sliding down an endless slope. Dorran had found her hand, and he was pulling her up. She was glad she could hide her face in his shirt. She didn't want to meet his eyes. "I'll make it up to you."

"Please." He was hoarse. "I only want one thing. Would you eat?"

He adjusted her so that she sat at his side on the bed's edge, then reached to the kitchenette and retrieved the bowl. Clare took it and stared into the warm stew inside. She didn't know how he'd managed to heat their food that morning—it would have taken a lot of effort to build a fire in the dirt outside the camper—but he'd done it. She picked up the spoon.

The stew felt as though it was choking her, but every mouthful seemed to spread relief through Dorran. When she was done, he took the bowl from her, set it aside, then gathered her into his arms. He kissed her forehead. It was gentle. Desperate. She leaned into him, resting against his shoulder, holding him as tightly as he held her.

"I didn't expect this to be so hard," Clare managed. "I was only focused on getting to Beth. Four hours there, four hours back. We were supposed to be home by now. But everything—the freeway, the bridges, Marnie—"

"It is worse than you could have anticipated." He sighed. "Myself as well."

She'd been so focused on her own pain, she hadn't considered how he felt. "This must be horrible for you too."

211

His fingers ran over her hair. "Do you remember, on our last day at Winterbourne, how I went to search the passageways alone? You were so angry when you found me."

"Still am," she mumbled.

That brought out a cautious smile. "I am sorry. I wasn't trying to exclude you from the work. Sealing the doorways was just an excuse. In truth, I was searching for the creatures."

She lifted her head, frowning at him. "Why?"

"Because I sensed we were close to leaving our home. And I felt so desperately unprepared. I needed more practice. I needed to *understand* them. I needed to be sure I knew what to do and how to protect you before we left our shelter."

She swallowed thickly. "I don't know if *anyone* is ready to handle the hollows. You're probably doing the best any person can."

"No. I am underprepared, and in ways I did not even expect. Every day, every moment, I fear I am on the cusp of a mistake I cannot recover from. You have been hurt. Now you have lost your aunt. And—" His voice caught. "I do not know how to make this right."

She closed her eyes. The words tumbled out of her before she could stop them. "Your shirt has a stain on it. On the collar."

"Ah. No wonder." He pulled out of the embrace, his expression tense. "I am sorry. I had thought I..."

He stood, staring around the camper. His eyes landed on cabinet doors, and he pulled them open, sorting through the contents. He found clothes in one of them. They sported bright colors and patterns and were sized to fit an older, plumper couple, but Clare and Dorran had only brought extra jackets, no change of clothes. Dorran pulled a plain green shirt off its hanger, then slipped out of the top he was wearing and discarded it in the camper's corner. As he pulled the replacement over his shoulders, Clare caught sight of the bandages on his wrist. Guilt twisted her stomach. She'd forgotten about the bite.

"Dorran." She held out a hand, calling him back. As he sat at her side, she took his arm and ran her fingers over the bandage's edge. "Does it still hurt?"

"No."

She squinted at him, trying to read his expression. There was a lot to see; the fear still lingered, along with nerves and painful vulnerability. But the impassive mask had been shed. He was no longer trying to hide from her.

"I love you," she whispered. "I really, really do."

His eyes flickered. Deep joy, relief, adoration. He leaned toward her, closing the distance, and Clare kissed him unreservedly.

She still hurt. But she no longer felt alone. And that made more of a difference than she had expected.

"Rest now," Dorran murmured, and brushed stray hair out of her face. "We are safe here. You can sleep."

She wanted to. Spending the day in the camper with Dorran, knowing he would hold the nightmares at bay, hugging him tightly as feeling slowly seeped back into her... It sounded good. But the reality of her world wasn't so simple. She braced herself against the despair that wanted to crawl back into her. "I don't want to give up on Beth."

"No," he said. "I thought perhaps you would not. Then are you ready to return to the car? We can look for another way across the river."

"Yes." Smiling felt foreign, but not bad. "Thanks for not listening to me yesterday. I don't think I could forgive myself if we'd just driven home."

They looked through the camper before leaving. It gave Clare a strange feeling; they had borrowed a stranger's home for the night, and Clare didn't feel right leaving it messy. She flipped the sheets back into an approximation of neatness and put their plates into the sink. It was bordering on laughable when the camper would likely never be inhabited again, but it made her feel better.

Dorran found a day's worth of long-life food and tea bags in one of the cupboards, then stopped beside the closet. "Anything here that you would like?" he asked.

"As long as it fits, I won't complain." Clare felt grimy, and she knew Dorran must as well. She flipped through the woman's clothes, looking for something that might be comfortable and practical. The dresses would be hard to run in. Most of the blouses were too light. She eventually found a knit top that she thought would wear okay, even if it was too large. They carried their prizes bundled in the blanket as they stepped out of the RV.

Cold mist bit into Clare's exposed skin. She couldn't tell if it was just an early morning frost or whether the temperature was dropping again. Her breath misted, and she was grateful for the warm breakfast in her stomach. Smoke rose from a stack of charred sticks where Dorran had heated their food.

They slid into the car. The radio still played its static. It struck Clare as an acutely sad thing that it had been sitting on the dashboard all night, still trying to make contact. She watched it for a moment, then reached forward and turned it off.

Dorran didn't speak, but she could see the worry gathering in his eyes as his brows pulled down.

"It's okay." The words were painful, but she smiled through them. "If we couldn't get through to her by now, I doubt we will. It's easier not to have it there as a constant reminder."

He nodded and handed the folded map to Clare. Her eyes blurred as she blinked the tears back. By that point, she was almost certain they were just going through the motions. It had been nearly two days since she'd last heard from Beth. The bunker would be empty. But she still had to get there, just to know she had. To be certain. To know she'd done everything she could.

In the distance, something inhuman wailed. Dorran stared into the mist that curled across the field. "It might be wise to begin moving."

"Yes, that's probably a good idea." She traced lines across the map. "Try the second path across the stream again. The water might have gone down overnight. While you're doing that, I'll see if I can find an alternative."

CHAPTER 28

DESPITE THE COLD, DESPITE the sore muscles and stiff neck, and despite the implications of the silent radio hanging over them, Clare felt more like herself that morning. The man at her side was familiar and safe, not the stranger he had felt like the day before.

The car rocked across potholed ground, splashing fresh mud over its already spoiled paint, as they moved toward the river. Clare ran her finger across the map. She knew she had to find a way forward, but she hadn't been in that part of the country in years; her trips along the road had always ended at Marnie's house.

We need a high bridge. Not something low. Not something suspended a few feet above the water. A bridge with at least five meters of clearance.

The car slowed, and Clare looked up from the map. They had

arrived back at the water's edge. The river had subsided a little overnight, but not nearly enough. The sign declaring the bridge's name peeked above the frothing water, its metal bent slightly by the force of the deluge. Everything else was still invisible.

Dorran turned to Clare, patient but waiting for direction. She chewed her lip as she traced lines on the map.

Wait...Marnie.

When Clare made her weekly visit to her aunt's farm, she was greeted by three things: hot coffee, fresh cake, and gossip. *Scratch that. Four things. Her cats always ended up in my lap somehow.*

She managed a smile. The memories were bittersweet: sitting by the old stone fireplace, two cats already squished together in her lap and a third jonesing to get up. Marnie sitting in her favorite rocking chair and holding on to her cup as she chatted, her hair falling out of its bun and her cardigan a little crooked, but looking so happy that none of it mattered.

Clare latched on to that image. She held it in her mind, savoring it, trying to make its goodness overwrite her last memory of her aunt. It did...a little. She thought, with time and effort, she might be able to remember her aunt without feeling sick.

Marnie had loved gossip. But not the kind other people usually spread. She didn't talk about who was having an affair with who, or how so-and-so's child had been expelled, or about how the neighbors had fallen into a public argument. Her gossip could have been described with one word: wholesome.

She'd told Clare about the neighbor who snuck into the local church's garden early on Saturday mornings so that they could trim the plants and fix anything that looked untidy. About how two teenagers working at the grocery store had been making eyes at each other for weeks and the boy had finally gotten up the courage to ask the girl out. And about Mr. Peterson's private bridge.

"He invited me to see it last week," Marnie had whispered conspiratorially. "It's the loveliest little bridge I've ever seen. Or I guess I shouldn't call it little! It's so high off the water that I was afraid of falling. There isn't a bridge close to his house, you see, and he loves to go into the forest on the other side of the river to pick wild mushrooms. The men from the nearest farms all got together one weekend and helped him build it. It's good to know his friends care for him so much."

"Marnie told me that Mr. Peterson has a bridge." Clare grabbed Dorran's hand, excitement making her heart jump. "It wouldn't be on the map, since it's a private property. But it's high. Maybe high enough."

"Good." He grinned as he put the car into reverse and backed away from the overflowing river. "Which way?"

"Uh…" That was a problem. Clare didn't actually know Mr. Peterson. Her entire knowledge of the region came from her aunt. She bit her lip as her smile faded. "Hm."

"It's all right. Take your time."

Think, Clare. Where would he live?

He was a farmer—she knew that much. But almost everyone along the winding rural road was a farmer of some kind or another.

What else did Marnie tell you about him?

Two years' worth of visits swam together in her mind. She hunted, furiously, looking for any hint or clue buried inside the chats.

"Mr. Peterson's dog had puppies! Nine healthy golden retrievers." "Mr. Peterson down the road asked for some cuttings from my hydrangeas." "I'm thinking of getting a new mailbox. Mr. Peterson replaced his for a lovely bright green one, and I notice it every time I drive to town. It makes me want to up my game."

Clare's eyes snapped open. "Turn left on the main road," she said. "Marnie drove past Peterson's property on her way to town, so it has to be down that way. He has a green mailbox."

The car swerved back toward the street. Clare hoped the mailbox clue would be enough. The street was long, and their trip was already carrying them close to the edge of the map; if they had to drive much farther to reach Peterson's property, she wasn't sure how easily they could find their way back to the route to Beth's.

That wouldn't have been a problem in the old world. She could have looked up their location on her phone, and even if that hadn't worked, she could have stopped at a service station or a house for directions. Now, she only had Dorran to rely on, and he only had her. Everything they needed had to come from what they knew or what they could find.

We'll make it work.

Dorran drove quickly. He watched his side of the road, and Clare watched hers, both of them making note of every mailbox they passed. Doubts began to crowd into Clare's mind. That little bit of trivia was at least two years old. Peterson might have changed his box since then. It might have come down in the snows. Clare saw at least three mailboxes that were either leaning dangerously or half-submerged in the muddy ground.

There were precious few remnants of humanity left. They passed two cars, one off the side of the road, one parked in the middle of the street with its doors open. Dorran slowed the car as they eased around the obstacle, but they didn't stop for either vehicle.

Then Clare caught a flash of green up ahead and tapped her hand on the dash. "There! Stop!"

Dorran pressed on the brake as they neared. The mailbox was shaped like a house, with a brass knob to open the little door below its peaked roof. The whole shape had been painted a bright green. It was exactly the kind of thing Marnie would have liked.

"Well done, Clare," Dorran murmured, and turned into the driveway.

Their progress slowed. The dirt track was a mess of half-dried mud. Twice, the tires began to spin, and Clare had to mentally brace herself for the idea of pushing their way out before the car got itself free.

The house came into view ahead. Like Marnie's, the small building was situated near several sheds. She nodded to Dorran, and he turned off the driveway to coast over the waterlogged grass. They gave the house and its buildings a wide berth. Along the weatherboard side, Clare saw what she thought were the remains of hydrangeas. *Marnie's cuttings.*

Past the house was a hobby orchard and a pond. They were harder to navigate around. The sound of rushing water became clearer the farther into the property they drove. Willows cropped out of the ground, some that looked half a century old. Clare's hatchback hadn't been designed for off-road driving, and it tilted horribly as it struggled over the root-pocked ground. Dorran's face was tight with concentration. Clare gripped the sides of her seat, squeezing the nearly dried fabric.

Then, abruptly, they were at the river. Willows surrounded them. Their leaves were gone, and the draping branches created stark lines against the mist. Through them, the overflowing river frothed against its banks. She couldn't see a bridge.

"Stay here. I'll search," Dorran said.

Clare felt uneasy about leaving their shelter. As long as they were in the car, they had a layer of metal protecting them from anything outside, and no matter how claustrophobic it made her feel, it was still better than the alternative. They weren't exactly in the forest, but the trees were still grouped closely together and could very easily be hiding hollows.

But they were stuck until they could find the bridge. And that would be faster on foot.

"I'm coming." She opened her door before Dorran could object. Cold air wound against her. She didn't think it was her imagination anymore; the world was growing colder again. She prayed the snow would hold off for at least another day.

The rushing water was louder than it had seemed inside the car. Clare drew in lungfuls of the crisp air and held her hand up to block the sun as she squinted down the stream's length. It twisted out of sight in both directions. Clare moved close to the water's edge and, crouching on a rock, dipped her hands into the stream. The water was achingly cold, but she had felt grimy all morning and splashed water over her face and arms.

As she shook droplets off, she thought she could glimpse something made of stone to her left, half-hidden behind the river's bend and the trees. She signaled to catch Dorran's attention and began following the riverbank.

As she stepped around the bend, she found herself facing Peterson's handmade bridge. The banks were steep and narrow at that point, and the bridge was high enough to poke above the water. Just barely. Liquid ran over its lowest points, where the stones connected with the ground, but the bridge's middle arched up at a gentle angle to put it above the water.

"Ah," Dorran said as he caught up to her.

Clare rubbed at the back of her neck as disappointment turned her stomach sour. The bridge had been built by farmers, not engineers, and it showed. It had been made high enough to stand above the badly engorged river, but it hadn't survived the water's barrage. A deep hole had been carved in the right-hand side where the stonework had crumbled.

"We could still walk over," Clare said. She dropped her hands, feeling useless. "But then we'd have no car."

The bridge had initially been wide enough for Clare's hatchback to squeeze over. Now, less than two feet of it remained at the damaged section. The wooden support beams were visible, poking up from the water and showing where massive slabs of stone had once belonged.

"Maybe it will still work." Dorran pressed Clare's shoulder as he stepped past her to examine the structure. "We could repair it."

She narrowed her eyes, dubious.

"Not properly. Not with stone." Dorran stopped as close to the water's edge as he could and crouched down, peering at the exposed support beams. "But we could wedge it with branches and logs. The supports are still there. If we can fill the hole sufficiently, the car should be able to drive over it."

"Okay." She stepped back, trying to envision it. The hole was facing the flow, which should help hold the branches in place. That meant they only had a four-foot area to fill…and to make stable enough that it could support a car's weight. "Okay, that might work."

"We'll *make* it work."

CHAPTER 29

THE WILLOWS AROUND THE river provided an abundance of fallen wood. Most of it had been caught up by the melted snow and swept downriver, but many branches had been caught in shrubs and against roots.

Clare picked the thickest branches she could, then dragged them back to the river's edge, where Dorran broke them into size with a well-placed stomp or the ax. He leapt across the submerged segment of bridge, then perched on the edge of the hole as he lodged the wood between the supports and the remaining stones.

"Be careful." Clare dropped off another armful of dead wood. Dorran seemed precariously close to the edge, and she didn't like how shaky some of the stones were. He raised a hand to acknowledge her, then returned to kicking at a branch to get it level with the rest of the bridge's surface.

This has to work. Please. It has to.

A scream broke through the still air. They both froze, turning toward the forest on the other side of the bridge, where lingering fog crawled between the trunks. The noise hadn't been close. It hadn't been human either.

Dorran motioned for Clare to come closer. "Give me what you have. It will be enough. We shouldn't linger here any longer."

Clare stretched to pass Dorran the remaining sticks across the water, then backed up to the car and reached through the open door to get the crowbar. She swung it at her side as she scanned the area: the willows surrounding them, the steady rushing water, and the sparse forest on the bridge's other side. Dorran moved in quick, sharp bursts as he fit the remaining branches in between the ones he'd already placed. Then, with one hand resting on what little remained of the wood railing, he stepped onto the temporary surface. The woods creaked and bowed under his weight, but they didn't break, and they didn't dip more than a few inches.

"That should be enough." Dorran jumped over the water to join Clare on the spongy ground. "Let us try the car now."

She nodded, but couldn't stop herself from staring at the engorged stream. The water moved quickly and it would have to be freezing. She didn't like to think about trying to swim against it…or keep her head above water for that matter.

"You should cross the bridge on foot," Dorran said. "We stand a better chance with less weight in the car, and you can help guide my path across."

She frowned. "How come your plans always end up with you carrying the most risk?"

"Because I am abhorrently selfish." He found her hand, lifted it, and kissed her fingers, laughter sparkling in his eyes. "And because I secretly hope it will impress you."

"Hah." Even though Dorran still held her hand, her fingers felt cold. She shivered. "How about *I* drive and impress *you*?"

"I would rather see you on solid ground." Another kiss. "Don't worry for me. I am not afraid."

A second wailing cry echoed from the forest. Clare pulled Dorran close, hugging him tightly, relishing the feel of how warm and solid he was. Then she stepped back, swallowing the ache in her throat. "Okay. Okay. But…be careful. Please."

"I will." He stepped into the car.

Clare waited until the motor started, then she turned to face the bridge. The water grasped at everything it touched, obsessively trying to tear it away. Even as she watched, a clump of dead grass and soil broke free from the bank to her right. It tumbled into the water, breaking apart and vanishing under the makeshift bridge repairs.

She couldn't stop visualizing what might happen if the bridge couldn't hold the car. It would tumble and roll, dragged under by the rapids, the pressure fighting any attempt at escaping the vehicle while icy water flowed inside like a waterfall.

Stop it. Dorran believes this will work. Trust him.

Clare held the crowbar close as she leapt across the submerged patch of bridge, stretching to avoid getting her feet wet. The stones crunched under her feet as she climbed to the highest part of the arch. The bridge wasn't long—twenty feet, if that—but it was a lot less stable than she would have hoped. She couldn't see any concreting between the rocks. Peterson and his friends seemed to have built it the old-fashioned way, using simple gravity and tight packing to keep it stable. It was no wonder the river had ripped sections free.

She eyed the gap as she passed it. The wood was packed tightly, with flat branches on top to give the car something solid to drive over. But it still left her feeling queasy. Some of the gaps would be large enough for a tire to become stuck in. And some of the branches didn't seem strong enough to carry much weight at all.

Clare faced the car. She could see Dorran behind the cracked windshield, his eyes glinting through the shadows. She nodded to tell him she was ready.

The car crept forward. Its front wheels disappeared into the submerged section, and Clare bit back a scream as the car's front drifted to the side. But its tires found purchase again, and a second later, they were back on the dry stones.

"Okay." Clare backed up, one eye on the uneven ground beneath her feet and one eye on the car. Dorran slowed as he neared the crumbled section. "Okay, okay. We can do this."

She motioned for him, adjusting the car's trajectory to move over the thicker pieces of wood. They creaked as weight compressed them. Little flecks of spray, splashed up from where the river hit the stones, grazed Clare's cheeks. The water's angry rumble, the creak of trees behind her, the whistle of the cold wind—she pushed it all to the back of her mind and zeroed in on the vehicle, and the man, she couldn't afford to lose.

One of the branches snapped. The car lurched down, and Clare yelped. It didn't fall far, though. Dorran, eyebrows low and lips pressed together, froze in his seat. The car hung there, its front right-hand corner dipped down toward the water, then Dorran tried creeping it forward again. Slowly, the car rose out of its hole.

He's almost there. Almost…

Clare continued to beckon, her heart in her throat, barely noticing as her slow paces backward put her feet into the water submerging the end of the bridge. The car's front wheels were almost onto solid stones.

The car horn blared, deafening. Clare locked eyes with Dorran. He pitched forward in his seat, teeth bared, eyes wild with fear. He pressed on the horn again, staring at something over her shoulder.

Reflexes took hold. Clare ducked and felt claws snag on the back of her knit top. She pivoted and swing her crowbar at the same time. The metal connected with something fleshy and angry chattering exploded around her.

"Clare!" Dorran had his door open, but he was trapped in the car. One end hung precariously over the collapsing branches. The other was butted up against the opposite side of the bridge, with no room for him to escape.

Clare stepped back a fraction of a second too late. Teeth bit into her shoulder. She screamed and tried to pull out of the hollow's grip, but the jaws only tightened. Long, spindly arms slid around her chest and her abdomen, its spiderlike fingers tapping over her as it locked her into an embrace.

Pain ran through her shoulder, arcing down her arm. She did the only thing she could think of: she threw herself backward and used her weight to crush the creature between herself and the stone bridge.

She felt the teeth break. Two of them stayed in her flesh, the impact embedding them. The monster's jaw fractured, but it seemed impervious to the pain, and its scrabbling hands continued to tighten around her.

Clare lifted her crowbar. She couldn't see the creature pinned under her, but she could feel it. She clenched her teeth as she stabbed the metal down at her side.

The crowbar pierced through the creature's flesh, finding a gap just below its ribs, and hit the stones below. Dorran leaned on the horn. The blast was deafening, but it worked. The hollow flinched at the noise, and its arms lost some of their tightness.

Clare rolled, breaking free of the creature's embrace. She hit the edge of the bridge. The splintered edges of the broken railing scraped her hip as she passed over it.

"Ah!" Clare clutched at the stones to stop her momentum. She felt her legs go over first. The water grabbed at them, pulling with more force than she'd thought was possible. Her good arm latched around the remaining wooden railing. The structure cracked. She hung, one arm holding on to the support, the other scrabbling at the stone wall, trying to find a purchase to pull herself back up. Her shoulder burned, sending pain streaking up her neck and into her arm.

The hollow chattered. From Clare's position, nearly off the

bridge, she couldn't see it—but she could hear it. The thick sluicing noise of a body being lifted off the metal pole. Then the tapping, the noise that had haunted her dreams, creeping closer. Its sunken face appeared, leering down at her. Its bony fingers landed on top of Clare's hand.

The car's engine roared. She heard the crack of breaking branches, then the car slammed into the hollow. The monster tumbled away, and in its place was Dorran, leaning out of the open car door to reach for Clare.

He grabbed her arm and pulled. Clare screamed as damaged skin was strained. Then she was back in the car, her legs hanging out of the door and her torso across Dorran's legs.

"Hold on."

One hand rested over her back, holding her in place. She gasped as the car lurched forward. A loud smacking noise told her the bumper had connected with the hollow again, then they bounced as the wheels jolted over its body.

Clare scrambled to get herself fully into the car. The open door knocked against her legs as the hatchback careened. Another screeching, wailing noise split the air, then they were back on steady ground, shadows from the trees flowing over them.

Dorran kept his eyes on the path ahead, his face grim as he swerved. Clare used her good arm to drag herself into the passenger seat and pulled her wet legs close to herself as Dorran slammed the door. She braced one hand on the dashboard, shaking, and stared at flashes of illuminated trees through the windshield. There was no road leading through the forest. The trees were thin enough to drive between, but they had to weave. Gray, bony shapes flitted in the side mirror, chasing after them, then the mirror disappeared as Dorran clipped a trunk. He kept the pressure on the car for a minute, until the wailing cries had nearly faded, then pulled to an abrupt halt in a small clearing.

"Clare." He pulled her close, his hands running over her arms and her face. He was ghost white, and perspiration glistened across his face. "Clare, I—I—"

"It's okay." The pain in her shoulder wasn't bothering her as much, but she didn't know if that meant it wasn't as serious as she'd thought or if she was just going into shock. She laughed, but it came out thin and oddly pitched. "We're over the river. About time, right?"

He had one hand braced on the side of her head as though she needed holding up. His shaking fingers hovered over her shoulder, where blood stained the knit. "Just relax. This will be all right. I will get the kit. Medicine for the pain—"

"Not yet." Distant, screeching cries echoed through the forest. She was acutely aware of how close they were to the bridge and how little space they had between them and the monsters. "Keep driving. Get us out of the trees, and try to lean left, if you can. That's where the main road is."

He looked conflicted. "Clare—"

"Go on." She took his hand, squeezed it lightly, and pushed it back toward the wheel. "I've had enough of those monsters for today."

CHAPTER 30

"SWEETHEART. CAN YOU HEAR me?"

Clare jolted awake. Chilled air stung her cheeks. She blinked, disoriented, and saw the car's door was open. Dorran stood in it, one hand resting on Clare's arm, his eyes tight with concern.

"Sorry. Did I fall asleep?" Clare lifted a hand to rub tiredness from her eyes, and pain blazed along her shoulder and back. She grimaced.

"Shh. Come. Lean on me."

Dorran unbuckled the seat belt, then strong arms were around her, lifting her out of the car. Clare squinted against the pale light that cut into her eyes. She didn't know how long she'd been out, except that the afternoon was fading. An empty road stretched in both directions, but Dorran carried her off its side, to where he'd laid their blanket beside a small, crackling campfire. "Where are we?"

"Somewhere safe." He lowered her onto the blanket, and Clare shivered. The fire hadn't been alive for long, but its warmth felt good, and she moved closer to it.

"Where did you get the wood?"

"There are some small trees farther up the road." His fingers moved around her face, gently pulling hair out of the way. "Don't worry. They are not large enough for hollows to hide among. We can rest here a moment."

She blinked, and the scene came into better focus. The road was long and straight. Dead, thigh-high grass filled the space to either side, interspersed by tenacious trees that had found a home in the poor soil. In the distance, at the car's back, were the rolling, hilly mountains that she associated with Marnie's area. They must have been driving for hours.

"I am sorry," Dorran said. He was pulling supplies out of the car. "I would have stopped earlier, but there was nowhere safe."

"Yeah." Clare slowly turned her neck, trying to loosen tight muscles without hurting her shoulder. "It's all pretty thoroughly forested around that area. Did you see any other hollows?"

"Yes." He crouched at her side, opened the first aid kit, and began picking through supplies. "A few dozen. Most stayed off the side of the road. They don't like the car's noises. Several tried to charge at us, but we were too fast for them to catch."

Clare chuckled. She still felt dazed. As a child, she'd loved visiting Marnie with Beth. They'd always watched for wild animals on the drive to her property. Roadkill was common, but they usually saw live animals as well. She guessed hollows had become the new animals to spot.

"Here." He handed her a cup of water and two painkillers, then his fingers moved around the collar of her knit top.

She flinched as the fabric was peeled back from the drying blood.

Dorran muttered under his breath. He used scissors to snip through the weave so he could pull it out of the way.

"How's it looking?" Clare drained the cup. She hadn't realized how thirsty she'd become.

Dorran took the mug back and refilled it, along with a pot of water he set beside the fire to heat. "I never should have left you outside the car."

"Mm. One of us had to drive it over the bridge. And I still think you had the more dangerous job. I was just slightly less lucky this time."

His eyes were sad, but he tried to smile as he placed a pair of surgical pliers into the pot to sterilize them. "This will hurt, I am afraid. There are…fragments inside the wound."

"Oh." Clare's face twisted. She remembered feeling the teeth break out of the hollow's jaw. "Right, yeah, get those out, please."

Once the pot boiled, Dorran used a cloth to retrieve the pliers, waited a moment for them to cool, then began work on Clare's shoulder.

The tooth fragments made hideous sucking noises as they came free. Clare breathed through her mouth, shaking, her whole arm on fire. She refused to let herself cry. It wasn't any worse than the bite on Dorran's wrist, she told herself. If he could cope with it, so could she.

"That's the last of them." Dorran sounded relieved as he dropped the final bone fragment into the grass. He opened the bottle of antiseptic and doused the wound. This time, Clare couldn't smother a cry. Dorran held her still as she kicked and swore, then stroked her hair as the agony subsided.

"That was good. You did well. Very well."

"Thanks." The word came out muffled as Clare let her face rest into his shirt. She didn't feel like she was doing well. She was exhausted in a way that sleep wouldn't fix. She wasn't looking forward to returning to the car, but as the sun ticked closer to the horizon, she knew they had no choice. She tried to imagine where they were on the map, but her mind came up blank.

Dorran kept one arm around her as he took bandages out of the kit. The pain subsided to a steady ache as he covered the cuts, then gently tugged the torn sweater back into place.

"Okay." She felt boneless and shaky, and spoke with more conviction than she felt. "Onward we go."

"Not just yet." He ran his fingers over her neck. "We need to eat. Let's take advantage of the fire to enjoy some warm food."

The day was chilly and the car was missing its heater, and Clare couldn't object to sitting in the warmth of the fire. Dorran tipped out the boiled water and used the saucepan to heat their food. They had stew again, but he also brought out a can of peaches, which he cooked until their juice had thickened into syrup and the fruits were on the edge of falling apart.

They each had a spoon but ate out of the same saucepan perched carefully between them. The cuts still ached, but

Clare was starting to feel more peaceful. The area was quiet—almost eerily so. No insects bothered them, though she knew the long grass must have been full of them before the snows. The sky was a deep, hazy shade of gray, and visibility wasn't good. She could see the mountains in the horizon, but none of their definition.

"Do you think it will snow again?" she asked Dorran.

He sat with his legs out in front of him, one arm propped behind her back. "Most likely. Before the world changed I would have said the snow would be light, though. But now? I really cannot predict it."

"Do you know where we are on the map?"

Dorran didn't answer immediately, and Clare felt a twinge of panic that they might actually be lost. But then he said, "Not exactly. As far as I can tell, we went off its edge after passing the river, but I have been holding our course northwest to pull us back toward our original path."

"That's good." She scooped up more of the warm peaches. "I should be able to place us if we can see a street sign."

Dorran fussed over her as he got her back into the car, fastening her seat belt, wrapping the spare blanket around her legs, and refusing to let her help pack up. He stomped their fire out and returned their supplies to the car's back seat. The stop hadn't been long, but Clare was grateful for it. To be out of the car, to be able to stretch and breathe fresh air, was a luxury she wouldn't have expected to miss.

The idea of having a camper like the one they had stayed in at the campsite was sweetly tempting. A real bed. A kitchen. Room to stand, to walk, to stretch, without being vulnerable.

And a massive liability. Hitching a camper behind their car would chew through fuel and make them too slow for any kind of rapid escape, like at the bridge. Clare had to grudgingly admit that the luxury wasn't worth it.

As Dorran drove, the open plains began to return to hills. A road intersected with the path they were on, and Dorran slowed as they neared it. An old, weather-beaten sign told them they were driving along Murray Road. Clare shook the map out with one hand and scanned it.

"Here!" She grinned as an almost painful relief crashed through her. Not only were they back on the map, but they were closer to Beth's than she'd dared let herself hope. "If we turn left, we can get onto the freeway. It would only take twenty minutes to reach Beth's from there."

"Dangerous," Dorran murmured.

"You're right. Let's go straight instead. That keeps us on the rural roads." Clare traced the path, lips twitching as she calculated the time. "It's not much farther...probably no more than an hour. We should be able to get there before it's dark, right?"

"I'll follow your directions." Dorran smiled, but he didn't look as happy as Clare had expected.

She frowned at him, trying to understand what was making him tense. *Beth's house is in a suburb. Is he worried about getting past the hollows?*

"We'll have the masks," Clare said. "If we park right out in front of Beth's house, we can get to the bunker and back in less than a minute. That should be quick enough to slip past the hollows before they get too pushy."

He nodded, but his expression didn't change. The awful guardedness was back in place, a careful construct of serenity.

Clare pursed her lips. *That wasn't the problem. What else, then?*

The answer came quickly and with it, a rush of uneasiness. He wasn't worried about getting to the bunker; he was worried about what was inside. He expected Beth to be dead. And he was probably right.

Clare tried to imagine what they would find—Beth, suffocated, dead, lying on her bunker floor. Or maybe nothing at all, except perhaps a splash of blood on the front step. She didn't know which would be worse, but they were the only two possibilities that seemed in any way likely. The idea of knocking on the door and hearing Beth's answer was more akin to fantasy than true hope.

And Dorran was afraid of what the loss would do to her. With good reason too. She'd fallen apart at Marnie's house.

Clare tightened her hands into fists on top of the map. She wouldn't put him through anything like that again. She knew what the bunker likely held; she'd been preparing herself for it ever since leaving Winterbourne.

But, then, she'd expected Marnie to be dead too. That hadn't made the encounter any easier.

As long as they were still driving toward Beth's, there was hope. It was small, but it still existed, and it held the grief at bay like a crumbling dam. She could tell herself Beth was gone, but until she saw it with her own eyes, it didn't feel like reality.

Beth had been the closest family she'd known since their mother had passed. Thinking about a world without Beth in it was innately wrong.

But she's gone. Almost certainly. Almost guaranteed. Gone like the rest of them.

"Let me drive," she said.

Dorran shot her a concerned glance. "Your shoulder is hurt."

"That doesn't matter. You've been driving for longer than you should have. And anyway, I know the area around Beth's house. I'll be able to navigate it better."

"Hm. All right. Take some more pain tablets first."

They exchanged places quickly, out of the car and back in within thirty seconds. Clare reflexively pulled her seat belt into place as she settled in the driver's seat. It was a habit she would have to forget, she told herself. In this new world, the risk of crashing was outweighed by the possibility of needing to escape the car in a hurry. Still, it felt comforting to have the strap looped over her shoulder and waist.

Dorran was a solid presence at her side. His expression was placid, but the tension around his shoulders and back told her the approaching confrontation was pressing on him as much as it was on her. She rested one hand on the center console to rest it, and Dorran placed his over hers.

The road stretched, straight as a ruler, with very little around it. Clare squinted as she tried to make out distant shapes through the haze. She imagined she could see the freeway to their left. And up ahead, structures that had to be buildings.

I made it, Beth. I came for you.

CHAPTER 31

THEY WERE APPROACHING THE suburb from a different direction than the way Clare used to drive, but as they drew closer, she began to recognize landmarks. A cell tower dominated the skyline, even though the lights around its top were blank. In the far distance, she caught a shape through the fog that was too square to be a house—the water tower.

As they neared the suburb's outskirts, indulgent farmhouses began to crop up. The sprawling, modern structures were a relief after nothing but the sparse fields and barbed wire fences. Clare thought she recognized some of the cross streets.

"Better to keep the speed up, I think," Dorran said. He still looked relaxed, but his voice was clipped. "They come out when they hear noise."

"Right." She saw a flicker of motion in her rearview mirror. Something with four arms peered through a topiary arrangement.

They passed off the straight, rural road and into a more formal street with gutters and sidewalks. The houses changed noticeably; they were cheaper than the rustic mansions and huddled on compact blocks of land. The last time Clare had seen them, they had appeared uniform but modern and neat.

The suburb occasionally saw snow in winter and the gardens were designed to cope with it, but Clare guessed the snowstorms must have been as brutal to Beth's suburb as they had been to Winterbourne. Gutters were littered with fallen branches. In some areas, the roads were still flooded thanks to debris blocking the drains. Clare saw smashed windows everywhere she looked. They left her uneasy. The holes created access points to the houses, which in turn meant ample nests for the hollows.

She didn't want to linger but was forced to slow as the roads threw up obstacles. Evidence of the last day, and the panic it caused, was everywhere. Cars rode up onto the sidewalks, hitting garden fences or crumpling against streetlight posts. Others had been abandoned on the road, doors hanging open. Clare managed to get around one by rising up on the sidewalk herself, but then had to put the car in reverse as a fallen oak blocked the road.

"It's okay." She spoke half to reassure Dorran and half to reassure herself as she twisted to watch the street behind them. "The streets all connect with one another. We shouldn't get stuck."

In the distance, through one of the broken windows, she thought she saw eyes glowing in the red backwash of her car's lights. The monsters were keeping their distance at least. Clare wondered if she and Dorran were the first humans they had seen since the stillness.

How long did this area last after my phone disconnected? An hour? Maybe two? Long enough for people to try to escape.

Two spilled suitcases lay outside an open door. Clothes tumbled over the path, still wet and beginning to rot, a reminder of how quickly the world had ceased.

Clare corrected the car's path to take them down a clear street. Twilight caused the cookie-cutter houses and dying lawns to blend together, forcing her to squint to see. Clare made herself loosen her death grip on the steering wheel. Her palms were wet with sweat. Dorran's pose was relaxed as he sat back in his seat, but his eyes were constantly moving below heavy eyebrows and he ran his thumb over his lips.

Beth's house was near the back of the development, in an area with larger plots of land and less manicured gardens. When Clare had first seen it, she'd laughed. Beth's home was surrounded by posh, expensive buildings, but she'd still chosen a house with a half-wild garden and irregular windows. Clare had said, "You can take the girl out of the country, but you—"

"Hush, you," Beth had said, ushering Clare into the house. "I need my neighbors to think I'm a respectable suburban lady."

But the nonconformist building helped Clare to see it while she was still two blocks away. A huge pine stood in the backyard, poking above the rooftops like a flag. She fixed on it, eyeing the dark pillar as she struggled through the choked streets to reach it.

Beth might have wanted to fit in with the Joneses living all around her, but when it came to her private backyard, she hadn't been able to hide her true nature. She loved gardens. And not the sparse shrubs and succulents that were the staple around her; she grew flowers, vines, and trees with wild abandon, and the tame front yard hid a wonderland planted behind the house. The bunker hadn't been the only addition that would have raised eyebrows.

Clare slowed at an intersection and butterflies ran through her stomach. She knew the turn; she'd taken it a hundred times—the washed-out wooden fence to her left, the bank of rose bushes to her right. It felt almost as much like home as her own suburb.

"Okay," Clare muttered, and turned the wheel.

Everything was familiar, but at the same time, it had all changed. The lawns were dead. Branches had come down and there was no one to remove them. The windows were all cold and empty in a way Clare hadn't ever seen before.

She passed the house owned by the woman with three huskies, but the kennels were quiet and empty. The dogs had to be dead. Eaten, probably by their owner. Nausea clenched her stomach. Dorran seemed to sense it; his hand rested on her shoulder, warm, comforting. Clare breathed deeply as she coasted past the house.

The children were missing from the yard they always seemed to congregate in. Three tricycles were left abandoned on the lawn. Clare wondered if they now made up part of the group that tormented Beth in her bunker. *What would a toddler's fists sound like beating against the metal door?*

Clare forced her eyes to move farther along the street, toward the house she knew the best. It was darker and quieter than normal, and perhaps a little more worn down than Beth would have let it become, but in some ways, it also looked unchanged. Clare had the sudden idea that she could climb the two steps to the wood door, hear her knocks echo through the rooms, and wait on the clatter of excited footsteps coming to let her in, just like she used to.

Then she blinked and saw the car crashed outside Beth's home. It had come off the road, crushed her mailbox, and ended its trajectory against the tree that shaded Beth's living room in summer. The tree, a weathered old maple, stayed standing; the car's driver's seat was empty, but a thick streak of dark liquid smeared across the windshield. Its back end hung onto the road, stopping her from parking directly outside Beth's.

"Stop in the middle of the road," Dorran suggested. "It will be easier to drive away quickly if we need to."

Clare nodded, feeling foolish. She'd been subconsciously looking for another parking space between the other cars. Old habits die hard. There was no one to care if she blocked the street, but she still felt like she was doing something wrong as she put the car into park.

Dorran turned in his seat to reach the car's supplies. He resurfaced with three masks: one for himself, one for Clare, and one for Beth.

Thank you, Dorran.

He didn't believe they would find Beth alive. But he was still going through the motions, willing to see the journey to its end, willing to try for the best outcome for Clare's sake. A thin smile struggled to hold as she took her mask and stared at the slightly dented mesh.

She didn't feel ready. She'd had two full days to think and worry and hope; it still hadn't been enough. She pulled the mask on and the world dimmed under the mesh and folds of fabric.

Dorran passed her the leather jacket and gloves. They were still grimy from their first trip to the car. She strapped them on, using their makeshift ties to fasten the gloves to the sleeves and cover every inch of skin. Dorran mimicked her motions beside her. His breathing was fast and faintly ragged. She wondered if he felt the same thrum of fearful adrenaline that was pulsing through her.

"Ready?" His voice was low, intense. One arm was poised to open his door.

Clare took a slow breath. "Wait. One moment." She twisted around to find the radio she'd discarded in the back seat. She knew it would be futile, but she was too frightened to stop herself. She switched it on and checked it was locked into the right frequency.

"Beth? It's me. We're here for you. Please reply."

Nothing but white noise responded. She hadn't expected any different; she'd only known that she had to try. She placed the radio on the dashboard, not willing to turn it off, then turned toward Beth's house.

Their path would lead them down the narrow passageway between the right-hand side of the house and the fence, through the side gate, and into the backyard. She twisted, scanning the street, looking for motion. It seemed clear. She didn't expect it to stay that way for long, but they didn't need more than a couple of minutes.

Dorran took a breath, and Clare felt he was on the cusp of saying something. Then he shook his head. Clare reached across the space between them and took his hand. He leaned closer, until their masks bumped together, and through it, Clare glimpsed his eyes. They were intense, filled with fear, sadness, and adoration.

"We'll be quick," Clare said. "Don't worry. As soon as we're sure Beth is gone, we're leaving."

He nodded. "Whatever happens…know that I love you. So much."

He squeezed her hand. Clare held it in return, suddenly afraid to let go. Then they both turned toward their doors, and in unison, the latches clicked as they opened, and they stepped out into the silent world.

CHAPTER 32

THEY EACH HELD A weapon of choice. Clare had lost her crowbar at the bridge, so instead she took up the fire poker. She hadn't consciously planned it, but she realized she gravitated toward long weapons. Knocking the hollows aside was easier than feeling a blade become buried in skin. Dorran brought his ax, its head already stained dark brown. He carried it one handed, held at his side.

Beth's front gate barred their path. Clare couldn't shake the feeling of surrealism as she neared it. Beth had been pedantic about her gate; even though it was only waist height, she'd never left it unlatched. She'd been afraid of strangers breaking in, and she believed a shut gate would act as a deterrent. Clare had never bought into the theory. But Beth had been resolute about it. And here, at the end of the world, her gate remained shut.

The metal latch screeched as Clare opened it. She left it ajar, knowing their retreat was likely to be quick.

The small brick house stood ahead. Now-dead vines grew along the side walls. Plain cloth curtains blocked the front windows, hiding the comfy chairs and quirky paintings from neighbors' eyes. Clare couldn't count how many hours she'd spent inside the home with her sister, sometimes arguing about things that now seemed inconsequential or laughing as they watched cheesy comedies. She'd known seeing Beth's house would raise emotions for her. She hadn't expected them to be so strong.

I came for you, Beth. I'm sorry it wasn't sooner.

Down the side of the house, moving quickly and rolling their feet to minimize noise on the rough pebble path, Dorran and Clare hung close together. A low, steady chattering noise floated across the fence and manicured lawns. It wasn't too close, not yet, but still closer than Clare would have liked.

A second latched gate opened into the backyard. The trees, shrubs, and flowers, Beth's pride and joy, filled the area. They were looking worse for wear, just like everything else in the new world. But many of them were still green. It was a little spark of joy in Clare's heart.

At the garden's back, between two twisting crape myrtles, was the bunker. Its entrance was discreet. Just a square metal door standing between the trees. A concrete tunnel behind it disappeared underground at a ninety-degree angle. The door was closed.

"Okay." The lump in her throat was choking her, but she squared her shoulders. Seeing the shut door answered the question that had plagued her since she'd lost the radio in Winterbourne's shed. Beth had chosen suffocation over death at the hollows' hands.

Stay with the plan. The longer you spend out here, the more danger you're putting the both of you in. Look inside the bunker; it's the only way you can be certain. But no matter what you find in there, you're turning around immediately and going back to the car. There isn't time to bury her. You can grieve on the drive home.

Beth had kept a spare key for the bunker in case Clare ever needed to use it in an emergency. When Beth had shown Clare where to find it, Clare had tried to turn it into a joke about paranoia. Now, she was only grateful for her sister's forethought. She knelt at the stack of pots running along the back wall and pulled out the second-largest one. Woodlice and tiny pale worms squirmed away as she turned the pot over. Taped on the underside was a discolored silver key.

Dorran stayed in the garden's center, turning in a slow circle as he watched the surrounding wooden fences and the main gate. Clare moved to the bunker's door. She was shaking. Tears stung her face behind her mask.

Look inside the bunker, then leave.

She made to slot the key into the lock and felt a jolt of shock as the door creaked. Clare pressed her fingers to the cold metal and pushed. The door drifted inward. It wasn't locked, like she'd thought. Someone had opened the door, then carefully closed it behind themselves.

Beth. So you chose to let them in after all.

She felt Dorran watching her but wasn't able to meet his gaze.

A screaming, chattering wail came from somewhere near the road. Clare shook her head. She couldn't afford to be wasting time. She stepped into the stairwell, taking a short, sharp breath as she did.

The smell was immediate and repulsive. The stink of urine. The sour scent that she'd come to associate with hollows. And, beneath it, the sweetly poisonous tang of rotting flesh.

I don't want to see it. I don't want to see her dead.

But she had to. They had risked their lives to get there. She took another step down. The metal stairs echoed under her feet. Clare knew there was a light switch on the stairwell's wall and felt for it, then remembered that the generator had died. The plastic switch turned uselessly under her fingers. She continued on.

The pit below was perfectly dark. Thin light—tinted red as the failing sun struggled to press through choking clouds—came through the open door and created an insipid rectangle of illumination at the base of the stairs. Inside that were three small drops of something dark. Another step, and Clare staggered against the wall as the smell became worse. She was nearly choking on it. The air was stale and seemed to stick to the inside of Clare's lungs. Another three step, taken too fast, and she was nearly at the base of the stairs. The drops of blood were clearer. Her eyes were adjusting to the darkness. Slowly, she turned her gaze toward the rest of the room.

Cans and bottles lay on the floor. A small pile of clothes had been discarded in one corner. The couch in the center of the room was lumpier than Clare remembered it being. Near the stairwell was the TV, an old-fashioned boxy shape with a DVD player. Clare still remembered the films Beth had bought for her bunker. Her "I'll never get tired of these" collection, all cheery rom-coms and slice-of-life series.

Clare stopped at the base of the stairs. Her skin prickled. The bunker was cold, and she strained to see through the gloom. Dorran had remained at the top of the stairs, standing guard, but now he followed. His footsteps seemed to beat in time with her heart. She turned left. Beth had said she'd had flashlights. A cylindrical shape rested on the small table opposite the TV. Clare grasped it with shaking, sweating hands and felt for the button. She found it. Her little circle of light exploded over the opposite wall.

"Oh," Clare moaned.

Beth's tiny bunker was in chaos. The metal shelf that held her food and water had been knocked down. Its corner rested against the table and its contents were spilled across the floor. The couch had appeared lumpy. Clare now saw why. Something had cut into its fabric, and the deep slashes spilled billowing stuffing free.

The metal walls had shiny dents in them. The door to the bathroom had been broken down. It lay in splinters. Scraps of papers were everywhere—on the floor, on the tables, moving in little eddies when air from the open door disturbed them. The radio Beth had used to communicate with Clare lay on the floor beside the TV, its plastic shell cracked.

And there were dead hollows. Four of them. At least, as far as Clare could see. Two had been mangled so badly it was hard to tell where one began and another ended. The third one lay facedown on the floor, a kitchen knife embedded in its skull. Its head was tilted to the side, facing the door. Clare turned her flashlight toward it, and its eyes twitched in the sudden light. Its jaw gaped a fraction of an inch wider.

Clare pulled her mask off and let it drop to the floor along with the crowbar, then pressed a damp hand to her face. She had been ready to see her sister's body. But it wasn't there. Instead, she found only confusion and chaos. And she couldn't make sense of any of it.

Dorran moved silently as he took the flashlight from Clare. She lowered her hands and forced herself to look again as Dorran examined the scene.

"What..." He shook his head.

She opened the doors. They came in. She fought.

A swell of pride for her sister was quickly followed by grief. Beth had fought, but she couldn't have escaped. The suburb was teeming with hollows, and the sounds from the scuffle would have drawn in a wave of them. Her eyes dropped to her feet. The floor was saturated with blood. More blood than she thought the remaining bodies could account for.

They ate her. Clare felt herself choking and grasped at the unraveling threads of her mind as she tried to pull herself back together. Beth hadn't died cowering. She had taken down four of the monsters before succumbing. That was admirable for anyone.

The nearest creature twitched again, its fingertips curling up a fraction. It wasn't dead, but it was so close that Clare was amazed it was still moving.

Dorran placed a hand on Clare's back. "Turn around," he whispered.

"What?"

"I need to take care of this. Turn around."

She faced the wall above the table. The metal had been damaged there too. Tiny scratches that had probably come from hollow fingernails marred the metal.

Two loud whacking noises echoed through the room. Clare flinched. The hollow stopped croaking. Clare took slow breaths.

That's it. You saw the bunker. You can get out now. Run for the car. Don't look back.

Her eyes were blurred with unshed tears, distorting the marks on the wall above the desk. Her breath caught. The scratches appeared in little bunches. They were too controlled to be from hollows.

"Dorran. The flashlight."

He directed the light toward where she pointed, and Clare squinted against the glare cast off the metal.

The lines weren't scratches from fingernails, like she'd first thought. They had been cut with the sharp edge of a screw. The implement lay on the ground just below the table, its tip worn down from the usage. Beth had written an address into the wall.

CHAPTER 33

"HELEXIS TOWER, FLOOR 12, Inner City."

Clare ran her fingers over the words as she read them. The lines were all jagged from the force of being cut with a screw, but they were in Beth's hand, she was certain. Beth had a particular way of forming *E*s that was unmistakable.

"Is the location significant to you?" Dorran's voice was a whisper. He kept glancing up the open stairwell beside them. They had already spent longer there than they should have.

"I know the city. I've been there a few times. But I've never heard of the tower. Why would Beth write it, though?"

"And on the wall, not on the paper." Dorran indicated the scraps of white littering the ground. Pages torn out of books. Scraps from the notepad that was now flung against the opposite wall. If she'd needed something to write on, there was an abundance of material.

The answer came to her quickly. "Because she wanted me to see it. She knew I would come for her, but that I wouldn't have enough time to sort through the papers on the ground. So she left it on the wall, where I couldn't miss it."

Except you nearly did miss it, the little voice in her head whispered. *If Dorran hadn't made you turn around, you wouldn't have seen it at all.*

But it was the only theory that made sense. A message scrawled on metal. Something that couldn't be erased, scrunched up, or burned. Placed beside the exit. It had to be for her.

She pressed her hand to the metal. Her breathing was ragged and her heartbeat sounded too loud. The fact that she didn't understand the message didn't matter. Beth had tried to communicate with her.

"Clare. Mask." Dorran stayed facing the stairwell. He'd gone very still, and his whisper held a note of warning.

She grabbed the fencing mask from the floor and pulled it over her head, then stepped up to his side. At the top of the stairs, framed by a square of harsh light, stood a disfigured silhouette. Its elongated head tilted to the side as it stared down at them.

Damn it. I promised him we wouldn't stay too long.

Clare, without moving her eyes from the figure, felt the cloth around her neck and the gloves tied to her sleeves. They were secure.

It can't recognize us. It won't attack. We can slip past it if we're careful—

More silhouettes appeared behind it. With the light diffused behind the creatures, she couldn't see their expressions. But she could hear the hunger and anger as jaws stretched open to chatter at them.

The blood, she realized. *They smell the blood down here. They're going to attack.*

The hollow lunged toward them, uneven footsteps ringing on the metal stairs. The internal door was propped open beside her. Clare moved quickly, grabbing the door's edge and forcing it closed. She staggered as the cuts in her shoulder burned. The metal, designed to be airtight, was heavy and resisted being slammed. Clare grunted as the creature hit the other side of the door. She put her shoulder against the metal, trying to force it shut, but a gray arm stretched through the gap. Grasping fingers coiled around the door's edge, hunting for her, flailing through the air. Then another hand. Then another. Dorran swung his ax. A limb sprang free, a streak of thickened blood arcing through the air. He kicked at another hand to force it back through. Another three scrabbling arms came to take its place.

How many are there?

Clare gasped as her boots scraped on the concrete. The gap widened. Dorran moved to Clare's side, putting his shoulder against the door to keep it closed. The pressure on the other side was immense. Screams and the ceaseless chattering shook the room. Clare couldn't think. She put her head down and pushed with all of her strength, trying to drive the door closed against the wall of flesh. Dorran flinched as fingers plucked at his arm. The hollows didn't care that their limbs were being crushed. Their hunger and rage were mindless.

Mindless...

Clare's eyes turned to the radio in the room's corner. The door ground inward an inch, and she leaned farther into it to force it back. "Can you hold it?"

Dorran gave a short nod. Clare closed her eyes and stepped away from the door. She felt a stab of fear as the metal grated inward, but Dorran dug his feet into the floor and forced it back. She could see muscles straining even under the jacket.

She darted around the abnormally long arms. The fingers caught at her as she ran past, scraping over her arm, and the screaming, chattering throng became louder as the limbs chased her. She dropped to her knees beside the radio and pressed the power button. It stayed dead.

"No, no, no..." She ran her fingers over the cracked plastic. Dorran knew how to repair the machine, but she didn't. She turned it over and saw a dark hole in its back.

It wasn't broken. It was missing its batteries. She put her head down close to the ground and searched for them. Two were under the table. A third had rolled near the couch. Clare snatched them up and forced them into the radio with shaking hands.

"Clare," Dorran said. He strained against the door, but it was bowing inward an inch at a time. Faces pressed into the gaps between the arms. Hissing. Jaws clicking as they rolled in their sockets. Demented eyes glinting in the flashlight's beam.

"Almost," Clare called back, but the word became choked in

her throat. She could barely see through the mask. *There.* The final battery was half-hidden under a sheet of paper. Clare could have cried as she grabbed it. It slid into its slot, and she scrambled back to Dorran as she turned the radio on.

One of the hollows spilled through the door. Its torso stretched forward, its arms swinging toward Clare. Its hips had become pinned in the gap. Dorran grunted as he forced the door back an inch, and Clare thought she heard the hollow's bones fracture. She grabbed his ax off the floor. It was heavier than she'd expected. She lifted, staggered, and brought it down over the hollow's head.

She'd been trying to decapitate it, but her aim was off. The skull split horribly as the ax embedded in it. Clear cranial fluids ran out of the cavity, dripping down the handle. Clare yelped and released her hold on it. The hollow stayed upright for two more seconds, its eyes rocking wildly in its skull, then it slumped forward, limp.

Clare snatched up the radio and put her back against the door next to Dorran. Desperate, she fumbled over the box's settings. It hadn't been left on Clare's frequency. Beth must have been searching for another broadcaster before she opened the door.

To her horror, new noises came from the bodies packed against the other side of the door. Wet noises. Chewing noises. The dead hollow shuddered, then its body began to slide back behind the door.

"Come on. Come on." The door shuddered, making it nearly impossible to control the little dials. Clare shoved back, digging her feet into the ground. Dorran gasped with exhaustion. Then Clare finally got the right setting and turned the switch to start the broadcast.

The radio's pair waited back in her car. And it was turned on. Clare tapped against the microphone, knowing the sounds would be magnified. It wasn't enough, though. She tapped harder, scratching her gloved finger over the fine mesh. Then she lifted it to her lips and screamed into the microphone, "Go away!"

That worked. Clare heard her own voice, ragged and full of fear, projected from the car on the street. The chattering wails abruptly fell silent, and the roving arms fell still, their fingers still hooked around the door, splayed over the metal walls and the floor.

Clare cupped one hand around her mouth to minimize what noise escaped into the room and spoke into the radio, starting at a whisper and gradually increasing the volume. "Get out of here. Get out of my sister's bunker. Out of my sister's yard. Leave us alone. Get out!"

The arms withdrew, the thin skin scraping off against the door's edge. The chattering carried up the stairs as the hollows scuttled over each other to get outside. The bunker door shut, and the latch clicked, sealing it. Dorran took his mask off, and Clare quickly followed.

"Smart girl," he said.

Clare tried to smile as she stared at the black box cradled in her hands. "It got them away from us. But now they'll be gathered around the car, instead."

"Only as long as they can hear you." He pointed to the radio, and Clare turned it off. There was no sense in drawing hollows from the rest of the suburb as well.

Her legs had no strength left. She let herself slide down until she sat on the floor. A second later, Dorran followed, and together they stared across the ruined bunker.

CHAPTER 34

THEY SAT ON THE cold concrete floor with their backs against the door, both slick with sweat and hollow blood. Dorran took Clare's hand and held it tightly. Clare rested her head against his shoulder.

Beth had said it took several hours for the hollows to leave once they could no longer hear any noise. Clare hoped that would be true of the car as well. If they waited long enough, they might be able to get across the yard without being intercepted.

She already knew the wait would be painful, though. The small room smelled foul. With the door closed, there was no way to get fresh air in, and the odors seemed to build on themselves until she was afraid of gagging.

One of the hollows returned. Clare couldn't see much with their flashlight facing the opposite wall, but she felt Dorran tighten as the shuffling footsteps climbed the metal stairs. She held the radio in her lap, but she didn't try to use it. Every additional noise would only prolong their stay.

The hollow scratched around their door. The sound of fingernails on metal set Clare's teeth on edge, and she closed her eyes as she tried to ignore it. She and Dorran remained completely silent. After what must have been minutes but felt like hours, the scratching ceased, and the hollow climbed back up to the outside world.

Time stretched on. Clare tried to count the seconds in her mind, carrying a running total so she could guess the length of their wait. She lost count somewhere around half an hour.

Then Dorran dipped his head closer to hers and whispered, "When we reach the car, are we returning to Winterbourne?"

It was a loaded question, and Clare wasn't prepared to answer it. She glanced toward the five words scribbled on the wall. They shimmered in the dull light. "Beth wanted me to find her message. I'm sure of that. The address is important."

They were quiet for a moment as they made sure their whispers hadn't attracted any further attention. Then Dorran asked, "How far away is it?"

"I don't know the building. But the city is about three hours away on the freeway. Double that if we take the back roads."

Again, they fell into silence. A question hung between them. *Are we going?*

"Winterbourne's garden will need us back soon if the plants are going to survive." Clare adjusted her position against the door and flinched as her shoulder protested. "And getting through the suburb was challenging enough. The city must be absolutely overrun with them. Plus, we don't actually know what we'll find there. It's just an address. Maybe Beth was trying to tell us to *stay away* from it."

"Be honest." His fingers rubbed over Clare's own. "Are you trying to tell me you don't want to go, or are you giving me reasons for why I can refuse to take you?"

"The latter," she admitted. The flashlight's beam flowed over a stretch of gray skin in the early stages of decomposition. She tried not to stare at it.

Dorran waited. With anyone else, the silence would be uncomfortable. But Dorran wasn't using it to apply pressure; he was waiting for her to get all of her thoughts out. He wanted to know how she truly felt.

"It's just that…we didn't find her body. And the bunker's door was closed when we arrived. That is such a Beth thing to do. Shut the door on the way out." She smiled, but it vanished quickly. "And my mind just keeps swirling around that. What if she's still out there? And what if she left me directions for how to find her?"

Dorran nodded but still didn't speak. Clare had the horrible impression that he was staying quiet because his mental train had diverged from hers.

"What are you thinking?" Clare leaned into him, nudging his shoulder with hers. She could barely see his eyes in the dim light, but the emotions in them weren't happy. She swallowed. "Please. I want you to be honest with me."

He took a deep breath and held it for a beat. "I don't believe Beth left that message for you."

"Okay." She'd been braced for dissent, but it still felt like a knife in her stomach.

"I understand why...why you *want* it to be. But..." He glanced at her, and she nodded back, resolute, telling him it was okay to continue. "Beth was adamant that you should stay at Winterbourne. She did not want you to come here."

"But she knew I would anyway." Clare's voice rose louder than she'd meant, and she forced it back to a whisper. "And...and so she left it just in case."

"The address has no meaning to you." Dorran looked sad, almost apologetic for having to say it. "If she wanted you to find it, she would have included an explanation. Or even just your name, to make sure you would have no doubt about its purpose."

Clare shook her head furiously. She hated feeling like she was grasping at something hopeless. "Maybe she didn't have time. Maybe she fought off one wave of hollows and only had seconds to write down her destination before escaping."

Dorran glanced at the words. Clare looked, too, and felt her heart sink. The scores were jagged but not wild. The address had been written with care in neat, straight lines by a steady hand.

"If she had time to write the address, she would have had time to bring her radio," Dorran said.

"Maybe...maybe..."

"Perhaps she heard someone share the address on the radio and scratched it into the wall to remember it."

Clare tilted her head back and blinked furiously at the shadowed ceiling. "Yeah…maybe it's the address of a safe house. She might have been planning to go there."

"I think that is plausible," Dorran said.

Hope exploded in Clare's chest. She gripped Dorran's hand too hard. "We might find her on the road. That hollow with the knife in its head—it was still alive when we found it. She probably hasn't been gone more than a couple of hours. She might not have even left the suburb yet!"

Outside, a hollow screamed. Clare realized she'd been too loud and bit her lip. They waited, listening, but nothing came back to the bunker door.

Dorran relaxed again and adjusted his legs to stretch them in front of himself. Clare tried to read his expression. The hope was a painful wildfire burning through her chest. He wasn't meeting her eyes, though, and she knew that wasn't a good sign.

"You don't think so," she said, prompting him, trying to fight the disappointment that wanted to leak into her voice.

"I think it is plausible that Beth would have a plan to escape. Possibly the address was a part of it."

His sentence had an unspoken *but*. He still hesitated, though. Clare closed her eyes and spoke more calmly. "It's okay. I won't get angry. Go ahead."

He released a held breath. "The hollow was still alive, but the blood was dry. Beth has been gone for at least a day."

"Okay." Clare pictured the hollow lying on the bunker floor, twitching, for that long. Beth must have thought she'd killed it when she'd driven the knife through its skull. But the hollows refused to follow human laws of mortality. They didn't seem to need their blood, or all of their brains, or their spinal cord, or anything else that should have been necessary for life.

"If the bunker had been empty and orderly, I would hold hope as well. But this was a fight." Dorran indicated to the dead monsters. "Fights create noise and draw more hollows. You saw how many were outside the door when we were trying to close it. Beth was remarkable to have killed four of them. Truly remarkable, especially for a sole individual with very little in the way of defense. But I cannot imagine she would have made it as far as a car. Especially not without leaving signs for us to see. The garden was undisturbed—no bodies, no blood, no churned dirt. The fight started, and ended, here."

She kept her head tilted back so he wouldn't see the tears gathering in her eyes. Both her mind and her heart hurt. She wished he wouldn't make so much sense.

"I am so sorry." It was not a platitude; his voice was full of pain. "I wish I could see it any other way. I wish I could justify a journey to the city."

"But we can't." Her mind was clearing, and the address, so full of promise a moment before, felt empty.

"Six hours to the city if the roads are not blocked. Then perhaps a full day of driving to reach home. We would need to stop for food and fuel. We would need to find a way through the city."

Beth's voice echoed in Clare's mind. *If you want to survive, don't take risks.*

"And we don't know what we would find when we arrive there." Clare's voice had lost its energy, but she tried to smile. "It might be a safe house. Or it might be nothing."

Underneath was an unspoken implication: *whatever is there, it won't be Beth.*

It hurt. She shook her head as she tried to focus on something more immediate, something more actionable. "What supplies do we need?"

"Clare…"

"What supplies?"

"We are low on all necessities, including gasoline, bandages, antibiotics, and food. We have enough water left for a day if we only drink it and don't use any for washing."

"And I *would* like a bath. I never realized what a luxury running water was until we didn't have any." Clare looked down at herself. On top of every other layer of grime, blood, and sweat, Clare now had cranial fluid sticking on her hand. She felt repulsive. The fact that Dorran still sat so close to her reinforced what she already knew: he was halfway to being a saint.

"I would not disagree with a bath either. I feel as though I am barely a step above the hollows I am fighting." Dorran chuckled.

Clare joined in, and the tension between them dissipated.

"It is in your hands." Dorran's voice was so soft she could barely hear it. "You know how I feel, but this is still your choice. I promised I would follow where you led, and I will. If you wish to travel to the city, if you feel you *cannot* return to the house without doing so, I will be there with you."

The city would be dangerous. She knew that without a shadow of a doubt. The streets would be worse than the freeway. The buildings would be many-storied death traps. The cities had been the first places to change, and their high-density populations meant there would be precious few chances to slip past the hollows unobserved.

They had made it through so much already. They were both injured and worn down—ready to return home, ready to consolidate and recover.

Dorran was watching her, his dark eyes filled with grief and love. She had lost her sister. She had to protect what she had left. Clare smiled, and this time, it didn't hurt as much. "Let's go back to Winterbourne."

He kissed her forehead, a soft murmur in the back of his throat, and she could feel the relief running through him.

"We don't have to give up entirely," he whispered. "We still have our radio. Beth knows your frequency; if she is out there, she will make contact."

It was a promise without hope, but it was all he could give her. Clare nodded. He pulled her closer and rested his head on top of hers. The bunker was cold, but Dorran was warm and safe. Clare closed her eyes. Her heart hurt, but she knew it wouldn't last forever. She just had to get them home.

Low on food, low on water, low on medicine. She turned the radio over in her hands. At the opposite wall, the fractured supplies shelf covered a plethora of cans and bottled water. Some had become broken during the scuffle, but there was still more than they could carry. "We can take some of Beth's food with us at least. And…I think I know how to get more bandages and antibiotics as well."

"That would help. The antibiotics, especially, are a priority." His eyes flicked down to her shoulder, and she knew he feared that they might make it home in one piece only to succumb to infection. Even if the condition afflicting the hollows wasn't contagious, that didn't mean their bites were free of bacteria.

Clare nodded. "Beth will have a first aid kit in her home. I don't know where she keeps it, but it's probably either in the kitchen or the bathroom. And I think we can use the radio to buy us a few minutes."

"Good. I'll collect the food."

Dorran left Clare beside the door as he stepped around the dead hollows. He found a discarded quilt and shook it out, then moved through the food, picking out cans that weren't damaged and placing them in the quilt one at a time to avoid noise.

Clare squinted through the low light to see the settings on the radio. During her time at Winterbourne, she had scrolled through some of the frequencies looking for other survivors. Their numbers had grown fewer with every day, but some broadcast regularly, sharing advice or simply looking to meet up with others to trade supplies. In among them, she'd found one channel that was unlike anything she'd heard before. It was a jumble of sound—white noise, interspersed with second-long clips of songs, sound effects, and voices. It felt uniquely like a product of the stillness—something that shouldn't have existed in the world before. It made her feel cold and unsafe.

She still didn't know exactly what it was or who broadcast it, but she had some guesses. The clips, even the voices, all sounded prerecorded. She thought it might be a radio station that had been left running after the world went quiet, and its system had malfunctioned to play each automated segment for only a second or two at a time.

Clare scrolled through the channels until she found it. Even with the radio's volume turned to its lowest setting the noises were unmistakable. She heard a laugh track, followed by a single beat of a song, then a man cheerfully saying "Teeth—!" interspersed with static.

Dorran had returned, the quilt tied together at the corners to hold their supplies. Clare stood to take her place at his side. They exchanged a look, then she slowly, carefully opened the door. Fresh air rolled through as the seal broke, and Clare breathed deeply as she leaned into it.

They waited there a moment, watching the block of light at the top of the stairs for any sign of movement. It stayed empty. Clare swallowed, then pulled her mask back over her face.

The hollow she'd killed lay just outside the door. The ax was still embedded in its skull and its eyes stared up at them sightlessly. Its lower half had been almost completely devoured. Clare gagged and looked away as Dorran bent and wrenched his ax free. He lifted the bundled supplies onto his shoulder while Clare found her fire poker near the wall. Together, they stepped over the fallen hollow to ascend the stairs.

Daylight was running out. Clare guessed they had less than

ten minutes of visibility left. That wouldn't be good for getting out of the suburb, but she was sure they could make it work as long as they could reach the car. The garden seemed empty, but it was hard to be certain when the plants had lost their tones in the neutralizing dusk.

They moved quickly and quietly as they crept along the house's side. As they neared the front yard, Clare caught motion in the shadows around the silhouette of her red hatchback. She put her hand out to stop Dorran and they held still, not even breathing, as they watched the creatures clawing at their vehicle. Clare waited until she was certain they weren't looking in her direction, then moved forward again, bent low as she sprinted around Beth's fence to reach the neighbor's yard.

Shapes appeared in the gloom ahead, stepping out of the plants, from around the cars, and through the open doors lining the street. Eyes glinted in the low light. Clare wondered if, like animals, the hollows were more active at dusk. She ran, Dorran keeping pace behind her with long, nearly silent strides. They only stopped at the stairs leading to the neighbor's front entrance. A hollow set up its chattering cry, and the sound danced through the cold night air. Clare looked up at Dorran, a silent request for confirmation, and he nodded in return. She turned the radio's volume up to its maximum level.

CHAPTER 35

THE NOISE BLARED AROUND them, deafening. A second of piano. A second of a woman's sigh. A second of what sounded like cutlery scraping over a plate. A second of a child laughing.

Clare shoved the radio into the massive bush beside the house's front steps. The plant had managed to survive the cold snap and its leaves were still thick and dark, and they hid the radio well. She and Dorran turned and bolted.

The hollows initially recoiled from the deafening sounds. Clare had been relying on that; it gave them precious seconds to get out of sight. They ran around the fence, paying less attention to how quiet they were now that the radio was masking their noises, and didn't stop moving until they were in the shadows of Beth's front porch.

Clare pressed her back to the bricks, Dorran's arm warm at her side, as they watched the street. Hollows crept toward the sound, scuttling like insects over the dead grass. Something heavy hit the awning above them. Clare's heart leapt into her throat and she flattened herself against the brick wall. Dorran's ax shimmered in the moonlight as he lifted it.

The sounds moved above them, weaving toward the awning's edge, then a hollow scuttled down the pillar to reach the yard. It didn't so much as look at them as it skittered between the shrubs and toward the fence.

The radio continued to play its broken track. The sounds of traffic. A man saying, "Good evening!" Part of a song that Clare thought she recognized. All blended together into the static until it was a maddening soup of noise. Clare knew the human voices would be most attractive to the hollows. As they converged on the shrub hiding the radio, she turned to Beth's front door and tried the handle. Like she'd feared, it was locked.

Dorran held up a finger. He passed her the ax and dropped the sack of food to the floor, then pulled his jacket off and wound it around his hand. He approached the nearest window and waited. It only took a few seconds for the radio to land on a noise that drowned out their movements: an angry foghorn. Dorran moved quickly, punching through the glass and scraping the shards away before the radio had a chance to switch to a quieter track.

Clare glanced behind them. One of the hollows on the street had frozen, staring in their direction. She held still, praying the masks would work. They did. The hollow turned back to the shrub.

Dorran jumped through the open window. A second later,

the front door clicked open. Clare entered, then they closed it behind themselves, and Clare pulled her mask off to clear her vision.

The wood-clad hallway was barely visible in the darkness but still sweetly familiar. She knew the paintings on the wall, even if she couldn't see them. Hulking couches in the living room seemed to be waiting for her and Beth to take up their usual places. It even *smelled* like home.

"Kitchen's that way." Clare swallowed around the lump in her throat and pointed to their left. "Spare blankets in the hallway closet. There are clothes in the bedroom, but only women's."

"That's fine. I can continue to wear this; it is not torn, only in need of a wash. Get something for yourself."

Clare went to the bedroom first. Beth was only a size larger than her, and they had the benefit of liking the same colors. Clare threw open the wardrobe doors. A need to linger, to see and hold the clothes, burned through her. It might be her last chance to feel close to her sister, and that thought hurt. She blinked furiously. They had seconds, not minutes, and goodbyes were a luxury she couldn't afford. She took an outfit indiscriminately and tucked it under her arm as she jogged back to the hallway.

She found Dorran in the kitchen with the pantry doors open. Anxious Beth always kept her home well stocked "just in case." Clare had also kept stores of long-life food, but at least she'd had a good reason. Her house was rural enough to be cut off from the shops in deep winter. Beth's suburb never saw more than a dusting of snow.

Clare wished she could apologize for every time she'd laughed at her sister's paranoia. Because, that day, it was saving them.

Dorran had untied his bundle of supplies on the kitchen counter and was adding extra food to it as he searched for the first aid kit. Beth's bunker had been well stocked but lacked variety. They picked up extra pasta. Cans of sauces, cans of fruit, bottles of condiments. Clare found a box of chocolates at the top of the cupboard and couldn't hide a guilty smile as she added it to the pile.

A knife block caught the light in the back of the room. She picked out one of the longest blades and tucked it into her jacket's pocket.

Clare didn't know how long the radio would hold the hollows, but she doubted it would be long. Just like they had at the barn, they would probe at the radio and either realize it couldn't lead them to anything edible…or break it. Clare crossed to the window and tugged the curtains back. The radio, muffled, continued to play. She couldn't see any movement.

She leaned close to Dorran and whispered, "I'll search the bathroom. Keep looking here. See if there's anything else that might help. Flashlights or matches or anything of the kind."

He nodded and they split up. Clare followed the hallway into the bathroom and went straight for the cabinet above the sink. She pulled the mirrored front open and squinted at the contents. There was no first aid kit. Instead, a truly staggering array of bottles and cardboard boxes filled the space.

"Beth, you hypochondriac," Clare muttered under her breath. She snatched the bottles up and turned them over, trying to read their labels. Medicine for anxiety. Medicine for headaches. Medicine for indigestion, for dry skin, for oily skin. A box of antibiotics, partially gone. She pocketed that one. Sedatives. Stimulants. Cold medicine. A box of bandages that also went into Clare's pocket. Sunburn lotion. Earache relief. And a whole row of herbal complexes that Clare couldn't afford the time to sort through. And that was only on the first shelf.

She'd known Beth liked visiting her doctor. Now, she was starting to think the doctor had been enabling Beth more than helping her.

Clare closed the glass door and bent to see if there was anything underneath the sink. As she ducked, she caught a glimpse of something in the mirror. Clare froze, her heart jumping, and slowly lifted her head again to see her reflection.

The past few days hadn't been kind to her. Her hair had become matted and oily. Her face was grimy, even though she'd washed it in the river just that morning. The knit top's collar was crusty with dried blood and threads were hanging loose from where they had been pulled. She looked thinner than she remembered. And she wasn't alone.

A hollow stood behind her. Its back was arched, shoulders thrust back to jut its chest forward painfully. All of the bones in its body looked like they had been twisted and extended beyond where they could stand. Its arms flexed behind its back. Both knees turned in, hobbling it as it tried to shuffle toward her, its neck pulled back and its chin tucked in so that it could meet Clare's eyes in the mirror.

She turned, trying to yell, but the noise caught in her throat. She raised the metal bar ahead of herself defensively. But the hollow wasn't charging. It backed away with a short, shuffling step. The bloodshot eyes twitched as they looked from Clare's face to the metal.

"Please," the hollow rasped.

Clare's stomach turned cold. Deformed as it was, she still recognized the creature. Thin patches of gray hair clung to its head. Its skin was wrinkled, its naked breasts sagging. And one of its fingers, contorted behind itself by the twisted bones, still wore a wedding ring.

Clare had met her twice while visiting her sister. Annie, the older woman who lived down the road and owned three huskies. Beth had talked about her fondly. She was a sweet woman, Beth said.

She hadn't become mindless. There was awareness in her eyes and misery pulling at her face. She had probably come to Beth's house seeking help, slipping through the open front door and locking it behind herself. But Beth hadn't been there; she'd been in her bunker. And Annie had become trapped by her own mutations, her fingers twisting until they could no longer turn a handle.

Clare felt paralyzed. She couldn't hear Dorran under the noise from the radio, but she knew he wouldn't be far away. Like her, he'd assumed all of the hollows had been drawn outside by the noise. But Annie wasn't like her counterparts; she wasn't blindly hungry. At least a part of her was still human.

The cracked lips parted again, and the hollow whispered through a near-crushed esophagus, the words slurred and distorted: "Please…help…me."

Clare opened her mouth. A horrible sense of despair weighed on her. *What kind of help could make any meaningful difference? I can't change this. I can't reverse this—*

The woman's mouth worked, saliva pooling over her chin as she struggled to form the words. "Let…me…die."

Tears spilled over Clare's cheeks. She looked down at the metal bar she gripped in her hand. Then she shook her head urgently, almost desperately.

You have to. She's in pain. How long has she been here, wishing she could die, but too hobbled to end it herself, not even able to open the door? She can't do it. You have to.

Clare imagined bringing the metal down on Annie's head again and again, as many blows as it took to stop the twitching. She wanted to scream.

Dorran was close. She could call him. He would take care of it for her. Again.

That wasn't fair. She already relied on him too much. She needed to be strong for him. To be prepared. To carry her share of the burden.

She raised the metal bar. Her grip was weak. The metal shook. She wouldn't be able to do it. She couldn't carry through.

Clare choked on a sob as she dropped the fire poker into the sink. Annie took a halting step closer, her expression pleading.

A weight rested in her pocket. *The knife*, she remembered.

Clare pulled it out and felt the cool metal handle. "This…this, uh…should be faster."

"Please," the woman gasped.

Clare stepped near to her. Nearer than she wanted. Near enough to smell the stench and to see the cracks in the skin where it had stretched too far. She lifted one shaking hand and placed it on Annie's opposite cheek to hold her head still. Then she brought the knife up and positioned it under the tilted chin.

The lidless eyes looked strangely gentle. They weren't afraid.

"I'm so sorry," Clare whispered, and thrust the knife up.

Hot blood poured over her hand. Annie's eyes rolled up in her skull. Clare tried not to scream or cry or be sick. She needed to do the job properly. She twisted the knife, digging it in as far as she could, until Annie's body went completely limp and tumbled to the ground.

Clare backed up and stood by the sink, body heaving as she retched and sobbed.

CHAPTER 36

"CLARE?" DORRAN STOOD BY the hallway cupboard, sorting through sheets and towels as he searched for anything useful. His expression tightened as he saw her swollen eyes, then flicked down to her hand, which was painted red with blood. The concern turned to terror. He crossed to her in five quick steps. "You're hurt. Clare—"

She shook her head. She couldn't stop crying. She'd thought she'd had the measure of this new world, but the encounter with Annie left her feeling dead inside. Dorran held her hand, turning it over as he looked for cuts, and she pulled free from him. Her tongue felt swollen and inflexible. "I'm fine. We need to go."

He looked tense, his lips pressed into a tight line as he stepped around her, scanning her, his hands running over her shoulders and back. "What happened? I should not have left you alone. Was it a hollow?"

"We need to go" was all she could manage. She moved past him, into the kitchen, toward their collection of supplies heaped in the center of the quilt. She tried to pick some of the cans up, but Dorran gently pushed her hands back down.

"I have this. Just follow close to me. This will be all right, my darling. We will be all right."

The radio still played its discordant clips, the audio loud enough to crackle through the rooms and mask their voices. Dorran brought the corners of the quilt together and tied them. He heaved it onto his shoulder, then reached out his other hand to hold Clare's. She didn't want the blood to get on him and shook her head no.

"Yes," he said, and took it anyway.

They moved through the house and carefully opened the front door. The radio abruptly fell silent, and they both froze. The quiet only lasted a heartbeat before it resumed, a man laughing, followed by three notes from a commercial's jingle.

They're breaking it. She could picture the creatures prying at the radio, trying to open it, trying to either make sense of or silence the voices.

Dorran paused in the open doorway as he searched the street. Daylight was gone, and the moon was weak. Clare hoped he could see better than her; she was struggling to parse the shadowed shapes. He kept scanning the environment, one hand holding the supplies on his shoulder and the other clasping Clare's. They half walked, half ran along the flagstone path and through the gate. Clare's red car seemed to have gained a few new scratches on its paint while they were in the bunker, but she couldn't see any signs that the exposed engine had been tampered with, at least.

Something wailed to their left. Clare turned and caught sight of the hollows gathered around the shrub. At least, what had once been the shrub. There were more than thirty of the creatures. They swarmed the area, clawing at the ground, clawing at the house, clawing at each other. The shrub had been torn apart, branches stripped and discarded. They fought over the radio. Some of them had started digging a hole in the ground to get under the shrub's roots.

Clare slipped through the passenger door as Dorran threw the supplies in the back seat and vaulted over the motor to reach his side of the car. The hollows were starting to pay attention, but Dorran was efficient. He dropped into the driver's seat and turned the key, and the creatures scattered as the headlight flickered on.

As the car pulled forward, Clare had time for a final glance back at Beth's house. Its windows were cold and empty, just like every other building in the street. She hated seeing it like that; it had always been warm and inviting when Beth lived there. Now, it only looked abandoned.

Dorran took a sharp turn, and she had to brace herself against the dashboard to keep stable. This new cross street was narrower but quieter. She could feel Dorran watching her, his dark eyes careful and worried. "Tell me. Are you hurt?"

"No." She couldn't stop her eyes from burning, but at least her voice was steadier.

"Please, my Clare. I need to know you are telling the truth."

"I am." She stared down at her hands—one white, with grime under its fingernails. One smeared with red. "It's not my blood."

He exhaled deeply. "Thank heaven. What happened?"

Again, she saw the misery in Annie's eyes. She couldn't tell Dorran everything—not yet. It still hurt too much. "There was a hollow in the bathroom."

He hissed between clenched teeth. "I am sorry. I should have searched the house before I left you alone in it. Why didn't you call me?"

"It wasn't dangerous. It couldn't move much."

"I could have killed it for you, though. Protected you."

She tried to smile. Her muscles seemed to have forgotten how to. "It's okay. It was over fast."

"My poor Clare."

She couldn't look away from her hand. The blood was slick. It stained her clothes where she rested her hand in her lap. "I have to get used to it. I have to be stronger than this."

Dorran turned another corner. Without the map, he was driving blindly, but Clare still had a sense of their direction. They were getting close to the end of the suburbs. More hollows were creeping out of the houses as they passed, none yet eager enough to approach the car. Dorran was quiet for a moment, then spoke, his voice low and careful. "Do not mistake hard-heartedness for strength. To live in this world and to hold on to your humanity, your compassion, your joy—I believe that is strength. And more valuable than being callous enough that death never haunts you."

She clenched her teeth, trying to keep her emotions inside, but they escaped as a whine. Dorran's hand came over to stroke her hair as she cried. She leaned into the touch.

It only took a few minutes for Dorran to navigate out of the suburb. A marshy area, the ground glistening with water and ragged with weedy trees, separated them from the next town over. Dorran slowed the car to a crawl, then turned to feel in the back seat. Their radio still spat static, so he turned it off. When he shifted back, he held one of the bottles of water, which he offered to Clare.

"Open your window and lean out to wash your hand."

She rubbed her sleeve over her face to wipe away the dampness. "We shouldn't waste water."

"This isn't a waste. Go ahead."

She took it and wound down the window. It only made it halfway before becoming stuck, but it was far enough. She washed as much of the blood from her hand as she could manage. Flakes still stuck under her nails and stained her sleeves, but it was better.

"Thanks." She smiled, and he smiled back. A distant howl echoed from the suburb behind them, and Dorran pulled their car farther down the road. His headlights washed over the black, shrubby trees, and in the distance, more buildings blocked out the speckled stars. "We'll need to stop for the night, won't we?"

"Well..." He lifted one shoulder in an apologetic shrug. "I was hoping you would have an idea of somewhere nearby we could stop. Somewhere safe from the hollows. We could have spent the night in the bunker, but—"

"Yeah," Clare said, thought of the decaying bodies, and shook her head. "No."

"Hah. That is how I felt as well. Take a moment; breathe deeply, try to release some of the tension. I can continue circling as long as needed. When you are ready, see if you know of any locations nearby that we could secure well enough to sleep."

Clare chewed on her lip, her mind working. There were endless houses around, but she didn't trust any of them. Even if they found one with intact windows and enough material to barricade the glass, she couldn't be sure it would be secure. The hollows had wormed their way inside Winterbourne through the roof; a locked door was relatively little disincentive.

The trailers the previous day had been a lucky find. But that had been in the country, where habitation was scarce and the picturesque mountains attracted tourists. Now that they were past Beth's house, the area became more densely populated. It wasn't as bad as the city would be, but it was bad enough that they couldn't drive for more than a few minutes before passing through clusters of buildings.

They needed somewhere remote. Preferably somewhere that would have been abandoned before the stillness even occurred.

Clare found the map under the radio and unfurled the well-worn paper. She frowned at the patches of brown and green. Dorran said he could keep circling as long as she needed, but Clare knew he was being more generous than he should. They couldn't afford to waste fuel, but at the same time, they couldn't sit still. She needed a destination.

If Beth did get out…where would she have spent the night?

Clare shook her head, trying to push the idea aside. She knew it was nothing but a desperate bid to escape her grief that made her imagine her sister's safety, and she couldn't lean on hypotheticals to make decisions for her and Dorran's safety. It didn't matter whether Beth might have driven toward the mountains or toward the river—

The river.

"I have an idea," Clare said. "Turn right at this intersection."

She did her best to navigate them away from anywhere that was likely to be choked: strip malls, business districts, and town centers. The area gradually became more closely packed as they moved toward the city's outer suburbs. But Clare was leading them to one very specific location, a place she'd visited with Beth several times as a teenager.

"It should be somewhere close." Clare squinted from the map to the street ahead. "Beth and I had a tradition. Twice a year, we spent the afternoon on a riverboat. *The Adelaide*. It runs tours along the river, but it always moored here, in Glenbrook."

"A riverboat?" He sounded intrigued. "If it's separated from the shore…"

"The hollows won't be able to reach us." Clare nodded, switching her attention from the map to the road. "Remember when they fell into the pond at Winterbourne? They thrashed, but they couldn't swim. Unless the ones here have learned somehow, the river should be moving too quickly for them to get close to the boat."

"It's a good plan." Dorran took a turn Clare indicated.

The moon's light was dulled by clouds and their single headlight didn't show the road as clearly as she would have liked. Still, she thought she could recognize some of the businesses they passed. The town was old, its strip mall shabby and its houses leaning toward run-down, but at least the streets were wide, and Dorran didn't have any trouble getting around obstacles. Clare caught glimpses of the river through the buildings. Occasionally, twisted shapes darted between the houses, barely catching in their headlight.

Unlike the earlier stream they had forded, this one was naturally wide and slow moving. She was crossing her fingers that the wider banks had contained the extra water and that the flow would have started to slow as the melted snow washed out to sea.

She wasn't disappointed. As they turned down a narrow street lined with weatherboard houses, Clare caught sight of an empty parking lot to their right. A brightly painted sign on the street corner advertised the *Adelaide*. A cartoon duck pointed down the lane, exclaiming, *Fun for the whole family!*

"Down there," Clare said. She leaned close to her window, hoping her instincts hadn't led them to a dead end. She had faint memories of the boat's timetable. On Sundays, the day the quiet zones had started overtaking the world, the *Adelaide* didn't begin its tours until eleven in the morning. If she was right, it would have been close enough to the city that the area would have gone quiet before any passengers had the chance to board.

Dorran let the car slow as they neared the grassy river edge, and Clare grinned. The two-story boat was exactly where she'd hoped to find it, drifting at the end of a wide wooden pier. The *Adelaide* seemed to have survived the bad weather with minimal damage. White and blue paint sparkled in their headlight, and a bright red paddle wheel stood out behind it like a cheerful marker.

Dorran parked the car facing the boat. Their headlight washed over the dark windows and open upper deck. Clare watched for any sign of movement inside, but it seemed vacant. There was activity behind them, though; through the mirrors, Clare could see hollows creeping out from between houses.

"What do you think?" she asked Dorran.

He flashed her a warm smile. "I think you are brilliant. This will be more secure than anything on land."

"And it should have running water and heat."

"I may never want to leave." He glanced behind, toward the eyes that caught in the red backwash of light. "Gather anything you want to bring. I will use the horn to buy us some time, and we will run for it."

Clare pulled her mask on and reached into the backseat. The riverboat should have most of what they would need to make their night comfortable, so Clare only brought things that would be in short supply: food, flashlights, their toiletries, the radio, and bedding. Then she picked up her own fire poker, as well as Dorran's ax. "Ready."

The hollows scattered as the horn blared through the still night air. They threw their doors open and leapt out. The pier wasn't long. The riverboat's side hung close to it, bumping against the wood with every gentle swell of the water, and Clare felt a spark of doubt as she searched for a way to board. Normally the boat had a ramp to climb up. But with the tour never started, the ramp hadn't been deployed.

Dorran took it in stride. He didn't slow down as he neared the end of the dock, but increased his speed and sprang for the railings. The river was engorged and the boat floated more than a foot higher than it normally did, but he managed to hook himself on the white metal bars and haul himself over. He moved to the gate, kicked it open, and crouched down to offer Clare his hands.

She threw the supplies at him first, then risked a glance over her shoulder. The hollows crept after her, their overgrown nails clicking on the wood. Clare swallowed thickly and jumped. Dorran caught her, throwing his body weight back in the same motion, so he ended up on his back with Clare sprawled over him. They lay there for a moment, laughing giddily, Dorran with his arms around her, before the chattering broke through their relief.

Dorran rolled to the side, carefully lowering Clare onto the wooden deck. He gained his feet in a graceful rolling motion, pushed the gate shut again, and peered over the boat's railings. Clare joined him, and they watched the monsters pace along the pier's edge, clawing at the painted walls whenever they drifted close enough.

"I don't think they know how to get up," Clare said. One of

the hollows reached forward and tried to dig its nails into the boat's side, but only succeeded in scraping it.

Dorran watched them for a second, his lips twitching, then walked along the boat until he found the immense rope mooring it to the dock. He unraveled it, spilling out as much length as he could, and let the river's slow current carry them downriver. By the time he tied it off again, the *Adelaide* no longer touched the dock.

"Better not to have to worry at all," he said, and helped Clare pick up their supplies. "We could both do with some undisturbed sleep."

CHAPTER 37

THE *ADELAIDE* HADN'T CHANGED since Clare had last seen it. The upper deck was partially covered with rows of plastic benches bolted to the floor. Clare remembered sitting there with Beth, who had put them as far from the railings as possible, despite how phenomenally safe the boat was. It had a wide, flat base, moved at a molasses pace, and barely even rocked on the water. Clare was glad to be able to visit the boat again, even under their current conditions.

She turned on her flashlight and led Dorran through the door to the lower deck. Round windows overlooked the river on all sides, though with the moon half-obscured by clouds, she only glimpsed glimmers of light on the rippling water. Most of the floor was taken up by tables and chairs, and a bar with a large freezer chest stood beside the staircase and hallway at the room's back. Clare pointed out the areas she remembered. "Bathrooms are down that hallway. The captain drives from the little room up top. I think there are kitchens somewhere—probably not large, but they should have running water and maybe some other supplies."

"I'll make sure we're alone," Dorran said. "Stay here. I will be back soon."

Ax in one hand and flashlight in the other, he disappeared down the hallway that led to the bathrooms. Doors creaked as he searched inside. Clare exhaled and stretched, flexing muscles that hadn't seen much use over the previous days. The lower deck had carpet that might not have been the cleanest but was still better than the car's. The riverboat was virtually immobile in the water, which was a mercy, because the slowly moving shadows left Clare unsteady enough as it was.

She approached the bar and glanced over the supplies. A chest freezer had been positioned against the wall. She tried opening the lid in case the food inside might still be good, but it was locked.

Probably for the best. Its contents would be thoroughly thawed and rotting by now.

Clare placed her supplies on top of the freezer chest, then returned to the floor. She found an area she liked in a corner and pushed the chairs out of the way, then she began shaking out their bedding. With only two pairs of arms and the need to carry food as well, they hadn't been able to bring much. Still, two quilts were better than nothing—and they were the ones from Beth's house, which hadn't yet had a chance to become dirty. She laid one out as a cushioning underlayer and reserved the second for a blanket.

Dorran returned from the hallway. He shot her a quick glance before turning to the stairs leading to the upper floor. Clare didn't like his expression. It had lost the easy relief he'd held just a moment before. She followed him to the narrow metal stairs and stared up them, listening as he moved through the second deck.

Did he see something? She looked right. The hallway held four doors: two bathrooms and two doors simply labeled *Staff*. She opened both bathroom doors, but they were empty and unremarkable. She tried the room at the end of the hall.

Inside was a kitchen, just as narrow and poky as she'd expected. The ship must have brought most of its food prepared. The stove was tiny and wouldn't have been able to serve a quiet day's worth of customers, let alone a full one. Four microwaves stacked on the shelf gave Clare a clue of how the food was really heated. A counter ran along three walls, cluttered with bowls and utensils.

And blood.

Droplets streaked across the walls. A bloody handprint marked the fridge. A pool of it had collected on the floor and dribbled down the drain.

Clare's heart missed a beat. The blood looked dry, but she knew that didn't signify any kind of safety around hollows. She tilted her head up, to where Dorran was searching the upper floor.

A sudden, deep rumble rose from under her feet. Clare yelped and pressed her back against the door. It took her a second to understand what was happening. Lights blinked on through the kitchen and the fridge started rumbling. Dorran had turned on the power.

She hoped that was a good sign and moved back along the hallway and toward the stairs. Dorran was already coming down, his movements relaxed. "It's clear."

Clare released a breath she hadn't realized she was holding. "You saw the blood in the kitchen, didn't you?"

"Yes." He nodded to the space above them. "There is also blood in the captain's room. From my best guess, some of the staff must have been onboard when the stillness moved through. With no other food to hunt, they must have killed each other. I cannot find any sign of a final survivor. My guess is it might have climbed over the side to find better hunting grounds in the town."

"That would make sense." The staff had probably been on the barge for hours before the cruise started, prepping the area. Clare wondered how many there had been. The captain, almost certainly. A cook. At least one or two assistants. She moved to look into the bar and found a speck of blood on one of the bottles. At least it wasn't as gory as the kitchens.

"Do you feel safe enough?" Dorran asked.

Clare nodded. Her mouth was dry, but Dorran had searched the ship, and she knew him too well to think he wouldn't be thorough. Despite the signs of violence, the riverboat was likely the safest place they could stay that night.

"If you don't mind, I'll leave you for a moment to wash up,"

Dorran said. "The bathrooms are small, but they will probably be easier to clean in compared to the kitchen."

"Definitely." Clare went to their bundle of supplies and found their spare clothes. With the promise of running water, she suddenly cared about the gory kitchen a lot less. She split into the women's bathroom while Dorran took the men's.

The taps gurgled for a moment before releasing a stream of water. Clare placed her fresh clothes on the closed toilet lid and stripped out of the dirty ones. The bathroom was cramped and she had to come up with some creative contortions to wash herself, but at least it had almost everything she needed, including soap and a hand towel. The first step was to scrub the red stains out from under her fingernails, rinse them, and scrub again. She finished bent over the sink, shivering, as she doused her hair under the tap. They didn't have shampoo, so she had to use soap to wash the grease out. She knew it wouldn't be great for her hair's health. She didn't care. She was *clean*.

When she emerged, Dorran already stood at the other side of the boat, staring through a window at the moonlight glittering across the water. He looked good, with his wet hair slicked back and dressed in clean, if not crisp, clothes. He'd washed the old ones and draped them over the back of a nearby chair to dry. Clare came up behind him and wrapped her arms around him.

He hummed lightly as he rested his hands over hers. She kissed his back through his shirt, then let him pull her around so he could hold her properly.

"How is your shoulder?" he asked.

"Fine. It's not hurting anymore." That was almost true. It had stung like a nightmare when she washed it, but otherwise it wasn't bothering her as much as she would have expected.

"You are very pretty," Dorran murmured.

She grinned against his chest. "I don't know about that. But I don't look like a human garbage truck anymore, at least."

"You were also very pretty before you washed," he said.

"Liar."

Dorran laughed and rested his head on her damp hair. "I would not lie to you. My beautiful Clare."

The rest of that night was the happiest Clare had felt since leaving Winterbourne. Dorran braved the kitchen to heat their food over the stove. Since they'd found Beth's supplies, there was no need to ration it. Clare ate the creamy pasta dish until she thought she couldn't eat any more, took some of the antibiotics she had found in Beth's bathroom, then settled into the bed, warm and curled up at Dorran's side. The engine rumbled below them, a gentle melody that meshed with the lapping water. They turned the lights off in their section of the boat but left the heating on.

Cradled at Dorran's side, it was possible to forget all of the painful parts from the previous few days: Marnie, Beth's bunker, Annie. Each time one of the memories encroached, Clare pressed her face into Dorran's shirt and focused on how warm and solid he felt. He seemed to know what she needed and responded by sleepily running his hand across her back until she relaxed.

The hollows returned several times that night. They paced the shore and the docks, chattering, searching for a way to reach the riverboat. They never lingered more than a few minutes, though. Occasionally the riverboat creaked, its motor clicking over and old metal joints flexing as it warmed. Even knowing that they were safe, Clare still slept lightly enough to startle awake at the noises.

CHAPTER 38

MORNING CAME TOO SOON. Clare emerged from sleep to the sound of rain pattering over the boat. Dorran was already awake but lay on his back and stared at the water-flecked window above them as he played with her hair.

"Morning," Clare mumbled. "Bad weather, huh?"

His smile was full of a good mood. "Not the nicest. Do you want to wait for it to clear, or get an early start?"

She rubbed sleep out of her eyes and sat up. The idea of staying in the riverboat was tempting. It was warm. It was safe. Clare could easily picture them turning it into their private oasis.

But she still felt the faint squeeze of pressure. They had to get back to Winterbourne's garden before the plants died from cold or lack of water. The riverboat was a beautiful, seductive limbo. But unlike Winterbourne, it was not sustainable, and any loss of momentum could be disastrous.

Well, I just called an outdated riverboat seductive. That has to be a new low. Clare smiled to herself. "I'm ready to leave now, if you're up for it."

Dorran looked pleased. "Of course. With luck, we will be home before nightfall."

She stretched, popping some of the tension out of her back, and flinched as the bite in her shoulder flared. Dorran noticed. He reached for the jacket draped over the nearby chair and pulled the bottles of antibiotics and painkillers out of its pocket. "Here. I'll get you some water."

"I'll get it." She took the tablets he tipped into her hand and rose, rubbing sleep out of her eyes. "It would be nice to have another wash before we get back to the car."

"Good idea. Take your time."

Clare made her way across the dining area and into the hallway while Dorran began rolling up their bedding. She shut the bathroom door behind herself and squinted at her reflection. The day was early and the bulb above her felt insipid. But the sleep had done her good. She looked less haggard.

She cupped water into her hands to swallow the tablets, then turned on the hot water and shook out the still-damp hand towel. At least the ship's heater kept the rooms at a nice temperature.

Clare swayed as the floor moved under her. She frowned. Held in place by the taut rope fastened to the dock, the riverboat hadn't shifted at all the previous night. She turned the taps off and opened the bathroom door.

Down the hallway, the kitchen's light swung from the sudden

movement. She turned in the opposite direction, toward the seating area, and felt her heart skip. Beyond the rounded windows and through the blur of rain, the scenery was moving.

"Dorran?"

She jogged toward where she'd last seen him, at their bed. The space was abandoned, the blankets left in a pile on the floor. She turned in a circle, hunting for him among the old-fashioned tables and patchily painted walls.

He wouldn't have left without me. Of course he wouldn't have. He has to still be on the ship. Right?

She trusted Dorran more than any other person, but panic threatened to choke her. The boat wasn't moving fast, but it was caught up in the river's flow. Each second carried it farther from the dock and their car.

Something slammed against the door closest to the riverbank. The window was blurred by rain and Clare couldn't make out the shape on the other side. Her hands felt empty. She needed a weapon. Her fire poker was missing from where she'd left it on the table the previous night. So was Dorran's ax.

The door screeched as it was forced open faster than the runners wanted. Dorran leapt through, then slammed it shut again. Something hit the other side. A gray hand pressed into the glass. It smeared droplets away as the fingers dragged down toward the handle.

Dorran grappled with the lock, engaged it, then took a step back. He was breathing heavily and rain flattened his hair and dripped off his jaw. He didn't take his eyes off the door but held a hand out to Clare as she crossed to him. "We are not alone after all."

The door handle rattled. Through the window, Clare saw heavy-lidded eyes. They met hers, then moved to Dorran, seeming to examine them. Then the hollow stepped back, fading from sight.

"What happened?" She gripped Dorran's hand. It was cold and wet, but he squeezed back.

"I heard a noise outside. That creature was cutting through the rope. I couldn't stop it in time." He shook his head, his eyes thunderous. "I can't believe I didn't find it last night. I looked *everywhere*."

Clare slowly turned to face the bar. "Oh…oh no…"

She'd tried to open the freezer chest the night before, only to find it was locked. Now, the lid stood open, the supplies she'd placed on top scattered across the floor. The box was easily large enough for a human to huddle inside. She pictured a body curled into a fetal position, unblinking eyes staring into the darkness as pale hands held the box's lid down while Clare tried to lift it.

Dorran choked. "No. Surely it couldn't have been hiding there the entire night."

"It would have been dark, cold, and damp. Perfect for a hollow. And I put our supplies on its lid. It couldn't open the seal without knocking them to the floor and waking us. It *waited* for us to be out of the room." Clare couldn't keep still. She turned, looking across the windows, hunting for any motion between the trails of water. "How was it cutting the rope? Was it chewing through it?"

"No. It had a knife. I tried to force it overboard, but it slashed at me."

Her mouth was too dry and her voice came out raspy. "It's one of the smart ones."

Normal hollows didn't use weapons. And normal hollows didn't have the intelligence to hide through the night. It took something special to bide its time and to cut off their only escape before making any move. Their weapons had been taken, probably thrown overboard. Suddenly, the noises during the night felt a lot more ominous. Clare pressed her hand to her throat, her mind buzzing. Metal rattled behind them.

There's a second door.

The riverboat had two entrances to the lower floor on opposite sides of the ship. Focused on the place she'd last seen the hollow, Clare hadn't even thought of the second entry. The hollow must have crouched as it circled the ship; that was why she hadn't been able to see it through the windows. Clare dropped Dorran's hand and raced for the door, knocking chairs out of the way, eyes fixed on the handle as it turned.

The door rattled open before Clare reached it. She had a stark impression of the creature that stood in the entrance. He'd lost his uniform but kept the name badge. It had been pinned to his chest, the needle running through his skin, the little plastic tag bearing a bright green script: *Hello, I'm your captain, George.*

Strips of skin were missing from his chest and left arm. The shape of the scores told Clare they had come from fingernails, probably from one of his old coworkers. Naked, the skin had sunken deeply across his ribs, but his stomach was bulging. His eyes were heavy lidded, but his lips were gone, leaving him with a permanent grimace.

Clare was moving too quickly to stop her momentum. The captain lifted his hand. A serrated kitchen knife, still carrying flecks of long-dried blood, glinted in the early morning light as he stepped through the door.

There wasn't enough time to stop the collision she was set on. Clare did the only thing she could think of. She extended both hands out as she neared the captain and slammed them into his chest.

His flesh was cold. Wet from rain. Leathery. She felt each rib under her fingers, the bones hard but brittle, bumpy like broken stones.

The impact forced him back out of the door. He brought the knife down. It caught on the edge of Clare's sleeve, tearing a hole in the fabric, but didn't meet her skin.

Dorran was there before she knew what was happening. He followed up her push with his fist, connecting with the captain's jaw, sending him staggering back until he hit the railings. Clare yanked Dorran back inside and wrenched the door shut. She forced the lock into place. A second later, the handle rattled again.

"Are you hurt? Did he catch you?" Dorran grabbed Clare's hands, turning them over, examining the place the knife had snagged her shirt.

Clare shook her head. "I'm fine. But he's going to try again. Where are the other doors? How else can he get in here?"

Dorran kept his hold on her as he scanned the space. "The stairs to the second deck. I don't know how else."

Something scraped the metal behind them. They both turned to face the wall. Through the windows, all they could see were the railings, the rain, and, in the distance, the shifting riverbank. Clare knew what must be happening outside. The captain was climbing the walls.

Dorran darted to the stairs beside the bar. Metal clanged as he ascended them three at a time, and then, a moment later, the clatter grew closer as he descended again. His face was tight. "There is no lock."

"What?"

"There is only a door. The lock has been removed."

Clare dragged her fingers through her hair. "Do we... Can we..."

They had no weapons. She had no doubt that the hollow would have removed anything else they could use to defend themselves, as well. She looked toward the windows. The banks were at least twenty meters away on each side. Beyond them, shielded behind a layer of plants, were homes. Even if they swam for shore, she didn't think they would last long once they reached them.

"We'll barricade it," Dorran muttered. He snatched up one of the closest tables and dragged it toward the narrow stairwell. "Get chairs."

"Right." The dining area's chairs were all cheap wood and fake leather, but they were relatively hardy. Clare grabbed two at a time and hauled them to Dorran, who alternated stacking them with the tables. He jammed them between one another, locking them into place, and filling every gap he could reach. The door on the upper deck slammed. Dorran picked up a final table and flipped it to lean its weight against the pile. Then he stepped back, and they both stood, breathless, as they watched their barricade.

The table blocked Clare's view of the stairwell, but she could hear the captain. Each footstep reverberated off the metal. He stopped after six paces. She heard a clatter as furniture jostled, then a bang as it stuck. The table bulged out an inch as he tried to push it, then shuddered as he tried to pull. Clare exchanged a look with Dorran. A frustrated snarl echoed from the stairwell, then the door slammed again as the captain returned to the upper deck.

Dorran bent close to whisper into Clare's ear. "Wait here. Call me if he returns to the stairs."

She tried to ask where he was going, but he moved into the hallway before she could speak. Silent as a wraith, he disappeared into each door, turn by turn. Clare kept one eye on him and the other on their barricade. She couldn't hear the captain any longer.

He's smart. He hasn't tried to talk, not like Madeline did, but he remembers how to use knives, and he remembers the way around the ship. Maybe he kept part of his humanity, but not all of it.

Dorran reappeared and gave Clare a brief nod. "There are no other doors. We should be secure as long as he can't dismantle the stairwell blockade."

"Okay." Clare licked her lips, her heart hammering. "What do we do now?"

CHAPTER 39

THROUGH THE WINDOWS, THE scenery continued to change slowly but unrelentingly. One of the doors rattled, then fell silent again as the captain scoped out the remaining entrances to the paddle-boat's central area.

Dorran ran his hand over his face, wiping away the remaining raindrops. He took a moment to answer Clare's question. "We don't have access to the engine room any longer; I don't know how we can return to the car."

How far are we from it now? A kilometer? Two? How far will we have traveled before we can get to shore?

Clare blinked furiously. Of all the things she could grow attached to, she hadn't expected it to be a grimy, half-broken vehicle. But that car had saved them. It had carried them for days without complaint. Despite how precarious its repairs had felt, it hadn't failed them.

And it held most of their supplies, including the radio. Except for the blankets, food, and masks they had brought onto the ship, everything was in the hatchback.

She wanted to repeat her question. *What do we do now?* But she knew that wasn't fair. Dorran didn't have any more answers than she did.

They could try to swim to shore, but it was hard to know what they might find once they got there. In a best-case scenario, they might find an abandoned vehicle with its keys still in the ignition close by. Alternately, they could be stranded in an unfamiliar location, resourceless and weaponless, hampered by wet clothes, and surrounded by hollows. Then her mind came up with a worse scenario. The hollows might hear them swimming and crowd along the riverbank, grasping for them anytime they tried to climb up. *What would happen then? Would we be forced to swim until we drown?*

Clare's brain began to freeze with anxiety. She closed her eyes and focused on the concrete information she knew. "Eventually, the riverboat will have to hit some kind of obstacle. Maybe other boats. Maybe fallen trees that were washed into the river from the flood. They will give us a way to reach shore."

"We have our masks," Dorran said. "As long as we are cautious, we should be able to find more supplies, maybe even transport. Do you know which way the river is carrying us? Toward home, or away?"

"Um." They'd left the map in the car. Clare grimaced and tried to visualize the landscape. "Away, I think."

"Then we will hope we stop sooner rather than later."

They both looked up as the door above them slammed open. Again, the blockade rattled. Clare clenched her fists at her side until they ached. But the tables and chairs remained locked together, and after a minute, the captain left.

"We should eat," Dorran said. "If the boat becomes caught, we may need to leave immediately, and I don't know how soon the next opportunity for rest might be."

Or how much we might be able to carry with us. Clare's palms were sweaty from stress. As long as they'd had the car, she'd felt at least somewhat secure. It could shield them. It could move faster than the hollows. Home had never felt too far away. And they'd given it up for a night of comfort on a riverboat.

Dorran disappeared into the kitchen. She heard the scrape of cans being opened. Clare wrapped her arms around her torso and stood guard by the bar, alternately watching the barricaded staircase and their course through the rounded windows.

The river curved lazily, and the boat drifted near to the shore. Through the trees, Clare caught glimpses of riverside houses. Most were old and covered in chipped paint, but they were interspersed with luxury properties. The area was in the process of being modernized, and the tiny, old houses would probably have cost a lot a few weeks ago when money still mattered. Clare thought they might be drifting closer to the city, which meant more streets, more houses, and more hollows.

Please, don't run aground. Not yet.

The river straightened, and Clare released her breath as the boat's rails grazed against the riverbank and kept moving.

A body moved in front of the window, and Clare flinched. The captain had appeared, fast and silent, to block her view. One hand reached out to caress the glass. His lipless teeth seemed to be grinning, though his heavy-lidded eyes held no humor. He leaned close to the window, his breath leaving traces of condensation on the glass as he stared at Clare, rainwater dripping from his hooked nose.

She took a step back but didn't try to hide from him. She had to watch the river. Had to make sure they weren't about to become trapped.

Dorran approached her silently and passed her a bowl. It was heaped with warm porridge, canned peaches, and canned berries. Clare doubted she could finish it all, but she knew why the serving was generous. It would be their last reliable chance to eat for a while.

"I'll watch the river," Dorran said.

Clare gratefully sank into one of the chairs, facing away from the unblinking captain. She scooped porridge up absentmindedly.

They alternated watch shifts through the morning. For most of it, the captain stood outside, staring at them. Occasionally he lifted the knife and drew it across the window, letting the dulled steel scrape across the glass. Twice he left to circle the boat again, trying doors and rattling their barricade. But he always returned to the window, his sunken eyes brimming with hunger and hatred.

The cheap, old houses began to vanish, and the exclusive riverside retreats increased. Private jetties jutted into the water, sometimes with small boats attached. Once, the riverboat scraped against a dingy. Clare felt the tremors run through her feet. The *Adelaide* didn't normally venture into that part of the river, but stayed in the more scenic areas farther upstream.

They passed a tree with a human skull suspended from its lowest branch. The skull had been speared onto it, with the wood passing through under the jaw and poking out through the eye socket. Clare couldn't stop herself from wondering who it had belonged to—a human or a hollow.

Morning eventually gave way to afternoon. The boat moved painfully slowly, dragged along by the lazy current. The river was starting to swell, though, moving them faster as the fresh rain engorged it. The downpour was unrelenting.

Clare and Dorran rarely spoke. It felt wrong to disturb the rhythmic tapping of raindrops on the upper deck, the nearly inaudible sloshing of water displaced around the boat, and the quiet hum of the motor.

Then they left the outer suburbs and entered the stretch of river that passed through the city. Tall bridges arched overhead. Single-story shops became apartments, then skyscrapers. The river was wider, but more crowded.

Clare and Dorran stood side by side, staring past the leering captain to watch the boat's course. Clare pressed her hand to her throat as they bumped into an abandoned motorboat. It hadn't been moored—its owner might have been out on the river for an early-morning cruise when the city was enveloped by the quiet zone—and they knocked it free from the dock it had been snagged on.

They were still moving, but Clare didn't know if they could get through the city without becoming caught. The docks and the boats weren't the only hazard in their path. Branches, parts of swept-away houses, and even a few cars had been washed into the water from the flood. Their riverboat had a shallow base, but it was wide. All it would take was a large enough object in their path to bring them to a grinding halt.

Then what? When I imagined leaving the boat, it was in a rural area. We could have seen what was coming toward us at least. Here, even if we manage to find a car, there will be no way to drive it out of the city.

She could see glimpses of streets between the high-rises and historic buildings. They were crowded with cars, like she'd expected they would be. An unending wall of vehicles, banked up on each other, impenetrable.

Clare lifted her eyes toward the buildings. In the distance, a flash of color made her breath hitch. She leaned closer to the glass, craning her neck as the captain tried to obstruct her view. An office building had blocked her view, and already, she was beginning to doubt what she'd seen. Then the office building drifted out of the way again, and Clare saw seven blue letters perched at the top of a dark-windowed skyscraper. They would have been nearly invisible against a clear sky, but with rain clouds thick above them, the name stood out in sharp relief.

She clutched Dorran's sleeve, breathless. "Helexis."

His eyebrows drew down. "I see it."

The tower was at least four blocks away. Close, but at the same time, painfully far. Clare lowered her eyes to the streets. They were chaos. The dim early afternoon light reflected off a dozen tangled vehicles and a felled crane.

Dorran's gaze followed the same dance hers had, flicking from the tower to the street, building scenarios and running calculations in his mind.

And already, in just those few seconds, Clare felt them start to drift away from the tower. The river's flow had felt too slow when they were waiting for an escape. Now, it felt too fast. The building was four blocks away. If they waited even another minute, it would be five.

"Are we going?" Dorran asked. He was tense, his dark eyes intent.

She opened her mouth, then closed it again. Beth would have had a reason to write the message into her bunker wall. Helexis Tower might be a safe haven. It might hold other survivors who could help them, protect them.

Or it might be barren. Clare imagined running through four blocks of hollows only to meet a dead end.

But they were so close to it. So close that it almost felt like fate.

"Yes," she whispered.

Dorran snapped into motion. He darted across the boat to where they'd made their bed the night before and snatched up their jackets. "Masks," he barked, sliding one over the table for Clare to reach. "Be quick but secure it tightly. We need to find a way around the captain too."

As Clare fit the dark mesh over her face, she glanced at the hollow. He watched them, curious, head tilted. The serrated knife glittered as rain dropped over the blade. He was too smart to be fooled by the masks, she knew. "I can buy us at least a minute."

"That is all I need." He was already back at her side, fastening gloves over her hands, then bending to check her pant legs were tight around her ankles. As he stood, he slid his own mask into place. "We don't have much time. We need to go now."

Helexis Tower had fallen out of sight, masked by the myriad of buildings clustered between it and the river. Clare jogged to the door on the right-hand side of the boat, the side opposite to the tower. She unfastened the bolt and wrenched it open. The metal made a deep clattering noise as it slid along the runners, and Clare glanced over her shoulder.

The captain was already gone. She knew he must have flattened his body to the ground as he raced along the deck. She left the door open as she and Dorran bolted for the exit the captain had stood by just seconds before.

There wasn't enough time to be cautious. Clare unlocked the door and threw it open. As they stepped through, she caught sight of the captain coming through the right-hand doorway. She wrenched her door closed behind them but didn't lock it. "Try to find us a way to shore!"

The captain hit the door. She felt the handle rattle under her fingers and held it tightly. It was a gamble, she knew, but it was the only way to hold him inside the room. Locking the door would only send the captain scuttling back through the cabin and onto the deck. Instead, Clare teased him, allowing him to pull the barricade open half an inch before slamming it closed again. He was stronger than she'd expected. She had to lean her weight into the metal to keep it shut.

Dorran moved toward the ship's front in long, fast strides. It only took him a second to return with a loop of thick rope carried on his shoulder. He leaned across the railing, watching the scenery passing them by as he waited for an opportunity.

The door scraped back, and when Clare tried to shove it closed again, the latch failed to catch. The captain had thrust his knife through the gap, jamming it open. The wet blade jostled just below her elbow. *Damn it. Be quick, Dorran.*

Almost as though he could hear her, he unslung the rope, braced himself, and threw the loop. She heard a faint *thud* as it hit something, then Dorran leaned back, muscles straining, as he fought to close the gap.

The knife slid back through the door. The captain tried to replace it with a hand, but Clare slammed the door into it, crushing his fingers. He pulled the hand back inside. Clare forced the door closed and felt the latch fall into place. "Dorran!"

"Ready!" He turned back to her and stretched out a hand. Clare pushed away from the door and ran to him. He caught her up, lifted her, then together they tumbled over the side of the boat.

She took a sharp breath, then pressed her lips together, expecting an icy rush of water to surround her. Instead, they hit a dock. Even cushioned by Dorran's body, Clare had the air forced out of her and couldn't stop a cry as her shoulder jarred.

They rolled and came to a stop. Clare pried her eyes open. Dorran had caught the rope's loop on one of the dock's pillars to pull the boat within jumping distance, but without the other end secured, the vessel was already drifting away.

The captain appeared, crouched on the railing like a bird of prey, eyes flashing as he peered down at them. He looked ready to leap, but Dorran moved forward, blocking the end of the dock, hands raised in preparation to rebuff the attack. The captain's teeth parted to release a hiss, and hatred flashed through its eyes. Then, reluctantly, he slunk backward, disappearing into the ship.

Dorran waited until the boat was out of reach, then slumped back. He turned to Clare, his words a whisper that almost disappeared under the pounding rain. "Are you all right?"

"Yes." She crept to his side. They waited a moment, listening. Nothing came down the dock toward them. Nothing appeared between the buildings. Clare could only hope the rain had masked the noise of their disembarking.

The riverboat continued to drift, carrying its captain with it. Clare wondered where it would end up. Trapped somewhere downriver, perhaps. Or if it was very lucky, it might make it all the way to the ocean, carrying its loyal captain onto far rougher seas than the ship had been designed for.

Dorran's hand wrapped around her own. Even with the gloves in the way, it was a comfort. He helped her stand, then they turned toward the city and the tangle of metal and glass that hid Helexis Tower.

CHAPTER 40

CLARE'S BREATHING ECHOED INSIDE the mask. She tucked at the fabric around her neck, making sure it was tight and that none of her skin would be visible. The rain had already soaked through her jacket, and her skin crawled as icy water ran over it.

They began to move along the dock. Its end connected with a concrete platform, with stairs leading up to a brick-patterned street. That part of the city had been designed for tourism. Overpriced eateries faced the water, and a small shack nearby offered to sell tickets to a river taxi.

The area was showing its age. Water stains marked the concrete and sun exposure had discolored the eateries' signs. As they climbed onto the street, Clare saw dark stains scattered across the brown, interlaced bricks. The frenzy of the quiet zones must have caused people to spill their drinks.

No. Not drinks. Her stomach turned. *Blood.*

The stains were the only remnants of what must have been a massacre. She held Dorran's hand. He squeezed back. They couldn't risk speaking, but she was grateful to have him at her side. She didn't think she would have had the courage to step into the city otherwise.

The brick street ran along the river's edge, sometimes widening to make room for a children's play area, sometimes being encroached on by overturned plastic restaurant chairs. It felt strange to see it so empty. Straight ahead, the bricks led between two apartments to reach the first real road. There wasn't much light with the angry clouds choking the sky, and the towering apartments conspired to block out the little that there was. The walkway between them was dark enough to be night.

Dorran bent close so that she could hear his whisper over the drumming rain. "I think speed will be to our advantage. We stay together but move quickly. Agreed?"

Clare nodded. She wanted to keep holding his hand, but it would slow them down too much, so she reluctantly let go. Her fingers felt empty. She flexed them, wishing she had some kind of weapon to hold. She might find something inside the restaurants if they took the time to search them. But that carried too much risk. Every minute they were exposed only invited more danger.

Was this a mistake?

Helexis Tower was only five blocks away. She had to keep her eyes fixed on it and not look back.

We didn't have anywhere else to go. This is our best chance. Isn't it?

She was acutely aware that the tower had the ability to save them, or destroy them. They were too deep into the city to walk out intact. Five blocks to the tower was likely all they could manage, and even that was a terrible risk.

Dorran was silent at her side. She had led him farther than either of them had planned. He had never even wanted to leave Winterbourne, but he had, for her sake. Every step of the path had been her decision. Clare prayed she hadn't brought him to his death.

Their pace quickened from a walk to a jog as they crossed the stained bricks. They put their heads down as they passed between the buildings. Clare could feel their presence over her, smothering her like a heavy blanket. She hazarded a look toward the structure at her right.

Faces pressed against the windows. Emaciated bodies bobbed as the apartment's occupants, trapped inside their rooms and without enough wits to know how to open the doors, paced. They watched the two humans below them, hands slapping the glass, hungry and frustrated. Clare's eyes moved higher up the building. There were dozens of them. Never more than one per room, though. It was like what she'd seen in the cars; the hollows would hunt in loose packs in the wilderness and forest, but when trapped in close quarters, the weaker members would be eaten.

Those would have been family once. Best friends. Parents and children on a vacation, excited to visit the city, enjoying their views over the water.

She turned to face the road again, eyes burning.

Cars blocked the street. Two had crashed, their tires riding up onto the sidewalk and their crumpled hoods hanging through a store window and bending around a streetlamp.

Clare stopped at the intersection and looked in both directions. It was impossible to hear or see clearly through the rain and the mask. Motion drew her attention toward a store window, but it was only a plastic shopping bag caught on the shattered glass and swinging as the wind tugged at it.

Maybe the city won't be as bad as I thought. Maybe the quiet zone moved over it very early in the morning, and most of the hollows are trapped inside their homes.

Helexis Tower was a block to their right and five ahead, if she hadn't lost her orientation. Straight ahead, the road was littered with remnants of a broken jewelry store. A car had run through the corner window and sparkling glass shards were jammed into cracks in the road. Rings, necklaces, and bracelets, worth a small fortune, lay ignored among the once-white stands and scraps of pamphlets. Clare cautiously approached the street. Glass crunched under her boots. She stopped beside a streetlamp, scanning the environment, breathing heavily.

A hollow chattered, but the sound was muffled and came from above. One of the apartment dwellers. They turned right, circling the wreck of the car that had broken the store, and followed the sidewalk.

That road had been closed off to cars and converted into a market. Clumps of something black and sticky stuck to bright sheets of plastics—decayed flower bouquets, she thought. Clare recognized food stands, one which had been knocked over. Its deep-frying vat of oil had spilled across the road, but the worst of it had already been washed away, and what remained was turning dark as grime and grit absorbed into it. Then, past that, a collection of mannequins stood guard. A telephone booth had been set up as a kitschy changing room for a street fashion display.

The cluttered stalls made Clare anxious, but the road was free from cars. Dorran led the way, weaving between the stands. Something scraped beneath Clare's shoe. She looked down, expecting more glass, but saw she'd stepped on a gold coin. A woman's purse lay nearby, dropped mid-transaction. The markets had been open at the time the quiet zone had passed through, then.

But the streets seem deserted. Are the masks working? Did something chase the hollows away? Or are we just lucky? It feels like we've already pushed our luck as far as it will go, but I won't complain if it holds a little while longer.

Dorran's mask kept moving in steady arcs, scanning the streets, but Clare noticed he kept glancing up for a second at a time before pulling his attention back down. He hadn't seen the city before, she realized. Or any city. She didn't know what the family's Gould estate was like, but if it was as secluded as Winterbourne, his only exposure to the outside world would have been through books, stories from his uncles, and the views he had on their biyearly pilgrimage between the properties. Her heart ached for him. She wished she could have shown him the world the way it had been before the hollows.

Sticky noises rose from their shoes as they stepped through the oil. Up ahead, the mannequins blocked their path. Clare hated the way the bald heads were tilted at angles, as though listening to the rain. Hands were raised into inscrutable gestures, smooth indents marked the places their eyes belonged. Their poses were elegant, but their clothes weren't. Bohemian styles and pastel shades were discolored. They hung off their mannequins awkwardly, wet, sad, and torn. Clare wondered where the rips had come from. *Humans grasping and writhing in agony as they tasted the stinging air Madeline Morthorne talked about? Hollows scrambling after their prey?* More than half of the statues were overturned, their poses still elegantly classy as they lay facedown in the puddles.

Clare shivered as they passed the figures. They didn't have faces, but they still looked too human. Then, behind them, hinges whined. Clare froze. Their luck had run out. A low, sickeningly familiar chattering noise floated through the air.

She and Dorran turned. The changing booth, a repurposed telephone booth with blacked out windows, had an *occupied* sign hanging from the door. The wooden plaque rattled as the door swung outward.

CHAPTER 41

THE WOMAN INSIDE THE booth fixed Clare with her one remaining eye. It was bulging and red, and Clare thought she knew the cause. Sharp bony spikes, like stalactites, filled the empty socket. She'd lost her blouse and pants, but her business jacket still clung to her narrow shoulders. It flapped as she lurched forward. One leg had grown longer than the other, giving her an exaggerated limp. The bloodshot eye moved from Clare to Dorran, and the jaw widened as she chattered.

Dorran tapped Clare's forearm. It was a small touch to shake her out of her shock and get her to move. She pressed her lips together and gave a tiny nod, and together they began backing away.

The hollow took another staggering step forward. The jaw worked, and her head tilted curiously. Clare risked a glance down to check her gloves were still tucked into her jacket sleeves, and her socks covered any trace of skin. She was hidden under the layers of clothes. But the hollow was growing excited. Its chattering became louder and the jaw moved faster, swiveling in loosened sockets, as she stumbled forward recklessly.

Can it tell we're human? Can it hear our breathing? Smell us? Recognize the way we walk?

Another subtle tap from Dorran. They were backing away, but the hollow's unsteady gait was closing the gap. They needed to run. She shot Dorran a final look, wishing she could pick out some expression under the mask. He tilted his head in her direction, the only response he could give. Then they turned as one and began running.

Mannequins skittered across the street as they were kicked out of the way. The hollow howled. Through their own pounding footsteps and the steady pattering rain, Clare heard the creature's feet slapping on the ground as it chased them. Its limp gave it a distinctive, nightmarish gait. One loud smack, then a quick scrape, repeated. Clare focused on their path, squinting through the fabric, mesh, downpour, and thin fog to see their path ahead. A deep fear of becoming cornered had taken root in her.

They had to leap over a cascade of rotting fruit to escape the closed-off market street. On the main road, cars became a hazard. They had to split up to weave between the vehicles. Guttural chattering followed them. Two cars had collided ahead, hedging Clare in, and she leapt onto the hoods to slide over. Dorran reconverged with her. The hollow thudded into a car behind them, and Clare clenched her teeth as nails scraped over metal.

Up ahead, the blue *Helexis* sign loomed out of the sky. Two blocks away. A stitch was forming in Clare's side as she struggled to draw air through the wet mask. She could make it two blocks. They were close.

Close to what?

She tried not to obsess over the thought, but it was the only thing her mind could focus on. Helexis Tower might be their salvation. But it could just as easily be an abandoned building. A locked door. Or, worst of all, a tower full of nothing but hundreds of closed doors, all holding a single hollow impatiently scrabbling to be let out.

Stop thinking that. It's too late to go anywhere else. Just get to the tower. Beth had a purpose in sending you there.

In the desperate part of her mind, she imagined Beth pulling the tower doors open and beckoning her inside. She tried to tell herself it was a fantasy, that she couldn't believe Beth was still alive, that she was setting herself up for disappointment, but the idea stuck in her mind like a fiery beacon, bright and tantalizing.

They were a block closer, and the sidewalks were clear. To their right were boutique clothing stores sporting immense display windows. Clare gasped as something hit the glass. Two hollows pressed against the window. Fractures already ran across the surface from repeated beatings.

Keep running. Don't look back.

The distinctive *slap-scrape-slap* noise was now mixed with other pounding feet. She couldn't see them, but at least half a dozen of the creatures had joined in the pursuit. Some gaits were staggering. Others were long and gaining.

One block. Just one block.

She kept her eyes switching between the road under her feet and the blue letters marking their destination. Breathing was painful, a dry, tacky film developing in her throat.

They rounded the final corner. Only a four-lane road separated them from Helexis Tower. The blue letters shimmered high above them. Her eyes followed the building's length. It was dark stone, built within the last ten years and designed to be minimalistic. Hundreds of large, blank windows were the only relief in the smooth walls. Buried in the tangle of stylized architecture and classical buildings, it was plain enough to avoid almost all attention. Clare could have walked past it a hundred times without giving it a second look.

Then her gaze reached the juncture where the building connected with the sidewalk, and she choked on her own breath.

Before, she'd marveled at how empty the city was. She'd thought that perhaps the quietness had passed over it while most people were still inside their buildings or that the hollows had been killing each other.

Now, she saw she'd been wrong. The city wasn't empty. The hollows weren't dead. They had just been distracted.

The tower's base teemed like a beehive. Thousands of bodies pressed together, climbing each other, scrambling to reach the stone walls. The entire lower floor had been engulfed. An eerie noise rose from the swarm. Hands patting stone. Hands patting flesh. Rasping breaths, so many that they merged into an unending whirr.

Clare's feet faltered. She stared at the tangle, her mind freezing as shock and panic swallowed it. The nearest hollows, the ones on the fringe, turned. Eyes flashed. Jaws widened.

Dorran pulled on her hand, dragging her to the side, toward one of the shops. Clare felt the tug of fingernails snatching at her jacket as the hollow from the telephone booth caught up to them. The shock got her moving. She matched Dorran's pace as they raced toward one of the window displays. It had been a high-end accessories store, full of mannequins brandishing purses that had probably cost more than Clare's car. Dorran aimed for the window and twisted his body as he neared it. His shoulder hit first. A jangling crack rose from the glass as it shattered. Clare followed in Dorran's wake, relying on the layers of clothes and the mask to protect her from the razor-sharp edges.

She landed on the platform inside the window and staggered. Dorran still held her hand and pulled her close to keep her upright. He reached for the nearest mannequin and wrenched its arm off. Its wig went flying as it tumbled back. Dorran turned and swung the limb like a club. The hollow was already halfway through the hole he'd created. The impact was fierce enough to crack the ceramic arm and force the hollow into the shards of glass still protruding from the window's frame.

A glut of blood spilled from the hollow's face. Her business jacket trembled as she tried to squirm free, and fresh blood ran from where a jagged piece of glass cut through her cheek.

Dorran lifted the ceramic again, but he didn't need to use it. As the woman slid free from the glass, she crumpled to the ground, lifeless. Clare could guess what had happened. The cranium bones were growing out of control through the empty eye socket. They had probably already been putting pressure on the brain, and the impact had been enough to sever something important.

Dorran looked down at the mannequin's limb, crackled and marred with a splatter of red, then dropped it. He was breathing quickly and still kept a tight hold on Clare, as though he was afraid he might lose her if he didn't.

A deep, screaming howl echoed from the street. It was repeated, then joined by chattering screams. The hollows around the tower had heard the commotion. Clare could imagine the swarm turning to face them. Scrambling forward. Teeth bared, arms outstretched, riled by the smell of blood.

"We need somewhere to hide," Dorran hissed. "Somewhere defensible."

Clare was already moving. She pulled him deeper into the store, past the display stands and around the counter, which held a box of new shipments not yet unpacked. The store would have some kind of back room—something with a lock, she hoped.

The space was larger than it had looked from outside and, despite the wall-length windows, dark. She had to squint through the gloom, hunting among the stacks of displays and the deceptive shimmers from a dozen metal embellishments and chains. Glass scraped as bodies crawled through the broken window. Low, eager chatters floated through the still air.

There! A narrow door, neatly hidden behind a jewelry stand, was tucked into the back of the room. Clare ran for it. A heavy *thud* behind them told her a mannequin had been knocked over. Clare grabbed the door handle and wrenched it open. She'd only managed one step into the room when a shape lurched out of the darkness. The hollow slammed into her, knocking her back.

The light was too poor to see anything of it, except for the dirty-blond hair around its face and the knobbly fingers that scraped over Clare's mask. It had to be the store's employee, Clare thought; she'd become trapped in the storage room after retreating there during the stillness.

The impact pushed Clare backward into Dorran's chest. They both staggered. Then Dorran yanked her aside, pulling her out of the hollow's grasp. Clare hit the ground. Cold, fresh air grazed across her sweaty cheeks as the mask was jolted free. Frantic, she grabbed it and tried to pull it back on.

Dorran grunted as the woman bit into his arm. His jacket was thick, but the creature wasn't deterred. She clung on as he grappled with her.

The crowd from the street had caught up to them. As Clare tried to tuck the mask's cloth back under her jacket collar, hands wrenched it free. She gasped as something heavy landed on her chest. Dorran yelled. She couldn't see what was happening to him. Only that the room was a mess of limbs and unblinking eyes. She tried to roll away from the hands she knew would be coming for her, but they tangled in her hair and yanked her back.

Static boomed through the space. It was so sudden and so

loud that Clare's first thought was that it was inside her head—that she'd fractured her skull, maybe, or that the pain had broken something inside of her. But the hollows froze, their chattering falling quiet, their glinting eyes all flicking toward the store windows.

The static was replaced by a young girl's voice. "Please."

It was loud enough to make Clare flinch. The hollow holding her hair shrieked and its fingers loosened. The pressure on her chest relented. The voice was replaced by more static, and the chattering returned. This time, it was furious, bordering on panicked.

Something grabbed Clare's arm, and she reflexively pulled away.

"Shh," Dorran hissed, bending low over her.

The static transformed into a scraping noise. It reminded Clare of a spoon being swirled through a metal bowl. It only lasted for a second, though, and then it was replaced by the static again.

It's the radio station. The one that only plays fragments of noises. Someone's broadcasting it over the city.

The hollows around them were moving. Miserable howls filled the space as they tried to escape the noise. They bumped into each other, clawing at the walls, at the floors, and at the displays in their urgency to hide. Clare saw her mask near her foot and snatched it up. She pulled it over her head and held it in place. Dorran lifted her to her feet. He kept one arm around her as they moved through the shop.

They bumped into countless bodies. Cold, clammy, still damp from the rain. The hollows barely paid them any notice, though. The noise was painfully loud, even through the mask. A second of music, the bass shaking the floor. A second of a man's voice: "Today—" A second of howling dogs.

She and Dorran blindly pushed their way through the creatures, aiming for the broken window. As they neared it, sudden bright light burst across the street. Clare squinted but didn't stop moving. She stumbled over the windowsill, the wet glass threatening to slip from under her boots, then caught herself against the wall. She turned toward the source of the noise.

Helexis Tower stood on the opposite side of the street. A floodlight on its roof pointed down toward the boutique store. The radio station blasted from it, deafening but effective. The hollows that had been clustered around the building were scattering. Some ran wildly down the streets, others hunted for peace inside the buildings, seeking out open doors.

Someone is in there. Holding on to her mask with one hand and Dorran with the other, Clare couldn't stop grinning. *Beth knew what she was doing. It's not a dead end.*

The spotlight's angle adjusted to surround them in light. Clare held up a hand to shield her eyes, blinded. She felt Dorran squeeze her shoulder. Together, they began moving forward. It was impossible to see properly. She nearly tripped as she stepped off the sidewalk and onto the road. The spotlight followed them, surrounding them like a halo.

Hollows screamed, but the noises seemed to be growing more

distant. They were drowned out by the incessant, deafening radio. A second of laughter. A second of a classical composition. A second of a woman saying "power." Clare had thought the station was disturbing when she'd first heard it, and it still creeped her out. But she didn't stop smiling, not even when her feet got caught on the curb outside Helexis Tower. She couldn't see, but she could feel Dorran holding on to her, and she knew the tower had to be straight ahead. She reached out and touched the bronze door under her glove.

CHAPTER 42

CLARE SQUINTED HER EYES open. The floodlight's angle meant window ledges cast shadows over the tower's base. They stood at a bronze, windowless door. A bar ran across its front, and Clare pressed on it. The bar shifted a fraction, then stuck. Clare pushed harder, leaning her weight on it. The door remained locked.

Dorran turned to face the street and raised a hand to shield his eyes. She couldn't see his expression under the mask, but she could hear the tension in his voice as he yelled over the cacophony. "They are still out there."

"The hollows?"

"Yes. Most are trying to hide. But some are moving closer again."

"Damn." She tried the handle again, rattling it, then beat her fist against the door. She thought she heard something clattering on the other side. Then the bar dropped under her hands and the door swung open.

Clare sucked in a sharp breath. Through the glaring light and the mask's haze, she saw her sister waiting on the other side of the door. Beth, golden hair pulled back into a bun, dimples forming in her cheeks as she smiled, her arms held out in an invitation. Clare reached toward her. Then she blinked. There was no Beth. Inside the building stood a man.

He took Clare's outstretched hand and pulled her through the door. Dorran followed. Then the stranger shoved the door closed, enveloping them in darkness.

"One…uh, one moment."

Clare blinked furiously. After the harsh light, the building's inside was dim enough to make her blind. The windows had been blacked out, she realized. She heard the scrape of metal as the door's lock slid into place, followed by quick footsteps moving away from them.

"Clare?" Dorran asked.

She reached for him and found his hand. He gripped it tightly.

Then, suddenly, the lights above them flickered to life. Clare inched closer to Dorran as she stared about the space.

They were in a vast foyer. At their feet, marble tiles had lost some of their gloss, but none of their importance. A half dozen matching marble pillars rose up to meet the high ceiling. A reception desk—easily wide enough to hold four staff without crowding them—stood not far away. On either side of it, security gates blocked them off from the elevators and a wide stairwell.

Like Clare had guessed, the windows had been covered, some with cloth painstakingly taped over them, others with cardboard.

Comfortable waiting chairs were arranged on a thick rug, and modern paintings—the kind that were mostly shapes and splashes of color, not pictures—had been arranged tastefully over the otherwise-empty walls.

The broadcast continued to boom, but it was mercifully muffled inside the building. Clare hunted for their companion and found him near the reception desk. Everything in the foyer seemed sleek and discreet, expect for the black wires running to a laptop resting on top of the desk. The man bent over the computer, clicking feverishly. The radio abruptly fell silent. A second later, a whine came from outside as the spotlight was shut off.

After being drowned by noise, the silence was almost overwhelming. Clare took a deep breath and heard it echo in the cavernous room.

The man straightened and turned toward them, hands clasped ahead of himself, and Clare was finally able to see him clearly.

He stood a little taller than her but couldn't have been over thirty, she thought. Bronze hair was brushed into a tidy side part, though it was reaching the point where it needed a trim, and strands had been knocked out of their careful arrangement. He wore a crisp white shirt and beige jacket, both a few sizes too large. Pale skin and sloped shoulders made him seem much less threatening than he might have otherwise been.

A nervous, frightened smile cracked his face, and Clare thought she saw moisture shining in his gray eyes. "You came."

Clare didn't know what to say. She was acutely aware that she was dripping all over the elegant marble floor. In the back of her mind, she kept hunting for signs that there were more people in the tower—noises, the sound of footsteps, voices—but all she heard was silence.

The stranger unclasped his hands, then pressed them back together again, swallowing thickly. "Uh, may I, if you don't mind... Could I see your faces?"

Clare realized she was still wearing her mask. She pulled it off and brushed wet hair away from her forehead. A second later, Dorran removed his.

The stranger's smile widened, his eyes creasing nearly closed, and he stepped forward. Before Clare knew what was happening, arms were around her, pulling her into a fierce hug. Ragged breathing filled her ear. It had been a long time since Clare had felt contact with a human other than Dorran, and her instincts were to flinch back. At the same time, her subconscious wanted to lean forward. They had found another human. And that was something incredibly rare in this new world.

Dorran made a faint noise in the back of his throat and reached toward Clare, but before he could do anything, the man let go. He held his arms towards Dorran, who had no chance to react before he was pulled into a hug of his own. Shock flickered over his face. He sent Clare a desperate, confused glance, then awkwardly reached up to pat the man's back.

"You're here." The stranger only came up to Dorran's shoulders, and the words were muffled in his coat. Then the man stepped back, his face damp from their clothes, but his grin as wide as ever. "I was starting to give up hope—thank you. Thank you so much."

"I…" Clare felt lost. She didn't know what they were being thanked for, but the man had obviously been expecting someone. The idea that they were about to disappoint him made her nervous. She latched on to the question that had been lingering at the forefront of her mind. "Is…is anyone else here? Anyone by the name of Beth?"

"Oh, no, sorry. Just me." The man knit his hands together, his smile twitching. "Were you hoping to meet up with someone here?"

Clare's throat was tight, so she only nodded. She'd known Beth was gone. That had been obvious since the moment she stepped into the bunker and saw the pool of congealed blood saturating the floor. And, despite all of that, she'd held on to the tantalizing hope beyond all reason. Part of her wished she'd never been forced to find out the truth. She choked, and Dorran's hand found her arm, but she refused to let herself cry.

"Ah, gee, wow. I'm sorry." The infallible smile finally dropped. "Well, they might still be coming. Don't give up hope. That's the real killer in this world. You've got to stay optimistic, stay hopeful, no matter what, right? Heaven knows it's been hard enough these past few weeks. Some days I just wanted to sit down with a bottle of whiskey and let the despair eat me. But I knew someone had to come eventually. And you did. Here you are." He folded his arms over his chest as the grin broke out anew. "You really came. Sorry…I still can't get over it."

Clare glanced up at Dorran. He met her gaze. His expression was placid. She recognized it—he'd worn the same face when she'd first arrived at Winterbourne. At the time, he'd seemed distant and cold. But now she knew better. He wasn't calm—the opposite. He had no idea what to do or say when confronted with a stranger, and to compensate, his every movement and expression became guarded.

Clare took a slow breath to calm her heart. She had lost Beth. But Helexis Tower hadn't been entirely a false hope. They were safe—at least for that moment. She made her tongue move. "Were you waiting for someone?"

"Well, no. I mean, I was. But not someone specific." He bounced on his feet, his brown eyes switching between Clare and Dorran. "*Anyone*. Just someone who would hear me and brave the city. I knew it was a big risk. Not a lot of people would be prepared to try it. That's why I had the loudspeakers and flood-light hooked up and ready. If I'd known you were coming, they would have been running sooner. I only realized you were out there when the hollows started screaming. Lucky I didn't take a nap, huh? I guess you heard my message?"

Clare frowned. "Your message?"

"To know to come to the tower? Or were you in the city for another reason?"

"Um." Another glance at Dorran. "Actually, we read the address. It had been scratched into a bunker wall. We had no idea what we would find here."

He chuckled. "Unorthodox. But hey, it worked, I guess? You came here, and that's all I'd hoped for."

A low, soft chattering noise came from behind Clare. She flinched and swiveled. At the same time, Dorran put a hand out and swept Clare behind himself. The room remained empty.

"It's okay! Don't worry!" The man lowered his voice and extended both hands, palm out, as though trying to pacify them. "They're outside. They can't get in. At least, they haven't so far."

Dorran slowly relaxed his guard. The scratching sounded closer than it was. Clare would have thought having covers over the windows would be comforting, but in reality, it left her feeling unsettled. She hated not being able to see the hollows— how many there were, how close they were. The chattering was growing louder. She suspected most of the dispersed creatures were returning now that the radio and spotlight were off.

"I'm sorry, I'm doing a really awful job as a host, aren't I?" The man broke into a nervous chuckle. "I'm Peter. Dr. Peter Wiesner."

Clare finally pulled her eyes away from the shrouded windows. "Doctor?"

"One of the theoretical ones. Not a medical doctor, I'm afraid."

"Oh. Uh, I'm Clare. And this is Dorran."

"Pleasure to meet you." Peter loped forward, hand outstretched, and shook Clare's, then Dorran's. His fingers were warm and shaking. From nerves or excitement, Clare wasn't sure. "Look at you; you're drenched. You must be freezing. And probably exhausted and hungry too. Let's go upstairs. It's going to be a lot more peaceful than down here. And I can get you some dry clothes. Nothing glamorous, but it'll be better than what you have."

Clare gave Dorran a final glance, checking he was happy

to travel deeper into the tower. He was already watching her, waiting for her decision. He sent her a small smile, and Clare returned it. Peter was already moving toward the reception desk, so they followed.

"Hey, Peter." Clare wrapped her arms around her chest as they crossed the vast, sparsely decorated foyer. "What is this place?"

Peter stopped beside the reception, where he'd set up his laptop. He took a moment to power it down, then slowly turned to face them, fingers knit, smile unsteady. "Well…it used to house a lot of businesses. It was a bit of a hub. But it holds a special significance for the current state of the world. I guess you'd call it ground zero."

Clare faltered. "You mean…"

"Yeah. It all originated here. The stillness, the monsters…" Peter took a breath and pulled a smile back onto his face with obvious effort. "I'll tell you everything. But let's get you somewhere safe and warm first. Follow me."

CHAPTER 43

AS PETER PICKED UP the laptop, a loud, screeching wail echoed from outside the building. The front door rattled, and Peter tucked the laptop under one arm. "You don't need to worry. The tower's secure. Well, relatively. There are some hollows inside but they're all locked in rooms. Those guys on the street don't ever leave, but when you get to the upper floors, you can't really hear them much anymore."

Peter stopped beside one of the security gates and pulled an ID card suspended from a lanyard from under his jacket. He swiped it over the reader, which beeped and flashed green. The gates swept back and Peter ushered them through before they closed again.

"You have power?" Clare asked.

"A generator. I've been restricting what it feeds juice to. No matter what I tried, I couldn't turn off the security system, so it's been leeching power. The elevators are out of service, though, so we need to take the stairs. Sorry." His smile was apologetic. "You've probably already done a lot of walking today. Do you think you could manage another twelve floors?"

"Just as long as we're not being chased," Clare said.

Peter laughed. "I like your spirit."

Dorran ran his fingertips across the marble walls as they started climbing. The stairwell was wide and elegant, an echo of the foyer. Every second landing opened into a new corridor with its own set of doors, each with a little plaque set beside it.

"Best to stay away from rooms you don't know," Peter said. "Some of them contain hollows. You can usually tell which ones because of the noise, but sometimes they're silent, and that can be an unpleasant surprise. I've locked all of their doors, though."

Clare gave a slow nod. She was feeling faintly dizzy, and not because of the stairs.

Is he telling the truth? Is this where the stillness spread from? She tried to swallow, but her throat was too dry. She already knew the disease wasn't infectious—if it was, she would have felt its effects weeks before—but she still felt itchy just touching the bronze railing.

She'd listened to all of the wild theories being bantered across the radio, but Clare had never believed she would find out the cause of the world's destruction. It had felt like something that was meant to be abstruse. Like black matter, it was a concept that wasn't ever supposed to be in the hands of average people.

Though…in this stillness, is anyone average? We all survived the end of the world. We're all remarkable in some way or another.

A hundred questions crammed themselves into her brain, but strangely, she was reluctant to pull any of them out. The idea of knowing more about the disease was frightening. She dreaded what the answers might mean for humanity's future.

As they passed the fourth floor, she began to shiver. Outside had been cold, but inside the building was worse. It didn't have heating and still clung to the chill from the snows. The exercise kept her core warm but didn't do much for her numb fingers.

The higher she climbed, the more she began to dislike the tower. It was too clinical, bordering on hostile. In some ways, it felt like Winterbourne's opposite. Winterbourne had never been welcoming, but it had held an excess of hostile emotions and passions. Helexis held none.

"Here we are!" Peter skipped as he came off the twelfth floor's landing. He nodded to the passageway ahead of them. "I've been living here. We have food and water, and the heater's running. It's not exactly homey, but, uh, I hope you'll make yourselves at home anyway."

Clare read the plaque by the stairs as she passed it. *Aspect Laboratories.* "You said you were a doctor?"

"I have a doctorate in molecular sciences. My dissertation caught the attention of Aspect, the company that owns this part of the tower, and I was given a grant to explore surgical advancements for eighteen months. Basically, they gave me office space, equipment, and money to live off. In return, they owned part of anything I created here and would theoretically make bank if I developed anything impressive." He laughed.

Clare felt faintly nauseated. She forced the words out. "Did your team…?"

"The stillness? No. I wasn't involved in it." He stopped beside a thick metal door and rested his hand on it. "But I know how it happened. It's a long story. Let's get you dry and fed first, all right?"

Clare mutely nodded.

The ID badge came out again and Peter swiped over the black box beside the handle. A quiet beep, a green light, then Peter shoved the door open and stood back for them to enter. "Well, here we are. The closest thing I have to home now."

The room was larger than Clare had expected. It wrapped along that half of the tower in a rectangular shape, with close to twenty windows overlooking the city. Most of the blinds had been closed or angled so that light could come in but the occupants couldn't look out. She could guess why. Spending weeks staring down at the mass of hollows surrounding you would be a poor way to live.

Furniture had been arranged in the area haphazardly. Desks were propped against walls or standing free in the room's center, most holding dead laptops, stacks of binders, and reams of notepaper. A kitchenette stood against the back wall with a jumble of mismatched couches arranged into a circle nearby. Bookcases had been stacked anywhere there was room. Most held textbooks and hefty nonfiction titles, but Clare was surprised to see an odd assortment of novels and board games mixed into them. Evidence that the room had been lived in was everywhere. Jackets and scarves hung over the backs of chairs. A pillow had been unceremoniously stuffed between a computer monitor and the painted brick wall. Chip bags and candy wrappers—the kind she expected to come out of vending machines—lay across the floor.

"Sorry," Peter mumbled as he kicked an empty chip bag under a desk. "Bit messy."

Clare tucked a strand of wet hair behind her ear. "It's not what I expected. For a lab, I mean."

"Oh, yeah, this is just our work area. The actual labs are on the floor above us. It's much more, eh, official up there. This is just where we developed our ideas. Or came to relax." Peter opened a cupboard near the door. "Aspect was pretty accommodating. They believed that the best ideas came from environments with no boundaries, so they let us get away with a lot. There are bathrooms and showers on the opposite side of the hallway, along with bunks for anyone who needed to spend the night here. Intended for time-sensitive projects, but of course a few of us were lazy enough to just live here."

Inside the cupboard was a medley of clothes. On one side were lab coats and white tank tops. On the other was what Clare could only imagine were lost-and-found items, including scarves and rain jackets. She glimpsed a man-sized purple onesie with rabbit ears. Peter quickly shoved it aside and dug through the lab coats. "All right…this should fit you, I think." He tossed a tank top and coat into Clare's arms, then squinted up at Dorran. "Big guy, aren't you? Try this. It'll probably fit. Tell me if it doesn't."

Dorran wordlessly accepted the clothes.

Peter ducked past them and dug through the stacks of paper

on one of the desks. "We weren't supposed to leave these lying around, but people did. Never thought I'd be grateful for lousy standards, eh?"

He held out two of the lanyards. Clare took the one offered to her. It displayed the photo of a red-haired, plump man named Michael Billings. She glanced at Dorran's. His was from Pauline Rosch.

"Bathrooms are this way." Peter pulled the door open and pointed to the signs on the opposite side of the hall. "There are showers if you want. Towels in the cupboards. We don't have any hollows on this floor, so you don't need to worry about that. I'll go foraging for some food. Just let yourself back in when you're ready."

Without waiting for a response, he turned to the stairs and began jogging down, his bronze hair bouncing with each step. Clare watched him disappear, the lab coat draped over one arm and the ID badge clasped tightly in the other. She glanced at Dorran and lowered her voice. "He's a bit of a whirlwind, isn't he?"

Dorran looked exhausted. He glanced down at the clothes he held. "I'm not *that* big."

Behind them were two doors: one for the women's bathroom, one for the men's. Clare nodded to the nearest door, the women's. "Can we stick together? I don't really want to be alone in this place."

"Yes. Please."

The door beeped as Clare used her badge to let them in. The bathroom was spacious bordering on excessive, with a larger shower than the one in Clare's old home, a double vanity unit, and a vase holding fake and slightly dusty flowers. Clare put her clothes on the sink, then went digging through the cupboards for towels.

"Are you okay?" Dorran leaned his hip against the sink's edge, his dark eyes following Clare's movements.

"Yeah." It was a lie, but one she felt compelled to cling to. In reality, Clare's insides were in turmoil, tied up so tightly that she felt like she might be sick. She'd installed so much hope into the tower—hope about what it might hold and what it might mean—that the reality felt like a punch to the stomach. There was no colony of survivors, just one man. No forming resistance, just a monolithic tomb. No Beth. No *hope*.

Dorran took Clare's hand, lifted it, and tenderly kissed its back. Then he used it to pull her closer and wrapped her in a hug.

"I know I shouldn't have gotten my hopes up." She mumbled the words into his wet jacket, not even sure if he could understand her. "Of course Beth didn't make it here. I just…"

"I know. It still hurts."

Clare blinked burning tears back. She refused to let them fall. Dorran needed her to be strong. But now that she had time to collect her thoughts, they were turning in a dark direction. The tower was surrounded. "Dorran…how are we going to leave?" She closed her eyes. "*Can* we leave?"

He didn't immediately answer. All Clare could hear were the faint hum of the lights and the irregular drip of water hitting the tile floor. Then he exhaled. "I do not have any answers. But don't give up hope. We are safe for the moment. We can rest. And if this man is to be trusted, we will know more soon. I do not think he wanted company here simply because he was lonely. There must be some greater purpose. Hold on to hope, my darling."

Clare nodded. Dorran pulled back just far enough to kiss her lips. The kiss was soft and lingering, and for those few seconds, Clare let herself fall into the sense of security he gave her. She and Dorran separated reluctantly and turned to getting dry.

They faced away from each other as they rushed to undress and get into the new clothes. That floor felt warmer than the ground level, but Clare was still shivering by the time she tied off her new crisp white pants. She pulled the lab coat over the tank top and glanced at herself in the mirror. If she'd had a pair of glasses and her hair had been dry and tied back, she would have looked like she'd stepped out of a pharmaceutical ad.

Dorran buttoned his own coat. He pulled off the impression better than Clare did, with his dark hair swept back and his heavy brows. He flashed her a tired smile and picked up their wet clothes.

Clare collected their waterlogged boots. "Ready?"

"Ready."

Barefoot, they left the bathroom. Clare used her badge to let them back into the main office area.

Peter stood by the circle of comfy seats and waved as he saw them. "You can hang those clothes anywhere to let them dry. Then come on over. We have a radiation heater. And the finest food that level four's vending machines could supply."

Despite the stress and exhaustion, Clare managed a chuckle.

There was something infectious about Peter's enthusiasm. She helped Dorran drape their old clothes over the backs of chairs and spare corners of desks. As she approached the couches, Clare felt the heat rolling off an old heater and stretched her hands toward it. The coffee table in the middle of the circle held a stack of food, including, to her delight, four apples.

Peter saw her staring, picked one up, and tossed it to her. "They're a little old and going mushy, but still good. You've probably been living off long-life food, right?"

Clare nodded as she clasped the apple in both hands and took a bite. It had lost most of its crispness. She didn't care. It was food and hadn't come out of a can or a bottle. She thought she could eat a dozen of them without stopping.

Peter tossed a second apple to Dorran, then dropped into one of the seats and pulled his legs up under himself. Dorran turned the apple over in his hands but didn't try to eat. He chose a double seat a little separated from Peter, and Clare took her place beside him. The radiation heater was close enough that she could stretch her legs out and warm her toes. She finished the apple in seconds.

"There's a trash can just behind you," Peter said, pointing over her shoulder. "We've got to be careful with waste. No garbage man to take out the trash, no cleaners to come through and sanitize the place... I don't know how long I might be living here. I've got to be careful not to turn it into a toxic wasteland. All it would take is a minor rat infestation and life could become very unpleasant."

"Right." Clare threw her core into the trash, then took a tissue from the table to dry her fingers. "I guess that's the kind of thing we need to think about these days."

"Exactly. It's amazing how busy my days can become with mundane tasks I took for granted before. I keep all of the trash locked in one room on a different floor. My work area has to stay hygienic."

Clare glanced behind them, where chip bags were still littered between the desks.

"Hah! All right, except for that." Peter rubbed the back of his neck. "In my defense, it's not mine. I can't bring myself to clean up my coworkers' areas. I lived with those people for the last year, and now, their clutter is one of the few parts of them I have left. I could have this room spotless...clear off the laptops and discarded jackets and trash...but that would be like erasing them from existence. And I can't make myself do it. Not just yet." He continued to smile, but his lips twitched.

They were circling around the most important subject—the quiet zones. The hollows. Clare did her best to ease them toward it in a gentle way. "Were many of you in the tower when...*it* happened?"

"Not many. To be completely honest, I was one of the lazy ones who lived here instead of driving home each night. So I was in the tower when everything went south. But most of my coworkers were at home or on their morning commute." He took a deep breath and folded his hands in his lap. "You'll want to know how it happened. It's a bit of a story, so settle in."

CHAPTER 44

CLARE LEANED FORWARD IN her seat. Dorran stayed perfectly still at her side, but she knew he was no less attentive. Peter turned his eyes toward the ceiling. He licked his lips and was silent for an agonizing minute as he collected his thoughts. When he started his story, his smile was shaky.

"So, you know a bit about Aspect Laboratories. It liked to pluck the brightest minds fresh out of university and give them eighteen months to prove their worth to the company. All expenses paid and complete freedom to do whatever we wanted, within certain ethical constraints, of course. At the end of eighteen months, we were released if our results were underwhelming. But people who performed well were given full-time positions at the company. Often very lucrative ones. Being picked for the program was the dream for a lot of students in the medical science field. It was seen as *the* place to be if you wanted to make a difference."

Peter picked up a bottle of water. He cracked the seal on the lid but didn't drink from it. Instead he screwed and unscrewed the top repeatedly. A nervous tic, Clare thought. He needed something for his hands to do.

"Nine out of ten students never amounted to much. Eighteen months sounds like a lot of time, but it's really not, and it's easy to fritter away on busywork if you're not disciplined. Aspect relied on the one out of ten who discovered something or invented something that would go on to make them millions. For a program that was largely unsupervised, it was surprisingly lucrative for them. I was given a grant for my thesis on robotics. I was trying to develop an artificial eye. Something that would provide feedback to the brain. Not proper sight—that's still a few years away. But my prototypes could feed in a sense of color, shapes, and lights."

"Couldn't you just"—Clare shrugged—"put a camera in there?"

Peter laughed good-humoredly. "That sounds like a great idea, huh? But the hard part is actually hooking it into the brain. And finding a way to make it comfortable and safe for daily use. While some parts of it were artificial, I found the product needed to be made from mostly biological material. But that's beside the point. My artificial eye probably won't ever see the light of day now."

He sighed through his nose as he turned the bottle over in his hands. "There were sixteen of us in the program at a time. I liked most of my coworkers. A lot of them were pretty eccentric. It's a cliché to say madness is just the other side of genius, but I think that's sometimes true. There was one guy, Bobby, who was given a permanent position in the company about six months ago. He created a new strain of antibiotics. Created, not found! The implications of that alone were immense. But the guy was one of the most disgusting individuals I've ever met. He kept a foot bath under his desk and used it constantly. But he never cleaned the water out. He just topped it up every other day. Each morning he came in, turned it on, and poked his feet into this disgusting slime of weeks-old foot soup. We used to joke that the antibiotic came out of that primordial sludge."

A flash of fondness passed over Peter's face, then faded. "Well, I had one coworker who seemed bound for great things. Ezra Katzenberg. He entered the program at the same time as I did, and I guess we became something like friends. We used to talk about our projects, use each other as sounding boards, commiserate, and celebrate, that sort of thing. He was intensely passionate. And I really thought he'd be one of the ones who got their name into the history books. His area of focus was molecular science. Specifically, molecular cures. You've heard of nanobots, right?"

Dorran was silent. Clare did her best to fill him in without making it obvious. "Tiny machines that can enter the body, right?"

"Pretty much. They were supposed to be the future of medicine. Microscopic robots that travel through our blood and tissue and repair a whole host of issues. Ezra got his grant for a thesis on nanobots. When he entered the program, he was working on a model that was supposed to be one of the first viable prototypes. Its whole purpose was to clear blood clots out of arteries. Basically, you injected tens of thousands of the nanobots, and they would travel through the vessels, searching for blockages. When they found one, they broke up the clot without the need for surgery. It would have been a huge leap forward for how hospitals responded to strokes and could replace the need for stents."

Clare glanced at Dorran. He still clasped the apple as he listened attentively. This world had to be painfully foreign to him, but he was absorbing everything Peter said.

Peter tilted his head back to rest it against his seat. "Ezra's biggest issue was that he couldn't duplicate the nanobots with any kind of cost-effectiveness. He needed thousands of them for each trial, and the costs were blowing out of control. A hospital's not going to pay forty grand for one dose of nanobots, no matter how effective they are. He was working on a few methods to bring the cost down. He just needed time. But, well, Saul got there first."

"Saul?"

"He was the black sheep. No one knew what he was working on, only that it had to do with advancements in surgery. For the eleven months Ezra had been developing his clot nanobots, Saul had been watching in secret and developing his own strain. He borrowed many of Ezra's discoveries to leapfrog his own research forward. And he found a way to make them cost-effective first." Peter shook his head. "He took them to the commissioners and graduated from the grant program."

Clare leaned forward. "But that's got to be illegal, right? Couldn't Ezra contest it?"

"Oh, he tried. I watched Ezra beat his fists against that metaphorical wall for weeks. Saul had been careful about how he adopted the stolen ideas. There was no direct proof of theft, so he could argue they developed their ideas independently. And Aspect…well, if we're being honest, they didn't so much care about what was sacrificed during the developmental stage as long as finished products made it to the market."

Clare glanced across the long room. So many people working so close together, sharing ideas, brainstorming… She could imagine intellectual theft would be not just easy, but common.

"Ezra didn't take it well." Peter scratched his scalp, knocking the carefully combed hair askew. "Not only was another man getting the glory for his hard work, but he was facing the end of his grant period with nothing to show. And people who flunk out of Aspect's program tend not to have good careers afterward, you know? By that point, he only had five months left. The rest of us all thought it was the end for him."

Peter finally pulled the cap off the bottle properly, took a drink, then rescrewed it and threw it back onto the table. In the distance, thunder crackled. Clare was suddenly grateful that the blinds on the windows were closed. She didn't want to watch the storm as it grew.

"Ezra spent a week away from the tower. To be honest, I was a little shocked when he returned. I'd thought he was gone for good. But when he walked through the door, he exuded a manic kind of energy. 'I know what to do,' he said as he started up his computer. I don't think he left it for nearly three days straight, survived off of energy drinks and coffee. There were plenty of workaholics among our group, but he outperformed the lot of them. It was like…" Peter waved a hand. "Like a religious experience for him. It wasn't about revenge. It wasn't about getting a position at Aspect. It was…*more*. As though he'd been given a purpose in life."

Clare frowned. "What was he making?"

"I was the only one who knew." Peter leaned a little closer and lowered his voice, as though the secret was still too sacred to share. "He didn't trust anyone else in the office. He'd been burned once by being too open, and it had made him paranoid. But he told me."

Thunder rumbled again. It was growing closer. The radiation heater seemed to have lost some of its warmth. Clare shivered and felt for Dorran's hand. He took it and threaded his fingers between hers.

"It was a step beyond his original nanobot creation." Peter's eyes were bright. "It was *biological*. He managed to make a machine that could replicate itself. It harvested carbon and metabolites from the air and multiplied, growing and splitting like a cell. It solved the cost issue. There *was* no cost. Give it fuel and it did all the work itself. That alone would have earned him a career at Aspect. But he didn't stop there. He didn't want to *just* create self-replicating machines. He wanted to save humanity."

"Save…" Clare's mouth was dry. She thought she could hear

it again: the scratching, the scrabbling, the noise of a thousand creatures clawing at the base of the tower.

Peter's shoulders sagged as he exhaled. He looked at his feet, his fingers interlaced but held limply so that they drooped. "I knew Ezra. He wasn't trying to…make *this*. He really, truly thought he was saving humanity. Free healthcare for third-world countries. Salvation for the terminally ill. He wasn't doing it for the glory. He did it because he believed it was what the world needed."

Lightning sparked through the slats in the blinds, streaking across the floor. Clare knew she was holding Dorran's hand too tightly. "What did he do?"

"He called them thanites. That's from the Greek *thávma*. Miracle. They activated our own stem cells and were supposed to regrow and repair anything that had been damaged. Teeth. Lost limbs. Surgically removed organs. Dementia. Anything."

Clare blinked, and she saw the waking nightmare she'd been living in. All of the hollows they had encountered. Excess skin. Excess limbs. Too many joints. Painfully human, and yet so desperately removed from their humanity.

"It went wrong. It wasn't supposed to leave the lab. But it got out somehow. On the sole of a shoe. On the hem of a lab coat. Somehow, one of the thanites was taken out of isolation, and once outside, it did what it was designed to do. It began to multiply."

In the distance, Clare thought she heard one of the creatures wail. She squeezed her eyes closed.

"Ezra didn't realize." Peter rubbed the back of his hand across his eyes, a quick, angry motion. "The thanites were small enough to be invisible. Designed to be dormant until activated. Without anyone knowing, they spread, and spread, and spread. From what I've calculated, it would have taken them about two months to populate the entire globe. Blown over oceans by the wind. Carried in airplanes. They are attracted to, and utilize, compounds that humans breathe out. They need carbons to grow, and those exist everywhere, but the thanites are designed to flourish in a human-heavy environment by utilizing metabolite combinations that are unique to us. That meant the thanites naturally clustered in places where humans lived—cities, towns, communities. Then, nearly a month ago, they were activated."

Lightning exploded directly over them, and the following thunder was deafening. She tried to reel her thoughts back in. When the stillness caught up to her, she'd been just inside Banksy Forest, an area far secluded from human habitation. Dorran would have been near the forest's other side, having left his family's camper hours before. They had both grazed dangerously close to thanite exposure. "So…Dorran and I weren't effected… because we were in a remote area when it happened. Because there weren't any people around, and that meant there weren't any machines in the air to infect us either."

Peter's smile was sad. "Are you hurt? I can see a bandage on your shoulder."

Clare glanced down at it. The off-white bandages, still damp, were visible under the lab coat. She licked her lips. "What—"

"Take the bandage off."

"I don't—"

Peter's smile remained unchangeable. "Just take the bandage off."

Slowly, numb fingers fighting against the movement, Clare pulled at the tape edging the bandages, and peeled the material off. Underneath were red marks left by hollow teeth. The skin had knit together and begun to scar.

"That's, what, a few days old?" Peter tilted his head to the side, and Clare was suddenly hit by the impression that his smile was empty, devoid of any feeling. "Normal cuts don't heal that fast. You didn't escape the thanites. No one did."

CHAPTER 45

CLARE COULD BARELY HEAR the storm through the ringing in her ears. She stood. The impulse to run was overwhelming, but there was nowhere to run *to*. Sickly heat rushed through her. She staggered to the trash and threw up.

Shaking, sweaty, she reeled back from the plastic container and was caught by warm arms. Dorran held her up even when her legs wouldn't.

She turned her head and saw the marks on her shoulder. A frantic terror gripped her. She dug her fingernails into the healing skin. "Get them out."

"Clare!" Dorran grabbed her hands, pulling them away.

Blood beaded in the cut she'd reopened. But it wasn't enough. She thrashed, trying to break free from Dorran's hold. "Get them out! *Get them out!*"

The hollows were all she could see. Saliva slick over distended jaws. Eyes missing lids. Ribs poking through their side, rubbing against raw flesh with every movement. It was coming for her.

"Get them *out*!" Her hand was slick with blood, and she wrenched it out of Dorran's. She twisted just far enough that he couldn't capture it again, then began digging.

"No!" Dorran slammed her into the ground. He lay over her, using his weight to pin her, holding her hands at her sides.

The impact was rough enough to shake some of the wildness free. Clare lay still, face pressed against Dorran's shoulder, shaking violently as she struggled to breathe. The pain in her shoulder began to make itself felt. She scrunched her face up but it wasn't enough to stop the tears.

Peter swore quietly. She heard him jog across the room and open a closet.

"Clare." Dorran waited a second, then shuffled up, resting his weight on his elbows so that he could look down at her. "Focus on me."

She didn't think she could speak, so she nodded.

Dark eyes flicked to her shoulder, then returned to search her face. "If I let you up, will you leave it alone?"

Another nod. Shame was coming in to mingle with the horror. Dorran waited for another second, then loosened his hold on her arms. Clare pulled them close to her body. The impulse to scratch at her skin was maddening. She could feel them inside of her—the machines, floating through her blood, burrowing into her bones. They itched.

What kind of changes are they making, hidden under my skin? In

361

her mind's eye, she saw hairs sprouting around her lungs. Teeth growing between her organs. Flaps of skin developing around her brain, pressing into it, crushing it.

She clenched her teeth as shivers ran through her. Dorran shifted to sit at her side, one arm at her back to hold her steady. A second later, a blanket was draped around their shoulders. Then Peter crouched beside them, unscrewed the cap from a bottle of water, and held it out to Clare.

"I'm so sorry." He looked like he meant it. Sweat speckled his forehead, which looked even paler than normal. "I was so eager to tell my story I didn't even think about how it might affect you."

"Please get them out." She'd promised Dorran she wouldn't dig anymore, but her fingers twitched, desperate.

"You…" He hesitated, seeming to weigh his answer. "Look, it's not going to be bad for you. You're not going to become like *them*. I'm really sorry. We can't get rid of the thanites once they're inside you. But they're in *everyone*. Me, you, everyone else out there, even your terrifying friend here. It's just a case of how badly."

Peter still held the water bottle out for her. He shook it, eyebrows raised. Her throat burned from the sickness. She hesitantly took the water and swallowed as much as she thought her stomach could handle.

"Wherever you were when the stillness hit, it must have been somewhere with a sparse thanite population." Peter rocked back on his heels, forearms braced over his knees. "You probably have less than a hundred thousand in you."

Clare choked on the water.

"Which is nothing!" Peter held his hands up, pacifying. "Those blighters out there? They have tens of millions. Maybe billions, for the worst ones. That's why they're becoming twisted from it. Millions of thanites, all trying to repair damage, all creating fresh damage with their overeagerness, then trying to repair that in an escalating spiral of disaster. You... Whatever you have is small enough that it's not deforming you. It's behaving more like it was supposed to. Repairing actual injuries."

"What about..." She swallowed and sat up straighter. Dorran rubbed her back, comforting. "What about inside? Could it be... growing...stuff where I can't see it?"

"Eh. Who knows." Peter glanced toward Dorran and cleared his throat. He quickly amended, "But almost certainly not. If you can't see anything on the surface, you're probably fine. Absolutely."

Clare looked up. Dorran's chin rested near her temple. His expression was murderous as he glared at Peter. It had been a long time since Clare had thought of Dorran as frightening, but Peter didn't know him like she did. *Even your terrifying friend there.*

"Look, how about we get you sat up?" Peter rolled to his feet. "We'll stop that bleeding and get you something else to eat. Something with lots of sugar."

"I don't need that." Clare pressed her eyes closed. "I just need to understand this."

"Sure, of course you do. But we can talk *and* not drip blood on the carpet at the same time, eh?" He winked at her, but Clare couldn't muster the energy to laugh. She let Dorran help her up, though. He moved her back on the couch and wrapped the blanket around her. Peter jogged to one of the cupboards near the door and searched through its contents.

Dorran nestled himself at Clare's side, one arm around her back, the other holding her hand in his. He stared at her shoulder, which oozed fresh blood.

"Sorry," she mumbled.

Dorran bent close so that only she could hear him. "Don't apologize for being human. If you want to know the truth, I was close to doing the same."

Peter reappeared beside them. He held a kit—plastic, modern, and larger than the one Dorran had kept in Winterbourne. He flipped the lid open and settled it onto the table, beside the pile of snack food.

"You're a couple, right?" He pulled his chair closer. "That's nice. It's good to see...I guess you'd call it *life*. Sounds awfully miserable, though, right? As though it's a surprise to see people being happy. I'm glad you are, though. D'you want to take care of this, big guy?"

Dorran mutely took the cloth from Peter and pressed it over the tear on Clare's shoulder. She flinched but didn't complain as he applied pressure.

Clare's brain felt as though it had been put on ice. Thoughts were frozen there, painful but refusing to budge. She took a stuttering breath. "Is it going to get worse?"

"Hah. I have no idea." Peter pulled his legs back under himself.

"Right now, I'm really just taking each day as it comes. I've been trying to calculate how many people might have survived the stillness. That's what they're calling it, you know? The stillness. At first, I thought it was a stupid name. There's nothing especially *still* about those hollows. I can't stand going down to the lower levels because of how loud they are. But now I'm starting to think it's actually kind of appropriate. The hollows aren't still, but the humans are. Once, you could turn on the radio, turn on the TV, turn on your smartphone or laptop, and have instant contact with other people. Now, you've got to search for it. Hunt through the radio, looking for any kind of life you can find. I feel it here, in the city, especially. You used to have to fight for even ten minutes of peace. But now…"

Fresh lightning, painfully bright, spilled through the windows. Clare found she couldn't pull her eyes away from the blinds. A horrible paranoia wormed through her. "We're in the city."

"Hm?" Peter lifted his eyebrows, following Clare's eyes to the window, then looking back at her curiously.

"The…the thanites—there are going to be more of them in the city." *Why didn't I think of this before? Why did I let us come here? Are they infecting us right now?*

Her throat burned and her eyes stung. She became convinced she could feel them, scratchy, rough, clinging to the mucus in her lungs.

Peter stared at the window. Clare wanted to scream at him. He'd pacified her before; she wanted him to do it again. To promise that, despite all signs, they would be safe.

"They're not active right now," he said.

Clare fought the urge to hurl her water bottle at him. "What do you mean? Are they infecting us? Are they going to *become* active?"

Peter blinked rapidly, seeming to shake off some bad memory, and chuckled. "No, no, don't panic. We're fine. I've been living here for weeks and I'm still human, see?" He held his hands up and wiggled his fingers, grinning broadly.

"But there are thanites here. You said they collected in cities. Is it a matter of time? Did you call us here so that we could die with you?" Clare leaned forward. She knew she sounded aggressive, but she couldn't calm down. Dorran's arm around her shoulders was normally comforting, but at that moment, it only made her frenzy more urgent. If she was being infected, then so was he. The image of his beautiful face, deformed, mutated, haunted her. She needed to expunge it. She needed Peter to tell her everything would be okay.

"Hey, hey, relax. I know how stressful this must be. And I can only imagine what you've been through already. But I swear, I wouldn't have called anyone here if the city were toxic. You're right, there are thanites everywhere. After the stillness event, they started to replicate themselves again. Like they were designed to. But they're not hurting us right now, and they never will, if I have anything to do with it."

She felt Dorran stir uneasily beside her. He was equally wary. Peter picked a candy bar out of the pile of food and tossed it to Clare. She caught it with her good hand.

"Eat that. Get some sugars into you, because you could probably really do with some right about now." Peter's smile was sad. "There isn't much left to my story, but once you've heard it, you'll probably understand everything a little better."

Clare gave a short, stiff nod, encouraging him to go on. Peter pointedly stared at the bar she held, and so she struggled to open it with shaking fingers. Dorran eased it out of her grip, tore the top off, and handed it back to her. He then reached for the first aid kit and examined the supplies while Peter resumed his tale.

"Okay. You know how the thanites were created. And you know that at one point during the development period, one of them escaped containment. Not one of the earliest models, but not the more recent ones either, from what I can work out. Once outside, it populated itself without Ezra's knowledge. Meanwhile, he was under immense pressure. The end of his grant was racing toward him and he needed a working model. He'd been so paranoid about having his work stolen that he hadn't breathed a word to anyone—not even the Aspect commissioners, or else they probably would have imposed more stringent safety measures. He'd confided some of it to me, but even I didn't know the extent of his experiments. About three weeks before the end of his grant, he woke me in the middle of the night."

The chocolate bar was too sweet. Clare's stomach threatened to revolt as she chewed it, and she put it aside half-eaten and picked up the water. Dorran splashed some antiseptic across the cuts, and she hissed. He murmured quietly as he dabbed the liquid, then began wrapping a fresh bandage across it.

Peter watched from a distance, shifting his position. He looked uncomfortable. The memories were probably unpleasant for him. To be so close to the source of the stillness and be unable to stop it...

"Like I said before, I spent most of my nights here. Not because my own work was very high pressure, but, well, I guess I was lazy." He laughed, but it sounded pained. "Easier to stay here in rooms cleaned by janitors than travel home to my own poky apartment. I guess it saved my life. Most of our other coworkers were home that night. Ezra had been routinely sleeping at the tower for efficiency's sake. He woke me around four in the morning and said he needed my help. He wanted a witness."

Dorran tied off the bandages but kept his hand resting over Clare's shoulder. She was grateful for their warmth.

"I guess I was excited for him." Peter took a deep breath, then let it out as a heavy sigh. "After how hard he'd worked, I was hoping his invention, whatever it was, would succeed. So I followed him up to the labs. At his request, Aspect had constructed several containment units. Airtight glass rooms where you could watch your experiments. Inside one of them was an older Korean woman. Wrinkled, wearing her best coat and hat, sitting on this white plastic chair patiently. 'Who's that?' I asked. 'My neighbor,' he said."

Peter chuckled, but the sound wasn't cheerful. "He must have been violating a hundred ethics regulations. You need all sorts of permissions for human trials, but I guess Ezra didn't have time. He needed proof of concept. And he was willing to cross a few lines to get there. He explained that his neighbor had a terminal lung cancer and had agreed to test the thanites. If they worked, they would repair the damage it had already created. 'It's very safe,' he kept saying."

Clare didn't want to hear the rest of the story. She could see the direction it was taking, and the nightmare was too close and too painful to stand. But Peter's eyes were turned to his feet, distant and tight as he unraveled his memories.

"He had to upload some code to activate the thanites. They might have been mostly biological, but they still had enough machine in them that they needed a command to switch on. Ezra explained what was happening as he worked. Thanites had been released into the room with the subject. They floated through the air, being inhaled and expelled with every breath but ultimately dormant. When activated, they would seek out a host. Their biological nature meant that they needed to find a hospitable environment to survive—specifically, a human. They could enter the body through any mucus membrane, such as those in the eyes, throat, and lungs. They would be nearly painless. Ezra would allow them to work for several hours and had a second code lined up to deactivate the thanites before his neighbor was allowed out of the room. Then we would run tests to see whether any repairs had been made, and if so, how much."

A shot of light came through the slats, thunder rolling after it. In that second of brightness, everything in the room took on an unnatural appearance; the chairs, the discarded jackets, even Peter took on an otherworldly glow.

"We watched and waited. For the first minute, nothing seemed to happen. The little old Korean lady kept sitting there, smiling patiently. Then—"

His voice choked as he stood. He crossed to the window and leaned against the sill, staring through the slats at the sky. When he turned to face them, his grin was resolutely back in place but strained. "Well, you can probably guess. And I'm sure you could do without the details. But it didn't go well. As soon as she started screaming, Ezra put in the deactivation code. Only, it didn't work."

CHAPTER 46

PETER PUSHED ONE OF the window's slats up with his finger and peered down at the street. His face twitched, and he dropped the slat back into place. "At the time, Ezra didn't know what had gone wrong. But, looking back, I have a pretty good guess. The earlier model of his thanites—the broken ones—had populated everywhere by that time. Including the air in the isolation chamber. Ezra had been feeding carbon and compounds into the room to grow the machines, without realizing he was essentially populating two versions, one which was already present in high numbers. The termination code worked exactly as it was intended, but only on the latest strain. It did nothing for the rogue version."

The rain had settled into a steady, drumming pattern. Lightning bursts were frequent but distant. The crackling thunder blurred underneath Peter's voice.

"As you can imagine, Ezra was frantic. He'd thought his thanites were harmless. Instead, he'd had to watch his subject, his friend, die in one of the most unpleasant ways imaginable. I was beside myself. Ezra kept pacing, swiping a tissue over his face to mop up sweat. It took us a while to compose ourselves enough to face what we'd done. It was a little after six by that point. Our early-bird colleagues would be arriving in an hour. Ezra asked me to help him hide the body. But before we could open the chamber doors, I got a phone call from my sister."

Dorran spoke, his voice so low that it barely disturbed the room's stillness. It was the first time he'd addressed Peter directly. "You were going to hide the body?"

Peter turned away from the window, blinking rapidly. "Well. It was complicated. No matter how many precautions you take, it's impossible to ensure complete safety in any kind of human trial. People do occasionally expire in the name of science. They're made aware of the risk before signing up, as Ezra's neighbor would have been. I know it sounds callous, but the reality is you have to endure occasional death in the pursuit of something that might save countless more lives."

Dorran was so still that he could have been a statue. "A woman was dead. Murdered. And you would have hidden it."

Clare blinked. "He's right. That…that's so…"

"Oh, no, no!" Peter held his hands up, chuckling. "I'm sorry, you misunderstood me. I didn't mean hide her body as in *hide* it. Not like in a shallow grave or anything. I'm not a criminal. We were going to cover the observation room's windows so that our coworkers wouldn't have to see it while we waited for the authorities to arrive."

Clare managed to smile. "Right. I guess I let my imagination run away on me."

"No, that's understandable." Peter came back to his seat and stood behind it, hands braced on its back. "Ezra wanted me to help him hide it from our colleagues. Can you imagine coming into work and seeing a woman with tumor-like growths across her face and hair pouring out of her mouth? It's enough to give anyone nightmares. But we didn't even get that far. My sister called me. She lived a couple of hours away. She'd heard the earliest news reports on her radio while walking her dog and wanted to make sure I was okay. And I turned to Ezra and asked him, 'Are you sure it's contained to the lab?'"

It was surreal to hear about the world's end told from the perspective of one of the people behind it. And to hear the news had reached him from such a mundane avenue. Clare frowned. "But if it started here, wouldn't you have known about it? There must have been screaming—"

"Not in this city. Not at that point. From when Ezra put out the activation code, it would take nearly three hours for the thanites in our area to respond. Because they work in tandem to come online, areas with the thickest population were more likely to activate sooner. The isolation chamber came on nearly immediately since Ezra had been feeding in fuel to artificially increase the numbers. Outside needed more time to respond. I think Beijing fell first, with New York thirty minutes later. It escalated from there.

"Ezra and I were relatively safe inside the airlocked room, since the space only held a limited number of thanites, unlike the test chamber and the outside world. We called our families and then the news stations, trying to get the word out to take shelter inside airtight areas. Our phones died pretty quickly. Then it was just us, trapped in the room, listening to humanity dismantle itself thirteen floors below. We stayed there until the following morning, when our thirst was so severe that we were forced to leave. By that point, the activation cycle had finished and any thanites that hadn't found a host were either broken or dormant."

Clare didn't want to imagine it. Secluded in Winterbourne, she hadn't learned about the mass extinction until weeks afterward. She didn't know if she could have coped with being aware of it as it happened—listening to it, perhaps even being able to watch it from a window—while unable to do anything to help.

"At first, the thanites only effected their brains." Peter's eyes were glassy. "It took a few days for the stem cells to start... *growing* things. The hollows on the first day looked much more like humans, though they lost their humanity pretty quickly. The brain stem was broken down and rapidly rebuilt, several times over. It removed most of the conscience, memories, personality. It also removed the need to sleep and the ability to feel pain. Well, no, that's not really correct. I believe they feel it. They just don't respond to it."

Clare saw Marnie again, swollen, her bellowing cries full of misery. She wanted to cry for what her aunt had gone through.

Thunder boomed, the closest yet. The lights flickered, then went out. Suddenly, the room was so dark that Clare couldn't even see Dorran at her side.

Peter swore under his breath. Clare heard him move between the desks. Items fell to the floor as he knocked them over, but he didn't try to right them. Uneasiness rose in her. "Peter? What happened?"

"Generator's out." He sounded like he was choking. A drawer slammed open. "Where the hell did I put it—"

More lightning. It flooded through the windows, turning the space into an oversaturated plate of whites and blacks. She caught a snapshot glimpse of Peter, digging through the drawer. He no longer smiled.

Clare slowly stood. She had the awful sense that Peter's panic wasn't due simply to the sudden darkness. "What's happening?"

"We'll be okay. It's going to be fine." The words were comforting, but the voice wasn't. Something heavy fell to the floor. Then Peter took a sharp breath. A moment later, a beam of light appeared as he turned a flashlight on.

Even without the harsh light, his face would have been colorless. He turned the beam toward Clare and Dorran, and they both squinted against it. Peter lowered the flashlight. "Come with me. Quickly. We need to restart the generator."

"Oh." Clare barely had a moment to catch her thoughts before Peter jogged for the door. She kept her grip on Dorran as they followed.

Peter forced the door open and waited just long enough for them to slip through in his wake before turning toward the stairs.

"Sorry. We're short on time. The generator's out, which means the backup locks downstairs are no longer engaged."

"The locks?" Clare stubbed her toe on the lowest stair and grimaced.

Peter turned his flashlight downward to help her see. "Helexis Tower has bolts on its ground-floor windows that can be activated remotely. It was meant to be cutting-edge technology...but it was designed to automatically unlock if both the power and backup generator died. A fail-safe in case of fire. No one expected we might have worse concerns than an inferno."

Clare blinked and pictured the swarm of hollows gathered around the tower's ground floor. Her voice turned croaky. "Can the hollows get in?"

"Technically? Yes." Peter turned the corner and entered the second flight of stairs. In the erratic light, Clare caught sight of thick metal doors blocking what had to be the lab. "But they would need to lift at the same time as pulling to get them open. And they haven't figured out how to yet. But...I'd really rather get the bolts reengaged than trust in their stupidity."

"This has happened before?"

Peter was breathless as he turned another corner. "Twice. Storms. Knocks out the generator." He paused to suck in a deeper breath, then continued racing upward. "Doesn't get any less stressful, though."

Their footsteps reverberated on the marble steps. Clare wondered how high they had to climb. A stitch was developing in her side. Beneath the footsteps, she thought she could hear wailing, banging noises. *The hollows. But not from the ground floor. Hollows trapped in rooms.*

They passed another landing and Clare saw what looked like a row of offices. Each of the doors had a frosted glass pane set in them. A blurred face pressed against one. She didn't have time to stop and watch; they were already turning onto the next flight of stairs.

Peter stopped, bent over, hand pressed to the wall as he sucked in whooping breaths. "Brains...over brawn... Should've done... more gym."

"Are you okay?"

His smile was strained. "Not far now." Then he set off again, still gasping, his face turning red.

Clare's own feet made a drumming rhythm that conflicted with Peter's. Dorran moved near silently. She could barely see him, but she could feel him, never more than an arm's length away. The idea of the hollows getting inside the tower weighed heavily as her mind generated visions of what that might entail. With no other exits, the tower would become a coffin built of stone and metal.

Peter skidded as he turned onto another landing and caught himself on the wall. Clare prepared to turn the corner and keep climbing, but there were no more stairs.

An immense blast of light came through the windows on either side of them. Clare had the sense that they were so high that the storm was no longer above them but surrounding them.

Peter shoved the flashlight into Clare's hands and wheezed in painful gasps as he fumbled to open the narrow metal door. She stepped to the side, pointing the flashlight to help him see.

Lightning came again, and Clare was too slow to close her eyes against it. For a few seconds, all she could see was a web of harsh white tattooed across her retinas. As she blinked, the swirling shadows from the tower's upper room returned to her. The lock clicked and Peter pushed the door open. The room held a medley of machinery Clare couldn't name.

"Here, please," Peter gasped.

Clare jogged after him and directed the flashlight where he pointed. A hulking, cylindrical shape—the generator, Clare guessed—took up part of the wall. Peter wrenched a lid up to reveal a blank dashboard. He pressed a button, then pulled a switch and stepped back.

Clare glanced around, expectant. In the flashlight's beam, she could make out bulbs in the ceiling. They stayed dead. The machine was quiet. The only noises came from the wind screaming against the tower's walls, the muffled drum of rain, and the near-constant, bone-shaking thunder.

"Come on, come on." Peter returned to the machine, pushed the button, and flipped the switch again. Sweat trickled around his wide eyes.

Clare felt the knots in her stomach tighten.

The hollows haven't figured out how to open the doors yet. They weren't smart enough. But not all of them are mindless. All it would take is one of the clever ones to be in the crowd, to realize the power had gone out...

Peter looked at her, and she could see her own thoughts reflected in his eyes. The dead generator was a ticking bomb.

CHAPTER 47

"MAYBE...MAYBE SOMETHING CAME loose inside it." Peter pulled a second cover off, this time exposing more of the machine's insides. Clare saw a tangle of wires and pistons. Peter ran his hands across them, wiggling wires, searching for any kind of weakness. Clare did her best to keep her flashlight focused on his work. His hands were shaking.

"Your fuse is gone." Dorran, unfazed, stepped past Clare and gently tapped one of the little glass cylinders near the control panel. "Do you have a replacement?"

Peter blinked at him, then began nodding. "Yeah, yeah, there should be replacements somewhere over here."

Dorran followed him to the back wall. Plastic trays were attached to an alcove above a counter. They began opening them and searching the contents.

"Bring the light over please?" Peter waved Clare forward.

He and Dorran were working on opposite ends of the counter, so Clare scoped around for the best angle. She found a chair, dragged it forward, and stood on it, so that her light washed down over their heads.

Something heavy banged below them, and Clare flinched. She tried to tell herself it was just one of the trapped hollows. The ground floor was so far below that, even if the hollows had broken in, she wouldn't know for several more minutes. The thought wasn't at all comforting.

"Found it." Dorran pushed away from the counter and jogged to the machine.

Clare leapt off her seat and followed. He worked quickly. The old fuse popped out and the new one slid into its place in seconds, then he pressed the button and pulled the switch, like he'd seen Peter do just minutes before. The machine made a choking, gurgling noise, then a deep, steady hum rose. Lights blinked on above them. Clare let her head sag, eyes closed in relief.

"Wow." Peter swiped the back of his hand across his forehead, his grin falling back into place. "You're a useful guy to have around, huh?"

Dorran made a noncommittal noise. He slipped his hands into his coat pockets and stepped behind Clare, a discreet message that he was passing the conversation back over to her.

She turned the flashlight off and handed it back to Peter. "Is there any way to make sure the doors stayed secure? Beyond, uh, waiting to see if anything comes up the stairs?"

"I'm sure you'll be happy to hear there is." Peter placed the flashlight on a counter and crossed to the wall. Eight little green lights shone from a display. "These babies reckon we're safe. They monitor the locks. If any of the windows were open, they would have turned red."

Clare nodded, relieved. Now that the urgency was gone, she was starting to feel shaky. "You said the generator went out twice before. Is it likely to do it again?"

"Uh…" Peter grimaced as he dragged his fingers through his hair. "Maybe. The storm definitely isn't good for it. But, I mean, as long as the hollows don't figure out what they need to do…"

The silence hung for a moment. The maintenance room didn't have any windows, but Clare could still feel the thunder shaking the building.

Peter worked his jaw, seemingly trying to balance what he said next. "On your way here…did either of you encounter any hollows that seemed…*more* than the others?"

"Yeah. Smart ones."

"Good. You already know about them." He folded his arms, rocking lightly as he stared at the generator. "I didn't want to fearmonger. As long as it's only the dumb hollows outside, I don't think we're in too much danger. They just push and beat their fists. But the smart ones are what I'm really frightened of. They won't be able to do much to get inside if the locks are in place. But if they see the power go out…if they figure out how the locks work…"

Clare shivered. "I've only seen a couple of them. Are they common?"

"No idea. There would have been a lot in the beginning. But now?" Peter slowly lowered the lids on the generator, running his fingers over the metal. "I know where they came from at least. The thanites work better with some blood types than others. People with AB-positive blood transform faster and usually have more pronounced mutations. On the other hand, people with AB-negative blood mutate more slowly and usually retain most of their mental functions."

Clare frowned as she tried to remember her own blood type. She was fairly sure it was A-positive. "AB-negative…that's the rarest, isn't it?"

"One of the rarest. It still accounts for something close to five hundred million worldwide, though."

"That's…"

"Insane, isn't it? To think there might be so many of them out there." Peter shook his head. "But there aren't. Not anymore. Losing mental function turned out to be a vital element for the hollows to survive this long. Imagine you started to turn, and you were aware of it. Your bones were splitting, your skin was tearing, your body was stretching. You're constantly hungry but the only food that appeals is warm, wet flesh. Meanwhile, your friends and family—everyone you loved—are gone, replaced by monsters. What would you do?"

Clare blinked. Her eyes burned. Dorran rested a hand, warm and steady, on her back. "I…I…"

"At that point, the only solution for a lot of them would be death." Peter's shrug was sad. "Put a stop to it before it grows worse. I don't think very many of those millions are left now. For some, they realized what the future would hold and killed themselves before they had to suffer any more of it. Others went insane from the horror of what was happening to their bodies... or were insane to begin with."

Clare glanced up at Dorran. His expression was stony. He didn't seem to want Peter to know about his mother, so Clare kept quiet as well.

"They're the most dangerous out of the hollows," Peter said. "Smart enough to problem solve, but also mostly crazy. I don't know how many are in the city. I doubt they'd be crawling around the outside of the tower—they'd realize the futility. But they might be in the houses or towers surrounding us, watching. And if they see the lights go out and realize the power failed..."

Clare glared at the generator. It was a large machine, made of metal, heavy and solid. But, in an odd way, it also seemed horribly fragile. It had failed before. It was likely to fail again. And maybe next time it wouldn't be fixable.

"Come on." Peter's smile reappeared, though it looked less steady than it had before. "Crisis over. Let's get back downstairs where it's warm and comfortable, and where we'll feel a bit safer behind some locked doors. You two must be tired."

As they left the room, Clare looked toward the window. She couldn't see the clouds in the darkness but she could imagine them—thick, rolling, black. The lightning seemed to be coming more often. The rain refused to lighten. "Did the thanites do anything to the weather?"

"They did. Good guess." Peter locked the maintenance room behind them, then beckoned them toward the stairs. "They're part machine, part biological. When they were activated—when the code passed between them—it created a tiny reaction similar to an EMP. Insignificant in small quantities. Remember, until then, the thanites were only tested in a lab. I guess Ezra had no way of telling what would happen when they were unleashed en masse. With billions of those reactions per square kilometer, the results were devastating. Phones went out, cameras, cars, planes. Anything that relied on a computer to function was suddenly dead. And it affected the weather. In most areas, temperatures plummeted. There were sudden snowstorms even in milder regions."

Clare's memory of driving toward her sister's was still clear. One moment, it had been a brisk but sunny morning. The next, she'd entered a snowstorm. Her phone had died. She'd seen a car off the side of the road, its doors open. The realization of how close she'd come to the activated thanites was painful. She'd probably only been spared by a few minutes. Then Clare imagined breathing the invisible machines in, and her throat closed up again. She pressed her eyes shut and waited for the reflex to pass.

It's psychological. You were never bothered by the thanites before you knew about them.

"Clare?" Dorran hesitated at her side, one hand held toward her. She tried to relax her face. "I'm fine."

Peter was nearly half a flight of stairs ahead of them. Clare quickened her pace. As they followed the twisting stairs back down to the twelfth floor, they passed the immense set of metal doors blocking the labs. Clare said, "You didn't finish your story."

"Didn't I?" Peter twisted to look back at her.

"After the stillness. After you realized the thanites had spread. What happened to Ezra?"

"Ah." Peter's mouth twitched down. "He didn't…*stay* long. One of our coworkers kept a gun in the office…for what reason, I don't know, but like I said, this place was full of eccentrics. We all knew where he kept it. And while I was trying to contact news stations and spread warnings, Ezra found the gun and used it on himself. I guess this world he'd created wasn't one he wanted to live in."

"You've been alone since then?"

He nodded briefly, and for a second, Clare saw a hint of despair in his eyes. Then he blinked quickly, and the familiar cheerfulness was back in place. "I had the radio. I listened to other people trying to get data on the situation out there. And I put out my own signal asking for help."

"So that's why you were expecting someone." Clare frowned. "It's been nearly a month. I'm surprised we're the only people who made it here. Have you spoken to any of the other broadcasters?"

They had reached the hallway to their offices. Peter pulled his ID tag out and unlocked the door. "Well, I didn't want just *anyone* to hear me. So I disguised my transmission. Remember the signal that played while you were trying to get to the tower? That's mine."

"What? The station that plays second-long clips of noise? I thought it was nonsense."

He laughed as he held the door open for them. "It mostly is! But once every four minutes, I include part of the address: *Helexis Tower, Floor Twelve, Inner City.* Spoken a syllable at a time. You would have to listen to the station for a while to realize those clips are connected."

Clare had hated the station. It unnerved her. But she'd had company and security with Dorran at Winterbourne. She imagined her sister's situation. Beth had been trapped in the bunker with nothing except her radio. Alone, despairing, unable to find any other signal, she might have listened to the station as her only source of human contact. She might have caught the hidden message. And blind in the dark, she might have scored the words into the metal walls.

"Oh," Clare moaned. Her mind was threatening to spiral, so she pulled it back with some effort. "What…"

Peter reached forward, looking concerned. "Uh, maybe eat some more of the chocolate. Or what about some water? The chairs are over here."

"No. I'm fine. I just…" She shook her head. "Why did you broadcast it like that? Why not just…*tell* people?"

Peter settled into his chair, though he still looked concerned. "Caution. To survive the thanites, you needed to be somewhere painfully lonely, or you needed to be in an airtight environment."

Airtight. That's why Beth was safe in her bunker, despite living in the suburbs. The room had its own air filtration system.

"That means an eclectic mix of people made it through the stillness," Peter continued. "Some were just normal folks who

386

happened to be on a camping trip or were in the right place at the right time. Others lived in seclusion, homesteads that were off the grid or so remote that they had to drive hours to reach a town. Those kinds of people are a mixed bag. On one hand, they can be a little intense. On the other hand, they are really good at surviving on their own, in the way the city people aren't."

Clare nodded. Without Dorran, she didn't know how long she might have survived. He was adaptable and skilled in a way she never would be.

"Then there's a third group of people. The paranoid ones. The ones who had bunkers, airtight panic rooms, or gas masks, and thought to use them." He shook his head. "They're surviving better than the city people, since they were actually prepared. But they're also the most dangerous group out there. They're more likely to have guns and to use them. I was frightened of inviting those kinds into the tower. It would be a gamble whether they would help me or whether they would shoot me dead, loot the place, and run."

"I guess I can understand that." Clare glanced up at Dorran for confirmation. His expression was unreadable. "But if it was such a risk, why did you send out the signal at all? If you wanted company, couldn't you have listened to the broadcasts and traveled to meet one of the survivors?"

"Not quite. I need to stay at the tower." His grin widened. "I didn't call you here because I was lonely. I called you because I need help. I'm working on a cure."

CHAPTER 48

CLARE'S HEART LURCHED. "A cure?"

"Ezra's research is all still here. The development details, the code, everything. Now, it's not my field of research, but...I'm trying to unravel it." Peter nodded toward the only computer that was turned on. "And I'm making progress. It's slow. But I'm getting there."

"Do you think you can reverse the mutations?"

"No. Not that, I'm afraid. Once the stem cells are activated, once *stuff* has grown, there's no reversing it. Or restoring the brain. What I'm trying to do is find a way to kill them."

"Oh." Clare tried not to be disappointed. Of course curing the hollows had to be impossible. They had changed too much to hope to bring them back. But the idea of killing them was difficult when they still carried hints of the humans they had once been.

"People are dying en masse every single day." Peter's voice caught, and he cleared his throat. "The ones who were traveling when the stillness happened are faring the worst. They were unprepared and don't have the skills to survive on their own. But the preppers are struggling too. They're taking too many risks. Some of them are treating this like a live-action fighting game, and their luck eventually, inevitably runs out. The group best equipped to survive right now are the ones who lived outside civilization: the homesteaders. But they're starting to vanish too. The hollows are wandering. Every night, they travel farther, looking for more food. Not even the most remote locations are safe anymore."

Clare chewed her lip. "I used to hear people on the radio. I'd tune in every day to listen to what they'd found and seen. But there are fewer and fewer of them all the time."

"Poor souls. You saw how many hollows were outside the tower, right? That's because of my own station. Hollows are attracted to radio broadcasts. The thanites are receptive to the signals—it was how they were activated. Anytime a survivor talks through their radio, they're basically calling to any hollows within a twenty-mile radius."

Dorran muttered something under his breath. Clare felt cold. She squeezed her hands together until the knuckles bulged.

Peter's eyes flicked between them, then he leaned forward and pushed the vending machine food a little closer. "Don't panic. It's not too late. There are pockets of people surviving, and we're going to give them the best damn chance possible. Humanity can recover from this. But only once the hollows are gone."

"People were hoping the hollows might kill themselves." Clare's tongue felt stiff, but she forced it to move. "That they might starve, or..."

"Yes. Eventually, they would die out. But...not quickly. They are capable of surviving with shockingly poor nutrition. The thanites make them almost immune to injuries, since it fast-tracks healing and destroys infection. Now, the thanites will eventually be deadly. The mutations will continue growing and spreading, unceasing, until it kills them in some way or another."

Clare remembered the hollows with bones growing into their skulls. She grimaced and nodded.

"It's already killing some of them," Peter said. "But not fast enough. I ran some calculations. At the current rate, it would take close to a year until the hollows stop outnumbering humans a thousand to one. At least five years until there are more humans than hollows. Perhaps twenty before the creatures go extinct entirely."

Five years until they stop outnumbering us. The queasiness crawled its way back up Clare's stomach.

"I don't know how many people are still alive, but it's not a lot. And less every day. We can't afford to wait until these creatures kill themselves. But maybe we don't have to."

"How?"

"I'm trying to create a code that will, in layman's terms, detonate the thanites. Wherever they've clustered in the body, I can make them react with each other and self-destruct. Done all at once, the chain reaction should be enough to kill the hollow host as well. Imagine a billion tiny explosions running through the body like a shock wave. Any hollows that survive the initial deactivation will be left vulnerable to infection. Theoretically, the world would be safe again in as little as a week."

"What's the *but*?"

Peter chuckled. "Hah. You're right, of course. There's always a *but*. I'm doing my best. I've been spending all of my time on it since the stillness event. But I'm still not there yet."

"What do you need?" Clare asked.

Dorran's hand found her arm and squeezed lightly, his attention still fixed on Peter.

Peter took a slow, deep breath, then let it out gradually. "I believe there is a research institute still functioning. In Evandale. From what I've gathered, there are five or six scientists still living there since the station was airlocked during the stillness. If I can get my research to a useable point, they might be able to take it, check it, and enact it. Something like this...it's not the kind of thing you want to launch unless you're absolutely, beyond a shadow of a doubt, certain that it will work the way it's intended. If it went wrong, even just slightly, it could kill every single survivor."

"So you want to get your research to them." Clare chewed her lip, thinking. "Are they listening to the radio? Can you send your data to them through it?"

"I've never heard them on the radio, though they may be listening. But, either way, it would take months to verbally communicate the code to them, as well as introduce a huge margin of error.

No, it needs to be through USB. I have a drive with everything on it. I need to pass it to them somehow." Peter glanced between Clare and Dorran. "I would have tried to take it myself, except the stakes are too high. If I were to die, the research would be lost with me. It probably sounds like I'm being selfish, but the truth is, without me, there is no cure. I have to avoid risks at any cost. Someone else needs to take the USB."

Dorran's hand tightened on Clare's arm. He wasn't happy with the turn of events.

"Oh…" Clare glanced between the two men. "I know this is important, but—"

"Don't worry! I'm not dumping the responsibility on you!" Peter chuckled and shook his head. "I'm not *that* mean. I know it's a big request. All I'm asking is that, when you leave the tower, you to take a copy of the code with you. If you encounter any other survivors on your way home, tell them where it needs to go. See if you can pass it along until it reaches the Evandale station."

Dorran's hand finally relaxed. Clare nodded, relieved. "That might be easier."

"Thank you. Truly. If anyone else arrives here, I'll make a duplicate USB and ask them to do the same. That way, even if one copy is lost or damaged, there should be backups." Peter beamed at them. "I'm still a couple of days away from my data being ready. Would you mind staying here for at least that long? There are bunks you can sleep in. Once the code is finished, you can leave anytime. Or stay awhile longer, if you need the rest. To be honest, it's nice to have company after so long."

The tower felt precariously unsafe with hollows clustered around it and the storm raging outside the windows. But despite that, Clare knew they would struggle to find a better situation between there and Winterbourne. As little as she liked the tower's clinical feel, at least Helexis had water and food, and the first human they had met since the stillness.

Peter clapped his hands on his knees. "You don't have to decide right now. Eat some food. I'll see about finding you something more comfortable to sleep in. And maybe some toothbrushes, as well."

He left the room at a brisk trot. Clare waited until the door clicked closed behind him, then turned to the man at her side. Dorran stared at the wall opposite them. He wasn't a chatty person by nature, but he seemed even more withdrawn than normal.

Clare rubbed his arm. "What are you thinking?"

He pressed his lips together, seeming to measure his response. Thunder rumbled, and the lights above them flickered. "I really do not know."

"Something's worrying you."

"Yes." His eyes looked sad. "Clare, this is so far beyond what I am familiar with. Tiny machines. USB drives that need to be delivered to parts of the country I have never heard of before. And this man, Peter…"

Clare waited patiently, knowing he needed a moment to collect himself.

At last, he shrugged, exhaling deeply. "It does not matter."

"Hey, I'll be the judge of that." She squeezed his hand. "You know you can tell me anything."

A thin smile ghosted across his lips, then vanished. "I used to rely on instincts at Winterbourne. I could tell when someone was in a bad mood; I could tell when someone was lying to me. But here, in this foreign world, surrounded by new concepts and new faces, I cannot know what to believe. And I am afraid jealousy is manifesting as hostility."

It took Clare a second to understand, and when she did, she blinked in surprise. "You're *jealous* of him?"

"Of course I am." He let her hand go. "He talks so easily. He is charismatic and intelligent. And he is adept at this world; he may even be capable of saving it. Looking at him is like looking at an exhibition of my inadequacies. And I wish I were handling it more graciously than I am."

Clare crept closer and wrapped her arms around him. She rested her head against his shoulder, trying to spread some comfort to him through touch. "You have so many strengths of your own. If I had to pick someone to cross the country with, I'd choose you every time."

"You are kind."

"I'm *honest*."

Dorran chuckled and kissed the top of her head. He rested there for a moment, and Clare listened to his heartbeat—steady, reliable.

"What do you want to do?" Dorran asked. "About this USB drive and the research institute."

It wasn't an easy question. Clare pressed her eyes shut. "I know where Evandale is. But I've never visited it. It would be a long drive."

"Longer than what we've already crossed?"

"Yeah."

Dorran's finger grazed Clare's cheek, brushing stray hair behind her ear. "How do you feel about his other suggestion, that we pass the drive to another traveler?"

"I mean...we could probably find someone eventually, but..."

He nodded, but Clare had the sense he wished he didn't agree. "It feels negligent."

"It doesn't seem right to carry the answer to the world's problems in our pocket and not do everything we could to get it to Evandale. We could pass it to another survivor, but it might take days to find someone, and they probably wouldn't want the responsibility any more than we do."

"He still believes other people may come to the tower. But his signal has been broadcasting for weeks, and we are the first to find him. How long would he wait for another traveler?"

The door beeped. Clare jolted and looked over her shoulder. Peter had returned, beaming as he carried two thick bathrobes. "Good news. The social media company two floors below us were *also* in the habit of spending nights in the tower. And, apparently, they were accustomed to luxury. I even found an unopened pack of toothbrushes."

"Oh, now *that's* some good news." Clare took the bundle of items from him.

"You remember where the bathrooms are, right? Just across the hall." Peter was already backing toward the desk with his laptop. "Otherwise, make yourselves comfortable here. I'm going to try to get ahead on my work. Meeting the pair of you has restored some enthusiasm, so I hope you won't think I'm too rude if I take advantage of it."

"Of course not. Do you need quiet while you work?"

"No, not at all." He laughed. "I'm used to being in a room full of people. It might actually help me Zen into it if I have some background noise. Help yourself to dinner, such as it is. I'll be right here if you need anything."

He sank into the desk seat and pulled the laptop an inch closer. Clare watched curiously. A change passed over Peter as he began to work. He opened a chart filled with numbers, and within seconds, the animated smile faded into tight-lipped focus. His eyes developed a glaze as he tapped at numbers. Clare had the impression that he'd tuned them out. It was fascinating, if a little unsettling.

She crossed to the window and nudged the blinds back. The sky was hidden by clouds, but Clare guessed it had to be night. The storm hadn't lost any of its ferocity. When she pressed close to the glass and angled her chin down, she could make out the edge of the horde assaulting the building. Very few of them were visible between the dark sky and heavy clouds. But, occasionally, she saw distant glints as they tilted their heads back at the perfect angle to catch some of the window's light on their eyes.

CHAPTER 49

SHE LET THE BLINDS fall back into place. Dorran stood by the chairs, watching her. She tried to shake off her uneasiness as she crossed to him. "I could do with a shower. How about you?"

"Mm. Very much."

Clare led the way, weaving between the desks to reach the hallway and the bathrooms. They took turns using the shower. Helexis's amenities were vastly more spacious than the riverboat's, but the water heater had been turned off as part of Peter's efforts to conserve fuel. Clare stayed in the freezing water just long enough to rinse the shampoo out of her hair, then rushed through the towel drying to get the robe around herself. She was still shivering when she stepped into the main part of the bathroom, where Dorran had finished brushing his teeth. He swept her into a chair, pushed the bath mat under her feet, and grabbed a fresh towel to dry her hair for her.

"I miss Winterbourne's fireplaces." Clare, teeth chattering, clutched the robe's lapels as Dorran squeezed moisture out of her hair.

He chuckled. "It had some attractive features."

"Do you miss it?"

She watched his expression in the mirror. He took a breath but didn't speak immediately, instead keeping his eyes focused on her hair as he combed it. "Sometimes. A little."

"You grew up there. It's normal to be homesick. Especially when the outside world is so much different from what you're used to."

"Do you miss your home?"

Clare still thought of her cottage occasionally, though it encroached on her thoughts less and less frequently with each passing day. She lifted her shoulders in a shrug, then let them drop. "I miss what it represents. My old life, where I could sit in the garden when it was sunny, and wave to the elderly couple across the street when they went out for walks, and buy a new book each Friday, then try to find somewhere to fit it on my bookshelf. But I wouldn't want to go back there."

"No?"

"I can imagine what it must look like. The plants would all be dead. The neighbors would be gone. I don't think there would be any life or joy left in it at all. This way I can preserve it, whole and undamaged, in my memories."

"I can understand that." Dorran put the brush aside and handed Clare a hair tie. As she pulled her hair into a ponytail,

Dorran opened the first aid kit on the table. The wet bandages marking her body were cut off and discarded in the bin, and Dorran began redressing the wounds that needed it.

The cuts on her stomach and thigh, less than four weeks old, had almost completely healed. Red lines marked where the skin had once been torn, but even they were fading. The bite on her forearm, still recent, was knitting together.

"I saw you were healing quickly, but I did not suspect it was tied to the stillness," Dorran murmured. "No sign of infection; no delays to progress, even after extensive blood loss and less than optimal nutrition. No lingering effects from the cyanide. I am not a fool enough to be grateful for the stillness, but at least this is one result in our favor."

A side effect of an infection I can't escape. Clare's fingers twitched. She clenched her hands into fists in her lap.

Dorran lowered his brows, his eyes sad. "I am sorry, my darling."

"It's...it's fine." Clare hoped, if she repeated it often enough, she might actually believe it. "We're safe, and we're still together, and that's the most important thing, right?"

He bent to kiss the top of her head, his fingers lingering over the tape holding a bandage in place.

Clare brushed her teeth while Dorran showered. When he emerged two minutes later, he was shivering almost as badly as she had, the dressing gown tied tightly around him. He patched his own scrapes and bandages quickly, closed the kit, then held out a hand. Clare took it as they returned to the office area.

She used her badge to open the door. The space felt vacant; Peter was still at his desk, head down, fully absorbed in his formula, but he looked painfully small compared to the breadth of the room. The rapid key tapping blended with the drum of falling rain. Clare hesitated as the door swung closed behind them, but Peter didn't even seem aware that they were there. It felt wrong to interrupt him.

They resumed their spots on the couch and picked through the vending machine food. The apples went first; they were both starved for fresh food. They split a packet of salty peanuts. Clare's stomach had finally quieted enough that she could eat, but she tried to moderate what she had. The foods were all high in salt and sugar. She pitied Peter for having to live off of it for a month.

Clare tried to rest, leaning against the chair's corner and stretching her feet in front of the heater. It was like trying to take a nap with a beehive directly above her head. Her mind whirred, frantic and confused, and the more she tried to ignore it, the worse it became. She needed something to do.

Peter had told them to make themselves at home, but she didn't like the idea of encroaching on any of the other desks. They held too many memories from their past owners. Just looking through the papers and touching the discarded jackets and trinkets would build up an idea of the man or woman who had marked that area as their own, and Clare didn't want to let that into her head. It would hurt too much.

The bookcase behind them held novels and games. Clare loved reading, but she didn't think she could fall into any of the books. The fantasy escape they offered felt empty. She leaned close to Dorran and whispered, "Bed?"

He nodded, smiling, and Clare felt some relief. It couldn't have been any later than eight, but she thought sleep might at least soften the anxiety. Morning would bring a clean slate, and, she hoped, a clearer mind.

Clare rose and approached Peter. He hunched forward, his face intensely focused on the screen. Every few seconds, he tapped a key, toggling different cells and entering new numbers. Clare wondered if he had always been that intense. The way he stared, unblinking, made her think it was a lifelong habit.

An open binder stood on the desk's edge. The name on it was familiar: Dr. Peter Wiesner. He'd left his research notes for the bionic eye out on the desk. She guessed it really was difficult to let go of the past. The eye must have been his passion for more than a year. She knew it would have been a challenge to pick up a different scientist's work at a moment's notice.

Clare rubbed the back of her neck, uncomfortable with interrupting him when he was so involved with the spreadsheet, but he seemed oblivious to her. She waited until the silence was unbearable, then cleared her throat. "Peter?"

"Oh, hey, how's it going?" He leaned back, and immediately the grin brightened his face.

"Sorry, I hope I didn't disturb you—"

"Nah, it's fine. I could do with some distraction from this mess. It's enough to fry my brain."

Clare chuckled. She tilted her head toward Dorran, who

stood beside the chairs, patient but watchful as always. "We were thinking we might head to bed, unless you needed help with anything?"

"That sounds like a plan. I could probably do with some sleep too." Peter stretched as he stood. "I'll show you the bunks. Open the door for me, would you? I need to put out the light."

Clare pushed on the door to the hallway and waited. Peter tapped some keys on the computer. Every bulb went out—not just in the work room, but in the hallway as well. The only light came from the emergency exit sign above the stairs. Clare flinched as the red glow doused the space in a sickening ambience.

"Sorry, I know it's a bit creepy, but it helps save fuel." Peter's teeth flashed red in the backwash as he joined them at the door. "The lights are halogen, but I don't get to choose which floors to keep on. I can light the entire building or none of it, hah."

Clare tried to smile in return, but it came out crooked. She'd learned to hate the darkness. Darkness meant danger; it meant being blind, being lost, being hunted. The exit light was just enough to see her companions, the walls, and the shiny elevator doors at the hallway's end, but it felt worse than having no light at all. Something inhuman a floor below them howled.

Peter stepped around them and followed the hallway past the bathrooms. His voice sounded unnaturally distant. "You guys probably want to share, right? This room's the nicest. It has its own heater and a window. Not luxury, I know, but...well, we take what we can get, huh?"

The sensor pad beside the door beeped as he unlocked it and

402

propped it open, then reached inside to turn on its lights. The room was small but neat. A bunk bed stood against the left wall with a minimalistic plywood cupboard and a desk opposite. The space showed signs of having been lived in at one point; a mug sat on the windowsill, and the wastebasket was half-full.

Peter hesitated in the doorway. Clare thought he looked uncomfortable. She stopped by the desk and faced him. "Whose room was this?"

He dragged his thumb over his lower lip, his eyebrows tight. "Um. It was Ezra's."

"Oh." Clare's skin crawled. She looked over the space again. This time, she could pick out all of the artifacts Ezra had left behind. A shimmer of grease on the edge of the mug from where his lips had touched it. A poster of a diagram tacked onto one of the walls. A stress ball that had fissures running across its surface from months of abuse. The wastebasket was full of scraps of paper with indecipherable equations scrawled over them in a painstakingly neat hand.

Peter hunched his shoulders and folded his arms across his chest. "Look, how about we swap? You'll probably be more comfortable away from all of this."

Clare glanced up at Dorran for his input. He gave a very small nod, indicating the decision was up to her. "We don't mind sleeping here."

"Are you sure?" Peter shuffled nervously. "I know today hasn't been a great day for either of you…"

She forced a smile. It was just a room. The fact that Ezra had once slept in it shouldn't make any difference. And from the look of it, Peter was more uncomfortable there than she was. "Absolutely. I'm looking forward to trying out the heater."

"Okay. Okay, good." He nodded, glancing around the place. "There should be some spare blankets in the cupboard. You remember where the bathrooms are, right? If you need anything, I'll be next door."

As the door closed, Clare released her breath and unhooked the ID badge from around her neck. She hung it on a hook near the cupboard and approached the window. Very little was visible below. She turned her eyes up and was just in time to see a sliver of the moon before it was swallowed by clouds. They seemed to be moving quickly. Racing, even. She looked aside and saw the mug on the sill was still half-full of coffee. "Are you sure you're okay here, Dorran? We could probably sleep in the main office if we wanted."

"I don't mind." He came up behind her and threaded one arm around her waist. "As long as you are comfortable."

"Here's good. Let's get some rest."

"Hm." He dipped down to kiss the top of her head. "May I make a request?"

"Sure."

"Stay close to me tonight."

"Of course I will."

They found a foot heater by the desk and turned it on. The beds were single and bunked, but Clare felt as though even that small gap was too much of a separation. Dorran seemed to share her feelings. He gently pulled her after himself into the bottom bunk and coiled around her as they settled in to sleep.

The bed was narrow, but they fit together well; Dorran's arm curled protectively around her back, Clare's head tucked into his throat, their legs tangled. Clare tried to let her mind drift away. She was tired—she could feel it in every fiber of her body—but her mind wasn't ready to relax. Ferocious winds created a high-pitched whistle outside their window. The storm spread crackling lightning around the tower, so close that it seemed to charge the air she breathed. No matter what she tried to think about, her mind kept turning back to the thanites.

Peter said the machines were too small to be detectable without a microscope. But Clare was sure she could feel them. Scraping against her veins as each beat of her heart pulsed them deeper into her body. Digging. Squirming. Alive, like a parasite she could never be free from. In her lungs. In her bones. In her brain.

Eyes staring blindly into the darkness, she whispered to Dorran, "I feel like I'm going crazy."

He was silent for so long that Clare began to think he'd fallen asleep. The wind rattled a pipe outside their window and it sounded like someone knocking to be let in. Then he pulled her tighter against himself, his breath ghosting across her ear. "It feels as though the whole world has."

Her eyes were full, threatening to overflow as she stared at the mattress above them. "If you ever want to split up—"

"Never."

"But if I'm becoming a burden—"

"You're not." A kiss on her cheekbone, featherlight. "You are very precious to me. I know how you feel. Fractured. I wish I could do more to help; you deserve a better life than this."

She found his hand and held it over her chest, close to her heart. "You've done so much. You deserve someone stronger."

"I have known many callous people in my life." She could feel his smile against her cheek. "I like you better."

She didn't trust herself to talk without her voice cracking, but she still smiled. "Thanks, Dorran."

"Try to rest, my dear Clare. I'll always be here for you when you need me."

Thunder rolled through the walls. Clare could feel the vibrations in her bones; the storm seemed to be growing stronger.

She closed her eyes, but her mind immediately moved to the generator. *If it goes out during the night, will Peter know? How long will unlocked windows guard against the horde outside?*

The warm weight of Dorran's arm rested over Clare's stomach. She focused on it, paying attention to the way it shifted minutely every time he breathed. His presence, his quiet steadfastness, had always been calming.

The thanites are in him too.

Clare bit her lip until she tasted the sting of blood. The pain worked as a distraction for a minute, but her brain turned back to its spiral of stress like an addict seeking its fix.

The tower and its fallible security system. The hordes outside. The question of when they would leave and what they would do once they did. The USB and its promised cure…and its threat of malfunction. Ezra's folly.

Clare's eyes drifted toward the windowsill. Lightning flared, painting a silhouette around the old occupant's mug.

Something isn't right.

She tilted her head to see Dorran's face. Eyelashes twitched as he dreamed, and a trace of tension hung around his brow.

Something's very, very wrong.

She didn't want to disturb him. He'd had less sleep than she had. And, even as her heart galloped and metallic fear flooded her mouth, she knew she was overreacting. It was paranoia, symptoms of prolonged stress finally breaking through the dam. That knowledge wasn't enough to make it stop.

Feverish sweat beaded over her skin. She was having trouble breathing. Suddenly, the arm curled over her was smothering more than comforting. Clare moved gingerly as she eased herself away from Dorran. He stirred as she left, the fingers spreading and hunting for her warmth. She pulled the blankets over his arm and stood back, waiting. He didn't wake.

Cold water. She would go to the bathroom, wash her face, drink, take a moment to collect herself in private. The floor was chilled despite the heater, and Clare found a pair of Aspect-branded slippers under the bed and slipped her feet into them.

At the door, she gave Dorran a final glance. He remained still. The paranoia plagued her, warning her not to leave him, warning her that if she let him out of her sight she might never see him again. She felt nauseated and closed her eyes, breathing deeply.

Then she took the ID badge off the hook by the door and slung its strap around her neck as she let herself out.

The hallway was quiet. No light came from under the door to Peter's room. Clare shuffled along the hall toward the bathroom. As she reached for the door, she looked toward the exit sign that bathed her in its sickly glow.

Something's wrong. Something's very wrong.

She knew where she needed to go. Clare passed the bathroom and moved to the stairs leading up, toward the lab on the thirteenth floor.

CHAPTER 50

HER FOOTSTEPS ECHOED OFF the marble stairs. Clare bit her tongue and rested one hand on the wall. It was ice-cold, but she didn't pull away. With the light as low as it was and the stairs foreign, she clutched at any sense of stability she could find.

Gale-force winds assaulted the tower, and Clare imagined she felt the structure tilt. She closed her eyes and waited for the sensation to pass. The queasiness in her stomach took a while longer. When she resumed climbing the stairs, each step was more cautious.

It's a tower of stone and metal. It was designed to withstand this.

Thunder cracked, loud enough to make her ears ache. She wished she'd woken Dorran. She looked over her shoulders, down the stairwell, and toward the hall saturated in hellish red light, then continued climbing. He needed rest. The stairs turned into a landing between the floors. She passed around it and began climbing the second flight.

The change in atmosphere was palpable. The air was colder. Clare felt cut off from the floor below—and from the only life in the tower.

No, that's not true. There's plenty of life here.

She could hear banging noises reverberating down the stairwell. It wasn't coming from the lab, but from the floor above it. The other people—*changed* people—locked in rooms across the building.

Her chest felt sickeningly tight. The thirteenth floor loomed ahead. Even before she reached the landing, she could see the massive steel doors blocking the pathway. A plaque had been affixed to the metal: *Restricted Area, Authorized Personnel Only.*

Clare clutched the badge around her neck. Whoever Michael Billings had been during life, she hoped he'd had access to the labs.

The banging noises were louder, blending in with guttural howls. The floor above held more than one hollow. She held the ID up to the black box beside the steel doors. It beeped faintly. The light flashed green. The doors drew back, wrapping her in a gust of freezing air.

Inside was pitch-dark. She squinted, hoping her eyes would adjust. A heavy body slammed into the floor above, and she flinched. Clare took a slow breath and stepped into the blackness. As the door slid closed behind her, she reached out to find the light switch.

Her fingers grazed cold tiles. She felt forward, running her hand in cautious circles, breath held. A plastic ridge disturbed the icy ceramic. She found four switches and turned them all.

Lights came on across the space, starting above her head and flickering as they progressed along the room. They reflected off expanses of tile, glass, and stainless steel. The lab took up the entire floor. It seemed to never end. Clare's eyes fought for some kind of frame of reference, first focusing on one glass partition, then the glass behind it, then the glass behind even that. Dizziness swelled, and she turned to face the door she'd just come through.

How did people work here?

As her breathing slowed, she turned back to the room. Near the stairwell were a series of washing stations—sinks armed with seemingly endless antibacterial soap, a steel chute in the wall for dirtied lab coats, and bins still half-stuffed with plastic gloves. Past that was a decontamination room. The glass rectangle looked airtight and held a myriad of hoses.

The lab contained multiple sealed work areas. Each space had either windows, or half-glass walls. Some areas were as simple as tables holding petri dishes. Others looked like miniature workshops. Some held machines Clare didn't even have names for. Endless charts and whiteboards littered the area. The labs had been well used before the stillness.

Tiny bronze plaques had been fastened into the work area doors. They bore names and had been designed for easy removal to compensate for Aspect's high turnover.

She read the names as she passed them. Near the front of the room she found Michael Billings, the donor of her own ID card. His workspace had something that looked like an X-ray machine and not much else. A little farther beyond that was Peter's station.

Eye diagrams were stuck above the desk and the whiteboard was covered with complex calculations scrawled in a messy hand. The rooms were airtight and there was very little dust, but the desk still held a sense of abandonment.

Clare's heart beat faster as she moved deeper into the space. She knew eventually she would come across the name she dreaded, and needed, to see.

She found it at the back of the room. Dr. Ezra Katzenberg had one of the largest sections in the lab. The glass wall ran across nearly the entire rear of the room, and Clare could see more glass enclosures inside. She stared at his plaque for a second. The bronze name plaque glittered in the harsh light. She lifted her ID and swiped it, just in case, but the lock didn't respond. Then she noticed the usual red light was missing. Clare pushed on the handle and found, to her surprise, it had been left unlocked. The airtight door hissed as it unsealed itself and slid back to grant access.

Clare clamped a hand over her mouth and doubled over. The air was overwhelmingly foul. She leaned her forehead against the cool glass, taking tiny, sharp gasps between her fingers. Anytime she moved, her stomach threatened to revolt. All she could do was hold still and endure.

I shouldn't be here. This was a mistake.

She forced stinging eyes open and tried to take stock of her surroundings. Ezra's work area was divided into three sections. Her part, the observation area, was narrow but long. A desk had been set into one end, its dashboard looking like something out of a flight deck and with a cheap swivel chair tucked neatly into it. At the room's other end lay a heap of discarded lab coats, waiting to be taken out for cleaning.

The observation area ran the length of the two glass enclosures in the back wall. Eight feet square, they had frosting across the lower half of the glass, but Clare thought she could see a dark shape huddled in the corner of the area to her left. *Ezra.*

She swallowed the thick, metallic slime that had developed over her tongue and straightened. She'd come to see the orchestrator of humanity's fall. She was too close to back out.

Clare approached the containment room, her hands shaking as they clutched her ID tag. The door, airtight, had no access bar to swipe. She guessed it was operated by the machine on the desk to her left. The glass was blurred by greasy hand smudges, but she could still see inside well enough. She breathed through her mouth as she approached.

Ezra's body lay in the back corner, huddled over. A thick, torn gray jacket obscured his form. He was smaller than she'd expected. A crushed fabric shape had been discarded nearby. Clare tilted her head, trying to make out Ezra's form.

It trembled.

Clare's mouth opened, but any noise she tried to make became trapped in her throat. Her mind went numb. Full of horror, she reached out and tapped her fingertips on the glass.

The shape twisted, one blind eye staring at her, then lurched forward. Clare bit down on a shriek as it hit the barrier.

This isn't Ezra. Open palms slapped the glass and a wide jaw

413

gnashed, spilling saliva across the divider. Wiry gray hair grew from its face, poking through holes in the cheeks and throat and matting in slimy clumps. One eye had been lost. The other was scratched into blindness.

Clare curled her arms around herself and took a step back. Her attention flicked toward the discarded shape in the containment room's corner, and she realized it was a damaged hat with a pink fabric flower. Peter's words came back to her. "His neighbor…wearing her best coat and hat, waiting patiently."

"Oh," Clare whispered. The woman in the containment room was patient zero. Clare hadn't even considered that she might still be alive.

The woman slapped her fist on the glass, adding to the layers of grease she'd built up, and exhaled a rattling hiss through her choked throat.

Clare turned away. The observation room smelled foul, but it wasn't the kind of stench she'd learned to associate with the hollows. This odor was sour and yet sickly sweet, a unique tang that seemed perfectly designed to make her gag. *Rotting flesh. But not the hollow. That means…*

Her eyes landed on the pile of lab coats in the room's other side. They were shaped oddly. She took a step closer, then stopped. The toes of a sneaker poked out from under the cloth.

Clare tilted her head back, her heart thundering, her stomach in knots. Her legs didn't want to move, but she forced them forward, toward the shape. The smell grew impossibly worse as she neared it. She reached for the coat Peter had draped over his fallen friend, pressed the back of her hand across her mouth, and pulled the fabric back.

CHAPTER 51

THE COAT MADE A horrible tacky sound as it peeled away from the flesh it had fused to. Clare buckled over, nearly losing the war against her nausea, and had to face away from the body as she waited for the ringing in her ears to fade.

Do it. Get it over with quickly. See him, then leave.

She picked up the coat's collar a second time and tried to ignore the way the stiff fabric cracked as she pulled it back. She didn't stop until the body below was completely uncovered, then she stepped back, eyes leaking and rough sobs escaping between clenched teeth.

The room had been airtight. There were no maggots to devour the flesh, but it hadn't been immune to bacteria. The skin had swollen and burst in places. A dark, pus-like ooze seeped out from the form. His face was sunken and distorted, a small hole in his temple marking the spot the bullet had entered.

Despite all of that, the freezing temperatures had preserved him better than Clare would have expected. And he didn't look the way she'd imagined.

Ezra was large—probably over six feet—and plump. That was clear even after the decay. His cheeks had lost their tautness, but she thought his face would have been round in life. Black hair lay in a limp side part across his olive forehead. Full lips hung open, giving her a glimpse of the still-white teeth inside. He couldn't have been older than twenty-five.

When she'd pictured Ezra, she'd imagined a wiry, tense man. Someone ruthlessly efficient. Someone that fit her idea of an obsessed, delusional scientist. But Ezra's clothes, stained by decay, were casual. An oversized sweater hung over a T-shirt and jeans.

Why, Ezra? Clare tilted her head back, being careful to breathe through her mouth. *You knew the thanites better than anyone. You could have helped reverse this. Is the situation really so impossible that you believed the only way out was death?*

The hollow's fist landed on the glass. Each slap sent reverberations through the room, jangling Clare's nerves and making her skin prickle. She couldn't stop staring at the dead scientist. The man who had killed her aunt, killed her sister, killed nearly everything good.

Peter had said he was trying to save the world. She didn't know if she should pity him or hate him. Part of her wished he'd stayed to salvage what they could of the ruins. Another part of her knew, if he had been alive, she would want to see him dead.

His ID tag peeked out from under his sweater. It lay facedown, half-buried by the folds of decaying skin and fabric. She braced herself and reached down. The corner of the badge was clean. She dragged it out and flipped it over.

The plastic shimmered in the harsh white lights. Clare took a step back and stared down at the picture on the placard. Like she'd guessed, he'd been plump in life, and he was smiling. The picture had most likely been taken on his first day at Aspect, and she could feel the nerves and excitement radiating out of it. He looked like he'd probably been a cheerful soul in life.

Beside the photo was a name: *Peter Wiesner.*

Clare closed her eyes. *That can't be possible.* Her heart thundered. The sick, squirming uneasiness that had kept her from sleeping redoubled until she felt like insects were crawling underneath her skin.

Oh no, no, no…

The man she'd known as Peter carried an ID tag that didn't belong to him. He'd borrowed it from one of his neighbor's desks. She'd been so wrapped up in the stress and hope of reaching the tower, it hadn't occurred to her to question why Peter hadn't been using his own badge. Her subconscious had picked up on it, though. It had picked up on a lot of things.

Peter had given her Ezra's room. A coffee mug sat on the sill. If it had been there since the stillness, the coffee would have long evaporated. But it was still half-full. Because it had been sipped from just that morning.

Peter's desk held a binder of notes on the bionic eye. Not

because he was lamenting his lost project, but because he needed to learn about it to make his backstory credible.

Stupid. Stupid. There were so many clues. So many slips. How could you have overlooked them all?

She opened her eyes. Her vision had blurred. She looked down at Peter, the real Peter, the one who had befriended Ezra and had been present to witness the disastrous results of his companion's trial.

In those earliest hours of the stillness, as Ezra listened to humanity dismantle itself on the back of his mistake, he would have faced a choice. He hadn't wanted to die. But to live would make him the most hated man in the world. No survivor would have welcomed him into their home. Most would have wanted to see him dead.

He could have fled the city, adopted a new name, and buried his secret. Only one person knew he was responsible for the thanites. That person was in the same room as him, and Ezra had access to a gun. Perhaps that was the moment he'd killed Peter in a desperate bid to hide his crimes.

But leaving the tower would mean abandoning his research, living in a world overrun with hollows, scrambling to find food and shelter just like every other survivor.

Ezra was smart. Through the panic, a solution would have presented itself. With Peter gone and the city fallen, everyone who had known his real identity was dead. He would stay in the tower and continue working. Because he thought he knew how to fix his mistake.

He wouldn't be known as the man who destroyed humanity. He would be the one who saved it.

Peter afforded him an easy identity to adopt. They were friends; he knew a little about Peter's research and Peter's life that he could use to make his story more plausible. He could recount the experience through Peter's eyes, acting as an innocent bystander. As Peter, he was blameless for the stillness. But he still had the skills to understand the thanites—and disable them. He would be hailed as a hero. Humanity's savior. The identity he'd yearned for when he'd first conceived the miracle cure.

Clare shook. She backed away from the body and felt behind herself to open the airtight door. As she moved back into the labs and the door slid closed, the reek of rotting flesh faded and breathing became easier.

We can't stay here. Clare kept her head down as she moved through the empty work spaces. She hated herself for bringing Dorran to the tower. She hated herself for believing Ezra's lies. And she felt sick to her stomach as she tried to imagine the very few options they had to leave.

Clare stopped at the metal doors, her breathing ragged, and fumbled for her ID tag. In the distance, the lab's resident hollow moaned and slammed its fist against its glass prison. The door's panel beeped as Clare held the ID up to it. She paused just long enough to scan the lab, searching for any way she might have disturbed it or left a trace of her presence, then switched the lights out and stepped into the stairwell's landing.

As the door shut behind her, Clare tried to slow her breathing.

She needed to get back to Dorran. It had been a mistake to leave him alone. As she blindly felt her way toward the stairs, her mind ran through a hundred awful possibilities. Ezra knew the tower. He *controlled* it. He would know where the weapons were hidden, including the gun he'd used to shoot his friend. He controlled the lights and radio that would allow them to leave. And he controlled the thanites.

It's okay. He doesn't know what you know.

Clare's feet slipped from step to step, moving as silently as she could. Her heart seemed too loud. She prayed the noise was only in her ears, not echoing through the stairwell like it seemed.

She turned the corner and her steps quickened as she approached the hall connecting the offices and bedrooms. She just needed to get back to Dorran. No matter how bad the situation, they could get through it as long as they were together.

Clare stumbled to a halt three steps from the hall. The red lights from the exit sign washed across the space. A figure stood in the hallway, silhouetted but familiar. Ezra stared up at Clare. She couldn't see much of him except for the bloodred light shining off his eyes.

Clare froze. Every atom in her body felt like it was shriveling, recoiling. Her mouth opened, a reflex more than a choice.

Ezra tilted his head, and the red glow brushed over his cheek and lips. "Where have you been?"

CHAPTER 52

EZRA'S WORDS SENT CHILLS running across Clare's back. They were spoken lightly, with almost a singsong cadence, but with no genuine friendliness in them.

She felt as though she were standing on the edge of a cliff, fighting to keep her balance. She had to speak. She didn't know if she was physically capable. But Ezra was watching her, head tilted, red-washed eyes unblinking. She couldn't see his hands.

There's a gun somewhere. The gun that killed Peter.

"I...I was hungry." Her voice wavered. She didn't know how well he could see her in the stairwell, but she didn't dare step any closer. The perspiration and shaking lips would give her away.

"Ah." Ezra's face tilted in the opposite direction, hiding his expression again. The silence was so complete that she could hear his breathing, featherlight. There was no trace of kindness in his voice. "But there was food in the office."

"I…" Her voice threatened to break. She swallowed. "I wanted an apple. I thought there might be some in another floor's vending machine."

Ezra didn't move. Clare wished she could see his face. The silence terrified her, and she rushed on, desperate. "I miss fresh food so much. It'd been weeks since I'd had any. I know I shouldn't have left my room, but I couldn't sleep, and I thought…if I could just have one more apple…"

"Did you find one?"

The words were a whisper. Clare's stomach tightened. Her nerves were prickling, on fire, her subconscious screaming at her to run, that something bad was coming, that she was in a cage with a tiger. "I…I…"

A click made her flinch. One of the bedroom doors opened and bright white light washed across Ezra. Finally, she could see his face. The harsh lines around his mouth. The way his bronze hair had been combed back. The tightness in his features.

Dorran stood in the open doorway. His expression was unreadable as his dark eyes moved from Ezra to Clare. "Is everything all right?"

"Hah." Ezra's pale face twitched, and a crooked smile grew. "Of course it is. Your companion decided to go for a midnight roam. You should keep a better eye on her."

Dorran held his hand toward Clare. She hurried to him, grateful. Ezra blocked the hallway and she had to pass so close to him that she could smell the tang of aftershave. She kept her head down, but she felt his eyes following her. She took Dorran's hand and slid close to him, half-hidden behind his arm.

Ezra blinked slowly. His smile hadn't budged. "Best not to do any more exploring tonight. There are too many rooms with hollows inside. If you want apples, tell me, and I'll get them for you."

"Yes," she managed.

The smile widened a fraction, then dropped. "Sleep well."

Clare tugged on Dorran's arm, pulling him back into their room. The door clicked closed. Clare released her breath and keeled forward to rest her forehead against Dorran's shoulder.

He wrapped his arm around her. "Are you all right? What happened?"

Clare took a breath to answer, then bit her tongue. She reached around Dorran to turn the room's lights off. As darkness swallowed them, she looked toward the base of the door. The red emergency light sent a thin band of color through the gap between the door and the carpet. The line of red was interrupted by a shadow. Ezra stood outside, so close that she could have touched him.

"I went looking for an apple," Clare managed.

Dorran followed her gaze. She could barely see him in the light coming through the window, but his eyebrows lowered. Clare lifted a finger and pressed it over her lips, and he gave a single nod.

His voice was relaxed and easy. "You shouldn't explore alone. Stay here with me for the rest of the night."

Thank you, Dorran. "Yeah."

They crossed to the bed and Dorran shook the sheets out. They sat on the edge of the mattress, facing the door. Dorran's arm circled around her to hold her possessively. Clare clung to his hand. Together, they watched the door. Minutes ticked by. Thunder crackled. Clare flinched, and Dorran squeezed her hand, wordlessly reassuring. Then the shadows outside the door shifted as Ezra paced away. Clare waited, straining to listen, but she didn't hear Ezra's own bedroom door open.

Dorran dipped his head so that he could whisper into her ear. "What happened?"

"That's not Peter. It's Ezra."

The hand holding her twitched. She heard him open his mouth, but he didn't immediately speak. Clare knew he must want to ask, *Are you sure?* But he didn't.

While they were still in Winterbourne, he'd made a promise to never doubt anything she told him again. He hesitated for only a second before asking, "What did you see?"

She briefly told him about the things she'd uncovered in the labs above them—Peter's body, his ID badge, the hollow kept alive in the observation room.

"Damn it," Dorran muttered.

"I should have known he wasn't being honest," Clare said. "Remember when he was telling his story and he mentioned hiding his neighbor's body? When you called him out on it, he backtracked and tried to say he was just hiding her from sight. I bet he only said that because he realized it put him in a bad light.

He would have covered up her death if the stillness hadn't interrupted him." Clare shook her head, incredulous. "I can't believe I didn't see it sooner."

"You had no reason to doubt him before this. Nor did I."

Clare tilted her head up to see Dorran's expression. He was frowning. She wondered if he was thinking along the same lines as her: that he'd been mistrustful of Peter. Dorran had discounted it as jealousy, and Clare had assumed he was just uncomfortable around strangers, but she wondered if his instincts had been picking up on the things she hadn't noticed.

"He said he spent the morning of the stillness calling news stations," Clare said. "He claimed he tried to get the word out and tell people to find airtight places to hide. But I watched the news that morning. So did my sister. No one had any idea what was happening. I bet he never called anyone. He wasn't focused on saving people; he was in damage-control mode, which meant keeping quiet. He just edited that part of his story because he knew it would sound bad."

"Which also explains why he was so unconcerned about how quickly the USB would reach Evandale. People are dying every day, and he pretends to care, but the truth is that he is more concerned with shoring up his own position. It does not matter to him whether the stillness is ended in a week or six months, only that he comes out of it blameless."

"Did you notice, when he spoke about Ezra, he praised his brilliance and tried to mitigate his faults? Even when he was trying to paint Ezra as another person, he couldn't stand to speak badly about him."

Dorran was silent for a moment. His fingers traced over hers, creating soothing patterns. Clare tried to focus on them and not on the red glow seeping under the door.

"He will be dangerous," Dorran said.

"Yeah. He has a gun. And he used it once before to keep his secret. Dorran…" She swallowed. "I don't think he believed my excuse. At best, he had doubts. I think he's paranoid."

A hint of terse protectiveness entered Dorran's voice. "I only caught the end of your conversation. Did he say anything to threaten you?"

"No. But I don't know what he would have said if you hadn't come out then." She remembered the intense, almost unnatural look on Ezra's face. "I think he's afraid of you."

"As he well should be," Dorran muttered. "I will see him thrown through a window before he lays a hand on you."

Clare chuckled, but then her smile dropped. The extent of their situation was starting to dawn on her. "I don't think we can leave Helexis Tower without his help. He controls the speakers and the spotlight. There's no way to get through the hollows without them, and I don't know how to turn them on."

"And he will not let us go if he thinks we know his secret."

The stress was almost unbearable. Clare wanted to move about to expend some of the overflowing energy, but she made herself keep still. Ezra wouldn't hear their whispers, but he might hear footsteps.

"We can't leave the room again tonight," she said. "We can't give him any more reason to doubt us."

"Is there any way to regain his trust?"

"Maybe." Clare chewed on her lip, her mind racing. "He's paranoid, but he has an ego too. He doesn't just want to destroy the hollows; he wants to make sure people know it was his doing."

And, for that, he needed witnesses. People who would know him as Peter, who could watch him work on the cure and help deliver it to the Evandale research station. That was why he'd sent out the broadcast. And why he had been so friendly, so kind, so eager to please. Clare and Dorran had been intended to carry accounts of him across the country as they journeyed home.

Dorran said, "We are the only people to arrive in the weeks he has been broadcasting."

"Right. And that's probably the strongest factor in our favor right now."

Dorran rested his head next to hers, his eyes still affixed to the door. "What do you propose?"

"We stay here tonight. Tomorrow, we walk into the office as though nothing happened. I'll try to find a way to talk about other survivors we met on the way here and how we're hoping to meet up again when we leave. If I can do it in a natural way, it will put the idea in his mind that people will be waiting to hear us talk about him."

"And imply that word of his cure will spread quickly if he entrusts the USB to us."

"Exactly. He'll be more reluctant to kill people who promise to sing his praises to the world. That might be enough of a temptation to outweigh his doubts."

They shared a look. In the dim light, Clare hoped Dorran wouldn't notice the fear she was trying to hide behind confidence. The plan was weak, but they didn't have any alternatives. It was their only card to play.

Too much depended on factors outside of their control. How paranoid Ezra truly was, whether he still had enough morals to shy away from killing innocents, how desperate he felt. Clare tried for a shaky smile, and she thought the smile she received in return was just as unsteady.

Dorran said, "As long as we can get out of the tower, we can get to the river or onto the rural roads, and we should be all right."

Clare nodded. "We can do it. We can make him think we're his allies."

"And until then, we stay close together, yes?"

"Yes."

He kissed her lightly. "Try to get some rest. I'll keep guard."

CHAPTER 53

CLARE SLEPT FITFULLY. IN her dreams, she repeatedly saw Ezra's face, bathed in the red light, grinning up at her. She woke sweaty and shaking, only to be lulled back to sleep by Dorran's gentle whispers as his fingers ran through her hair. He stayed sitting on the edge of the bed, facing the door. The second time Clare woke, she offered to take over the watch, but he just kissed her and told her to go back to sleep.

The storm raged through the night, and by the time dawn came, it hadn't abated. The clock on the wall told her it was eight in the morning and Clare felt less groggy. If not for that, she would have believed it was still deep night.

"Good morning," Dorran murmured as she sat up. He was crouched by one of the drawers but slid it closed and returned to sit next to Clare on the bed. Dark shadows clung around his eyes and he looked leaner than the day before, but he smiled at her.

Clare brushed hair away from her face as she blinked at the room. "Is everything okay?"

"Yes. I was looking for anything we might use to defend ourselves." His shoulders rose and dropped in a weary shrug. "This room has nothing sharper than a pencil and nothing heavier than a book."

Ezra probably hid any weapons before he started his broadcast. Clare dropped her legs over the edge of the bed to sit at Dorran's side. "We'll have to go out soon, won't we?"

"If we don't want to seem suspicious, yes." Dorran was quiet for a second, then said, "He came past the room four times last night. He stopped just outside the door but didn't try to come in. I would be surprised if he slept at all."

For a moment, they stayed on the edge of the bed, staring at the thin door separating them from the rest of the facility. Then Clare inhaled and straightened her back. "It's only going to be worse if we put it off."

"Mm." Dorran picked up the lab coat Clare had worn the day before and held it out to her.

They dressed quickly. Clare tied her hair back and checked herself in the room's mirror. She looked pale. She hoped Ezra wouldn't notice. As they approached the door, Dorran took her hand and whispered, "Stay near me as much as possible."

The hallway was empty. Clare couldn't stop herself from glancing toward the stairs to their left. The storm was muffled in the hallway, but she could still feel the reverberations through her bones and still sense the building swaying under her feet.

Dorran used his ID to unlock the work area's door. Clare held on to Dorran with one hand and clenched the other into a fist as the door swung open. They stepped through, and she blinked in the sudden light.

"Good morning, good morning!" Ezra sat at his desk, his hair messy and his grin wide. One hand rested over the laptop's keys, obviously interrupted in the middle of typing. The desk was littered with empty energy drink cans. He tilted his head a little as he watched them. "I hope you had a good night's sleep. Except for that little excursion, ha!"

"Yes." Clare made herself smile. She'd expected Ezra to be quiet or suspicious of her, the way he'd appeared the night before. Instead, he was almost bouncing with cheerfulness. In some ways, it was even more unnerving. "Um, sorry for waking you."

"Oh, don't worry about that." He waved her apology away. "I was already up. Though I'll say you gave me quite a fright, appearing on the stairs like that. I'm almost done here. Why don't you get some breakfast? I went and found more apples for you, Clare, so you won't have to go scurrying over the building anymore."

Clare looked toward the seating area. A small pile of apples had been arranged into a pyramid shape beside the previous day's stack of chips and chocolate. She did her best to look enthused. "That's really kind, thank you."

Ezra returned to his laptop, his fingers moving at a blinding speed as he built code. Clare exchanged a look with Dorran. He lifted his eyebrows. She gave a small nod, and they approached the food.

Clare's throat was tight and her stomach upset, but she still ate. They couldn't afford to raise suspicion. As far as Ezra was concerned, it was a normal morning.

The heater was already on, and Clare sat near it as she worked her way through an apple. She barely tasted it. Dorran ate as well, and positioned himself carefully to keep Ezra in his peripheral vision without making it obvious he was watching. Ezra didn't so much as lift his head from the laptop.

Clare threw away her core, and Dorran passed her another apple. "Eat," he murmured, bending close to make sure the man at the desk wouldn't hear. "You may need the energy."

She was sick of both apples and nuts by the time she was full. She downed a bottle of water and tried to relax. It was impossible as long as Ezra was in the same room. Still, though, he didn't look up from the computer, and Clare didn't dare interrupt him. She felt awkward just sitting there, and turned toward the bookcase. She picked up a novel indiscriminately—a well-worn thriller— and opened it to a random page. She stared at it without reading.

Is he faking? Or does he genuinely not suspect? Maybe he's telling the truth; maybe he seemed off last night because I startled him. Is it possible he isn't worried about what's in the lab?

That seemed impossible, but on the other hand, Ezra seemed completely relaxed. He would either need to be an exceptional actor…or his nonchalance was genuine.

A chair creaked, and Clare flinched. Ezra leaned back at his desk, arms reached high as he stretched his back. He sagged back down with a hearty sigh, then unplugged something from the laptop and stood.

The familiar smile greeted them as he sauntered toward the chairs. Clare knew, if she was going to establish trust, this was the time to do it. She put the book aside and leaned forward, affecting friendliness. "Dorran and I were talking about our plans for when we leave here. We know a group of survivors less than an hour away; we thought we'd stop by there and see if any of them would take the data to Evandale."

Ezra dropped into a chair opposite and pulled one leg up underneath himself. "That sounds great. Did you meet many people before you reached the tower?"

Clare desperately hoped he wouldn't hear the lie in her voice. "Yeah, quite a few. I'm looking forward to checking in on them and making sure they're okay. And telling them about your cure." *Easy, easy, don't oversell it.* "I think it's really brave. To pick up Ezra's project and…and try to make things right. A lot of people would have just run. But you didn't. And I think that's admirable."

His face lit up, though he tried to shrug it off. "Hah. Well. There isn't anyone else who could have done it, and…it's not for me. It's for everyone surviving out there, you know?"

Clare nodded, encouraging. "They'll be grateful. I know I am. To think we could have our world back… It's more hope than I ever let myself have before."

"It's going to be a long road. But we'll get there. Humans are nothing if not resourceful."

You especially.

"That's what I was just coming to tell you." Ezra lifted his hand. A silver USB drive sparkled in his palm. "I pulled an all-nighter and I think I finished my code."

"You…" Clare stared at it. "Really?"

"Uh-huh. I don't know if it will work yet. It'll need testing, but that's all up to the people at Evandale now. You two can leave as soon as you want."

Clare's heart flipped. It seemed too good to be true. She dared a glance at Dorran, but his expression remained inscrutable.

Is it possible…Ezra wants to get us out of the tower just as much as we want to leave? His smile was broad and easy. Clare hunted for signs of tension underneath but couldn't detect any. *Maybe he doesn't want a confrontation. Maybe he just wants us gone.*

"We…uh… That's amazing." She fought to phrase herself diplomatically. "We…we're really looking forward to going home. We could leave today. Take the USB as close to Evandale as we can, find someone who will carry it the rest of the way, and, uh…"

"That sounds marvelous." Ezra glanced over his shoulder, toward the window. "The rain is pretty bad, but I can give you some waterproof covers. And load you up with food. And, of course, use the spotlight and radio to give you protection for as long as I can. I think you have a really good chance of getting out of the city."

Please. Please let this be honesty. Please let him keep his promise.

"Thank you," Dorran said. The words sounded warm, but Clare knew they cost him a lot of effort. "You have been a generous host."

"Ah. Just doing what I can to better a messed-up world." Ezra tucked the USB back into his jacket pocket and clapped his hands. "How soon do you think you'll leave? You could go right now, if you wanted. It's probably smart to get a head start early in the day. Maximize your hours of light, such as it is."

Clare licked her lips. "That's a good idea. I'm ready to go."

"Fantastic. Let's get you some supplies. Come with me." Ezra bounded out of his chair and moved toward the door. Clare's hope was tempered with a sense of foreboding. She didn't like the idea of following Ezra into strange parts of the building, but she didn't have an excuse not to.

Dorran's smile had faded, and his eyes were sharp. He took her hand, and together they stood and followed Ezra across the room.

"Where are we going?" Clare asked.

Ezra held the door open for them, rocking on the balls of his feet, one arm directing them toward the stairs. "Just up to the lab."

Clare nearly faltered. A sickly sense of dread rose, pumping through her veins, making her light-headed. "Oh?"

"The hazmat suits will be a good way to keep you dry through the rain and protect from the hollows, and we can get a container to keep the USB dry. Oh, I haven't shown you guys the labs yet, have I?" Ezra thrust his hands into his pockets as he sauntered toward the stairwell. "I used to love working up there. When all of the rooms were full, it was like a buzzing beehive. Everyone working on their own tasks, but also working as a group. If one of us was having trouble, we could tap on the glass and get our neighbor to help us brainstorm ideas."

"Sounds like it was fun."

"Oh, absolutely." He took the stairs quickly, jogging up two at a time and swiveling on the landing to watch them follow. "I miss those guys."

Clare was torn between reluctance and trying to appear enthusiastic. Her smile was growing painful. She matched Ezra's quick pace, and Dorran stayed at her side, shadowing her.

Ezra stopped at the metal doors and waved his badge over the reader. "Here we are. The hallowed labs. Try not to touch anything. I don't know what all of my coworkers were building, and there might be some monster viruses in test tubes or something."

The lights blinked on, moving through the vast room in waves, and Clare had a painful sense of déjà vu from the previous night. Her hand was sweaty, but she didn't let go of Dorran, and he didn't try to release the hold.

"Beautiful, isn't it?" Ezra extended a hand toward the rooms. "Aspect poured literally millions into this space. They could afford to, considering some of the stuff that came out of it. Each new hire had a space custom fitted for their needs. Mine was pretty simple—just a counter, some proprietary tools, and some tubes to grow the biological components. Ezra got a whole wall to himself."

Ezra led them through the room, seemingly happy to take his time and admire the contents of each chamber. The closer they drew to the final room, the tighter Clare's nerves wound. She was sure she hadn't left any evidence of her presence there. She'd turned out all lights, closed all doors. There was nothing Ezra could use to prove she knew about—

No. A spike of panic, sharp enough to turn her momentarily blind, speared through Clare. Her heart missed a beat, then redoubled its efforts as its flight-or-fight instincts kicked in. Dorran felt the change and sent her a concerned glance. She opened her mouth, but there was no way to communicate her fear to him.

She'd left Peter's body uncovered.

No. No. Why didn't I pull the coat back over him? Why did I leave him exposed? Did Ezra see? Is that why we're up here?

Ezra's path was leading them steadily toward the chambers at the back of the room. In a few more paces, he would be close enough to see Peter's uncovered body. Clare pulled on Dorran's hand, stopping their progress. Her voice sounded too tight. "Peter? I, uh, I can put the USB in a bag I have. We won't need the case."

He turned to face her, his smile horribly wide. "No. I guess you don't."

CHAPTER 54

EZRA'S HANDS CAME OUT of his pockets. A glint of metal accompanied them. Clare didn't even have time to breathe before he aimed the pistol at Dorran's chest. Ezra's smile seemed as though it had been fused to his face. "Get into the chamber."

Dorran lowered his center of gravity. It was a subtle change, but one Clare had seen before. He was braced to attack.

"Uh-uh, no." Instead of pointing the gun at Dorran, Ezra leveled it at Clare's face. "Move and she pays for it."

Dorran bared his teeth. Ezra took a step back, but his aim didn't waver. "Go into the right-hand chamber. Both of you. The door is unlocked."

The atmosphere felt thick enough to choke on. Dorran was wound tight, his grip on Clare's hand strong enough to hurt. She could see the muscles in his face twitch as he ran through their choices.

But there *was* no choice. Nowhere to run. No way to defend against the pistol. Clare moved first, stepping toward the glass wall, and Dorran reluctantly followed.

She coaxed shaking hands to turn the handle. It beeped as it opened, and the stench of rotting flesh flooded around them. She heard Ezra gag behind her and shot him a glance. He held one arm across his mouth and nose, eyes squinted nearly closed, but the gun remained steady. "Stand by the door there. The right-hand one. Don't move."

It put them closer to Peter's body than Clare wanted. She tried not to stare at him. Even bloated, even decayed, his face had a friendly quality to it. She wished *he'd* been the one to greet them at the tower. Her chest ached.

The computer on the opposite side of the chamber was already turned on. Ezra backed toward it, never taking his eyes off them, and pressed a button. The chamber door clicked and a hissing noise told her an airlock had been released.

"It's open. Go in."

To Clare's surprise, he sounded subdued. Sad, even. *It might not be too late to reason with him. He's a murderer, but he's also desperate.* "Ezra—"

"In!" he barked.

She pushed on the door. It glided inward, and Clare stepped through. Dorran's narrowed eyes stayed fixed on Ezra as he moved behind her. As the door closed, it clicked, and Clare knew it had locked.

Ezra lowered the gun with a heavy sigh. He tossed it onto the counter, almost carelessly, and pulled the roller seat out. Instead of sitting in it, he stood at its back, hands braced on the fabric and head bowed.

The containment room was void of any furniture. Its back walls were white-painted concrete. The floor was tile. The front wall was glass, as was the barrier separating them from the adjacent chamber. Clare glanced to her right. The other chamber had been unusually quiet, considering what lived in it. The lower half of the glass was frosted, and Clare edged closer, trying to catch a glimpse of their companion.

Ezra sighed a second time, then pushed his chair closer, until it was directly outside the door. He sat in it, facing them, and folded his hands in his lap as he leaned forward. The harshness had left his face. He looked gaunt and tired, and his lips twitched as he glanced between them. "I don't know how to say this. But...I hope you will understand. I am so incredibly sorry. For everything."

Clare licked her lips. She had never felt so much pressure to choose her words well. "Ezra...we can fix this."

He lifted his head, and his eyes glistened. "Can we?"

"We'll never speak a word of this. You have my promise. And I don't break promises."

One side of his mouth lifted into a lopsided grin. "You're nice. That's been the hardest part. When I put out the signal, I was hoping some crazies would show up. Because you'd have to be crazy to listen to a radio that played nonsense, right?"

Clare didn't understand. She swallowed and tried again. "I don't think you want to kill us."

"No, I don't." He dropped his head into his hands, fingers digging through his hair.

"And you don't have to. We won't cause you any trouble. We…we just want to leave peacefully. We won't take any of your supplies."

He didn't move. Thunder crackled outside the walls. She was so sick of it. The constant noise, the constant energy, charging the air, making her head buzz and her muscles ache. One peal barely died before another one began. She wanted to scream.

Keep it under control. Stay patient. He's responding to kindness. Do this for Dorran.

Dorran stayed at the back of the room, head down, shoulders bowed, hands behind his back. They had an unspoken understanding. Ezra liked Clare. He didn't like Dorran. He was *afraid* of Dorran, and fear could be dangerous. So Dorran sunk into the darkest corner of the room, where he blended into the gray walls, forgotten. He was good at it. Clare guessed he'd learned to be inconspicuous at Winterbourne, where it would have been a survival mechanism used around his mother. Out of sight, out of mind, out of danger.

Clare stepped up to the glass and rested one hand on it. She made her voice as gentle as she could manage, head lowered. "Ezra, this will be all right. You're not a murderer. And…we don't want to push you to that. You can step back and unlock the door. We'll go straightaway. You won't ever have to worry about us again. I'm sorry for making you worry in the first place."

He leaned back. His face had been handsome, but now it was

creased with deep lines as his expression twisted. Lips pulled up as though he was trying to smile, but Clare thought it was more of an attempt not to cry. "You're nice. I'd hoped I would get one of the crazy prepper types. Someone who was a drain on society, so I could lead them straight up to the labs and not feel guilty about it. But you...you looked so relieved to be here. And sad. And scared. And I couldn't do it."

Clare didn't like the turn the conversation was taking.

Ezra dug his fingers into his hair. A drip of saliva fell from the grimacing teeth. He took a shuddering breath and leaned back, wiping his sleeve over his chin. "I want you to know I'm not a bad person. Everything...all of it, *everything*, it was always to help people. My thanites would have saved millions of lives. If Aspect hadn't put such an unrealistic deadline on my work, if I hadn't been pushed as hard as I was, I could have been more careful and it never would have gotten out of the lab. It wasn't my fault!"

He stood and began pacing. Clare didn't know what to say. He seemed to want her to agree with him, to absolve him of blame. "I understand."

"What was I supposed to do?" He threw his hands out. His eyes bulged. "Wait for the committee to approve human trials? My grant was up at the end of the month. It would have all gone to waste, been trashed—or, worse, they would have stolen it, just like Saul stole my earlier work. That snake grew fat off my blood and sweat. I couldn't let that happen again. So I took a risk—not for my sake, but for humanity's sake, you understand? I couldn't have known what would happen. It wasn't my fault. I was trying to do the right thing! The stillness affected me just as much as anyone. And Peter kept screaming at me, 'What have you done? What have you done?' And I—I—"

Clare's eyes drifted to Peter's bloated, rotting corpse and the tiny bullet hole above his temple.

"I'm not a bad person." Ezra swung back to her. "If I were… if I were…I'd have taken the coward's way out. But I didn't. I stayed. Because I'm the only one alive who can fix this. I really can! I've been working nonstop these last three weeks. And I think I've got it."

"I believe you." Clare was so close to the glass her breath misted over it. "You're a good person. Which is why you'll let us leave."

"Oh. Clare." He stepped closer. His hand touched the glass's other side, pressed over where hers rested. The urge to recoil washed over Clare, and she fought to suppress it. "I was really thinking about sending you and your friend away. I fought with myself over it, telling myself that I could wait for a different traveler to find the tower…"

She leaned in close, matching his pose, hoping he wouldn't see how badly she was shaking. "It's not too late."

He exhaled, head drooping. When he lifted his face, moisture shone in his eyes and sweat beaded on his forehead, but his expression was smoother. "No, Clare. I can't wait for someone else to find the tower. It could be weeks, and every day, more people are dying. Please listen closely, and I know you'll understand. Sacrifices need to be made."

"Ezra—"

His eyes bored into hers, unrelenting. "This purpose is greater than you, and it's greater than me. You can help save countless lives. Wouldn't you like that? Don't you want to be a hero?"

She nearly choked on the words. "I want to be *alive*."

"I know. I know. I don't want to hurt you. I'm a gentle person. I'm not here to kill you, I promise."

Clare opened her mouth, then closed it again.

Ezra saw the doubt in her face and lowered his voice to a plaintive whisper. "I need help with the code. If we do this right, both of you can leave the tower unharmed. I'll even use the sirens to chase the hollows away from the doors. You can be free, just like you want."

She licked dry lips. "What type of help do you need?"

Peter nodded toward the chamber beside them. "When I realized, last night, that you knew what really happened—" His voice caught, and he took a second to collect himself. "I realized I was out of time. So I worked as hard as I ever had to finish my code. I came up to test it on her. And look; it worked."

Clare dreaded what she might see, but she had to know. She stepped closer to the glass dividing her from the second chamber.

"Oh." She swallowed the nauseated moan that wanted to escape.

The hollow was barely recognizable. White bones and red gore mingled in confusing and horrific ways. She had to take a second look to figure out where the creature's head was.

It was as though the hollow had been butchered. Except the

splits in the skin seemed to have started on its inside. Pus-like liquid seeped out of the holes. Flecks of flesh dotted the floor and walls. *Like a million tiny explosions went off inside its body.*

"The code works," Peter said. His grin, lopsided, grew as he followed Clare's gaze. "It deactivates the thanites, which in turn kills the hollows. She went down in just twelve seconds—and she stayed down."

Clare stepped back from the glass. Bitter bile filled her mouth. It was physically painful to smile, but she made her muscles work. "That's…amazing. You really did it."

"Yes. But I'm afraid it's not ready yet. There's still too much uncertainty."

Guessing where the conversation was leading, Clare began to nod. "So now it needs to go to Evandale. We can take it."

"No." A sharp note entered his voice. It was harsh enough that Clare flinched. Ezra's expression darkened, and even though he lowered his voice, it didn't lose its edge. "This was *my* discovery. *My* code. They won't get their hands on it."

He's possessive. He had his research stolen once; he's determined to keep the glory this time. "Okay. That…that's fine."

Ezra ran his hand over his jaw and turned his eyes toward the ceiling. They glittered in the artificial light. "I know it will work against the hollows. There's only one uncertainty. Will it be safe for humans?"

His gray eyes flicked down to meet Clare's. Her stomach dropped. She shook her head, backing away from the glass. "Ezra…no."

"I'm almost certain you'll be fine." He dropped his hand and crept closer. "You'll have barely any thanites compared to a hollow. And I think I've rigged up the destruction to cause minimal damage to a human host. I'm certain it's safe. Almost. We just need to be sure."

Clare wanted to scream at him *You thought the thanites would be safe when you activated them,* but she forced the words back down. Antagonism wouldn't save them. She tried to hold on to her composure, keep the gentle cadence in her voice. "Don't do this to us, Ezra."

"*Someone* has to test it." Now, it was his turn to sound coaxing. He spread his hands. "This is why I was hoping one of the crazies would find me. It crushed me to see how friendly and hopeful you were. But I can't afford to wait for someone else to stumble on the tower, you understand? If we have any hope of rebuilding our world, we need to eliminate the hollows as quickly as possible. And if that involves some risk, or even some sacrifices, well, it will be worth it."

Clare's throat had tightened. It made breathing difficult and thinking even worse. A warm hand rested on her shoulder. She looked up to see Dorran at her side. He was no longer trying to vanish into the background; that meant he thought the war had been lost.

"Look, if I'm right, you'll be fine." Ezra spread his arms, a smile twitching across his features. "And I'm *sure* I'm right. The thanites have been my life for the last year. I know how to handle them. How to destroy them. So, here's the deal. You get through this test, and I let you leave, unharmed."

You finished the code in a one-night, energy-drink-fueled binge. At least take the time to double-check it! Clare opened her mouth, but the words failed her. All she could think of was the dead hollow in the next chamber, its body ripped apart from the inside.

"*Trust* me," Ezra said. "I know what I'm doing. Heaven willing, it will work, and you can walk out of here by this time tomorrow."

She shook her head furiously. Dorran's hand tightened over her shoulder.

"Well, it's going to happen whether you want it or not." The smile twisted into something bitter. "So if one of you wants to volunteer to go first, now's the time to speak up."

CHAPTER 55

DORRAN STEPPED FORWARD. "I will."

Clare grabbed his sleeve and yanked him back. "No!"

"This will be all right." Dorran turned to face her, his wide shoulders blocking Ezra from sight. He ran his fingers across her cheek as he brushed loose hair behind her ear.

Hot tears spilled over her lids. She let them fall unchecked. "No, please, Dorran, don't. We have to stay together."

"Shh. Trust me." He bent to kiss her. Warm lips, salty with her tears, lingering. As he pulled away, he whispered, softly enough that it wouldn't carry, "Wait until he is away from the room, then go for the gun."

Dorran raised his eyebrows, and Clare's breath caught. *He has a plan.* She leaned into him, searching his eyes, silently asking for confirmation. He gave a very small smile as he stepped back, then turned to face the glass separating him from Ezra. "I'm ready."

"Good. Good." Ezra backed toward the control panel. His fingers shook as he adjusted its settings. Clare's focus drifted from the buttons to the pistol perched on top of the panel. Ezra seemed to have forgotten about it.

Go for the gun when he leaves the room. When? How are you going to make this work, Dorran?

"This is what we're going to do, big guy." Ezra faced them, one hand poised over the switches. "You'll move into the second chamber. You won't try *anything*. You understand? No heroics, no attacks, nothing sneaky. Because if I get even a hint of reluctance, I'll press this button. That's going to activate the thanites in your friend's chamber."

Clare shivered, and Ezra tilted his head to give them a piercing stare.

"You know what that means, right? There are still plenty of thanites floating through the air. Even if you got the upper hand on me, you'd have to watch your girl turn into one of those mindless, soulless creatures you've been killing. So no fast movements, because it would be awfully easy for my hand to slip. Right?"

"I understand."

Clare wanted to reach out to Dorran. His voice was flat, and it seemed to cost him effort to keep it that way.

Please, Dorran, whatever you're planning, be safe.

"You, Clare, step back against the far wall. Yes, just like that. Don't move." Ezra waited a second to make sure she was following his instructions, then pressed a button. The chamber's door hissed as the seal was broken, then whirred as it slid open. Dorran stepped through. Uneasy itches crawled over Clare as she watched him go.

As Dorran stepped out of the room, he subtly reached behind himself, holding his ID tag out of Ezra's view. He slipped the plastic card into the closing door. It caught, its cord dangling, as he stepped away. Clare's breath hitched. The ID tag lodged in the door's lock, leaving the glass panel a millimeter ajar.

"Into the other chamber." Ezra hadn't noticed. His attention was wholly focused on Dorran, and the strain in his voice betrayed his stress. His hand hovered over the button, fingers trembling. The unit beside them opened with a muffled hiss.

Ezra gagged as the air inside was released. Clare couldn't smell it, but she guessed the hollow must reek as badly as Peter's corpse. Dorran's expression remained impassive. He gave Ezra one slow, calculating glare, then stepped into the second chamber. The door hissed closed, and Ezra nodded as he removed his hand from the control panel.

"Good. Good. All right." Ezra rocked back on his heels. He looked happy. "I was hoping you'd volunteer, big guy. You look strong enough to brush off any side effects. You should be fine."

Dorran glanced toward the dead hollow at his feet. He folded his arms and faced the glass, silent, unreadable.

Clare couldn't so much as breathe. Her pulse was deafening, her eyes burning. She held perfectly still, not even letting herself look down, terrified that movement might draw Ezra's attention to the door's lock, where the ID tag was pinned.

Clever, Dorran. But how are you going to get him to leave?

"Good, good…" Ezra typed on his computer. Code flashed across the screen. "You won't need to do anything, just stand there."

Come on, Dorran, you don't have much time. What's your plan?

Dorran steadfastly faced forward, refusing to meet her eyes or give her any clues. His instructions had been to wait until Ezra was gone before running for the gun. But Ezra wasn't showing any sign of leaving. He was typing on his control panel.

And Dorran still refused to look at her.

A terrible idea occurred. He wasn't trying to barter with Ezra or manipulate him or coax him outside, because he knew it wouldn't work. Dorran expected Ezra to leave the room…*after* the experiment.

"Wait," Clare choked out. She hit her palm on the glass wall between her and Dorran. The deep reverberations rattled through her enclosure. "Stop!"

Ezra ignored her. He lifted his head, and shadows haunted his cheeks and the hollows under his eyes as he smiled at Dorran. "Good luck."

He pressed a button. A sharp blue light flashed at the top of the chamber. Clare thought she heard a high-pitched note ringing from the room, but the sound was so piercing she couldn't tell if it was real or in her imagination.

Dorran crumpled. The effect was instantaneous; one second, he was standing straight, reliable, unyielding. The next, he was gone. He landed heavily, facing away from Clare.

Ezra's eyes widened, his smile frozen, as he watched in cold fascination. His finger didn't lift from the button.

Clare slammed her shoulder into the door. The lock, propped open by the name tag, gave way as she forced the glass open. She launched into the main room, desperation and fear driving her.

"Wait—" Ezra swiveled, shocked. His finger came off the button. The high-pitched noise faded. "You—"

Clare's fist hit his jaw. He slammed into the wall and dropped, one hand cupped over the bruised skin, his eyes wide.

The gun was within reach. Dorran had wanted her to get it. He'd expected her to use it to protect herself if he never came out of the test chamber. But Clare ignored the weapon. Dorran lay on the cold tile floor, horribly still, and every other necessity paled in comparison to her need to get him out.

She wrenched the USB out of its slot, physically removing the code. Numb hands scrambled across the dashboard, trying to remember which switches operated the doors. She found what she thought was the right one. Turned it. Air hissed as the chamber's airlock opened, and the awful scent of drying blood mingled with the already foul air.

Clare reached toward the open door. Something hard slammed into her legs, upending them. She fell and hit the tile floor hard. Bitter blood ran across her tongue as she bit the inside of her cheek. She rolled and was just in time to avoid the chair Ezra slammed down toward her.

He stood, hunched, breathing heavily, his hair falling into disarray. The chair rose as he prepared to deliver a new blow.

Clare kicked her foot out, and he yelped as she hit his shin. The chair dropped. Ezra stepped back, wary, and Clare again tried to reach for the glass door. Ezra lunged forward and grabbed her ankle, dragging her back.

"Don't," he barked. "You'll contaminate the sample."

It took her a second to understand what Ezra meant. *The sample. Dorran.* Anger rose, blooming out of her stomach and pouring into her lungs like molten lava. Clare swiped at him, curling her hands to use the nails like claws, fighting to get him off her. His elbow jabbed into her chest, sending a spasm of pain across her ribs. Then a forearm pressed over her throat. In an instant, her air was cut off.

Clare struggled. Ezra was larger and heavier than her and used his weight to pin her down. The smile, frantically wide, filled her vision. Then Ezra yelped. The pressure disappeared from her throat, and Clare dragged in a gasping breath. She rolled over.

Dorran was no longer in the chamber. He stood over Ezra, eyes blazing and lips pulled back in a snarl. Vivid blood dripped over his face.

Clare scrambled to her feet. She was just in time to catch Dorran as he staggered. She wrapped her arms around his chest and set her feet to hold him up.

Ezra had fallen with his back against the control panel. His skin was white, sweat beading over his face, a vein pulsing in his throat beneath the scores Clare had left. One hand raised the gun.

"Out," Dorran gasped.

Clare pulled them both left, toward the door leading to the main part of the lab. A *crack*, so loud that her ears rang, boomed around them. The massive glass panel fragmented, a spiderweb of cracks growing over it as a bullet punctured through.

They ran into the labs. Clare kept her arm around Dorran, supporting him as much as she could. His breathing was labored. That frightened her. So did the blood dripping off the tip of his nose and over his lips. But he matched her steps as they ran for the door.

Another crack and one of the tiles on the back wall exploded. They skidded to a halt at the doors. Clare slammed her tag into the sensor, and as the metal sheets slid back, they darted through. They sidestepped to put the solid concrete wall at their backs as the doors whirred closed.

The hallway was too dark to see anything except the outline of Dorran's profile. Clare held his arm, her fingers digging into his jacket sleeve. "Tell me where you're hurt."

"I'm fine." He was still gasping. "We need to lose Ezra."

The red glow of exit lights flowed through the stairwell in both directions. Clare bit her lip. "How far can you run?"

"As far as you need."

She remembered following Ezra toward the generator the previous day, and the way he'd turned red and breathless. "We can go up. He's not fast on the stairs. It will buy us a couple of minutes."

"Good." Dorran caught her hand and pulled her forward.

Using the red light as a guide, Clare took the stairs two at a time. She stayed conscious of Dorran beside her, silently counting his steps and listening to him breathe. He didn't sound good.

Beneath them, the lab doors banged open. Clare clenched her teeth. Her mind ran through the building, hunting for any way out. The hollows surrounded the ground level. She had no idea how to control the lights and audio system to drive them off. They could hide in one of the rooms, but that was, at best, a temporary measure. Ezra knew the building. Ezra controlled the surveillance and the security systems.

We can't hide. We can't leave. Can we fight?

She didn't want to be a killer. The hollows were one thing, but this was a human—a living, thinking, sensitive human. She didn't know if she could look him in the eyes and end his life.

Is there any choice? Dorran was in no shape to fight. He moved unsteadily, eyes half-closed. He didn't want to tell her how bad it was, but his pain was palpable. She had to protect him, no matter what the cost. *I need a weapon. Something that can compete with a gun.*

In the three weeks he'd been trapped, Ezra must have gone through the entire tower. He'd marked the rooms with hollows inside. If there were any weapons, he would have found them, and most likely hidden them. He'd known his transmission would draw irrational, dangerous people. He would have been prepared. He would have ensured he had the strongest upper hand possible.

Not quite. There's one weapon in the building he didn't hide. The hollows.

They reached a landing and Clare pulled on Dorran's hand to keep him from turning the corner. The thump of feet on marble stairs rang from below. They sounded heavy; Ezra was already flagging. A different kind of thumping came from behind them. Clare turned toward the hallway.

Rows of doors lined the walls, with the red exit light above their heads radiating its grim color across the space. Something unseen beat its fists against the nearest door. Red masking tape had been used to draw a large X across the surface.

"I need you to trust me," she hissed to Dorran.

He gave her a crooked smile. "I always have."

"When I say go, unlock that door and open it."

Clare left him beside the occupied room and jogged along the hallway. Ezra must have already searched the space; doors stood open, exposing sterile meeting rooms and abandoned lecture halls. Inside the second conference room, she found a fire extinguisher half-hidden behind a dead potted fern. She wrenched it out of its holder and removed its safety pin as she returned to the hallway.

Dorran waited beside the door. Clare paused behind him to listen. The footsteps were drawing closer. Close enough, she thought. She nodded to Dorran. He nodded back, then turned the lock and pulled the door open.

CHAPTER 56

A HULKING, MISSHAPEN CREATURE spilled into the hallway. Drooping, pendulous flaps of skin pooled over each other, swinging as the hollow turned toward Clare. She had just enough time to see its beady eyes flash red in the exit light, then she pulled on the extinguisher's handle.

White foam exploded across the creature. It bellowed, a deep, reverberating tone that shook the air around them. Clare moved a step nearer, the extinguisher shuddering in her hands, and the hollow's howl intensified as it retreated.

Clare knew the monster had spent most of a month in isolation, and she'd hoped the sudden stimulus would be too much for it to cope with. Her gamble paid off. The hollow staggered toward the stairs, and Clare followed it. As they neared the top step, Clare lifted the extinguisher and slammed its base into the hollow's chest.

The creature howled as it fell down the stairs. Horrible

crackling noises rose as its fragile bones broke. Clare stepped back, breathing more heavily than she'd expected, and stopped at Dorran's side.

A surprised cry rose from Ezra. Clare closed her eyes, half of her praying the strategy would work, the other half dreading it. A gunshot echoed from the landing below, followed by a second. Clare waited. She was greeted by silence.

One bullet to kill Peter. Two bullets chasing us out of the lab. Another two to kill the hollow. He should have one left.

"Up," Clare whispered, dropping the fire extinguisher. "We need to find another hollow."

Dorran followed her onto the stairs. New noises rose from the lower floor. Ezra, swearing. The hollow had upset him. *Good.*

Her legs burned and her chest ached from where she'd been hit, but Clare didn't slow down. The hollow hadn't stalled Ezra for long. They stopped at the fifteenth floor, and Clare slunk forward, listening. She couldn't find any red tape on the doors. The floor was silent.

Dorran gave her a short nod, his hair shining in the red light, and they turned back to the stairs. Clare could no longer hear Ezra's footsteps below them. That worried her.

They took the next two flights in long strides. The stairs ended in a narrow foyer with windows on either side. Harsh lightning illuminated the room in sporadic, painful flashes. A single door stood in front of Clare. It looked familiar. She turned and saw a solid wall where the stairs were supposed to continue. They had reached the highest floor.

She pressed a hand over her mouth as she tried to swallow the overwhelming sense of panic. They were cornered. There was nowhere to hide on the highest level, and no hollows—just the maintenance room. They would be sitting ducks.

"Back down," she hissed. She didn't know if they had time to make it to the floor below before Ezra caught up to them or what they would do once they reached it. She just knew that they needed to keep moving.

She fought to keep her footsteps light, so she would hear Ezra's approach before he was on them. As they neared the landing, she pressed her shoulder against the wall and leaned forward to glimpse around the corner. There was no sign of Ezra, either on the stairs or in the hallway. The level was suspiciously quiet.

Maybe he realized we were trapped. Maybe he's hiding around a corner, waiting for our inevitable retreat. A point-blank shot.

He only had one bullet left, though. He couldn't hit *both* of them. Clare put her hand against Dorran's chest, pushing him back behind her as she slunk around the corner. The next flight of stairs was empty. She moved silently, holding her breath, straining to hear any human noises: the rustle of a jacket, the squeak of a shoe, a breath. The storm continued to rage around them, drowning out any of the subtler noises.

"Clare." Dorran's hand fell on her shoulder, halting her. "I hear something."

She frowned, listening. She could hear the storm. She could hear creaks as the wind's pressure made the metal tower sway. She could hear drumming rain. "What is it?"

He leaned close, his breathless voice in her ear. "Mechanical, I think. It blends into the thunder, but it is something different."

Clare took another step. She was nearly at the carpet. A faint light blinked at the other end of the hall. She hadn't seen that light before and it took her a second to realize where it came from.

He brought the elevators back online.

Ezra had realized they could outmatch him in speed, so he'd taken that advantage away. But it gave Clare an opportunity. She grabbed Dorran's arm. "We need to shut off the power. Quickly!"

He turned back toward the stairs, Clare following closely behind. She could make out the mechanical noises of the elevator gears turning as it drew closer. They skidded around the corner and onto the highest floor. The door to the maintenance room was locked, but it was only made of wood. Dorran lifted his foot and kicked. The wood cracked as it splintered, and when he kicked it again, the door burst inward, the lock left embedded in the doorframe with a halo of broken wood.

"Get the lights." He was already fumbling for the lids on the generator.

Clare felt for the switches beside the door and turned them. Rows of lights blinked on overhead. Dorran bent over the generator, his face full of hard angles and his hands buried inside the machine. The lights stayed on for all of two seconds before they died with a long, drawn-out whine as the power drained out of the building.

The darkness was oppressive. Clare closed her eyes and tried to remember the last time they'd visited the highest floor. Ezra had brought a flashlight. After fixing the generator, he'd placed the flashlight on the workbench, and she didn't remember him picking it up again after that. Clare moved toward the surface, clipped her hip on the edge of a pipe, and hissed.

"Clare?"

"Just a moment." She found the bench and ran her hands across the surface. Her fingers found something cylindrical and cold. Light exploded around them as she turned the flashlight on.

"I think we're okay." She moved back toward Dorran, her ears trained on the lower level. "I think we cut the power before he could open the elevator doors. He'll be trapped in there until we turn the power back on."

"Good." Dorran turned so that his back was against the generator and slid to the ground. He exhaled deeply as his long legs stretched out.

Clare dropped down beside him. She finally had a chance to get a good look at him, and what she saw filled her with quiet dread.

Blood ran from his nose and lips, though it was already drying. It was tacky in his hair too. He'd taken on an awful gray shade. His beautiful eyes were deeply shadowed and duller than she was used to.

Clare ran her fingertips across his cheek as gently as she could, and he leaned into the touch. "Does it hurt?"

"No."

There was an undercurrent in how he carried himself that made her think he was lying.

"Oh, Dorran." She trailed her fingers over his chin, where the blood had cracked. "What did he do to you?"

Dorran closed his eyes. He looked exhausted. "Don't worry about that. We just need to find a way out of the tower."

Clare bit her lip and turned the flashlight across the space, scanning the room. Ezra seemed to have spent a lot of time up there, probably trying to keep the generator running. Bottles of water lay discarded on workbenches, along with thick manuals and open boxes of supplies.

If we can find his computers and figure out how to activate the lights and alarms, we might be able to leave while he's trapped in the elevator.

Her stomach coiled. Leaving Ezra to starve might be even crueler than unleashing hollows on him. Clare tried to balance her perspective as her mind, panicked, darted between ideas. Ezra would probably figure out how to get out of the elevator. She just hoped that wouldn't happen too quickly.

Dorran suddenly moved. He bent over, facing away from her, and retched. The flashlight's beam picked up bright red blood pooling over the ground, and Clare clutched at her throat. "Dorran?"

He held up a hand, asking her to wait. The fingers shook.

Please, Dorran, please hold on.

The panic was rising like a tsunami. She didn't know what had happened to him, and there was precious little she could do to help. She couldn't even give him time to rest. Each minute inside Helexis was an extra minute Ezra would be working on opening the elevator.

Leaving the tower was only one issue. Even if they figured that out, Clare didn't know what they would do afterward. Dorran wouldn't be able to run much farther, or even walk. She wasn't strong enough to carry him. Blocked roads meant not even a car could help.

She felt like she was being pressed in on all sides, with no routes to escape.

Dorran slumped back against the generator. The muscles in his face were slack. *He's dehydrated. That, at least, is something I can help.* Clare crossed to the bottles she'd seen on the workbench. She found an unopened one and broke the seal as she returned to her companion.

"Dorran?" She crawled to his side, afraid to touch him in case she somehow made him worse. "We have water. It might help."

"Mm." His eyes cracked open. "Thank you."

"Shh, don't try to talk. We'll be okay. I…I'll…"

Clare wanted to promise him she would solve everything. That he didn't need to worry. That he just needed to stay alive, and everything would be all right. She felt like a liar.

He drank slowly, then lowered the bottle while it was still half-full. "Is there a cloth anywhere?"

"Hang on, I'll find one." Clare sprang back to her feet. The room was cluttered, but for all of its chaos, she couldn't find any fabric. She took up a knife and used it to rip the sleeve off her jacket, then returned to Dorran and offered it to him. "Sorry, this is all I could find."

"It's perfect." He poured water on it and used it to clean his face. Clare huddled at his side as he worked. His other arm slipped around her shoulders, and for a moment, Clare was transported back to a better time. When they had been at Winterbourne, they had often sat like that in front of the fire, on the rug, legs stretched toward the flames, Dorran's arm around her. She leaned her head against his chest to complete the picture. She wished she could pull back the smells from those earlier times too—clean linens and burning wood, instead of the blood, metal, and stress that surrounded her.

Dorran threw the cloth away. He'd cleared the blood off his face, but she could still see some of the stickiness in his hair. The gray shade wasn't improved. She wrapped her hands around his arm, desperately holding him against herself.

"Don't be afraid." He tilted far enough to kiss the top of her head. "We will make this work. We always do."

"We always do," she echoed.

All the while, her subconscious was tracking each passing second. Dorran needed rest, but the amount she could give him—a minute or two at most—seemed horribly inadequate. She stretched them as long as she dared, counting the seconds, pushing for just a little longer.

A noise echoed from deeper in the building. Clare squeezed her eyes closed, praying it was just the metal complaining under the storm's strain. If Ezra had gotten out of the elevator, they were sitting ducks. The flashlight at her side gave them a little bubble of light. She could turn it off and let them take shelter in the darkness. But, even then, that would only delay the inevitable. Ezra would be coming up to restore the generator. If they tried to run, they would meet him on the stairs.

The stairs...that's what it sounds like. Footsteps on stairs. Hundreds of them.

A deep, thrumming echo rose through the building. It was faint, but persistent. Clare squeezed Dorran's hand, her breath catching. "I think we need to put the generator back on."

He pushed away from the floor, staggered, and leaned against the generator. "Light, please."

She turned the flashlight around to help guide his hands. He'd taken the fuse out, and carefully refit it. The machine began to whirr as lights flickered on above them.

Clare looked toward the display panel Ezra had shown them above the generator. Six little lights tracked which windows were locked, and which were open. Five of the lights were green. One was red.

Dorran followed Clare's gaze. He took a slow breath. "We are out of time."

Clare stepped back from the machine. Her mind ran through every option, searching for some way out. The stairs. The windows. The locked rooms. The elevators.

The elevators...

"Can you run a little more?" she asked.

He nodded, and Clare gripped his hand to keep him at her side.

They moved back down the stairs, this time pushed by a fresh sense of urgency. Each second, the noises echoing from the floors below grew louder.

Clare staggered to a halt on the fifteenth floor. At the opposite end of carpeted hallway, the elevator doors were open. A block of light flowed out. It was a sharp contrast with the shadowed walls and red exit sign. As she watched, the doors slid closed.

"Ezra?" Her voice caught. She squeezed Dorran's hand, her fingers clammy, and took a step toward the elevator. "Please, listen...just for a moment. We can't afford to fight each other anymore."

He couldn't have gone far. She took the hallway in slow, measured steps, passing rows of closed doors. Her nerves were raw. At the back of her mind, she kept track of the chatter rising from the stairwell. It was closing in on them, already too near.

"We have to work together if we have any chance of surviving." She was nearly at the elevator, and yet, there was no sign of Ezra. If he was near, he was keeping quiet.

He can't have gone up; we would have met him on the stairs. Did he go down? Back to the workroom, maybe? Or the labs? They were nearly at the elevator. Clare reached a shaking hand toward the buttons.

"Give it back."

Clare swiveled. Ezra stood at the opposite end of the hall. He stepped out of the stairwell, gun aimed at them.

"Ezra, please. We don't have much time." Clare held her hands up. "The hollows—"

467

"The USB!" The gun shook. "You can't take it! Give it back!"

"I—I—" Clare threw her mind back. It felt like an eternity ago that she'd talked to Ezra about the USB containing his code. *Do I have it? I don't remember. When was the last time I saw it?*

"Give it to me!" A fleck of spittle flew from between bared teeth. He'd been pushed to his limit, to the point where madness started to seep through the cracks in his composure. Clare had felt what it was like to be pushed to that edge herself. She knew how bitter and frightening it was to teeter on that line, unsure of what was real, unable to trust her own mind.

"You can come with us." She held a hand out to him.

The noises in the stairwell were a cacophony. Ezra didn't show any awareness of them, though. His whole attention was directed toward Clare, eyes wild and desperate.

Then the shadows in the red-tinted stairwell suddenly morphed. They began to tremble, then dance, then explode in a frenzy of movement. Clare sucked in a sharp breath. "Behind you!"

Ezra turned just as the swell of hollows rose out of the stairwell in a wall of frothing limbs and gaping mouths. The gun fired, spending its final round into the crowd. If it hit any mark, it was quickly swallowed under the frenzy.

Dorran dragged Clare backward, away from the swarm. They hit the elevator doors. Clare reached out blindly and pressed the button.

Ezra staggered back, but he'd reacted too late. The hollows poured over him. A piercing scream cut through the hallway as he disappeared under the scrabbling, chattering bodies. Clare flinched away. She didn't want to see. But she had no way to block out the sound.

The scream rose, louder and louder, seemingly endless. It cracked into a raw howl. Then abruptly fell silent. The noise was replaced by the endless, quiet chattering noise, huffing breaths, and the wet smack of raw flesh between teeth.

The elevator doors slid open. A soft *ding* echoed through the hallway.

A dozen heads turned to stare at Clare and Dorran. Unblinking eyes shone in the light.

Clare clutched Dorran's hand. Together, they stepped backward, into the elevator. Most of the hollows were occupied with their feast, but additional heads rose from the heap to stare at them. Clare reached one shaking hand out and selected a floor on the panel, then carefully pushed the Close Doors button.

The nearest hollows began skittering forward. One of them carried a dripping mouthful of red pulp. The chattering was curious. Eager.

Clare mashed the Close Doors button.

The hollows sped up as they neared. The leader rose out of its crouch, its elongated arms stretched toward them, eighteen fingers reaching for Clare's face.

The doors slid closed. Bodies thudded onto the barrier. Fingers scratched at the metal, scrabbling along the seams as they looked for a weakness.

Then the elevator began to drop, pulling them away from the swarm and their feast.

CHAPTER 57

CLARE SLUMPED, RESTING HER forehead on the metal doors, pulling air into oxygen-starved lungs.

Dorran chuckled as he rubbed her back. "You did it."

"I did...*something*." Clare lifted her head. She blinked at the panel of buttons, dazed. In her urgency to escape the hollows she hadn't paid any attention to which button she'd pressed. She now saw she'd chosen the eighth floor. Ultimately, she suspected it didn't matter much. There would be hollows in every level of the tower by that point.

Only four floors didn't have access from the elevator: the maintenance room, the labs, and two other restricted levels. The lights above the door flashed as they counted down to eight. The elevator drew to a halt. Its doors slid open with a soft ping.

Mercifully, the hallway was sparsely occupied. Shapes moved through the stairwell at the opposite wall. Two stopped to stare at the elevator as the doors opened. Clare hit the Close Doors button again. The hollows had only just started to move toward them before the metal barrier slid shut.

"We should be safe in here, at least." Clare stepped back to lean against the railing on the rear wall. "They won't be able to get in unless they figure out how to press the buttons."

Dorran sighed and sank to the floor. He'd kept pace with her, but it was clear it had taxed him. He held out his hand, and Clare sat at his side.

"Rest with me a moment, then," he said. "We have some time before we need to plan our next step."

She knew what must be going through his head. They might be safe in the elevator, but it was a limited reprieve. With no water, their lifespan could be counted in days.

If they were in any other environment, they might have been able to outlast the hollows. The monsters would lose interest eventually and wander off for better pickings. But Helexis's power was still running, and the recording continued to play. As long as it broadcast its broken message, the hollows would be compelled to mill through the building. Forever.

Clare leaned her head against Dorran's shoulder. Her eyes burned. She tried to stay present and focused on their situation, but her mind kept sliding back to Ezra. The shock on his face as he turned toward the hollows. The screams.

Dorran brushed loose hair behind her ear, then ran his thumb over her cheek and down to her jaw. Clare closed her eyes and let herself sink into the touch.

"I'm sorry," she mumbled. "I shouldn't have turned the power off. It's just made everything worse."

"We were in a precarious situation. I don't know if I would have done any differently."

She chuckled. "You're too forgiving. Sometimes you just need to tell me I was an idiot."

He laughed as well, then pulled her a little closer. They were both dirty, the once-white coats thoroughly ruined. Clare didn't care. It was good just to be close to Dorran.

"My darling." He took her hand and stroked it thoughtfully. "I think we perhaps have less room for remorse in this new world. Our choices will have vastly worse consequences. Simple mistakes can result in life-altering outcomes. Sometimes even death. But as the consequences grow worse, our fear must be proportionally less. Do you understand?"

She frowned. "Maybe. I think?"

"Regret had a purpose in the world. It helped us to learn from our actions, to do better next time. But now, the room for error is so small that regret offers no advantage. Do you have room to regret five things a day? Ten? If you try to carry that weight, it will smother you. To survive, we must release ourselves from remorse."

"Dorran…"

"I am telling you this because you will need to be prepared. I have a plan."

She tilted her head back to look up at him.

"It will mean you leave alone."

A spear of ice-cold panic pierced through her chest. She grabbed the hand that was holding hers. "No. We either leave together or not at all."

"Shh." He kissed her forehead. "Don't be upset. I have thought this through, and it is the only option I can see. My darling, I am spent. I have no strength left to run. But I can create a distraction for you, to buy you time to get out of the city."

Distraction. He meant *sacrifice.* Being eaten. Using his own blood as a lure as Clare slipped away.

Fear and anger swelled through her. Clare twisted around. She grabbed Dorran's head with one hand on either cheek, forcing him to look at her, and snapped, more loudly than she'd intended, "*No.* That is *not* happening. We leave *together.*"

His eyebrows rose, and Clare was horrified to see amusement flit across his face. His hand slid around the back of her neck and pulled her in for a kiss. She didn't try to fight it.

"I love you so dearly." His lips, bitter from blood, grazed hers before he settled back against the wall. "You are brave and smart and stronger than you think. I know you can survive."

"Didn't you hear me? I'm not leaving without you." Clare's voice cracked.

Dorran left his hand on the back of her neck, the thumb tracing small, gentle circles. "My darling Clare. You have no idea how badly I wish I could give you everything you want. But I am not able to go further."

Sitting so close to him, pressed against his body, it was easy to see the toll the last day had taken on him. His skin's awful ashen color. New creases lingered across his brows and mouth. The darkness around his eyes was deepening. She pressed one hand to his chest and, through his shirt, felt how cold he was. Tears began to fall. "No, no, *no*. I'm *not* leaving you."

"Shh. Listen carefully. You can do this. Take the elevator to the ground floor. I will go out ahead of you. Draw their attention. I will see if I can lead them away from the windows. Then you will need to escape as quickly and as quietly as you can."

"Dorran, stop."

"Try to get to the river. I think that will be the fastest way out of the city. Take one of the boats and get to a rural road, then find a vehicle."

"*Stop.*"

"You know the country well enough to get back to Winterbourne, don't you? And you know how to keep the garden running. Seal the doors. Defend yourself. It will be hard, my dear, but I know you can do it. I know you can survive."

Tears ran freely. Clare hit her fist against his chest, a weak punch that replaced her lost words. She bowed her head to rest it against his shoulder as she cried. "I'm *not* leaving."

"Shh. Shh, my darling." Hands ran over her back. "I know this is hard. If you need time, I understand. We can sit together awhile more."

Clare felt as though she were arguing against a wall. Every other time she'd fought with Dorran, he'd allowed her concessions. This time, though, he wasn't even giving her a chance to object. She clung to him, terrified and sick. "I'm not leaving you.

I'm not living in a world without you. That's what you said to me, remember?"

She felt him smile into her hair. "We were never equal in that quarter. I could not take this world without you. But I think you will be all right without me. We both knew that I was just temporary."

"How——" She leaned back, words choking in her throat. "How *dare* you?"

Dorran grinned at her. Clare wanted to be furious with him. It wasn't easy when there was so much affection and adoration shining in his eyes.

"You have been the best part of my life." His thumb came up to brush tears from her cheeks. "I wish I had told you that more. I wish I had done a lot of things better. I was so occupied with trying to be the kind of man you wanted…"

Crushing sadness was dousing the anger. "That's why you agreed to help me get to Beth's bunker, isn't it? Because…you thought you weren't good enough? Because you were trying to buy my love?"

The sadness in his eyes was the only answer she needed. "I am not the kind of man you would have chosen in a better world. I know that."

"Dorran, you idiot." She pressed her lips against his. It was a messy, frenzied, helpless kiss. She tried to push her emotions into it, trying to show him physically how she felt when her words failed. He responded, leaning into it, arms circling around her to hold her tightly. When she finally released his mouth, she leaned her forehead against his. "You're the best man I've ever met."

He looked aside. He never seemed able to make eye contact when he was complimented. Clare's heart ached for him.

"If I'd met you before the stillness, I would have thought I was luckier than I deserved." She traced her fingertips over the hard lines of his brows, down his strong nose, and across his lips. "If I'd met you before the stillness, I would have loved you just as deeply as I love you know. I would have loved your good parts and your flaws. I would have married you."

His eyes flicked back to hers. They held a deep longing. One of his hands left her back and wormed between them, to feel inside his pockets. When it came out, it held a ring.

"What…" Clare stared at it, shocked into silence.

"I…I found it when we passed that broken jewelry store. Not very romantic, I know. But I didn't want to give you any of the rings my family owned. I wanted something that wasn't tainted by them." He swallowed and blinked rapidly.

"Dorran…"

"I know it's foolishness. There are no priests to marry us. No one to care whether we were or not. But I just thought, perhaps…"

She wrapped her hands around his and held them against her chest as fresh tears spilled over. "It's not stupid. Give me the damn ring."

He pulled her tightly against him. They were both laughing, giddy, and she thought he might be crying as well, though it was hard to tell. He pulled her around so she could sit in his lap properly, resting against his chest with his chin grazing the top of her head. He placed the ring into her hand. Clare threaded it onto her shaking finger. "It's beautiful."

"Hm." He sounded happy. "It will be something to keep. To remember me."

She shook her head. "I won't need to. We'll get out of here. We'll figure it out. And when we get back to Winterbourne, we can be a proper team. Our own little family."

Dorran didn't respond. Uneasiness ran through Clare's stomach. She leaned back to see his expression. "I'm not leaving without you."

He blinked down at her, calm and loving and sad all at once. "You will need a distraction to escape the tower. There is no other choice. At least, by doing this, I can ensure you get out of the city unharmed."

"No."

"It's all right, Clare. I am content with this choice. Please... please don't make saying goodbye any harder than it already is. I don't think I can take it."

She shut her eyes and clung to him. "I'll make it as hard as I need to. You can't force me to leave."

For a moment, the elevator was silent. Clare could hear Dorran's heart, beating too fast under her ear. The crackling storm outside. The distant chattering of hundreds of hollows racing through the building. Dorran took a deep breath and let it out slowly.

"It doesn't have to be right now. You need time to accept it. I understand." He rested his head on top of hers. "We still have a little time."

She scowled into his shirt. Dorran seemed content to hold her and stroke her hair. He hummed under his breath, a slow, soothing tune. Clare sat still and let him enjoy what he seemed to believe was a victory. Her mind worked furiously. There had to be a way out. Something she'd overlooked. Some way past the hollows. Then all they needed to do was find a way to carry Dorran until they found a safe space with food and water for him to rest. There had to be *something*.

She ran her thumb over the ring, then turned her hand into a fist. Dorran thought she just needed time to adjust to the idea. He also thought she was stubborn; he hadn't seen anything yet.

Hollows screamed outside the elevator. Fingers returned to the door, scratching and prying. They stayed for several painful moments before their owners gave up and paced away. Clare wondered if there was anything left of Ezra. She had seen the creatures eat bones; by that point, he probably only existed as a stain on the carpet.

The building creaked around them. She couldn't see the lightning, but she could feel the thunder. Her mind circled around their options for what felt like the thousandth time, desperate, hunting. Their masks were lost in the office area, now overrun. They could not reach the maintenance room to turn off the power or Ezra's laptop to turn off the recording. And the hollows would not leave as long as it played. Maybe not even then.

Is Dorran right? Does one of us need to die to have any hope of escape? She squeezed her eyes closed. *Then we will both die here together.*

478

Dorran lifted his head. For a second, Clare believed he must have heard her thoughts, and prepared herself for another fight. Then he said, "What was that?"

"What did you hear?" She blinked against the harsh elevator lights. Time had slipped away from her, and her legs were stiff from sitting.

"An engine. I think."

Clare frowned. Now that she was listening, she thought she could hear it too. Underneath the thunder and chattering hollows were sounds like an engine being revved. But that couldn't be real; the city streets were impassable.

Then a car horn blared through the chilled air. That was unmistakable. Clare shot up, her pulse hammering, as she stared at Dorran. "Someone else came."

His wide eyes stared back. "It doesn't seem possible."

"They must have heard the radio signal."

The car horn sounded again, this time loud and long. The chattering in the building grew frantic. The driver was courting danger by advertising their presence so loudly.

They could probably see the unlocked window on the ground floor, she realized. With hollows running in and out of the building, they were looking for some kind of response from the tower's occupants in case the building wasn't deserted.

This is how we get out.

CHAPTER 58

CLARE FACED THE SHINY metal doors, her heart hammering. Eight floors below them was rescue. Who, what, or how, she didn't know, but they had no choice but to accept.

She pulled on Dorran's arm, getting him to his feet. He felt cold. As he stood, a drop of blood ran from his nose. He wiped the back of his hand across it, smearing it away. Clare clutched his arm. "We have to get to them. I know you're tired, but you have to fight a little longer."

"I—"

"So help me, Dorran, you're getting into that car, or else I'll throw *myself* into a horde of hollows."

He shook his head, a thin smile tugging at his lips. "Have I ever won an argument against you?"

"No, and you're not about to start now."

The car horn blared again, a series of quick, sharp honks.

The engine revved. Hollows had to be converging on the noise already. The stranger wouldn't stay for long.

There was no time for subtlety or strategy. Clare hit the button for the foyer, and the elevator started moving.

The ground floor will be full of them, and we have no masks or armor. Clare chewed her lip. Dorran found her hand and pressed it. Together, they faced the doors, and Clare took a stuttering breath. "I think we'll just have to run for it."

Dorran nodded. The hollows would know they were coming; the pinging elevator doors would make sure of that. But if she and Dorran kept their heads down and moved fast enough, they might still have some small element of surprise.

The car horn sounded again, and the noise held for several seconds. It struck Clare as a final attempt to make contact. A last warning. They were already out of time.

The elevator whirred as it came to a halt. Clare leaned forward, exquisitely aware that the next few seconds would save or ruin them. Dorran tensed at her side. She kept a tight hold on his hand, silently telling him to stay with her.

Slowly, agonizingly, the doors trundled open. Clare's first glimpse of the foyer sent tremors through her chest. It was worse than she'd expected. Two dozen sets of eyes turned in her direction. One mouth opened in a piercing hiss.

There was no time to hesitate. The doors were wide enough, and Clare leapt forward. Dorran matched her pace. She stayed close at his side and put her head down and her arm up to shield her face.

Teeth locked onto her forearm. She didn't try to recoil, but barreled on, using momentum to push through. Arms grabbed at her legs. She stumbled. Dorran yanked her back up. She couldn't see the windows, but she could remember which direction they had been in. Bodies were blocking the path. Too many. Far, far too many.

Then light exploded through the foyer. An engine revved as the car directed its high beams toward them. Hollows hissed and screamed as they ducked away from the sudden harsh light. Clare lowered her arm. She could see the open window. It had been tilted, a huge slab of glass hanging from its hinges and leaving a narrow gap at its base. She and Dorran ducked together and dove through.

The vehicle's horn screamed, deafening. It wasn't a car, Clare saw. Just twenty feet from the tower was a minibus. Someone had modified it. Angled slabs of metal had been attached to the front like a crude snowplow. The windows were covered with plywood bolted to the vehicle's metal.

The door burst open. "Get in," a voice yelled. Clare tried to look through, to see the driver, and had the impression of a blank, featureless face. *They're wearing a mask.*

She tried to slow so Dorran could go in first, but he shoved her ahead of himself. Arguing would have risked them both. Clare leapt up the raised front step, then turned and hauled him in behind them. The hollows were close on their heels. He wrenched the door shut behind them.

Clare and Dorran stood in the narrow walkway beside the

driver's seat, panting and staring at the creatures as they tried to claw their way through the door. The driver put the minibus into gear. Clare staggered as the vehicle moved and caught herself on the back of one of the seats.

Their rescuer was dressed all in black and wore a beekeeper's helmet with extra fabric taped over the mesh to hide their face. Gloved hands expertly turned the wheel as the bus skidded around. Clare felt it rise onto two wheels and gasped. It touched down facing one of the main streets running through the city. A channel had been carved through the banks of cars. Probably using the makeshift snowplow contraption to clear the road, Clare thought.

"Sit down and get your seat belt on," the driver snapped.

Clare obediently sank into a chair beside Dorran. A sense of unreality washed through her. She'd heard that phrase at least a hundred times from someone very dear to her. Even though the voice was muffled by the mask, the inflection felt painfully familiar.

She'd grasped at unfounded hope so many times in the past days that it felt wrong to reach for it again. She looked up at Dorran. He'd already fastened his buckle and watched her, brows raised in a silent question. Clare turned back to the driver, her heart fluttering like a frantic bird. "Beth?"

They hit one of the cars on the side of the road. The minibus kept moving, but the jolt was enough to nearly throw Clare out of her seat. She grabbed the chair ahead of her with a grunt.

The driver twisted around and pulled their mask off. The face underneath held scars Clare had never seen before. But the tilt of the eyebrows, the fire in the eyes, and the exasperated angle of the lips were all beautifully, wonderfully familiar.

"So help me, Clare, put your seat belt on before I strangle you with it."

"Okay." Clare knew she was grinning like an idiot. She also knew she was crying. She couldn't stop. Numb hands hunted for the belt and dragged it into its lock as Beth slammed on the accelerator, taking them away from Helexis Tower and out of the city.

ABOUT THE AUTHOR

Darcy Coates is the *USA Today* bestselling author of *Hunted*, *The Haunting of Ashburn House*, *Craven Manor*, and more than a dozen other horror and suspense titles. She lives on the Central Coast of Australia with her family, cats, and a garden full of herbs and vegetables. Darcy loves forests, especially old-growth forests where the trees dwarf anyone who steps between them. Wherever she lives, she tries to have a mountain range close by.

THE HAUNTING OF ASHBURN HOUSE

THERE'S SOMETHING WRONG WITH ASHBURN HOUSE...

Everyone knows about Ashburn House. They whisper its old owner went mad, and restless ghosts still walk the halls. But when Adrienne inherits the crumbling old mansion, she only sees it as a lifeline...until darkness falls.

As the nights grow ever more restless, it becomes clear something twisted lives in Adrienne's house. Chasing the threads of a decades-old mystery, it isn't long before she realizes she's become prey to something deeply unnatural and intensely resentful. She has no idea how to escape. She has no idea how to survive. Only one thing is certain: Ashburn's dead are not at rest.

THE HAUNTING OF BLACKWOOD HOUSE

HOW LONG COULD YOU SURVIVE?

As the daughter of spiritualists, Mara's childhood was filled with séances and scam mediums. Now she's ready to start over with her fiancé, Neil, far away from the superstitions she's learned to loathe…but her past isn't willing to let her go so easily. And neither is Blackwood House.

When Mara and Neil purchased the derelict property, they were warned that ever since the murder of its original owner, things have changed. Strange shadows stalk the halls. Doors creak open by themselves. Voices whisper in the night. And watchful eyes follow her every move. But Mara's convinced she can't possibly be in danger. Because ghosts aren't real…are they?

THE HAUNTING OF ROOKWARD HOUSE

SHE'S ALWAYS WATCHING...

Rookward House may be hours away from its nearest neighbor, but its newest owner can't escape the feeling that he's being watched. Still, Guy decides to camp in the crumbling old mansion while he does repairs. Surely nothing too bad can happen in the space of a week.

But there's a reason no one lives in Rookward House, and the dilapidated rooms aren't as empty as they seem. Forty years ago, a deranged woman tormented the family that made Rookward its home. Now her ghost clings to the building like rot. She's bitter, obsessive, and fiercely jealous...and once Guy has moved into her house, she has no intention of letting him go.

THE CARROW HAUNT

THE DEAD ARE RESTLESS HERE.

Remy is a tour guide for the notoriously haunted Carrow House. When she's asked to host guests researching Carrow's phenomena, she hopes to finally experience some of the sightings that made the house famous.

At first, it's everything they hoped for. Then a storm moves in, cutting off their contact with the outside world, and things quickly take a sinister turn. But it isn't until one of the guests dies under strange circumstances that Remy is forced to consider the possibility that the ghost of the house's original owner—a twisted serial killer—still walks the halls. And by then it's too late to escape…

CRAVEN MANOR

SOME SECRETS ARE BETTER LEFT FORGOTTEN.

Daniel is desperate for a fresh start. So when a mysterious figure offers the position of groundskeeper at an ancient estate, he leaps at the chance. Alarm bells start ringing when he arrives at Craven Manor. The abandoned mansion's front door hangs open, and leaves and cobwebs coat the marble foyer. It's clear no one has lived here in a long time... but he has nowhere else to go.

Against his better judgment, he moves into the groundskeeper's cottage tucked away behind the old family crypt. But when a candle flickers to life in the abandoned tower window, Daniel realizes he isn't alone after all. Craven Manor is hiding a terrible secret... One that threatens to bury him with it.

For more info about Sourcebooks's books and authors, visit:

sourcebooks.com

THE HOUSE NEXT DOOR

NO ONE STAYS HERE FOR LONG.

Josephine began to suspect something was wrong with the house next door when its family fled in the middle of the night, the children screaming, the mother crying. They never came back. No family stays at Marwick House for long. No life lingers beyond its blackened windows. No voices drift from its ancient halls. Once, Josephine swore she saw a woman's silhouette pacing through the upstairs room…but that's impossible. No one had been there in a long, long time.

But now someone new has moved next door, and Marwick House is slowly waking up. Torn between staying away and warning the new tenant, Josephine only knows that if she isn't careful, she may be its next victim…

VOICES IN THE SNOW

NO ONE ESCAPES THE STILLNESS.

Clare remembers the cold. She remembers dark shapes in the snow and a terror she can't explain. And then…nothing. When she wakes in a stranger's home, he tells her she was in an accident. Clare wants to leave, but a vicious snowstorm has blanketed the world in white, and there's nothing she can do but wait.

They should be alone, but Clare's convinced something else is creeping about the surrounding woods, watching. Waiting. Between the claustrophobic storm and the inescapable sense of being hunted, Clare is on edge…and increasingly certain of one thing: her car crash wasn't an accident. Something is waiting for her to step outside the fragile safety of the house…something monstrous, something unfeeling. Something desperately hungry.